'One kiss…'

'Your brother asked

'You don't have to keep my promises for me,' Layla interrupted. 'I shall be returning to Ishla a virgin.'

'We were talking about a kiss!'

'So what's the problem, then?' Layla said.

She soon found out.

Mikael turned her around to face him and she stood shivering in anticipation. She felt his hand on her shoulder and his face move to hers… And then she was lost, because nothing in her imaginings could have prepared her for arrogant lips turned tender.

His kiss was soft at first, as one hand rested on her waist, the other at her shoulder. Then she felt the slip of his tongue and the slide of his hand to the back of her head. It was shocking, it was sensual, it was the gateway to paradise.

One kiss and her lips were swollen.

'We agreed one kiss.' Layla smiled again. 'But now I know why it is trouble…'

Carol Marinelli recently filled in a form where she was asked for her job title and was thrilled, after all these years, to be able to put down her answer as 'writer'. Then it asked what Carol did for relaxation and, after chewing her pen for a moment, Carol put down the truth: 'writing'. The third question asked, 'What are your hobbies?' Well, not wanting to look obsessed or, worse still, boring, she crossed the fingers on her free hand and answered 'swimming and tennis'. But, given that the chlorine in the pool does terrible things to her highlights, and the closest she's got to a tennis racket in the last couple of years is watching the Australian Open, I'm sure you can guess the real answer!

Recent titles by the same author:

MORE PRECIOUS THAN A CROWN
THE ONLY WOMAN TO DEFY HIM
THE PLAYBOY OF PUERTO BANÚS
PLAYING THE DUTIFUL WIFE

**Carol also writes for
Mills & Boon® Medical Romance™!**

**Did you know these are also available as eBooks?
Visit www.millsandboon.co.uk**

PROTECTING THE DESERT PRINCESS

BY
CAROL MARINELLI

Published in Great Britain 2014
by Mills & Boon, an imprint of Harlequin (UK) Limited,
Eton House, 18-24 Paradise Road, Richmond, Surrey, TW9 1SR

© 2014 Carol Marinelli

ISBN: 978-0-263-25026-8

Printed and bound in Spain
by Blackprint CPI, Barcelona

PROTECTING THE DESERT PRINCESS

CHAPTER ONE

'PRINCESS LAYLA, ARE you excited to be...?'

Layla patiently waited as the little girl on her computer screen faltered while choosing her words. By video link Layla was being beamed into the classrooms of the girls and young women of Ishla. Each class took an hour and, by working hard, Layla managed to get to each classroom once a month. Here she encouraged the children to converse in English and to work harder on their schoolwork, and it was proving a huge success.

'Princess Layla.' The little girl tried again. 'Are you excited that you will travel to Australia with Prince Zahid and Princess Trinity on their honeymoon?'

At the word 'honeymoon' the class exploded into a fit of giggles and Layla did her best not to join in with them. This class consisted of ten-year-old girls and they were all terribly excited that the handsome Prince Zahid had married the English lady Trinity, and they were all only too happy to talk about weddings.

And honeymoons!

'Well done,' Layla said to the little girl when the laughter had died down. 'You asked your question beautifully. Yes, I am very excited that I shall be joining my brother and his bride in Sydney, Australia. Did you know that you are my final class before we leave on the royal plane tonight?'

Zahid and Trinity's wedding had been beautiful, and the whole of Ishla had joined in the celebrations, even though the shocking news had hit, just before the wedding, that Trinity was already pregnant.

Layla's rule was that so long as questions were politely asked she would answer as best she could. Some of the questions, though, about Trinity's pregnancy, had been more than awkward—and not just because the subject in Ishla was sensitive. Layla simply hadn't known the answers, and had begun to understand just how naïve she was.

Layla craved knowledge.

She had long dreamt of a world outside the palace walls.

Before Zahid had even known who his bride was he had agreed to allow Layla to accompany him on his honeymoon. As a future king Zahid could not be expected to entertain his wife all day, and of course it had been assumed that his bride would need a companion.

They were so deeply in love, though, that perhaps they would prefer to be holidaying alone—but there was no way Layla was going to give up her first and only trip out of Ishla.

Guilt gripped her.

Not because she might prove a bit of an imposition for a couple in love—instead the guilt was for what Layla was secretly planning to do when she got to Australia.

'Princess Layla, are you scared?' another little girl asked.

'A little.' Layla spoke a guarded version of her truth. 'After all, I have never been out of Ishla, and so I don't really know what to expect, but I am also very excited. It is going to be a huge adventure for me and I have been looking forward to it for a very long time.'

'Princess Layla…'

All hands were raised. Her students adored her. They always did their homework now, just for the chance to speak with their princess each month. There were a lot of questions, but Layla's father, King Fahid, wanted to speak with Layla before she left and so she brought things to a close.

'Now,' Layla said to the students, 'there is no more time for questions. Instead it is time for you all to wish me a safe journey.'

She smiled at their voices as they did just that.

'Will you miss us?' they asked.

Layla held up her finger and thumb and held them a small distance apart. 'This much,' she said. As they all moaned their protests Layla stretched out her arms as wide as she could reach. 'Or perhaps this much! All of you know that I will miss you to the moon and back.'

She would miss them very much, Layla thought a little while later, as she lay on her bed on her stomach, going through her computer and checking and rechecking details for the very last time.

Would her father even let her teach them again, after she—?

Layla halted her thought processes; she could not allow herself to think like that now. Whatever the consequences to her actions, Layla had long ago decided that she was prepared to bear them.

One week of freedom would be worth whatever punishment her father would serve out for her.

Layla was petrified about taking a taxi alone in Australia, but she had watched little clips on her computer over and over and was as certain as she could be that she knew what to do.

How she loved her computer!

King Fahid was getting older and, though no one in Ishla must know, he was seriously ill, so perhaps had not investigated Layla's teaching aid quite as thoroughly as he once would have. Fahid did not really understand the access to the world that the computer gave his daughter. Layla lived a very protected life and wasn't even allowed a phone—she had never seen a television.

The computer was to assist with her teaching. Fahid was pleased that his daughter was helping the young women of Ishla and that *finally* his rebel daughter seemed to be staying out of mischief's way.

Layla pulled up the page that she had been studying carefully for weeks now—ever since she had found out where the honeymoon was taking place.

There he was!

Layla smiled at his scowling, haughty face.

Mikael Romanov, Senior Counsel, was, according to everything she had read, an extremely successful barrister. According to the translation of his website, he was considered amongst the best criminal defence lawyers in Australia. Originally from Russia, he had studied law in Australia. Tough and ruthless, he attacked the prosecution on every point and all too often won.

Good, Layla thought. He would need to be tough and ruthless to deal with Zahid, and possibly even the King.

Layla typed in his name and read a translation of the latest news. Although Layla could speak and understand English, she could not read or write it.

Mikael was in the news a lot at the moment, defending a man accused of murder and other heinous crimes against his late partner. Layla had been closely following the case from her computer after she went to bed at night.

How she loved the news clips of Mikael walking out of court in his black robe and wig. He offered no comment or apology to the questions that were hurled at him. He seemed not to care that everyone was demanding to know how he could even consider defending such a vile man.

Perhaps Mikael would be glad to turn his focus to a family matter, Layla thought. Maybe he would welcome the break from his horrible client, because Mikael did not look happy.

Not once had she seen him smile.

Layla felt a small shiver as she enlarged an image and looked at his full mouth. It was the only soft feature in his face, and it had her tongue rolling over her lips. His hair was as dark as his skin was pale, and always his attire was immaculate. Oh, and his voice— *his voice*!

She clicked on a rare interview from a couple of years ago that she had recently found. It was Layla's very favourite one, and she listened to his deep, heavily accented voice scolding a reporter.

'Tread carefully!' He pointed his finger at the reporter though for Layla it was if he was scolding her and Layla made a biting noise with her teeth. Her smile was wide as she started at the screen. 'May I remind you of the unanimous verdict?'

She had not chosen Mikael for his beauty, and yet the more she looked at him, and the more she found out about him, the more Layla wanted to know. She looked into his serious grey eyes—cold eyes that made her feel warm.

Some of the pictures of Mikael Layla was not so keen on—for there were a few of him with very beautiful women by his side.

Many beautiful women.

There he was on a yacht, with a blonde beauty lying topless on a daybed—or Layla assumed she was topless, because where her nipples should be the picture was all blurry.

Layla found her lips were pursed, but then she shrugged.

Her brother Zahid had been wild in his day.

She did not want wild—she wanted fun and romance and dancing.

Of course she would return to Ishla intact.

There were simply some things that Layla wanted to experience before she married a man she did not love. She closed the computer and lay on her back, imagining a whole day spent in bed without having to dress or speak to another person. She thought of other things too, like a romantic dinner, sitting holding hands, and afterwards dancing—which was forbidden in Ishla. She imagined the brush of lips on her mouth… But then her eyes snapped open, for it was Mikael's mouth that she was imagining.

No.

Layla dismissed that thought.

Mikael was merely a means to an end.

And a commoner too!

She clicked on her laptop again, to see if any other foreign royals were visiting Australia, and sighed at the lack of news for there were a couple of foreign princes who looked as if they could be fun!

Jamila, Layla's handmaiden, knocked on the door, and Layla clicked onto a game of chess she was playing and then called for Jamila to come in and prepare her bath.

When it was ready Layla went through and stood by the sunken bath as Jamila undressed her and then held Layla's hand as she lowered herself in.

'The water is lovely,' she said as Jamila started to wash her. 'Jamila?' Layla's voice was just a little too high as she attempted to sound casual. 'Are you nervous about coming to Australia?' When Jamila didn't answer straight away, Layla jumped in. 'Because if you are I can speak with father. I am sure I would manage on my own.'

'I would be more nervous if you were in a foreign country without me to take care of you,' Jamila said.

Jamila adored Layla. She had held her the moment she was born—a few moments before Layla's mother had died.

Layla was the baby Jamila had never had—not that she could ever let Layla know that she loved her like a daughter.

Neither could Jamila tell a single soul that she secretly loved Fahid—the King—and no one must ever know about the occasional love they shared.

'Here.' Jamila handed Layla a cloth, which she took, and she washed her private parts as Jamila washed her hair.

Still Layla carried on speaking.

'Well, you should rest while we are in Australia,' Layla said. 'You deserve to have a holiday too.'

'Layla!' Jamila's shrewd eyes narrowed as she rubbed oil into Layla's long black mane of hair. 'What are you up to?'

'Nothing.' Layla shrugged her bony shoulders. 'I just think that it would be nice for you to have a chance to rest and relax.'

Layla said no more, but she *was* worried about how her plans might affect Jamila, who was old and very set in her ways.

Trinity and Zahid, Layla had decided, would just have to bear the chaos of her actions. After all, they had had their fun—but poor Jamila…

Layla swallowed and dismissed the gnaw of discontent. She certainly wasn't going to change her plans to spare a servant's feelings.

'You are too thin,' Jamila said as she looked at Layla's skinny knees jutting up out of the water, her slender arms wrapped around them.

'Jamila,' Layla said, 'I could fill this bath and you would still say that I was too thin. Do you remember when I was a baby and always hungry and you said that I was too fat?'

Jamila's hand paused as she went to rinse Layla's hair—Layla should not remember those times. Jamila thought of those little fat legs and arms and her round belly. Layla had been such an angry, demanding baby and toddler. She had begged for attention from her father and it had been denied her as he'd grieved deeply for Annan, the late Queen. Jamila had tried to comfort the little princess with food, feeding her cream, honey, anything that might stop the relentless sobs that filled the palace.

Such sad, sad times.

'Let us get you dressed,' Jamila said, quickly finishing Layla's hair. 'Your father wishes to speak with you before you leave.'

Layla had chosen a simple burnt orange cotton tunic for the journey, but Jamila prepared a silver robe and silver jewelled slippers for her to wear on her arrival as there would be some dignitaries to greet them. Her fingers, toes and ears were dressed in pretty jewels, and her long black hair was tied in a low bun which was worn at the side of her head.

'Dismissed,' Layla said to Jamila, and then frowned when still she stood there.

'You *will* listen to what your father has to say, won't you?' Jamila asked, for she too was worried at the thought of Layla beyond the palace walls.

'Dismissed, Jamila,' Layla said.

Alone, Layla stepped out onto the balcony. The sun was starting to set and the sky was a fiery orange. The desert was like molten gold and it was a sight to behold, a view that she loved, and yet she knew there was more. She looked up to the sky, through which she would soon be being carried to her long-awaited adventure.

She knew she was being bad, and yet she had tried so hard to be good.

Once this was over she would be good for ever, Layla vowed.

This was her last chance.

Four years ago, when she was twenty, Layla had been dressed in white and gold and led down the stairs to walk into a room and select her husband from the men who knelt there.

Hussain had been and still was considered the right choice. They had played as children, and her father had told her that marrying Hussain would bring many benefits to the people of Ishla. Yet as Layla had walked down the stairs she had remembered what a mean little boy Hussain had been, and she had collapsed and started to shout and scream.

The kind palace doctor had smoothed out the offence caused by explaining that anxiety had caused the young princess to have a seizure.

Layla smiled to the sky. She had not selected her husband that day.

It had not been a seizure, just her temper exploding as she had looked at her wrist and recalled one time with Hussain.

'How do you make a match burn twice?' he had asked when Layla was nine.

'Show me?'

Wide-eyed, Layla had watched as he had lit the match and blown it out and then dug the burning sulphur into her wrist.

Immediately Layla had slapped him.

Now she looked down to the small scar on her otherwise unblemished skin and wondered about Hussain's reaction if his wife were to slap him.

He had no doubt moved on from matches now!

Layla headed back inside and opened the drawer in her dresser. Feeling far into the back, she removed the wrapped parcel she had been hiding.

Opening it, she held in her palm the black ruby named Opium. It had been gifted to her at birth by the King of Bishram and must surely be worth quite a lot.

Layla hoped that it was.

She had read that Mikael was expensive, and perhaps he would want to be paid.

Layla slipped the ruby into her tunic, worrying about something she had read on the internet about Australian Customs. She tried to tell herself that it would all be okay.

She made her way through the palace to her father's study, where Abdul, the King's chief aide, let her in. But Fahid dismissed Abdul so that he could speak to his daughter alone.

'Are you looking forward to your trip?' Fahid asked her.

'Very much, Father.'

'When you are in the hotel you will have your own room, with Jamila adjoining. Jamila is to take care of you there, but at all other times you are to be with either Trinity or Zahid.'

'I know that.'

'If you are in a restaurant then Trinity is to come with you if you need to go to—'

'Father!' Layla interrupted. 'I *do* know the rules.'

'They are there for your protection,' the King said. He looked at his daughter, whom he loved so very much. She was so contrary—floaty and vague, and yet arrogant too, just as her mother Annan had been. Layla was fiercely independent, and yet naïve from living her life within the palace grounds.

'Layla, I have not asked to speak with you to deliver meaningless words and a lecture. I really want you to listen to all that I have to say. Things are very different overseas—the people are different too. There is traffic...' The King winced as he thought of his daughter in a foreign city with fast-moving cars when she had never so much as crossed a road.

Layla saw his grimace and her heart went out to her father. 'I know you are worried for me, Father,' she said. 'I know that you have loved me from the moment that I was born...'

Again the King closed his eyes as Layla hit a still raw nerve.

He *hadn't* loved her from the moment she was born.

In fact the King had rejected Layla for more than a year. Sometimes Fahid wondered if that was why Layla was so rebellious and constantly challenged him, even if she couldn't logically know about that time.

He worried so much about her—especially knowing that soon he would be gone from his world. Surely Layla needed a stern husband like Hussain, who would keep her in line?

He would just miss the wild Layla so…

'Do you have any questions you wish to ask?' Fahid offered.

'I do.' Layla nodded. 'Father, I was looking up the customs in Australia—I thought I would find out who curtsies to me, who bows, and what gifts we should exchange, but instead I read that at the airport your property can be searched—even your body…' She paused when she saw her father's reaction. 'Why are you laughing?'

'Oh, Layla!' The King wiped his eyes as he tried to halt his laughter. 'That does not apply to *you*. Your retinue will take care of all the paperwork and luggage and our gifts are in the diplomatic pouch. You do not have to concern yourself with such things.'

'Thank you, Father.'

He rose from his seat and came over and took her in his arms. 'I love you, Layla.'

'I love you too,' Layla said, and hugged him back, but there were tears filling her eyes as she did so. 'I am sorry if I make you cross at times—please know that it doesn't mean I don't love you.'

'I know that,' Fahid said.

What the King didn't know, though, was that Layla was not apologising for her past.

Instead she was saying sorry for all that was to come.

CHAPTER TWO

'GREAT!'

Mikael had no choice but to pull to a stop as a policeman put up his hand and halted the morning traffic.

Even though he had more than enough on his mind, with closing arguments starting this morning, he flicked on the news to listen to the traffic report and hopefully find out the reason for the hold-up. He knew that he should have stayed at his city apartment, or even a hotel, instead of driving to his waterfront home last night, but he had just needed to get away from the case.

Mikael's remote beachside home was his haven, and last night he had needed to escape from the more pungent details of the case he was consumed by and breathe in fresh air and simply switch off.

It would be over soon, Mikael told himself.

'*Pizdet.*' He cursed in Russian when he found out that the reason for the delay was some visiting royal family, grinding everyone else to a halt.

Then he heard a little about himself as the news continued.

Mikael Romanov, SC, was surely going to lose this time…there was no way he could get his client off…

Then the calls in from listeners started and a character assassination ensued. Not of his client but himself.

'What sort of a person *is* Romanov?' an enraged caller asked. 'How can he possibly sleep at night?'

Mikael yawned with boredom and turned the radio off.

When his phone rang, instead of letting it go to voicemail, as he usually would, Mikael saw that it was Demyan and took the call.

'Any news?' Mikael asked, because Demyan's wife Alina was due to give birth soon.

'We have a little girl—Annika.' Demyan said, and Mikael rolled his eyes at the sound of his tough friend sounding so emotional. 'She's beautiful. Her hair is curly, like Alina's...'

Demyan went on to describe interminable details to Mikael.

All babies had blue eyes, Mikael thought.

'Congratulations,' Mikael said. 'Am I to visit while Alina is still in the hospital? What is the protocol?'

Demyan laughed. He took no offence. He knew that Mikael had no concept of family, for Mikael's upbringing had been even harsher than Demyan's.

'You don't have to come to the hospital,' Demyan said, 'but once this case is over it would be good if you could visit us before you disappear onto your yacht. I'm really looking forward to showing Annika off.'

'I'll be there,' Mikael said. 'It is closing arguments over the next couple of days, and then we await the verdict.'

'How is the trial going?' Demyan asked. 'It is all over the news.'

'Long,' came Mikael's honest answer. 'It has been a very long couple of months.'

It had been an isolated couple of months too.

He always pretty much locked himself away from

the world during a trial and, he admitted to Demyan, he was more than a little jaded from sitting with his client day in, day out.

'He's a fortunate man to have such a good solicitor.'

'Barrister,' Mikael corrected. 'One day you will get it right. Anyway, enough about the trial. Go back to your beautiful wife and daughter, I am very pleased to hear the good news.'

Rather you than me, Mikael thought as he ended the call.

When Demyan had told him that he was marrying again Mikael had offered to draw up a watertight pre-nup this time, given how Demyan's first wife had ripped him off for years.

Demyan had refused.

Fool! Mikael had not just thought it but had said it straight to Demyan's face, but he had been told that he was far too cynical.

Guilty!

Absolutely Mikael was cynical—he believed nothing anyone told him and had been proved right numerous times.

Mikael trusted and needed no one in his life, for he had never *had* anyone.

There were a few vague memories of a communal flat when he was growing up, but not one person in particular he'd been able to turn to. Mikael had been his own protector—even when he had found himself on the streets.

Especially then.

When he was a teenager Igor, a government worker, had stepped in and given Mikael an identity, a surname, an assumed date of birth and then a home.

Igor was the reason Mikael was driving to chambers

now to prepare for court—*he* was the reason Mikael believed absolutely in the need for a solid defence. For without one justice could never be truly served.

He did not want to think today of Igor; instead his eyes moved from the procession of royal cars to his dashboard, where the mileage read six hundred and forty-nine. He would be bored with his new toy by the time it read one thousand, but for now the low silver sports car was *his* new baby.

Finally the procession passed and the traffic inched forward.

Mikael arrived at chambers and spoke to Wendy, his clerk, for a few moments. His world had centred around this trial for a very long while, and all he wanted was the arguments delivered, the jury out, the verdict in and then to get away.

He'd take one of his toys to the water—he didn't even want crew.

Then Mikael changed his mind.

A couple of crew might be essential.

He had no intention of cooking or cleaning.

Perhaps Mandy could join him for a couple of days too?

Or Pearl?

Mikael soon put all such thoughts out of his mind and sat for a quiet period in his office, preparing himself for the day ahead and getting back to the real love of his life.

The letter of the law.

CHAPTER THREE

'I WANT TO drive that car!' Layla's slender finger pointed to a low silver sports car that gleamed in the morning sun as they passed an intersection.

'You can't drive,' Zahid said, but he did smile—it was nice to see Layla so excited and animated. Her face was up against the blacked-out window as she watched the world go by unseen, fascinated by it all.

'When can it just be us?' she asked. 'I am tired of all the formalities.'

'Soon,' Zahid said. 'Once we are at the hotel things will be more relaxed.'

'We can go shopping then,' Trinity added.

'Just Trinity and I?' Layla checked with her brother who, after a brief hesitation, nodded. 'Good.' Layla smiled. 'I want a red dress, red shoes, red...'

Her list went on until they were at the hotel.

Soon the Ishla royals and their retinue were taking up the entire top floor. There were guards at the lift and Layla paced her suite nervously, waiting for Trinity to come and take her shopping.

'Let me do your hair again,' Jamila offered.

'My hair is fine,' Layla said. 'You can go and rest in your room now.'

'I will wait for Trinity to get here.'

'You are dismissed, Jamila.' Layla said.

All Layla wanted was to be alone with her thoughts and to go over her plans for a minute or two before Trinity arrived.

Reluctantly Jamila went to her adjoining room. Layla looked at the lock on the door that stood between them and wanted to turn it.

She wouldn't have to turn it, Layla reminded herself.

A few hours from now she would be free!

Layla looked down at the streets below. Soon she would be down there amongst the noise and people.

She could see yellow taxis everywhere.

It was going to work!

'Enter,' Layla said when there was a knock at the door.

'Layla, you have to open it from the inside!' Trinity called.

'Oh!'

Fancy that.

Layla was ready to go, but Trinity seemed to have other ideas.

Zahid's last words to Trinity had been, 'Watch her.' She looked at Layla, dressed in a long silver tunic and jewelled slippers. Her black hair had been taken out of the bun and was loose and glossy. Her absolute beauty would turn heads everywhere they went.

'Would you like…?' Trinity hesitated—she was still very new to being Zahid's wife, and sometimes she simply didn't know how to speak to Layla, who was so different from Trinity's serious, rather more grounded husband. 'Would you like to borrow some of my clothes to wear while we go shopping?' Trinity offered.

'Borrow?' Layla screwed up her nose.

'I'm just concerned that in what you're wearing you'll stand out and people might stare.'

'But I always stand out,' Layla said, 'and people always stare. Come on—let us go shopping. I have been looking forward to this for a long time.'

They passed the guards and took the elevator down, and then stepped out onto the hot, busy street. Layla was more than used to heat, and walked quickly ahead.

'Slow down,' Trinity said. 'There's no rush.'

They wandered into boutique after boutique, but Layla was not really looking at the clothes—instead she was wondering how she could shrug Trinity off, for she was watching Layla like a hawk would watch its prey.

'I would like to try that,' Layla said, pointing to an ice cream shop.

'Sounds good.'

Still Trinity clung to her, and Layla's impatience was increasing. Yes, the ice cream was refreshing, but would Trinity ever just give her five minutes to be alone?

'Where to now?' Trinity asked once they had finished their ice creams.

'I might go for a little wander,' Layla said casually.

'Layla...' Trinity swallowed. 'Zahid said that I wasn't to leave you alone.'

'I am not a baby,' Layla said, 'I am twenty-four...'

But she went to cross the road without so much as looking and Trinity grabbed her back just in time.

'You have to wait for the lights to change before you cross.' Trinity pointed to the traffic lights as they turned green and they started to cross. 'I'm not leaving you alone, Layla. You can take it up with Zahid this evening if you want to, but for now...'

Trinity's voice trailed off as they walked across the

road and Layla looked to where Trinity's eyes had been drawn.

Perfect!

'Oh, look,' Layla said, walking over to the window of the baby boutique that held Trinity in its spell. 'Oh, Trinity, look at these sweet clothes—there is nothing like this in Ishla…' From Trinity's rapt expression, Layla knew her chance to escape was surely about to come. 'Let's go in.'

They did just that.

It wasn't just clothes on display but teeny-tiny shoes and socks, and little cashmere baby blankets too, and of *course*, the assistant told Trinity, they'd be only too happy to ship to Ishla.

'Why would you use a ship when we have a plane?' Layla asked, but Trinity wasn't listening—instead she was gazing at those little blankets and had the lost look in her eyes that Layla recognised from her cousins who had had babies.

Layla slipped outside unnoticed, pulling an envelope out of her bag as she did so. If Trinity saw her Layla would say she was just stepping out for some air.

On the street there was a yellow cab driving towards her, and Layla put up her hand as the clips she had watched on her computer had shown her she should.

It obeyed!

The driver did not get out and open the door for her, which made Layla cross, and she was glad that the window was wound down as the driver asked her where she wanted to go for it was a very smelly car.

Layla gave him Mikael's address. 'I need you to hurry.'

She *did* need him to hurry, for Trinity was racing out of the boutique.

'Layla, wait!' she shouted.

'I shall be fine, Trinity.' Layla threw the letter she had written in Arabic out of the window and shouted instructions to Trinity as the taxi pulled away. 'Get Zahid to read this and do *not* tell my father.'

She refused to feel guilty for ruining their honeymoon. Okay, maybe she felt a *little* guilty—but, Layla reminded herself, Zahid had had this sort of freedom for close to two decades when he had lived in England. Trinity had had it all her life.

Layla just wanted a week.

Mikael's day had not improved—not that he let anyone know it. He sat with his face impassive as he listened to the closing arguments from the prosecution barrister, who boo-hooed where Mikael had been expecting him to. A couple of members of the jury were even in tears. But then the prosecution hit him with an argument Mikael had not foreseen.

Deliberately Mikael refused to reach for his notes or react.

He just noted it in his head.

Tomorrow his response would be savage.

Tomorrow he would use every letter of the law that he had at his disposal.

'I'm gone, aren't I?' his client said before heading back to the cells.

'I haven't closed yet,' Mikael responded, though he gave no pep talk. He certainly wasn't here to reassure or make friends with his clients. All he required from himself was to offer the best defence.

It was a long walk back to chambers.

The press were waiting, with their usual questions, and Mikael duly ignored them. His mouth was dry and he wanted the cool darkness of his office, where the heavy drapes would be closed and he could sit in silence and make notes on all that had been said today.

'Don't ask!' Mikael warned his clerk as he stepped in.

Both knew that it was not going well, and that he would be here all night working on the final details before delivering his closing speech tomorrow.

'I don't know how to tell you this—' Wendy started.

Mikael turned and saw that his very efficient clerk for once looked a touch ruffled.

'There's a lady here to see you.'

'I haven't got time to see anyone now.'

'Mikael, I've tried to get rid of her...' Wendy let out a nervous laugh. 'I've never met anyone like her before—you simply can't say no. I even ended up paying for her taxi because she didn't have any money—the driver was about to call the police!'

'Wendy?' Mikael frowned, because he had never seen his clerk like this. Mikael dealt with the lowest of the low, and had only the best of staff around him—staff that were able to deal with the most difficult of people. 'Where is she?' he asked, glancing into the small waiting room.

'She's waiting in your office.'

'What?' She'd got past Wendy? This Mikael had to see. 'What's her name?'

'She won't tell me,' Wendy said, 'and she won't tell me what she's here for either. She refuses to discuss it with anyone but you.'

'Okay.' Mikael nodded. 'Don't worry. I shall sort it out.'

Mikael walked into his office and completely ignored his uninvited guest, who was standing by the window, looking out through a chink in the heavy curtains and watching the world go by.

Yet as much as he ignored her somehow Mikael was reminded of the rare beauty of the first glimpse of a new moon. Perhaps it was the way the light caught her silver robe or because she was so slender, but as he opened the bar fridge it was that image that was on his mind.

'Mr Romanov!'

Her voice demanded that he acknowledge her.

'Oh, sorry…' Mikael's voice was wry as, his back to her, he added a slice of lime and ice to a glass and then poured sparkling water. 'Weren't you getting enough attention?'

'I expect to be greeted.'

'Well, had you made an appointment then you would have been.'

He turned and looked at her, a golden ray of sun from the chink in the curtains serving as his spotlight. Her beauty was now possibly the biggest challenge of his day, for Mikael was momentarily sideswiped. Her black eyes were huge in her exquisite face, her hair thick and glossy, and her complexion quite simply flawless. His eyes roamed her face—as far as Mikael could tell she wasn't even wearing make-up. She was the first woman to actually stun him—so much so that when she held out her hand Mikael handed her his drink.

How did that happen? Mikael wondered as he turned again and made another drink—for himself this time.

'I am Princess Layla of Ishla,' Layla said, because, given Mikael's poor manners, perhaps he was not aware of to whom he was speaking.

'Really?' Mikael said.

Layla waited for him to continue.

'So *you're* the reason I was almost late for court this morning.'

'Excuse me?'

'Your convoy held me up,' Mikael said. 'Look, I don't know what your issue is—in fact I don't even *want* to know. I'm in the middle of a very complicated case and I am going on leave soon.'

'I know all about your case, but I need for you to speak with my brother. I want you tell him that I am taking a week off from royal duty and that he is not to look for me or inform my father.'

'Can't *you* tell him that?'

'I have written it all in a letter that he must be reading about now. I need you to reiterate the contents to him,' Layla said. 'If I speak with him it will get all emotional and I might back down—that is why I want you to do it for me.'

'You need an embassy.'

'No,' Layla shook her head. 'I do not want to make a big incident—unless I *have* to, of course.'

He heard the warning note in her voice, saw then the fire in her eyes, and he understood why Wendy had been unable to say no to her. She was pretty unstoppable.

Mikael, though, could not be manipulated. 'As I just said, I am near the end of a huge case. I'm not taking anything else on.'

'You will make one phone call for me,' Layla said. 'But first you can arrange for some refreshments to be brought in.' It had been a long afternoon of shopping after all.

Mikael felt the shock from the muscles in his face as they broke into a smile.

Was she for real?

'You want me to arrange refreshments *before* I make your phone call?'

'Just something light.' Layla nodded. 'Maybe some fruit, and also something sweet.'

Mikael pulled out a roll of mints. 'Here's your refreshments.'

She took one and popped it in her mouth, and he watched her eyes widen in delight as she rolled the mint across her tongue.

'I like.'

So too, Mikael decided, did he!

CHAPTER FOUR

'ONE PHONE CALL,' Mikael said.

But there was no way, Mikael knew, that this was going to go away with one phone call. He had only agreed to it because Layla had eked from him the first smile he had given in weeks.

He opened the curtains and invited her to take a seat.

'First, though—' Mikael went on, but Layla interrupted.

'I give you some details.'

'No,' Mikael said. 'First we need to discuss my retainer.'

'Retainer?'

'I'm very expensive,' Mikael said.

'Oh, you want payment up-front?'

'Absolutely.'

'I have this.'

Mikael was a master at keeping his face impassive—poker would have been a lucrative hobby if he'd so chosen—but even he was struggling as, from her tunic, Layla took out a stone that looked more like a paperweight and placed it on the desk between them.

'It is called Opium,' Layla explained. 'It is a rare black ruby that was gifted to me by the King of Bishram on my birth, so I would expect it to be worth quite a bit.'

Mikael said nothing at first. He just stared at the stone that was almost as beautiful as its owner and thought of her walking the streets with that in her pocket. After a long stretch of silence he picked it up and decided to put it in his safe for now, then he sat back at his desk and looked at her. 'What exactly are you hoping to achieve this week?'

'There are things that I would like to do before I marry.'

'Such as?'

'They are not your concern. All I want is a week of freedom from my duties and a week away from my family.'

'To do what?' Mikael persisted. 'If I'm to ring your brother then I need to know what you intend to get up to.'

'I would like to dance,' Layla said. 'It is forbidden in Ishla. And I would like to try an Irish coffee….'

'There *are* other drinks.' Mikael smirked.

'My brother mentioned Irish coffee once, many years ago. I thought it sounded nice that the cream stays at the top.'

'What else?'

Layla looked across the table at Mikael. For the first time in her life she felt a little… Layla tried to decide *how* she felt. Intimidated? She wasn't sure if that was the right word, but it had never entered her head that Mikael might say no to her request. More than that, though, the effect of his smile had unsettled her stomach in a way she did not understand.

Certainly she wasn't about to tell him all the adventures she was seeking—though her eyes did fall to his mouth, which she had briefly imagined upon hers, but then she met again the cool of his gaze. 'I don't know you well enough to tell you,' Layla said.

'How long have you been planning this?'

'For quite some time,' Layla admitted.

'Would your family have guessed that you were going to escape?'

'No.' Immediately she shook her head.

'"You're sure of that.'

'Very sure,' she said. 'I learnt a very long time ago that I get in trouble if I tell anyone my thoughts.'

'You can be honest here,' Mikael said, and Layla gave a hesitant nod—though her eyes said that she doubted it.

She did offer a little more. 'I tried to get my brother to take me to a wedding in London a few months ago—I was going to escape there, but he refused to take me with him.'

Sensible man, Mikael thought, feeling a knot of unease forming at the thought of her let loose in London—or even let loose here, for there was an innocence behind her arrogance, an inherent trust in the good of others that could so easily be shattered.

'How are your family going to react?'

'That depends,' Layla responded. 'I have made it very clear in my letter to my brother that he is not to inform my father that I am missing. If he does my father will have no choice but to create an international incident. That is avoidable, of course—I just need for you to reassure my brother that I will be safe and that I will return to the hotel one week from now.'

'What about your mother?'

'From what I have been told about her, she would approve.'

'Told?'

'She is dead, but apparently we are very similar, and if that is the case then she'd approve of my plans.'

'Where are you going to stay?' Mikael asked. 'Have you got friends…?'

'You will arrange that.'

'*One* phone call?' Mikael reminded her.

'Two.' Layla smiled. 'You are to make sure I stay somewhere nice and you will have to drive me there. I am not taking a taxi again; the man was very rude.'

'Possibly because you didn't pay him,' Mikael said. 'I'll ask Wendy to book you somewhere and she'll drive you to a hotel.'

They went over a few more details. There was nothing uncomplicated about Layla. She was twenty-four, he found out, and he checked that she was healthy, that she wasn't on any medication, or suffering any illnesses. He wanted to be sure that there was nothing that could be flashed up on the news about her life being at risk.

Physically, it would seem she was healthy—though certifiable, perhaps…

'They thought that I had seizure once, but I did not,' Layla said.

Mikael let out a tense breath as out of her lips popped another surprise.

'I was on my way to select a husband and I started to scream and shout expletives and then I fell to the floor. The palace doctor is kind and she told my father and suitors that anxiety had caused a seizure. But it was not a seizure. I was just cross.'

'Don't you ever try that trick on me,' Mikael warned her.

'It wasn't a trick.'

'Oh, Layla.' Mikael slowly shook his head. 'I'm quite sure that you are full of them.' He ran shrewd eyes over the cunning minx. 'Why did you choose me?'

'Because you are not swayed by emotion and you don't care what others think.'

'You don't know that,' Mikael said.

'You are hated by many for the people you defend.' Layla shrugged. 'Yet you do not look like a man who cries himself to sleep at night. Now, am I wasting my time or are you going to make that call?'

'Layla...'

'*Princess* Layla,' she corrected.

'I'd suggest,' Mikael responded, 'that if you really want to disappear for a week then you lose the title.'

'Mr Romanov—'

'Mikael,' he interrupted.

'Mikael,' Layla amended. 'I would like you to speak with my brother now.'

'Very well,' Mikael said, 'but you need to understand that I am near the end of a very complex case. I will make one phone call and have you taken to a hotel...' He briefly closed his eyes. 'I don't have time to babysit you.'

'Good.'

She smiled very widely then, and it was like a fist to Mikael's guts because the breath was almost knocked out of him when she did.

'The last thing I want this week is to be watched over.'

Layla didn't have a phone, but she did have Zahid's number. Mikael blocked his own number and then made the call.

He did not give his name, but explained that he was representing Layla and that her request for a week away from her family was far from unreasonable.

'You don't understand—' Zahid started.

'I understand that the laws in your land may be different,' Mikael interrupted, 'but—'

'You don't understand *Layla*.' This time it was Zahid who broke in.

Far from the fury and hysterics that Mikael had expected, Zahid's response was clipped. 'She will not manage alone.'

'Layla is twenty-four.'

'Which means for twenty-four years she has had everything done for her. *Everything*,' Zahid reiterated.

'Well, she seems very capable to me, and more than independent.'

'Could I speak with her?' Zahid asked.

Mikael looked over to Layla, who sat rigid in the chair, her lips pursed. 'Your brother wishes to speak with you.'

He expected her to shake her head, but instead Layla nodded.

'You don't have to,' he said, but she was holding her hand out for the phone.

'Don't give him my name,' Mikael warned her.

Layla had been right to get him in to handle this, Mikael thought, because whatever was being said in Arabic the conversation was clearly emotional. He watched as she stood and started pacing, shouting and crying, but then, just as he was going to take the phone from her, she switched to English.

'No, Trinity, I do not accept what Zahid just said and you can tell him the same. Yes, I have messed up your honeymoon—well, guess what? I don't expect to *have* a happy honeymoon. I *know* my honeymoon will be miserable. At least you get the rest of your life to be happy…'

Mikael's eyes widened a touch in admiration, and

then he suppressed the second smile to grace his lips in months as Layla continued.

'What does your pregnancy have to do with *my* life?' Layla demanded. 'I am supposed to put my *one* chance for freedom to the side because you are growing a baby…?' Layla gave an incredulous laugh. 'I never realised you were so precious, Trinity. Let me speak with my brother—clearly you are supposed to avoid the real world for the next six months.'

Mikael listened as she continued speaking to Trinity, who was surely pleading with her to go back before the situation got out of hand.

'I think one week of freedom is a very good deal,' Layla said. 'And I warn you: if you tell my father—if you look for me—then I shall take my barrister's advice and go to an embassy.' Layla handed Mikael the phone. 'My brother wants to speak with you again.'

'Whoever you are—' Zahid's voice was still supremely calm but it cracked near the end of his words '—please look after her.'

Mikael was just about to point out that that wasn't in his job description, but then he looked over to Layla.

How could he send her out onto the streets alone?

'She'll be fine,' Mikael said.

'I need your word.'

'Hey,' Mikael said, 'you're not my client.'

'I'll be paying your bill,' Zahid said, and Mikael ended the call and threw the phone on the desk and looked at his problem.

'You are trouble,' he said, and Layla smiled.

'I know that I am.'

CHAPTER FIVE

WHERE TO HOUSE the runaway princess? Mikael thought as her eyes lit on his chessboard and she walked across his office.

'Leave it!' he warned, because he played against himself and chess was part of his process when he was working through a case and needed fifteen minutes away from it at a time.

'But I can see checkmate!' Layla said.

'Layla!' Mikael warned again, and strode over. 'Leave it!'

He pointed his finger at her and blinked as her teeth made a biting noise and she smiled widely at him.

She was like a little wild animal.

Sex had previously been the last thing on his mind.

That would happen after the trial—*as soon as possible* after the trial—when Mikael would make up for all he had missed out on as he surfaced to the world.

Sex, though, was right at the front of his mind now—and starting to make itself known elsewhere.

'Come on.' His voice was brusque as he opened his office door. 'Wendy...' he called as Layla followed him out, but then Mikael halted. It would be easier to drop her off himself than explain it all to Wendy, so they walked together to his car.

'This is *your* car!' Layla clearly approved. 'It is very beautiful.'

'Thank you.'

'I'd love to drive it.'

'But then I'd have to kill you,' Mikael said, opening the passenger side door for her.

'You are much more polite than the taxi driver,' Layla said.

Mikael got in himself and before driving off called his favourite hotel.

He glanced over to Layla. Yes, he told Reservations, he would have his usual luxury suite.

'Right, I've booked you into a hotel. I'll cover it, and we can sort out money some other time.'

'You have your retainer.'

'I do.' Mikael sighed, imagining trying to cash a rare ruby. 'Put your seatbelt on.'

'Pardon?' Layla frowned. 'The taxi driver said the same.'

'And did you?'

Clearly not.

'You need to.'

It should have been easy to reach over and do it himself, except she started to laugh as if he was tickling her as he leant over to retrieve the belt and suddenly there was nothing straightforward about the way Mikael was feeling as his nostrils delivered to his brain its first hit of the exotic aroma of Layla close up.

'What *are* you doing?' She was giddy from the brief contact.

'Putting on your seatbelt.' He pulled the belt out, trying to ignore the scent of her and the sound of her laughter as he clicked it in. 'Don't you wear seatbelts in Ishla?'

'*I* don't,' Layla said. 'The same thing happened on the plane.' Then she turned and looked at him. 'Though it wasn't as much fun.'

Mikael said nothing. He just drove to the hotel. But he could feel her eyes on him.

'You're not a very happy person, are you?' Layla observed.

'It's not a requisite for my job.'

'You're not working now.'

'Yes, Layla,' Mikael said, 'I am. Believe me, it would have been far cheaper to get a chauffeur-driven limousine with a trained monkey in the back peeling grapes for you than to have me drive you.' He turned and saw her frown. 'You'll see the breakdown on my bill.'

'I want that monkey!' Layla said, then pouted when she got no response from Mikael. 'You didn't laugh at my joke.'

'I wasn't sure if it *was* one,' he admitted, but then turned and gave her a brief smile. 'It was a good one, though!'

They got out at the hotel and Mikael gave the parking attendant his keys, telling him he'd be out shortly and not to park the car. They walked through to check in.

'I'll see you to your room and then I need to go back and do some work.'

'That's fine.'

Heads were turning, Mikael realised, and not just turning. People were craning their necks to get a glimpse of Layla as she glided along beside him. As he checked her in under his name he explained that there was no luggage.

'You might want to…' He turned to see if she needed some cash but she was no longer beside him. Mikael saw her wandering into one of the hotel's boutiques.

'Excuse me a moment,' he said to the receptionist, and then strode through the foyer and into the boutique.

'I like!' Layla said, holding up a very glittery, very high shoe. She sat down and kicked off her silver slipper and held out her foot to him, just as the assistant called over that she would be there in a moment.

Even her feet were beautiful, Mikael thought. Long and slender and, yes, clearly irresistible—because with barely a thought he was helping her on with the shoe.

The sole of her foot was a soft as a kitten's paw and Mikael tried to ignore the feel of her skin and the scent of her hair as she bent forward as he tried to slip it on.

'It doesn't fit!' Layla exclaimed.

'You're like Cinderella in reverse.'

'Why doesn't it fit?' Layla demanded, because in Ishla her shoes were hand-made and fitted beautifully. *This* she could not even get her foot in.

'Because this isn't Planet Layla,' Mikael said. 'Come on.'

'But I want—'

'Layla.' His voice was stern. Mikael was fast losing patience as she followed him to the elevators. 'I don't have time to be taking you shoe-shopping, I deliver my closing argument tomorrow...'

Not that she'd understand that, Mikael thought as he swiped a card for the lift and handed it to her. 'You need to use this to take the lift and to get into your suite.'

'Thank you.'

'Twenty-fourth floor,' Mikael said, pressing the button.

'How did court go today?' Layla asked.

'Not very well.'

'He must be very difficult to defend,' Layla said.

Mikael shrugged and offered his usual response to that statement. 'Not difficult for me,' he said.

'It's an interesting case, though,' Layla said. 'Her silence is his defence.'

He had assumed that she was talking morally.

For once he was wrong.

'You really *have* been following it.' Mikael didn't even hide the slight surprise in his voice.

'Of course,' Layla said. 'I wanted to know who I would be dealing with.'

He showed her around the suite and where everything was, and then he showed her the phone. 'If you want anything ring—'

'You.'

'No, you ring the desk.'

'What if I need to speak with you?'

'Please don't need to speak with me,' he said.

He went to get out his business card but then changed his mind and wrote his personal number down on a pad on the desk.

'Emergencies only,' he warned, but she wasn't listening. She was at the window, her eyes glittering as she eyed the city streets below. He was starting to understand Zahid's concern—because how the hell would she manage out there?

'Can I ask that you don't go out tonight?'

She briefly turned and gave him a scoffing look. 'You think I did all this just to stay in my room?'

'Layla, I have a huge case on.' Mikael let out a breath. 'But tomorrow night I'll take you out.'

'Really?'

'Or possibly the next night.'

Layla rolled her eyes. 'Good evening, Mikael, thank

you for your help with my brother. You're dismissed for today.'

He could not dismiss her from his mind, though.

Well, he'd have to.

Mikael returned to chambers and finally sat down to work through his closing argument. If he was lucky he'd get a couple of hours' sleep.

Mikael was very good at shutting the world out when needed.

This was his passion.

Over and over the prosecution's closing he went, looking for holes, for the one little thing that might plant reasonable doubt.

He already had it—in fact Mikael had long known that it was *all* he had. Layla had got it exactly: the victim's silence was his client's only defence.

He might be getting more than two hours' sleep after all, he thought, and his mind briefly drifted to Layla. He wondered how she was doing in a strange city on her first night out of Ishla.

Not his problem.

He walked over to the chessboard to take a small break and stared at it for ages.

It wasn't even close to checkmate.

Was it?

Mikael looked again, for a considerably longer time.

No.

He made his move.

Mikael got back to his computer screen but there was a gnawing of anxiety in his mind. To ease it he picked up the phone and called the hotel and asked what had been charged to his room.

Several Irish coffees, toiletries and two peeled and thinly sliced apples, he was told for starters. But then that gnaw started to burn as he heard about the dresses and shoes that had also been charged to the suite, and that the car was almost ready to collect *them*.

'Cancel the car,' Mikael said.

Cursing, he reloaded his briefcase and headed out to his car, making light work of the dark city streets. At the hotel he tossed his keys at the valet and made his way up to the twenty-fourth floor—only to meet Layla, stepping into the elevator as he came out.

'Where do you think you're going?'

'I am looking for my driver...'

Mikael tried not to notice how gorgeous she looked in a tight red dress, and he also tried not to recall how soft her feet were as he saw that she had managed to get the shoes in her size.

Then he looked at black eyes that were almost crossing as they tried to focus.

'You're drunk!' Mikael accused.

'Am I?' Layla said, sounding very pleased with herself.

'No way are you going out tonight,' Mikael said, frogmarching her back to her suite.

'You can't stop me.'

'I'll call your brother, then,' Mikael said. 'Because *I'm* not going to police you.'

He pulled out his phone the second they got into her suite. There were glasses everywhere, and dresses and shoes; it was clear that Layla was seriously going all out for her week of fun.

'You will *not* call Zahid!' Layla roared. 'I am an adult. I am capable of making my own decisions.'

'Fine, then,' he snapped. 'But I'm warning you: it would be beyond foolish for you to go out in that state, but if you choose to then that's up to you.' He turned to leave and yet he couldn't. 'Where exactly are you planning to go tonight?'

'I want to go to a club—to dance.'

'With…?' Mikael looked at her and tried to ignore her gorgeousness, tried to be cross. And yet he was tempted to laugh. What did she do to his head? 'Have you got any money, Layla?'

'No.'

'Have you any idea of the trouble you could get into?'

She just looked at him, and suddenly it was very easy for Mikael to be cross—just not with her.

'My current client isn't the only bastard out there, Layla.'

'Mikael…'

'No, you need to hear this.'

'Mikael, help me!'

He watched her beautiful face pale and her hand clutch her throat.

'I think…' Layla said. 'I think that I'm…'

He got her to the bathroom just in time.

Never in his life had he done this, and never again would he do this, but Mikael stood holding her silky black hair as she knelt in the bathroom.

'I *should* ring your brother, you know.'

'I know,' she said. Unseen by her, Mikael smiled as she continued, 'But you won't.'

Yes, he really should ring Zahid and have him come and collect her—but instead he ran her a bath as he thought about her brother.

Mikael had been worried—and with good reason. Zahid must be beside himself.

Mikael was not a sentimental person—not in the

least—but surely a text to put him at ease could not cause any harm?

As he waited for the bath to fill Mikael fired a quick text.

Just to let you know, Layla is fine.

'Have a bath and wash your hair, and then I suggest you get some sleep.'

'Can you send someone in to wash me?'

'*Wash* you?'

She had no idea how to do it herself.

'I'll tell you this much…' He was breathing very hard as he massaged shampoo with rather angry fingers into her hair. He'd insisted she keep her underwear on—as if that would go down well with the defence! 'You're completely—'

He'd been about to say *spoilt* but he halted and thought about it as he rinsed the shampoo out of her hair.

She might be pampered, and way too used to getting her own way, yet Layla was the most unspoiled person he had ever met.

'There,' Mikael said. 'Your hair's clean.'

'Jamila oils it now.'

'There,' Mikael said again, a little while later. 'Your hair is washed *and* conditioned and now…' he moved in to pull the plug and met her lovely feet again '…I'll help you out of the bath. Then you're to dry yourself and put on a robe.'

'Okay.' For once she agreed.

He helped her out and she made sure that Mikael too was soaking as she toppled against him.

'I still feel a bit…' She didn't know how to describe it

as he handed her a towel. 'I think I like you,' Layla said, and Mikael's jaw gritted as she continued. 'Not just *like* you…it feels a bit different to that…' She turned as he walked out. 'Where are you going?'

'To do some work,' he said. 'Work that pays in dollars instead of stones.'

He was cross, Layla realised as he stalked out.

But lovely.

He didn't even look up as she came out of the bathroom.

'I know that I behaved badly tonight…it was just too enticing…' She looked out at the lights that still beckoned.

'You need to sleep,' Mikael said, 'and I need to work out what the hell I'm going to do with you.'

He didn't trust her as far as he could throw her—but not in a bad way.

Mikael went to the couch and took out his laptop and got to work as Layla made her way to the bedroom.

'The maids didn't put out a nightdress.'

Mikael closed his eyes for a second before answering. She was the most exhausting person he had ever met. 'Just sleep in your robe.'

'But it's damp.' She came out from the bedroom. 'If I sleep in damp clothes I'll catch a cold.'

'That's an old wives' tale.'

'I don't understand.'

Neither did Mikael, because a few minutes later he was naked from the waist up and trying not to notice just how long her legs were as she walked from the bathroom wearing his shirt and was finally safe in bed for the night.

'Mikael!' she called from the bedroom. 'Will you still take me out tomorrow night?'

Mikael didn't answer.

'Mikael…'

'Layla,' Mikael called back, 'could you really see checkmate?'

Silence.

'I want the truth—yes or no?'

'No.'

She started laughing and Mikael gave a wry smile. He'd add the extra twenty bloody minutes he'd spent staring at the board to her bill.

'Go to sleep, Layla.'

Finally she did as she was told and Mikael got on with his work, only pausing occasionally.

The sound of her soft snoring was actually quite relaxing…

CHAPTER SIX

LAYLA AWOKE TO the gorgeous scent of Mikael.

Or rather the gorgeous scent of Mikael's shirt, and she lay there remembering him bathing her and how cross but kind he had been. There was a flurry low in her stomach as she remembered toppling into him and smiling up at him, telling him that she liked him.

She still did.

Yes, he was a commoner, but she only had six days now and Mikael, Layla decided, would be her romance for the week.

Layla picked up the phone by the bed and ordered a thinly sliced apple, some mint tea and iced water and then padded out to the lounge, where Mikael was stretched out asleep on the sofa.

He looked so different asleep, Layla thought as she stood over him.

He appeared a lot less cross and he had shadows under his eyes like those Layla had had once had when she'd caught a cold. She looked at his chin. In all the photos she had seen he had been clean-shaven, but she loved his stubbly jaw.

Layla's eyes drifted from his face to his body, which was just as beautiful.

His skin was pale and his flat nipples were the same

dark red as his lips. She liked his flat stomach, and she blew out a guilty breath as she saw the snake of hair that led from his navel. She knew she should not be looking there and so moved her eyes back to his face instead. She watched him wake, his grey eyes frowning into hers. A look of concern darted across his face.

'Good morning!' Layla smiled down at him.

'What time is it?' Mikael asked with a horrible, panicked feeling that he might have overslept.

'Sunrise!' Layla smiled again and then turned when there was a knock at the door. Mikael watched as a trolley was wheeled in.

'You've ordered breakfast?'

'No, just something to cleanse my palate—my mouth is very dry.'

'I bet it is,' Mikael said, watching as she nibbled on her apple while walking over to the window.

'It's beautiful,' Layla said, looking out at the Sydney skyline. The Opera House looked gold in the morning sun and the whole city was gleaming and beckoning. 'I'm trying to think what to do today.'

'I've already decided,' Mikael said, picking up her glass of sparkling water and draining it. 'You're joining me at work.' He'd decided that just before dozing off. 'You can sit in the public gallery.'

'Really?' Layla beamed. 'How exciting!'

'And you're to behave and be quiet.'

'I *do* know how to behave,' Layla retorted.

Mikael looked at that mane of black hair and those very long brown legs and tried not to wonder if she had panties on; instead he turned his mind to think about clothes for her. Dressed in the silver tunic she had arrived in, or any of the clothes she had bought last night, she would bring the court down!

'We need to tone you down, Layla.' Mikael stood and rang down to the desk, not caring who needed to be awoken in order to facilitate his request.

'Why do I need to be toned down?'

'Because you don't want your brother to find you… And anyway,' he told her, 'today it's *my* turn to shine.'

'Oh, Mikael…' Layla smiled. 'I cannot wait.'

A selection of outfits was brought to the suite for Layla to try, and Mikael ordered coffee too.

'I'm hungry,' Layla moaned, coming out of the bedroom in a navy shift dress and screwing up her nose.

Mikael was putting his shirt back on—it was still warm from her.

'We'll have breakfast out,' Mikael said, because he liked to eat at his favourite café during a trial and he was not changing his routine for Layla. 'That looks nice.'

'*You* wear it, then,' she said. 'It makes me feel miserable.'

She selected another outfit and headed back to the bedroom. The pale grey linen suit looked very drab to Layla, but when she put it on the skirt was nice and short, and with a silver cami and the jacket's sleeves rolled up she liked it.

'I'm ready,' she said, stepping out of the bedroom and putting on her silver jewelled slippers. 'And I'm very, *very* hungry, Mikael.'

There was no chance of outshining Layla, Mikael thought, because she looked stunning. 'Don't you want to do your make-up?' he asked—because wasn't that what *every* woman did?

She wasn't every woman, though…

Layla shook her head. 'I will only wear make-up

for my future husband. Come on, Mikael, I need to eat soon or I will faint.'

'I won't be picking you up if you do,' he said.

Mikael's choice of café was a trendy converted warehouse that was frequented by his peers, who would all leave him alone, knowing that he wouldn't want small talk this morning or best wishes for the day.

'This is near the hotel where my brother and Trinity are,' Layla commented.

'Now do you see why I wanted you in different clothes?' Mikael said, and she nodded. 'Don't worry,' he added, 'even if we see them, you're having your week.'

Heads turned as they walked in. Not because Mikael was with a woman, more because Mikael was with a woman this close to the end of a trial—and what a woman she was!

Waving and smiling to anyone who caught her eye, Layla was surprised when they didn't wave back.

'Are you nervous about today?' Layla asked, but then the waiter handed her a menu. She looked at it for a moment and then handed it back to him. 'I can't read or write English,' she said, and beamed.

Mikael watched as Joel just about fell to the floor as she aimed her smile at him.

'I'll order,' Mikael said, because Joel would clearly be only too happy to go through the entire menu for her. 'Just fruit and pastries,' Mikael said, 'and two coffees—and two on sub. Actually, just a regular cappuccino for my guest,' he said, because he always had an extra shot, and a high-on-caffeine Layla he wasn't sure he could handle.

'You drink a lot of coffee,' she commented.

'Because I didn't get a lot of sleep last night,' he said,

and then realised what she meant. He had ordered four coffees. 'Two are on sub…'

Mikael let out a breath as she frowned. Just one easy conversation where he didn't have to explain everything would be welcome, but that wasn't going to happen this century.

'If someone needs a coffee and they don't have any money then they can ask if there are any on sub.'

She still looked bemused.

'Do you have homeless people in Ishla?'

'I believe so, but my father refuses to discuss those sort of issues with me.'

Those sort of issues.

Mikael was less than impressed when she wrinkled up her nose.

'They're people, Layla,' Mikael said. He didn't order those coffees without reason. How much easier would *his* life have been had he been able to get a warm drink or a sandwich just by asking. For a long while Mikael had scrimped or scavenged for every morsel. He remembered that every time he ordered food, and he did not take kindly to some pampered princess screwing up her nose.

'Of course they are people,' Layla said, 'but it is an issue, no?' She shrugged her shoulders, but not in a dismissive way. 'I am not to worry about such things, apparently.'

She looked over to him and Mikael realised that again he had misread her when she spoke on.

'But I do.'

The coffee was lovely, Layla declared, thanking Joel profusely for the shake of chocolate on the top of her frothy milk. 'What an amazing combination,' Layla said, as if Joel himself had invented cappuccino.

'You didn't answer me before,' Layla said once Joel had gone. 'Are you nervous about today?'

'I'm never nervous,' Mikael said.

'Never?'

'No.' He shook his head. 'I'm *prepared* for today.'

'Good! So I will start my magical week listening to you in court. I'm looking forward to it *so* much.'

She wasn't being sarcastic, but Mikael took a second to realise it.

'Layla—' he started, because what had seemed the most sensible idea when he had fallen asleep in the small hours felt more than a touch uncomfortable now. 'Some of the things that I say today…some of the things you might hear..'

'It's fine!' she dismissed.

'It's really not fine…' He breathed out, for today he was going to discredit the deceased. Today was not a day during which Mikael would be endearing himself to anyone. But immediately Layla waved his concerns away.

'I've been following the trial. I know what he did.'

'What he's *accused* of doing,' Mikael corrected, but she just shrugged.

'He should be fed to the dogs!' she said, and then looked straight at him. 'And in my country that isn't just a saying.'

The whole café seemed to fall silent as the impossible happened.

Mikael Romanov laughed.

At seven a.m. near the end of a trial.

'So,' Mikael said as their breakfast was served, 'apart from dancing and getting drunk, what else is on your bucket list?' He chose to explain that before she asked him to. 'Your to-do list.'

'Oh...' Layla smiled. 'This.'

'What?'

'This is on my list—I wanted to share a meal in a restaurant with a sexy man. But in my plan it was in the evening and we were holding hands.'

'This is a café,' Mikael said, 'and I don't hold hands. What else?'

'I'm not telling you,' Layla said, popping blueberries in her mouth.

'Go on,' he pushed, 'tell me.'

'If you take me dancing tonight I will tell you some more.'

'I'm not dancing till the jury is in,' Mikael said, 'and if today goes well then you'll be long gone by then.'

'Then you won't ever find out.' Layla shrugged.

'How about dinner tonight?' he offered.

'Somewhere romantic?' Layla checked.

'I don't do romance.'

'Oh. Well.' She shrugged again. 'Your loss. I might have to find another person to fulfil my wishes.'

When they arrived at chambers a rather bemused Wendy took Layla over to the court while Mikael showered and changed into a fresh suit, and then he sat for a long quiet hour going through everything in his mind, over and over. He scratched out phrases, honed in on words, re-examined every angle, just to plant that seed of beyond reasonable doubt.

As court resumed Mikael glanced up at the public gallery just once to check that she was there.

She was smiling down at him.

In black robes and a wig Mikael looked even more

incredible than he had when he had been on her computer.

His voice, when finally he commenced his closing argument, had the goosebumps rising on Layla's arms, for it was rich and deep and reached every corner of the courtroom. It was her privilege to sit, absolutely mesmerised, as Mikael set to work.

On many occasions throughout the long day Mikael rather wished that Layla had left, for what he had to say was not pretty.

There was a furious audible gasp from the gallery as he reminded the jury of a witness's testimony—an ex-boyfriend of the deceased had stated that she preferred her sex rough.

God, no wonder he was loathed by so many, Mikael thought as the lights in court seemed to flicker as social media lit up, demanding that Romanov's guts should be hated.

Still he did not look up to the public gallery.

'My client has never denied that intercourse took place before the deceased fell in the stairwell,' Mikael said. 'Nor has he denied that the sex was violent. But that was by mutual consent.'

Still he did not look up—even when the judge called for someone to be removed from the public gallery for shouting obscenities at Mikael.

He pointed to the gallery once, though, as order was restored. 'Up there is emotion,' he reminded the jurors. 'Down here we examine facts.'

The court broke for lunch and Layla hoped he would come and find her, so that she could tell him how well he was doing, but he was nowhere to be seen.

'Where's Mikael?' Layla asked Wendy, who was walking towards her.

'He just texted me and asked if I would take you to lunch.'

'Oh.'

'What would you like to eat?' Wendy asked as they stood in a café, and Layla frowned. It was so much easier with Mikael.

'What that man is eating,' Layla said.

'A burger?'

Layla nodded.

'With the lot?' Wendy checked.

Layla had no idea what she meant, but nodded.

Despite the company, it was possibly the best meal of Layla's life—and then it was back to court to watch Mikael at his savage best.

'My client has freely admitted that he was angry she had stayed out so late, and that she was drunk when she got home and an argument ensued. Arguments happen—so does make-up sex.'

The lights flickered again.

Hour by hour he shredded the prosecution's arguments, twisted words, questioned statements of so-called fact, reminded the jury of the amount of alcohol and drugs involved, inching them towards *his* conclusion.

'Did she ask the paramedics to get him away from her?' Mikael demanded. 'Did she plead with the treating doctors and nurses to keep this monster away? No, she did not. In fact, as we heard from the senior nurse who took her to the operating theatre where she subsequently died, she *asked* to see her boyfriend.'

Mikael watched as a couple of jurors frowned.

'Does that sound like a woman in abject terror? Does that sound like a woman who had been raped and beaten in a stairwell to you?'

Mikael was the second most hated man in Australia today.

His client was the first.

But for Igor he delivered the best defence he knew how.

CHAPTER SEVEN

MIKAEL WAS UNSURE of his reception when he knocked on Layla's hotel room door a few hours after Wendy would have delivered her back there.

'You were fantastic!' Layla opened the door, her smile beaming. She was back in her red dress and sparkly shoes. 'Oh, my, Mikael—you almost had me!'

'Almost?' he checked.

'That bastard is as guilty as hell but, *wow*, you were amazing!'

'You're the strangest woman I have ever met.'

'I was hoping to see you close up in your robes and wig. Why didn't you meet me for lunch?'

'Layla…' He was about to point out that it was only by some miracle that he'd even remembered she had no money and would have no idea what to do for lunch and so had contacted Wendy, but he left it.

He was relieved by her reception.

Pleased, even.

Layla had been right. He did not care what others thought of him—not a single bit.

He had today.

It was a relief not to have to justify himself.

'How was lunch?' Mikael asked instead.

'I had a burger with the lot and it was fantastic. Wendy isn't much fun, though, is she?'

'Wendy is an incredibly busy woman and it was nice of her to give up her lunch for you.'

'Give up her lunch?' Layla frowned. 'But she ate more than I did.'

She looked at Mikael; he was so very handsome. and she liked it when he smiled—which he was now. Layla knew it was rare, and that he was not a very happy person, and she loved the light it brought to his eyes.

'So what now?' she asked.

'We wait for the verdict.'

'I mean what happens *now*?'

'Do you want to go out for dinner?'

'Pardon?' Layla smiled.

'Would you like to go out somewhere nice for dinner.'

'Somewhere *romantic*,' Layla corrected. 'Yes, please, Mikael.'

He took her to a waterside restaurant. Yes, the view was to die for, and usually he would have asked for a table outside, but tonight their only view would be of each other, and he asked for their most intimate table.

'This is lovely,' Layla said as she slipped in to her side of a velvet booth. 'Oh, our knees are touching!'

'Better?' Mikael asked, moving his.

'No,' she said, because she'd liked the feel of his knees near hers. When he moved them back she smiled. *'That's* better.'

'Do you want wine?'

'I want champagne,' Layla said. 'The best one.'

'Of course you do.'

'Do you have any cigarettes?'

'I don't smoke,' Mikael said, reading the menu, 'and neither do you.'

'I'd like to try a joint.'

'Layla!'

'Zahid nearly got expelled from school when one was found in his locker, and since then I have wanted to try. Just one time.'

'It's illegal.'

'I know a very good defence lawyer!' Layla said, and her knees nudged his.

'You do!'

'Do you have a girlfriend?' Layla asked as the champagne was poured. Mikael declined; he only drank water when he was in the midst of a trial.

'I have girlfriends.'

'Anyone serious?'

'If there was then she wouldn't be very pleased right now.'

'It's just a romantic dinner,' Layla said, and closed her eyes in bliss as she tasted her first champagne.

'If you wanted romance then you chose the wrong man.'

'Why?'

'Because I'm not interested in romance,' he said, and then changed the subject. 'So, apart from drunken debauchery, what else is on your list?'

'I just want to kiss, to flirt, to be sent flowers—and then I will return and marry and be content that I had one magical week.'

He stared at her. It didn't seem an awful lot to ask, and he loathed the lengths she had had to go to and the very real trouble she might find herself in.

Serious trouble.

'I would like to spend a day in bed.'

'Layla,' he said. 'You can't go around saying that.'

'I'm only saying it to you…' She frowned at his concern. 'Always I have duties, and if I don't have duties then I am to join my father for breakfast or have my hair braided. I just want one day where there is nothing planned.'

He rolled his eyes as he realised her statement had been completely innocent. 'I apologise,' Mikael said. 'I thought when you said a day in bed…'

She thought that completely hilarious. 'I wasn't talking about *sex*! Don't worry, Mikael, I'm not going to do anything reckless—I know I have to return to Ishla intact…'

'Are we really having this conversation?'

'We are.' She smiled and looked at the purple marks that were still under his eyes. 'You look as if *you* could use a day in bed,' she said, 'for sleeping.'

'Well, that's not going to happen any time soon.' Mikael gave a thin smile. 'But once the verdict is in I'm going to have some time away.'

'On your yacht!' Layla said. 'With your blonde women!'

'You really did do your homework, didn't you?'

'I told you that I did.' She shrugged. 'So, how long do you think the jury will take?'

'As long as they take.'

'I loved watching you today…' she admitted. 'I kept hoping that you would look up.'

'I had other things on my mind.'

Now he had only Layla, and when her fingers nudged his Mikael took them.

'How is your game of chess going?' she asked, and they both smiled at her previous teasing.

'Can you play?' he asked.

'I am very good,' Layla said. 'I play with my father when he has the time, and often myself, but now I also play it online. It's fun—there is always someone in the world to play with and very often I win. Perhaps I could beat you?'

He saw the challenge in her eyes.

'Perhaps you could,' he said, 'if I had a migraine.'

Layla laughed. 'Don't dismiss me,' she warned.

And then she said something that meant he could not dismiss her—for it made them the same.

'I get bored a lot in Ishla, though it is better now that I can teach…' She gave a little smile. 'And now that I have a computer!'

Bored.

Mikael took her other hand and looked down at their entwined fingers to steady himself just for a moment. That word he could more than relate to.

He recalled his years on the streets—hour after hour to fill with nothing.

Day after interminable day.

He did not remind her she was privileged, he did not scold her with his eyes, for with that word she had him.

Mikael looked into her black eyes and saw the dance behind them, the intelligence that stretched beyond the world she'd been born to.

'Are you nervous about going back to Ishla?' he asked.

'No,' Layla said. 'I will be in trouble when I return—I accept that—but trouble always settles. I love my family,' she said, 'and I feel sorry that I have had to upset them to get what I want, but there was no other way.'

His hands were warm and dry and his fingers moved to the tiny scar on her otherwise flawless skin.

'What happened there?' Mikael asked.

'When we were nine Hussain, my future husband, showed me how to make a match burn twice.'

'Do you love him?'

'I don't know him,' Layla said. 'We played as children. I get to choose my husband, but I have been told, for the good of Ishla, that Hussain would be the wisest choice. My heart does not think so, though.'

He wanted to lift her wrist and kiss it better. Mikael had never felt anything like it before. But then Layla got too close.

'What are your family like?' she asked.

'I don't have any family.'

'Are your parents dead?'

Her question was so clinical he was able to answer.

'I don't know.' He didn't elaborate; instead he dropped hands and took up the menu, started to read out the choices, but she halted him.

'You choose for me,' she said. 'I want what you order—I want to try your favourite thing.'

'Is there anything you especially like or dislike?'

'I want to try whatever.'

So Mikael ordered for them. He taught her how to peel the fattest, plumpest prawns and their fingers played together in the warm water bowl.

'I love these,' Layla said. 'I want to eat prawns again.'

'Don't you have them in Ishla?'

'I don't know,' she said. 'I must ask my father to get some for me.'

Mussels, oysters—all were bliss. But Layla just wanted more prawns.

'I could live off these,' she said, and then very rapidly changed the subject back to where she wanted it to be. 'How can you not know if your parents are dead or alive? Can't you trace them?'

'Leave it, Layla.'

'But I want to know.'

'Well, I don't want to tell you.' Mikael refused to reveal anything. 'What do you want for dessert?'

'Prawns.'

After a draining black day it was a lovely night, and as he dropped her off at the hotel Mikael did the right thing: gave the valet his keys for a short while and saw her to her door.

'Aren't you staying tonight?' she asked as they approached her suite.

'I hope there's no need for me to stay,' Mikael said. 'Unless you're planning on going out again?'

'No,' she said. 'There is no need for me to go out tonight. I have had the best day and the best night of my life and I am feeling very content.'

'Good.'

'Well, almost the best day,' Layla said. 'But it would be even better if you kissed me.'

'I don't think that's wise,' he said.

'One kiss.' She smiled, swiping her door pass. 'Anyway, you have to leave me your shirt to wear—I still don't have a nightdress.'

'Your brother asked me to—'

'You don't have to keep my promises for me,' Layla interrupted. 'I shall be returning to Ishla a virgin.'

'We were talking about a kiss!'

'So what's the problem, then?' Layla said.

She soon found out.

Mikael turned her around to face him and it was a little like being in the car, with him trying to put on her seatbelt. Every touch had her awareness heightened. She stood shivering in anticipation as he positioned them. She felt his hand on her shoulder and his face move to hers, and then she was lost—because nothing in her imaginings could have prepared her for those arrogant lips turned tender.

His kiss was very soft at first, and one hand rested on her waist, the other at her shoulder.

Then she felt the slip of his tongue and the slide of his hand to the back of her head. She had not known that tongues kissed too. It was shocking, it was sensual, it was the gateway to paradise—and her hands went to his hair now as she matched his tongue. And then, whether it was his hand on her bottom or just the call of her groin, they moved in closer and *that* was the problem—one kiss led to more.

She could feel him hard at her centre, but more than that she could feel the strain of her breasts and the pull low in her stomach as Mikael kissed her ever deeper and then pulled his head back.

One kiss and her chin was red and her lips swollen.

'I'd better shave next time,' he said.

'We agreed one kiss.' Layla smiled. 'But now I know why it is trouble...'

He released her. 'I'd better go.'

'You need to leave my nightdress,' she said. 'Are you working tomorrow?'

'I am,' he said, 'but I'll try and finish early.' He was worried about her going out without him, but at the same time didn't want to curtail her. 'What are you doing tomorrow?'

'I have a very special day planned,' Layla said as he took off his shirt and handed it to her. 'I am not getting out of bed.'

'Oh?' Mikael waited for her to elaborate but she had clearly said all she wanted to on the subject.

She looked at him, naked from the waist up, and wanted more of what she had so recently felt. 'Can you kiss me now, so I can feel your skin?'

'Definitely not,' he said, putting on his jacket and pocketing his tie. 'Night, Layla.'

'I have another thing on my bucket list now,' Layla said as he headed for the door. 'I want to have an orgasm.'

'I'm going home.'

'Seriously, Mikael.' She saw him to the door. 'I thought you could only achieve orgasm with sexual intercourse, and even then only if you were lucky. Am I wrong?'

'Very wrong!' Mikael almost groaned. 'Goodnight, Layla.'

CHAPTER EIGHT

LAYLA AWOKE LONG after sunrise and lay in bed for a happy hour, just remembering Mikael's kiss and replaying it over and over, before ringing down for breakfast—only to find out that it was lunchtime.

'What would you like, Layla?' The staff thought she was wonderful, and the head chef was brought to the phone to help her with her order.

'I want someone to come and help me put on the television, and I want a thinly sliced and peeled apple to cleanse my palette, and then something nice to eat.'

'Such as?'

'Sweet,' Layla said. 'Some fruit. You choose for me. One other thing—can I get a joint from you?'

'No.'

'Okay, just some sweet milk to drink, then.'

Apart from when she had caught that cold from wearing damp clothes Layla had never spent a day in bed before, and she intended to enjoy it.

The maids delivered her food and Terrence, the butler, gave her a tutorial on the television's remote control, and Layla lay in bed, still in Mikael's shirt, dipping raspberries in white chocolate sauce and drinking milk laced with cinnamon and nutmeg while watching television.

It was fantastic!

She watched as the couple on the screen started kissing, and blew out her breath as she remembered her kiss last night with Mikael again.

She watched, eyes wide, as the man started to take off the woman's top, and started to blush as he undid her bra.

Oh!

Layla knew that she should not be watching this, that she should turn it off, but she could not stop herself. She wanted some lemonade from the fridge. Usually she would use the phone to get Terrence to fetch it for her, but she did not want to be disturbed and so, with her eyes not leaving the screen, for the first time Layla fetched a drink for herself.

The couple were now on the bed, with a sheet over them, and Layla just about choked on her lemonade at the noises they were making. She reached for the phone—not to call down to the desk, though; instead she called Mikael.

'I can't speak now, Layla,' he said. 'I'm about to have a meeting with my client's family.'

'Just one question?' she begged.

'One.'

'I am watching television and I think people are having sex in the middle of the day and they are not married to each other.'

'You're not watching television, then,' he said. 'You've put on the adult channel.'

God, he thought, another thing he'd have to have removed from her bill before her brother saw it.

'Oh!'

He heard her gasp of disappointment. 'Now they

are putting on the thing where they try to make me thirsty again.'

'That's a commercial.' He laughed. Okay, so she *wasn't* on the adult channel. 'Do you know the name of the show that you're watching?'

Layla told him.

'That's what we call a soap,' Mikael explained. 'They're not really having sex—they're just acting.'

'Well, it's very good acting,' Layla said. 'She looks how I felt when you kissed me last night. Are they dressed beneath the sheet?'

'I would think so.'

'But I saw the top of his bottom.'

'I have to go.' Mikael hesitated as Wendy buzzed. 'Hold on a moment, Layla.'

She would happily hold on, she thought—her show was back on and the couples were lying together and smiling.

'I really do have to go, Layla.'

'Just one more question…' She didn't get to ask it.

'Layla, the jury's returning.'

'So soon? But—'

Mikael had already hung up.

He met with his client, who was sweating. 'It's not good that they're back so soon, is it?'

'No,' he said.

'A little bit of hope would be nice.'

He did not respond. He had done his very best for the filth that now sat next to him. What hope had he given his victim that night?

Mikael sat, his face impassive, waiting.

'All rise.'

Mikael did.

* * *

Layla hopped on one leg as she watched the court reporter on the court's steps and Terrence stood beside her, navigating social media and giving her updates.

'The verdict's coming.'

'Oh,' Layla said. 'Do you think he'll be upset if he loses?'

'He rarely loses,' Terrence said. 'Probably…' Terrence paused. 'Okay, here it is…' He paused for a moment and then read out the verdict. 'Guilty.'

Layla gasped as pandemonium hit the courtroom.

'They're shouting abuse from the public gallery,' Terrence said, reading from a laptop as Layla watched the news. 'The judge is thanking the jury.'

'What are they saying about Mikael?' Layla demanded.

Nothing the court reporter or Terrence could find gave her a clue as to how he was feeling.

Mikael Romanov, the court reporter said, was, as always, a closed book.

Not even later, as he walked down the court steps and ignored the reporters, did his expression give Layla an inkling as to his thoughts.

'Send someone to tidy the room,' Layla said, 'and I want more fruit and chocolate sauce and champagne…' Rapid were her orders.

'Champagne?' Terrence checked. 'I don't think he'll be in the mood for celebrating.'

'*Now*, Terrence, please!'

Mikael's expression was unreadable as he walked back to chambers—just as it would have been had his client been found not guilty.

No one could ever guess what went on in his mind.

He de-robed and took a long drink of sparkling water. Then, a short while later, his car gunned from the car park and Mikael left in a puff of smoke, driving straight to the hotel, where he threw his keys at the valet and this time told him to park it. He took the elevator to her door.

'Enter,' Layla called, and he took out his swipe card and let himself in.

She was sitting up in bed, still wearing his shirt. There was champagne in a bucket and he hadn't had a drink in two months, and there was fruit and chocolate sauce. She understood him, Mikael realised, somehow she understood him—or rather she simply let him be.

'Are you upset?' Layla asked.

'No.'

'Because I thought you could just hide in bed with me. Not for sex. I have always dreamt of it, but today I found out it is really nice to sit in bed and just eat.'

'Okay…' Mikael's voice was a touch wary, but he took off his jacket and tie, shoes and socks, and then opened the champagne. He poured two glasses and joined her, but lay on top of the bed rather than getting in.

'How do you feel?' Layla asked, and Mikael thought for a moment before answering.

'Elated.' He turned and looked at her. 'There's no such thing as a bad day at the office for me, Layla. That bastard is going down for a very long time.'

He breathed out, stunned at his own honesty.

'Do you ever not try your best?' Layla's eyes narrowed as she asked a very brave question—one perhaps no one else would ever dare ask.

'I try my best for all my clients. I fight for them with everything I have.'

'Always?'

'Always,' Mikael said. 'And then, if they are found guilty, I know, as best I can know, that a guilty man has gone down.'

The champagne tasted nice, Mikael thought.

'Aren't you going to ask if it bothers me…?' He was surprised by the lack of the oh, so familiar question.

'Clearly it doesn't,' Layla said. 'I doubt many people could get you to do something you did not want to do.'

'You did,' Mikael said. 'I took you on when I didn't want to.'

'Ah, but you were attracted to me,' she said, and dipped a raspberry in white chocolate sauce. 'Intrigued.'

'I was,' he said. 'It doesn't trouble you, then?'

'Of course not,' she said, and instead of eating the raspberry herself she fed it to him, liking the feel of his lips on her fingers and the wetness of his tongue so much that she did it again as she spoke on. 'For a system to work, both sides need to be represented well. In some lands there is no such system.'

'How does it work in Ishla?'

'If you are found guilty of a crime you are either pardoned, removed or killed.'

'You can be pardoned?'

'Of course. It is at my father's discretion and once you are pardoned there is no grudge, no stigma. If you cannot be fully pardoned then you are removed from society till you can be fully pardoned.' She looked over at him where he lay on the bed, silent. 'Why are you smiling?'

'That's what you do to me,' he admitted. Maybe it was because she was here just for a few days—just a transient timeframe—which meant he could let down his perpetual guard a touch.

'Did you always want to study law?'

'No.'

'Why did you?'

Mikael shook his head. His guard wasn't that low. 'It's just as well you don't read and write,' he said, pulling her into the crook of his arm. 'You'd be running for prime minister.'

'But I can read and write,' Layla said. 'Just not English. But I am going to learn—it will be good for my work.'

'You *work*?' This he had to hear!

'Of course—though I don't get paid for it. My father was concerned because although the girls in Ishla were receiving an education their grades were far lower than the boys. We had a discussion and decided that I would speak with them once a month and encourage them. Now I speak to all the classes. Every day I have students, but I cannot know all their names. Their grades are improving,' Layla said. 'I'm very good at it and they love me.'

'You're modest too.'

She shrugged. 'I loathe false modesty. I tell my girls to be proud of themselves and their achievements.'

They drank more champagne in silence.

Sometimes she felt his mouth on her hair; sometimes she felt his fingers stroke her forearm. It was the most peaceful Layla had ever felt. He dozed, and she liked the thump-thump of his heart in her ear, liked the rise and fall of his chest, and she liked the view too—because she could see the outline of what had been pressing into her last night.

'What are you doing?' Mikael asked as her fingers moved to undo the bottom part of his shirt.

'I want to see the hairy bit beneath your navel again,' she said, but his hand moved hers away and held it and she watched with a smile as the outline widened and stretched.

'What made you want to study law?' she asked again.

'You're persistent, aren't you?'

'Very, very persistent.' Layla nodded. 'I always get my own way in the end, so it would be much easier on you to just give in now.'

It was tell her or let her hand go.

Speak or find her mouth.

Mikael knew what he would prefer, but she had invited him to her bed 'not for sex', and it had been the nicest hiding place he had ever had.

He couldn't even be bothered to put the news on and find out what was being said.

Okay, he'd tell her why he had studied law.

Some of it.

'When I grew up I had no family. I just remember a flat and lots of people, but there was no one there that I called a parent. There were other children and lot of fights, drinking. One night everyone was moved on and I started to live on the streets.'

'As a beggar?'

'And a thief,' Mikael said. 'When I was around twelve, maybe thirteen—I don't know exactly how old I was—a government worker helped me. His wife was dead and he took me in. I shared his home with him and his son, I got an identity, an assumed date of birth, and I went to school. I was always Mikael, but I took his surname.'

'What was it?'

'Igor Romanov,' Mikael said.

'He adopted you?'

'No,' Mikael said. 'I just took the surname. I was grateful to him, and worked very hard at school, but

I still got into a lot of trouble. I was very angry. But when I got the gold medal at school Igor suggested law.'

Layla lay there trying to imagine a life without her family. She missed her mother every day, and even though she had never met her she knew so much about her.

Imagine not knowing anything…

Mikael lay in the dark place in his mind that he didn't visit very often.

How he had fought to survive in a world where no one had cared if he lived.

Worse than that, though, had been the boredom—hour after hour to fill.

Had he not had chess, Mikael knew that he would have lost his mind. Day in, day out, night in, night out, hour after hour, he would sit with men older than him who taught him so well he could soon beat them—until people had started to pay for a chance to play him.

They hadn't paid much, but it had been enough to feed him.

That was when Igor had stepped in, having heard about this boy who was being paid to play chess. Mikael had carried on playing, but there had been books then, and study, as Mikael had fast made up the years of education he had lost on the streets.

Layla's persistent fingers had slid into the gap between his shirt buttons and now idly stroked the hair there. He went to move them, but from her breathing and the sudden stillness of her fingers he realised she was sleeping.

Mikael lay and watched the sun set over Sydney as the tension of the past few months receded.

'Layla…' He felt her stir, and despite having washed

her hair himself he could still smell the exotic scent when she moved. 'Would you like to go out?'

'Out?' Her hand pulled away from his stomach.

'Dancing.'

She was off the bed in a moment, and peeling off his shirt as she headed to the bathroom. Mikael had never known anybody get dressed so quickly.

'I've never danced,' she said excitedly as she pulled on her glittery shoes. 'What if I can't do it?'

'Oh, I'm sure you'll manage,' he said, ringing down for a driver and preparing to head out into the world instead of locking himself in for the night.

The trial was over; it was time for some fun.

CHAPTER NINE

He chose a very private, exclusive club, but as the driver dropped them off there was still a line-up for the less than perfect. They lifted the rope as soon as Mikael approached—but not before Layla had already bypassed the line.

She wasn't deliberately flouting the rules, Mikael realised, they had just never applied to her.

'I want to sit at the bar,' she said as they were led to a table.

'Fine,' Mikael said, because it was her night.

'I want to order.'

'Do so, then.'

'What do you want to drink?' she asked.

'They know my order,' he said

'A drink for Mikael and one Irish coffee for me.'

He just looked at the barman who, to his credit, only blinked once.

'Can I have some money to pay him, Mikael?' she asked.

'I have an account here.'

'I want to pay, though,' she said. 'I want to buy you a drink.'

With *his* money!

'Mikael!' A couple of silks came over. 'Didn't expect to see you here tonight. Bad luck—really thought you'd got him off.'

'So did I for a while,' Mikael said.

They chatted about work for a few moments, but all eyes were on Layla.

'Where the hell did you find *her*?'

'Don't ask.'

'She's stunning.'

'She's exhausting,' he said, and looked over to where Layla sat perched on a bar stool. She was wearing a cream moustache and chatting to the now besotted barman, who'd been foolish enough to say that he'd noticed her shoes as she came in.

'And now…' Layla smiled to the barman '…I take them dancing. Come on, Mikael!'

She *could* dance!

'It's so easy!' She beamed. 'So sexy!' She laughed. 'No wonder it is forbidden.'

As she danced and swayed Layla had possibly never been happier in her life, and her exuberance and sheer joy were infectious. So much so that the mood at the rather staid club lifted and a night that might have been spent commiserating over Mikael's loss seemed to have turned into a party—everyone was up and dancing.

'*You* are sexy, Mikael,' Layla said, wrapping her arms around his neck.

He was so lithe and so full of surprises—for she'd thought he would sit at the bar, but instead they'd moved together and danced into the small hours.

'Will you kiss me again?'

'Not here,' he said, and as the music slowed she leant against him.

'When we get back to the hotel can we do what they did on the television?'

Mikael frowned. It seemed a very, very long time ago since he'd been told that the verdict was in, and only when Layla spoke on did he remember she'd been watching a TV show.

'Can we act as if we're having sex but keep our panties on?' Layla asked.

'No,' Mikael said. 'And I don't wear panties.'

'Please?'

'No,' he said again.

'I'm tired of dancing now.' Layla sulked.

'Good.'

The driver took them back to the hotel.

'Thank you for taking me dancing.' She looked at him. 'Will you stay here with me tonight?'

Mikael had been thinking about the same thing all the car ride back to the hotel. 'Well, I've just had a chat with my self-control and, yes, I will stay here with you tonight.'

'Where are you going?' Layla said as they stepped into her suite and Mikael headed straight for the bathroom.

'To shave,' he said. Because she bruised like a peach and the kiss he wanted to give her would have her face in shreds.

Layla sat on the edge of the bath as Mikael rolled up his shirtsleeves, went through the hotel tray and then rubbed shaving cream in his jaw.

'I think I sweated,' she said.

Mikael shook his head a little at her way with words.

'I would like another bath.'

'Run it yourself, then.'

She met his eyes in the mirror and held his gaze, and the look between them seemed to go on for ever.

'Did you enjoy dancing?' he asked.

'Very much,' she said, 'but not as much as our kiss.'

Without another word she stood and turned. She put in the bath plug and added oils as if she was making a very complicated recipe, and Mikael tried to concentrate on shaving as she started to undress.

Off came the red dress.

Then she slipped off her shoes.

The razor hovered at a safe distance as Layla took off her bra and he saw her pert breasts and dark swollen nipples.

Her panties were next, and Mikael rinsed his face for a very long time. But even with his eyes closed all he could see was the silky straight triangle of hair.

He checked in again with his self-control as Layla spoke.

'Can you wash me again?'

'I think you can do that yourself.'

'I am sure that I can,' she said, 'but I like it when you do it.'

She did.

She wanted to be kissed by him again and she wanted the feel of his arms and the touch of his naked skin. Mikael turned around and she looked at him, wanted to see more of him.

'Can you remove your shirt?'

He did, and he was more beautiful than he had been asleep on the sofa because now he was awake, and she saw the stretch of muscles as he removed it. Her eyes did not guiltily jerk upwards from the snake of ebony hair this time; instead they moved down, and it was very clear that what she was feeling was matched by Mikael.

'You could take the rest of your clothes off,' she invited.

'I don't think so,' Mikael said, because someone had

to stay in control here and he guessed it would have to be him.

'I ache from dancing.'

'Ache no more,' he said, kneeling down.

Mikael washed her far more slowly than Jamila did. First he washed her neck and shoulders, and Layla closed her eyes in bliss at the feel of his fingers soaping her and the sound of him breathing.

Then he washed her arms, and it tickled a bit as he lifted one and soaped her. And then her breath caught as his hand soaped her breasts, one at a time and very slowly. Layla could feel her aching nipples and she looked down to where they were swollen and stretched. Her head was so heavy she rested it on his shoulder and started to kiss his neck.

His neck tasted wonderful, almost as nice as his mouth, and whatever he was doing with her breasts had her hungry to taste him some more.

'Move your mouth lower,' Mikael warned. 'If I have to face your brother it's going to be hard enough looking him in the eye without—'

He didn't finish, and Layla didn't really get what he meant, but as she pulled back she saw the red mark her mouth had made. She moved her deep kisses to his shoulder, licking, sucking and relishing the feel of her wet naked skin against his.

Mikael massaged her aching calves, and then his hand moved between her thighs.

'Jamila hands me a cloth for down there,' Layla said.

'Do you want a cloth?'

'No,' she said, but she was very honest as his fingers explored her intimate lips. 'Just touch me on the outside, though. I will be examined when I return.'

Mikael hated the thought of her being examined but said nothing.

With his free hand he lifted her mouth from his neck and kissed her as he had wanted to since the verdict had come in.

Layla felt the fierce passion of his mouth, the untamed desire of his tongue, even as his fingers stayed gentle. His tongue did to her mouth what she wanted his fingers to do. She was clinging onto his head, squeezing his hand with her thighs, urging him as he resisted. He worked her clitoris and her mouth, holding on himself as he felt her mounting tension.

'Mikael—' She pulled her lips back in panic, but he smothered her protests with his mouth, and she held onto his shoulders as *something* rippled through her, warmer than the water she bathed in and yet it made her shiver. Her thighs clamped around his hand and still he stroked her—and a shocked Layla came for the first time to his hand as Mikael fought to stay gentle.

He stopped kissing her and she rested her head on his shoulder as the *something* receded and a new calm invaded her.

'I think I *did* have a seizure that time,' she said. 'Oh, Mikael, did you have an orgasm too?'

'Layla…' he warned, because her questions were at times so very direct. But he was laughing as he picked her up out of the bath and took her to the bed.

'I can't touch with my hand what is not my husband's, but I want to see it.'

'Well, you're not going to,' he said. 'We're already heading into very dangerous territory.'

'Please, Mikael!'

'Layla, everyone has limits, and you're close to exceeding mine.'

'You will sleep in the bed with me, though?'

'Yes,' he said. Preferably with a padlock on his belt. 'I'm going to have a shower and then I'll be in.'

'Bring me your shirt.'

He was gone quite a time and Layla lay smiling until he came out. His trousers were back on and he had forgotten to bring his shirt out.

'Sleep naked,' Mikael said when she asked him to retrieve it. He was already climbing into bed. 'Live a little.'

'I'll catch a cold.'

'I'll keep you warm.'

It felt very nice to be against him, to feel his hand stroking her ribcage and to rest her head on his chest.

'Did you like your verdict party?' she asked.

'Was that what it was?'

'Yes.'

How much easier would his job be if he came home to *her* at the end of a trial? Mikael thought, and then halted himself—because he didn't like to think that way.

He was tired now. And maybe he was relaxed from the shower, or maybe it was because soon she'd be gone, but when she asked a question so pertinent, instead of evading it or changing the subject, he answered with the truth.

'Where is Igor now?' she asked. 'Do you still keep in touch?'

'No,' Mikael said. 'Just after I finished school Igor was shot and killed.'

'Why?' She went to lift her head, but his hand held her body down just a fraction and she chose to stay still, because he was answering her questions now.

'Street court,' Mikael said.

'Street court?'

'A woman with a very prominent husband was having an affair. One day her husband came home and nearly caught them, but the man escaped through the bedroom window. She confessed that she had been having an affair and her husband pushed her to name her lover. She and Igor had worked together for years, and the husband was furious and had him killed.' Mikael was silent for a long time. 'All the evidence pointed to Igor: the wife had confessed and named him, the husband had known they were friends. And yet, despite so much evidence, Igor was *not* sleeping with her.'

'You know that for sure?'

'I do know that for sure—because the person leaving her bedroom was me. I had met her at Igor's work.'

'She named *Igor*?' Layla was appalled. 'Why would she do that when it wasn't even him?'

'Because she knew what would happen—she knew that her husband would have him killed and she did not want to lose a good screw.'

His voice was so bitter that Layla shivered, and even if she had never heard that word before she knew what he meant. She lay there as Mikael continued speaking.

'I hate her more than the man who shot him. I hate her so much that when a witness comes on the stand I picture her and I tear through their answers. I make sure, if they lie, that I expose it on the stand.'

'This is why you believe in a good defence?' Layla asked.

'Absolutely.'

'So how did you get to Australia?'

'Demyan,' Mikael said. 'He's a friend of mine. I grew up with him but he had moved to Australia. I knew there would soon be a bullet with my name on it, so I called him and his aunt helped me get to Australia.'

Mikael got out of bed and went to get a drink. He did not want her shock and sympathy; he did not want the questions and the prolonged conversation afterwards.

He had told her—wasn't that enough?

'The woman you hate…?' Layla asked, and Mikael gave a wry smile, because she could easily don a wig and robe, so perceptive were her questions. 'Did you love her also?'

'Almost,' he said. 'Well, it was the closest I've ever…' He took a belt of his drink and then a very deep breath, wondering if Layla would notice his hesitation—because the way he had felt in the past didn't come close to the way he was feeling right now.

Not that she would notice.

She was putting on her shoes in bed and admiring her long legs—but what he didn't know was that it was for *his* sake.

She'd sensed that he no longer wanted to talk.

He had never met anyone like her. Mikael was far more used to women pleading for conversation, for emotion, for him to just open up a touch more.

Layla had had all three without even asking.

And the only thing opening up now was her knees as Layla offered a rather appealing distraction from his very dark thoughts.

'Can you kiss me down there?'

It would, Mikael decided, be his absolute pleasure.

CHAPTER TEN

MIKAEL WOKE TO the sound of Layla ordering her usual thinly sliced and peeled apple with mint tea and water.

'And coffee,' Mikael said. 'And cake.'

'Cake?' Layla frowned.

'Cake,' he said.

'Could we have some chocolate cake and coffee too?' Layla said to the chef. 'And I would like my slice of cake just a little bit warm, with lots of cream to pour over it.' She ended the call and gave Mikael a wide smile. 'I love this phone; it's just fantastic.'

'I thought you'd always be ringing down your orders in your palace?'

'No.' Layla shook her head. 'I just tell Jamila what I want and she gets it for me.'

'So Jamila's your maid?'

'My handmaiden,' Layla said. 'She has been with me since the day I was born.'

'Like a mum?'

'No!' She laughed at the very thought. 'You don't love servants…' Her face was suddenly serious. 'I do feel a bit sick, though, at the moment when I think of her. She will be so worried. Oh, poor Jamila!'

'Sounds a lot like love to me,' Mikael said.

'So,' Layla asked, 'now that the trial is over, do you get that time off you talked about?'

He gave a wry smile. His work had barely begun. There would be sentencing, appeals… He closed his eyes at the thought of it all for a moment.

'I have a very busy day today. I have to meet with my client, his family.' God, Mikael knew where he'd rather be.

'That's fine. I am going to take a ferry and I am also going to do the Sydney Harbour Bridge climb.'

Mikael lay there and told himself that Layla was twenty-four. She wasn't incapable. In fact she was possibly the cleverest person he had ever met…

And yet…

That gnawing of unease he had felt the first night when he had called the hotel to see what was happening was back.

It wasn't Layla so much who concerned him but others. She had been so protected it simply didn't enter her head that people might not be nice to her.

He closed his eyes as there was a knock at the door and tried to tell himself that he was overreacting, that of course she'd be fine out there without him.

Breakfast was delivered, along with something that Mikael was a bit embarrassed about now but had seemed a nice idea last night—there was a phone in the bathroom, after all…

'Flowers!' Layla was ecstatic 'And a card!' She opened it. 'What does it say?'

Mikael groaned. He'd forgotten in the moment when he'd ordered them that she couldn't read English, and now he'd have to read it out loud to her—but he waited till all the staff had gone.

'"*Layla, Thank you for an amazing end to a difficult day and an even more amazing night. Mikael.*"'

'No kisses?' Layla asked.

'Three.'

'Wow! Thank you! I will keep this for ever—maybe I hide it in my shoe or something, but I will find a safe place for it.'

'Layla, I don't want to get you in trouble...' Mikael halted. They were approaching the halfway mark of her week and four more nights were starting not to seem enough.

'Look, about today—'

'Mikael,' she interrupted, 'I want to have a day to myself. Please don't ask me to stay in the hotel.'

'Okay.' He pushed out a smile. 'You'll need some cash.'

'Yes, please.'

'Ask the hotel to organise a driver to take you wherever you want to go.'

'I'll be fine.'

'Take my number with you.'

She did.

She bought some white jeans and a top and some sandals from the boutique in the foyer, along with a handbag, and she was ready for her day of adventure.

Layla was worried that she might run into Trinity or Zahid, but at the same time she was determined that even if she did she would very simply refuse to return until her week was up.

She did not use the phone to organise a driver. Instead she decided to try taking a taxi again.

It was far easier the second time around, and she put on her seatbelt and understood that at the end she had to pay him.

Everything on her list Layla did.

She stood on the top of the bridge, being battered by the wind, and life felt so exhilarating that it was as if she were on the top of the world. Then she took a ferry to Manly and ordered a burger with 'the lot' and a can of lemonade, and she met some Dutch backpackers who were very serious but very lovely. They told her that she had to do the night-time harbour cruise while she was there.

'I don't know where to go,' she said.

'We'll show you.'

The cruise started long after sunset and went on for three magical hours. It was wonderful to see the Sydney skyline from the water at night. She could see the Opera House and the bridge all lit up. There was wine and a meal, though the prawns were not as nice as the ones she had had with Mikael, but she heard all the history—about Captain Cook and the convicts—and it was simply magical to sit with her new friends and listen, and feel the warm air on her skin.

She took a taxi back to the hotel, elated from a wonderful day out, tired and ready to have a bath and sleep. But as she opened her hotel door she jumped in surprise to see Mikael—and it was a Mikael that she had never seen before.

His face was grey and he did not return her smile when she walked in.

'Layla…' He was struggling to keep his voice even. 'Where have you been?'

'Doing the things on my list.' Layla smiled. 'I had a fantastic day.'

'It's after midnight.'

'I did a cruise…'

'And you didn't think to call me?'

'Call you?' She frowned. 'You said to only call you in emergencies.'

Mikael had had a day like no other. The moment he had got to work he had changed his mind and called the room, only to find that she had already left.

He had got through his work as best he could but had then cleared his desk for the rest of the week, berating himself for leaving her alone.

It had been a very, *very* long night, and now there she stood, her hair whipped by the wind, her cheeks pink from too much sun. He pulled out his phone and fired a rapid text as, unknown to Layla, he had each night she'd been there—though never as late as it was this time.

Just to let you know, Layla is fine.

'Who are you texting at this time of night?'

'Your brother,' Mikael said. 'As I have every night.'

'Why would you do that?' she demanded.

'Because he cares about you, Layla.' Mikael was having great trouble not shouting. 'Because he must feel sick wondering just how the hell you are and whether or not you are safe, and a text—one bloody text—must surely help, just as one bloody phone call might have...'

He stopped himself. The relief he had felt as she'd walked through the door had flicked to anger and he was not used to it, for he had never really cared enough about another person, or been scared for them before.

'You have no idea the trouble you will have caused for me!' Layla roared. 'My brother will be furious that I am with a man this late at night.'

'Well, you should have thought of that,' he said. 'Did it never enter your head that I might be worried?'

It truly hadn't, and her eyes told him the same—which only incensed him even further. 'You, Layla, are the most selfish person I have ever met.'

'Selfish?' she shouted. 'How dare you call me selfish? I bought you a snowglobe.' She went to get it out of her bag, except Mikael was picking up his keys. 'Where are you going?'

'You've got a nerve to ask.'

'Mikael...'

He didn't answer. Instead he left, and she stood in the lovely suite alone.

She looked out to the dark sky and waited for him to come back.

And waited.

'Where are you Mikael?' she said to the streets below the hotel.

She loathed it. And she was starting to understand—because she wasn't scared for him, she just missed him, and she didn't like the row that had taken place. She was cross, too, for him texting Zahid—and yet she was starting to glimpse why he had.

Mikael was angry for about another twelve minutes and then he pulled his car over and sat on the edge of the road. The fear that had clutched him all day didn't come close to the fear he felt as he looked at the clock on his dashboard and saw the time and the date: it dawned on him they were at the halfway mark before Layla returned to her family.

He sat there for a long time, because it took a very long time for him to process it. He had never known love nor loved anyone before.

He had cared for others—sometimes a little, sometimes a lot—but he had never actually known love, and now here it was.

He didn't want to get closer to her—there was no point, because very soon she would be gone.

When she called he didn't pounce; he did not want to feel the way he did. But he answered his phone on the third ring.

'I know it is wrong to call you so late…'

Layla gulped and he closed his eyes, for he did not want to be moved by her distress, and yet his heart twisted as she continued.

'But it is an emergency of my heart, Mikael. I can't stop crying.'

CHAPTER ELEVEN

SUNRISE FOUND MIKAEL back in her bed, but wearing only hipsters this time, with Layla asleep by his side. He inhaled the traces of bergamot in her hair—it was fading.

Nothing had happened last night. Layla had been crying too much and it had taken for ever for her to go to sleep.

He didn't love her, Mikael decided in the warm light of morning. Instead, he told himself, it was as Layla herself had once said—he was attracted to her, perhaps a bit infatuated.

His world operated much more easily when it was devoid of love.

He picked up the snowglobe she had given him as she stirred awake beside him and watched snow fall for the first time on the Opera House.

'It doesn't snow in Sydney,' he said. 'Not since 1836.'

'It's a global warming snowglobe,' Layla said, curling into him, loving the feel of her leg sliding over his. 'The weather is doing crazy things everywhere.'

He stared at the settling snowflakes, wishing that she did not make him smile so easily.

If he did love her, then it was a very pointless love.

'What time are we leaving?' she asked, and Mikael's

jaw gritted—because just to stop her crying he had suggested that today she check out of the hotel and they go to his home.

He'd rather hoped she might have forgotten his offer. Mikael's home was his haven. He had needed to be there the other night just to get away from the case, and he did not like sharing it with anybody else.

It was either here or to his city apartment that he brought women.

'I was just thinking about that,' he said. 'It's probably not such a good idea. There are no clubs or anything— just beach.' He'd hoped that Layla would decline, yet she seemed delighted with the idea.

'I would love to go to your home,' she said. 'And even if there aren't any nightclubs there shall still be dancing,' She smiled. 'Thank you!'

She felt calmer this morning. Last night had been horrible. After Mikael had stormed off she had realised just how selfish she had been—not just to Mikael. She was glad he was putting her brother's mind at ease but so terribly worried too, because Zahid would demand to know why Mikael had been with her at those times.

He would sort all that out, Mikael had said.

She hadn't believed him last night, but this morning she did. Because, warm and safe in his arms, she was sure that there was nothing he could not do.

'Before I take you to my home I have to go and see Demyan,' Mikael said. 'His wife has just had a baby and I need to visit. While I am gone you can sort out your stuff, and then I will come back and you can check out.'

'What present are you taking for the baby?'

'A snowglobe?'

'Mikael!' Layla scolded. 'That was my present to

you. You have to keep it for ever. Though you *do* have to take a present for the baby,' she said. 'We can go shopping and choose one, and then I would love to meet your friends. We can go on the way to your house.'

He said nothing, but Layla was becoming literally too close to home for him.

Checking her out proved just as complex as checking her in.

A case was needed for the rather remarkable amount she had accumulated, and even the chef came to say farewell to her. Terrence carried the flowers that Mikael had bought her.

It was only as they drove off that it dawned on Layla that she wouldn't ever stay there again, and as they passed the court she struggled to come to terms with the fact that the magical day she had spent watching Mikael was the only one she would ever have.

She had planned her getting here so hard, and had been so determined to have fun and to cram all she could into her one special week, but it had never occurred to her that it might kill her to say goodbye.

And that was just to the hotel staff.

It was starting to dawn just how hard it was going to be to say goodbye to the other.

For both of them.

They stopped at the very boutique Layla had escaped from and bought a cashmere blanket and some little clothes and waited as they were giftwrapped. Then they stopped at another boutique and bought a bikini and some beach dresses for Layla, before heading to Demyan and Alina's very luxurious penthouse.

'What is Demyan like?' Layla asked as they took the elevator up.

Mikael just shrugged, not quite comfortable with the cosiness of it all.

'Surely he's not as talkative as you?' she teased. 'What about his wife?'

'I have only met her a couple of times,' Mikael said. 'She seems more pleasant than the first wife, but the bar was not set very high.'

Back to cynical, Mikael told himself. It was safer that way.

'This is Layla,' Mikael introduced her.

Alina was sitting down, holding the baby, and Demyan looked as if he hadn't shaved or slept since they'd last spoken. Mikael tried to ignore the slight start of surprise on Demyan's face. He had never brought a woman to his friend's home before.

'Actually, this is Princess Layla, and she's on the run.'

'You said not to tell anyone,' Layla scolded. 'You said that I was not to use my title.'

'Demyan and Alina are fine,' Mikael said. 'Congratulations!' He gave Alina a brief kiss on the cheek and then peered at the baby. 'She's beautiful,' he duly said.

'It's okay, Mikael.' Alina smiled. 'I'm not going to breastfeed in front of you.'

Mikael actually smiled at someone who wasn't Layla. 'Okay, I will have a seat, then!'

Despite his reluctance to bring her along with him, Layla made the whole visit so much easier for Mikael. She handed over their gift to Alina and oohed and ahhed over the baby while Mikael and Demyan walked over to the bar, where they chatted for a while as they shared a congratulatory drink, speaking in Russian.

'She's gorgeous!' Demyan said. 'You are good together.'

'We are good together because she's temporary,' Mikael said.

'So was Alina,' Demyan said, and they shared a wry smile because Alina had started as Demyan's temp.

'Well, in this instance it really is temporary. Layla has to return to her family in a few days.' Mikael shrugged as if it really didn't matter. 'I'll probably be bored with her dramas by then.'

He very much hoped that he would be.

But he doubted it very much too.

'How is fatherhood second time around?' Mikael asked.

'Just as good,' Demyan said. 'Actually, better. I know a bit more what I am doing than I did with Roman. Alina is a natural mother.'

Even though they spoke in Russian this was all a foreign language to Mikael. What was a 'natural mother'? He looked over to his friend—a man he had had a fist fight with a few months back, when Mikael had suggested that he stop paying child support for his son, given that Demyan's ex-wife had told him that Roman might not be his.

Mikael had laughed then at Demyan's passion.

He was starting to glimpse it now.

'Why does she have to go back to her family?' Demyan asked.

'Because they love her,' Mikael answered, 'and because she loves them too.'

'Mikael—?' Demyan started, but Mikael shook his head.

'Don't.'

There was no point discussing it, for there was nothing he could do.

As they headed out to the elevator Layla was all smiles, but when the doors closed she rolled her eyes.

'What does that mean?' Mikael asked.

'You know.' Layla smiled.

'No.'

'All my cousins have babies, and you hold them and you smile, and you say the right thing, but...' Layla held out her palms in a helpless gesture. 'Then you run out of things to say.'

Very reluctantly Mikael smiled, but that was enough incentive for Layla to speak on.

'Now Trinity and Zahid are having a baby it will be the same with them. That was how I escaped. Trinity was watching me like a hawk, but I suggested we go in a baby boutique and once we were in I might just as well have not been there.'

'You don't like babies?'

'I don't *dis*like them,' she said, 'though they do freak me out a bit, with their big heads and eyes. I know I shall love mine, but really I would love more of this.'

'Of what?'

'Kissing and dancing,' she said as they stepped out of the elevator. 'Anyway, pregnancy isn't always a good thing...'

'Are you worried that it might ruin your figure?' He smiled.

Just when he thought he knew a little of what went on in her mind, Mikael found out there was so much more he didn't know.

'No.' Layla shook her head as they stepped out onto the street. 'I worry about death, given that it was pregnancy that killed my mother—she died giving birth to me.'

'Layla…' He went to catch her wrist but she shook it off.

'It is not something I wish to speak about,' she said.

'You can.'

'What's the point in that?' she challenged.

There was none.

They walked to the car in silence.

Layla was dreading a future with Hussain by her side.

Mikael felt suddenly ill at the thought of the same.

It was a bit strained on the drive to his property.

Layla was lost in her thoughts and Mikael glanced over several times, trying to work out what she was thinking. Layla wished she hadn't told him that, for she did not like to discuss her fears about getting pregnant, and there was nothing that could be done about them anyway.

So, as they left the city behind, rather than sit in pensive silence Layla nagged him to teach her to drive instead.

'Please, Mikael….' she said, for perhaps the twentieth time. They were miles from anywhere and there was barely a car on the road, just mile after mile of ocean, and then a low white property came into view and she glimpsed what must be his luxurious house. 'Please let me drive.'

'No,' Mikael said as they pulled up on his huge drive.

He took her case in and left it in the hall as Layla looked around.

It was like nothing she had ever seen—a green oasis, and the tropical bush land outside seemed a feature of the home.

The place gleamed with a mixture of modern appliances and a few treasured antiques. A huge black and silver globe hung in one corner, and Layla guessed rightly that it was perfectly angled.

'I am there,' she said, pointing straight to Ishla.

If only the world were really that small, Mikael thought as she clipped on high heels through his home.

It was terribly hard for him to comprehend that the last time he had been home Layla hadn't existed in his world.

'Oooh, I like your chess set.'

'Leave it,' he said, watching her fingers hover over his knight. It felt strange having her here—a streak of feminine beauty in a home that was very male. He did not like the way her eyes seemed to take in each ornament, or each book that lined the walls, and he tried to distract her with the delicious view.

As they walked through to the lounge there was a stunning view of the Pacific Ocean, with its waves constantly rolling in, and Mikael opened the French windows to let in the magical sound .

'Do you want to go the beach?' he offered.

'Maybe later.' She shrugged and with a complete lack of boundaries walked through the house to his bedroom, which looked out onto the water also.

'Where are the maids?' Layla asked with mild interest.

'I don't have maids,' Mikael said. 'I have someone who comes in daily when I am here and weekly at other times.'

'So it really is just us?'

He should be offended, Mikael thought as she snooped through his wardrobe and then into his study, except he couldn't be, for she simply had no concept of living alone.

She thought his home was very beautiful and absolutely intriguing. Unlike the palace, Mikael's walls were not lined with portraits of ancestors, for he did not know from where he came. Instead the art was modern, and Layla stared at a red line on the wall that was fractured in several places before continuing and branching out.

'What is that?' She frowned and peered closer.

'It's a lifeline,' he said, admiring his favourite piece. It had cost an absolute fortune and it spoke to him in many, many ways—not just about this past but about his clients, their victims.

'A lifeline?' she queried. 'Oh, you mean like this?' She held up her palm and then looked back at the painting and pointed to the first fracture. 'So is this you in Russia?'

'It's just a painting.'

It was more than that, though, to Mikael, and he looked at it and thought of the future and the next fracture that would appear when Layla left.

She wanted to know more—there was so much that she wanted to know—yet intuitively she knew that he had already shared more than he was comfortable with. It might take months, possibly years, to truly know him, and all they had were days.

'Layla…' Mikael broke the tense silence because there was a question that needed to be asked. If she felt a tenth of what he did then something needed to be addressed. 'Are you sure that you want…?'

She did not want his question—she did not want this tension that was building to a head—and so she interrupted him before he could say what he must not.

'I actually think I could paint that,' she said stepping back from the painting and nodding. 'If you got me some red paint I could do another one for you…' She turned and saw his rigid lips and kissed them. 'I'm playing,' she said. 'Well, sort of.' Because she was quite sure that she *could* paint it—after all it was just a broken red line! 'I love your home. It is very...' she tried to think of a word to use '...very Mikael.'

'So, what do you want to do?' he asked, because he didn't like her examining his things.

'I already told you—I want to learn to drive,' she said.

'Layla, it's not something you learn in a few days,' he explained. 'Wouldn't you prefer to be doing other things?'

She looked at his delicious mouth and then back to his eyes.

'Teach me to screw, instead.'

Deliberately he did not blink. Mikael knew she had picked up that word from him, and really he would prefer that she didn't return to Ishla with that in her vocabulary.

'That's not a great choice of word, Layla.'

'You said it the other night—you said that she didn't want to lose a good—'

'Lover,' he said, but that didn't work—because he had never been in love until now, and what was the point of falling in love when any day now she'd be gone?

'I want to come again,' Layla said.

'That's better.'

'I want you to come too. I want to see.'

Still he did not blink, but Mikael chose the safer option. 'I'll teach you to drive.'

He watched the smile play on her lips as they headed back out to his car. 'You think you won there, don't you?'

'I think I did.'

He turned the car around and went through a few

basics with her, but she just kept turning his radio on. 'Listen to me, Layla' he said, turning the music off for the third time. 'If I say brake then you are to brake—there is to be no arguing.'

'I know.'

'I'm in charge here...' Mikael warned, but he saw the press of her lips and the dark mood that had been building since last night inched towards breaking point. Was she serious about anything? he wondered, though he had enough insight to know he wasn't talking about driving.

A mini-tornado with black hair and eyes had spun into his life and changed every part of it, and she didn't even seem aware of the damage she would leave behind.

'Layla!' he warned as her fingers moved towards the stereo, and the anger in his voice was more than was merited, perhaps, but it came from within.

'Can I just remind you that I am a princess...?'

He climbed out of the car with his mounting temper and walked back to his sprawling home. She rushed after him.

'Don't walk away from me,' Layla ordered. 'Mikael. You do *not* walk away from me.'

She soon changed her mind when he turned and she saw the look in his eyes as he strode back towards her.

'Okay, you can go now,' she said, but he did not stop walking till he was right in her face.

'Never,' Mikael said, 'pull the princess rank on me.'

'But I *am* one.'

'Don't we all know it?'

'You're cross with me.'

'You—' Mikael was on the edge of losing his temper; he never did—nothing goaded him, *he* was the goader '—are the limit. Have the keys.' He tossed them at her.

'Better yet, I'll take you back to the hotel and leave you there. Better still, I'll take you back to the city and leave you on the street. I'm done.'

He bent down to pick up the keys from the ground and headed back to the car. It was better that he was away from her; she'd have his heart otherwise.

'Come on.'

'Where?'

'I just told you.'

'You can't leave me in the city.'

'I am,' he said.

'Everyone is looking for me.'

'You'll be very easy to find,' he said, and opened the door for her. 'In.'

'No.'

'In.'

'No.'

'Fine,' he said, 'then you get to stay at the house. I'm off to the hotel…'

He started the engine and she ran in front of the car.

He sat with the engine idling, in air-conditioned comfort, as Layla stood in the hot Australian sun, and he was a fool to even pretend that he did not love her.

Life, Mikael thought as she came round to his window, had been so much more straightforward without her in it.

She tapped on the window and waited as it slid down.

'Please don't go.' she pleaded, but he said nothing. 'I was playing and I should have listened.' Still Mikael stared ahead. 'I'm sorry,' she mumbled.

'For…?'

'Not listening when you were trying to teach me.'

He went to slide up the window.

'For being a princess.'

'You can be a princess, Layla, just not when it's the two of us. Do you get it?'

'I think so.'

Even *he* was having trouble defining it. 'When I say enough, or stop, or there is danger, you must listen to me without question.'

'You are just like my brother and father—'

'Please,' Mikael dismissed. 'Do you know, I'm actually starting to lean to their side? If they've had to put up with your dramas for the last twenty-four years I'm full of admiration, in fact, that they got you to adulthood alive.'

'We only have a couple of days and you spoil them by being mean to me,' she said.

'You forgot to stamp your foot.' He saw her tense, frustrated face as still she did not get her way. 'It won't work with me, Layla.'

'It worked before.'

'It won't work in the important things. Now, do you want to learn to drive?'

'Yes.'

'Who's in charge when you're a learner driver in my car?'

'You are.'

She climbed in, and this time Layla did listen.

Half an hour later they bunny-hopped back into his long drive…

'More to the left,' he said, his hand hovering over the handbrake, and wondered if he should take the wheel. But she righted the car—though a fraction too late.

'What was that noise?' Layla asked.

'My paintwork.'

'Oh.' She pulled to a halt, actually quite smoothly. 'How did I do?'

'Very well,' Mikael said, wondering why he wasn't jumping out of his car to inspect the damage; instead he leant his head back on the headrest and gave up fighting it.

Pointless and hopeless, perhaps, but in love was where he was.

She was the important thing.

Which meant that something had to be discussed.

And this time when he raised it he wouldn't let Layla interrupt him.

CHAPTER TWELVE

THEY UNPACKED HER case and Layla put on her new bikini. They had a swim at the beach until, salty and dusty with sand, they returned home hungry.

Layla was determined to make lunch herself.

Hair tied up, her new bikini damp, she was frying a practice prawn in butter with Mikael behind her, telling her to turn it when it went pink.

'It looks beautiful,' she said. 'I can't wait to tell my father about them.'

'Do you want to go back to Ishla?' Mikael asked the question he had tried to before, when Layla had been looking at his painting.

'Of course I do.'

She didn't even hesitate in her response, but Mikael persisted, knowing her answer had been automatic.

'Are you sure that you do?' He saw her face turn just a little and her lovely smooth brow was marred by a frown.

Until this morning she had not considered that she might have to say goodbye to people she cared about. Until now it had never entered her head that she might not want to go back to Ishla.

That she had a choice.

'Of course I am sure,' Layla said, though her voice suddenly said otherwise. 'I love my family.'

'I know that you do.'

'It would kill my father if I left.' Her voice started to rise as she pointed out the reality. 'It would honestly *kill* him.'

'Okay,' he soothed.

'I don't like that question,' she said. 'I don't like how it makes me feel inside. Please don't ask me things like that again.'

'I won't.' Mikael turned off the gas and, still behind her, wrapped his arms around her and held her till she relaxed back into him. But he could feel that her heart was racing—as, he guessed, was her mind.

'Go,' she said, because his words had unsettled her. 'Go and have your shower. I want to make lunch by myself.'

Mikael left her to it, mentally kicking himself and wondering if he could have handled that any better.

What the hell had he been thinking?

Suppose she'd said no, that she *didn't* want to go back?

What then?

Had he been asking her to be his *wife*?

Layla was determined to make a beautiful lunch—and she would if the butter knife she was trying to cut a tomato with didn't flatten it so.

And the onion had made her cry.

Or was she just crying?

Damn you, Mikael, for asking me that, she thought. *Damn you for making me stand here and cry and not want to go home to the land and the people I love.*

'Mikael!' She was suddenly angry and walked

through to the bedroom. She could hear the shower was on but had no qualms about walking in. After all, he had bathed her a few times.

What Layla saw, though, had her heart in her throat—and suddenly she wasn't angry any more.

He looked up and saw the shock on her face as his eyes lifted from where he had been concentrating and he saw her standing there, watching him.

Then he watched her as the shock changed to a delicious smile and she stepped into the shower with him.

'Continue,' she said.

Mikael wasn't sure that he could—until her mouth started working his chest.

'Is this why you have so many showers…?' she asked, and he gave a half laugh. 'I thought you were just very clean!'

She loved the tension in him, loved the feel of his wet skin, and she slipped out of her bikini and then boldly dropped to her knees and kissed up his legs… slow kisses that changed to frantic, because she wanted so badly to touch and to taste what she must not.

He almost pulled her up by her hair, but he wanted her to see this, and wanted her pleasure too. He took her hand and placed it over his, on the outside, so that she did not touch, but she felt the motion and the building tension.

'Oh…' It was the nicest thing she had ever felt.

He bent his knees a little and rubbed himself over her and Layla watched in fascination, till her thighs were shaking.

'Mikael…' Every stroke brought her closer, and then she watched as their hands stilled but his shaft didn't, and the moan that came from him as he shot over her was addictive, for she wanted to hear it again and again.

It was that and the shots of silver that spilled over her that almost brought Layla to her knees with her own lovely orgasm.

'What's that noise?' Layla gasped, at the sound of bleeping, but she was talking to thin air as Mikael had suddenly bolted from the shower. 'What is happening?' she asked, following him out. 'Mikael, what is that smell?'

Layla found out what a fire extinguisher was as a naked Mikael tackled the wok that she had left unattended.

'You're supposed to turn the gas off,' he said as he put the small fire out.

'You shouldn't have turned me on.'

She had an answer for everything, and Mikael stood back breathless and looked at the smoke on his gleaming walls. All he could think was that he was going to miss this.

'*I'll* make lunch,' he said. 'First, though, I'm going to get dressed…'

'Why?' she asked, wrapping her arms around him. 'I like us like this.'

So too did Mikael.

'Do you want to watch some pawn while we eat?'

He gestured to the chessboard and Layla nodded.

'You didn't laugh at my joke,' he said.

'I don't joke about chess,' she said.

But he realised she probably had not understood.

They had a very quick and less ambitious lunch, which consisted of tomato sandwiches with loads of black pepper, and then, naked, she took two chess pieces, shook them behind her back and held out her hands.

Mikael peeled open the fingers on her right hand. He

was black. There was a thrill of anticipation for Layla as he set the board up, and she lay on her stomach, propped up on her elbows. She had had the same flurry of nerves in her stomach when she had first played with a stranger online.

A better flurry, in fact!

'I don't want any favours,' she warned.

'You won't get them from me.'

Layla was white, within three moves it was Mikael attacking and Layla on the defence.

He watched as she removed his knight and then he swooped.

'*Mchfesa*,' she said.

Mikael could guess what that meant.

He set up again, and she opened as she had before, but again it was to no avail.

'I am *good* at this!' she said.

'You are.' Mikael smiled. 'But I'm better.' He wasn't pulling rank. 'I've played a lot.' And, as naturally as breathing, he told her a bit about his time on the streets and how chess had saved his sanity.

He didn't want pity, and he didn't get it from Layla.

'I have played a lot too,' she said. 'I would be out of my mind otherwise. Before I had my students, chess was the best company I had.'

Mikael looked up. 'Have you ever heard the saying, "at the end of the day the pawn and the king go back in the same box"?'

'No.'

She thought about it for a moment too long.

'Checkmate.' He smiled. 'You are too easily distracted. You need focus.'

'I will beat you one day,' she warned, and then he saw her jaw clamp down, because no matter how they hid from the world and got lost in their own they were constantly reminded that the clock was counting down on them.

But instead of dwelling on that Layla focused on the game. She opened differently and awaited his response.

'I'm thirsty, Mikael.'

'Then get a drink.'

She didn't. She moved into attack again and again, and suddenly they were game on.

'I'm *very* thirsty, Mikael.'

'Good,' he said, refusing to allow her to distract him. 'Shall I get up and run a tap?'

She shot him a look and stood up. Usually nothing distracted Mikael, yet as she returned and repositioned herself a very ripe nipple might have done. Had he had his time again he would not have made the move that he did. Not that his face told her that, and he hoped she wouldn't see the opening he had given her, but as he watched her fork him with her knight he realised she had.

'Your phone is ringing,' Layla pointed out as she sacrificed her queen.

'So?'

He let it go to voicemail as they played on, and soon her pawn had crossed the board and Layla had reclaimed her queen.

She smiled at him, but it wasn't returned for his phone was ringing again.

'What the hell does Demyan want?' Mikael's voice was irritated.

'How do you know it is Demyan?' she asked as he stood.

'He has his own ringtone.'

'That's sweet!' she said, and watched as he took the call.

The vague irritation in his expression disappeared and his face snapped to impassivity. She had a growing sense of unease as Mikael spoke in length to Demyan in Russian.

'What did he want?' she asked when he ended the call, and when he did not answer her straight away she knew that something was wrong. 'Is it the baby?'

'The baby's fine,' Mikael said.

But just as she relaxed he took her hands, and she knew she was going to hear bad news.

'Layla, Demyan and Alina were so curious about you that they looked you up. Your disappearance has just hit the press. The police are looking for you...'

'No...' she whimpered. 'No.' She shook her head. 'They won't find me here.'

'Yes, Layla, they will,' he said. 'The staff at the hotel will recognise you, and the booking was under my name. This is serious now.'

He let go of her hands, turned on the television and found the news.

There she was: black eyes, black hair, and a face that was unforgettable.

The police could be there in a matter of moments.

'We need to get you back.'

When she didn't respond he elaborated.

'Layla, it will be better for you if you return under your own steam than have the police find you.'

'One more night,' Layla begged. 'Mikael, please, I just want one more night.'

She was not manipulating him now; instead she was pleading.

'Just one more night and then I promise that I will

go back happy. I will never interrupt your life again, Mikael, if you will please just give me one more night.'

'One more night…' he said. 'We'll take out my yacht…'

He was already loading a cool bag with supplies: champagne, fine food—anything he could think of to give Layla the very best final night.

'Go and get dressed and sort out the clothes that you'll return to your family in.'

'Mikael?' She frowned. 'I'll get changed here, to-morrow, after our night.'

'We won't be coming back here, Layla. If we're going to leave then it has to be now.'

It was the most horrible thing she had ever heard, and she simply did not now how to respond.

'Layla?' He was very calm; he could see how much she was struggling. 'Come on,' he said, deciding to find clothes for her. Just now it had nothing to do with her being a princess that she could not dress herself.

She was simply trying not to break down.

They were heading to his car in a matter of moments.

'Mikael…?' She said as he opened the passenger door for her.

'You're not driving.'

'No, of course not.' She was suddenly serious. 'To-night, if I tell you to make love to me, if I plead with you that I don't care, please…'

'You'll be fine, Layla.'

She would be—he knew that.

But only for as long as she was in his care.

CHAPTER THIRTEEN

IT FELT LIKE the last night on earth.

Mikael sailed the yacht till it was far enough from his home that he was satisfied they would not easily be found, and then dropped anchor in a pretty cove.

He looked over to where she stood, leaning on the rail and looking out to the view, and he wondered how he could possibly give her the night of her dreams while knowing that tomorrow she'd be gone.

She could feel his eyes on her as she looked out at the view, at the gorgeous red sky. The next sunset she saw would no doubt be on her way back to Ishla.

Why had Zahid let her father know?

Tears stung her eyes because she had not wanted to hurt her father.

She remembered her threats to Zahid and Trinity that she would go to an embassy—she would never have done that, though. All she had wanted was a week.

'It is beautiful,' she said as Mikael came and joined her. But not even a sunset could soothe the hurt. Instead it made her want to cry. 'Why did they have to tell my father? Why did the police have to get involved?'

'I would guess they were very worried last night, when I didn't text and say that you were okay until so late.'

'I should have called and let you know that I was safe,' Layla admitted. 'It truly never entered my head. If I had had a phone there were a few times I would have liked to call you to tell you what was happening, but I don't have one.'

'I know,' he said, and put his arm around her shoulders. He looked out to the night and wished he could take away their row.

It had been no one's fault—she didn't know about public phones and, after all, he had told her not to ring him unless it was an emergency.

For Mikael, not wanting his day to be interrupted by her felt like a very long time ago.

'You were right to text Zahid, though,' she said. 'I was thinking about it after you left me alone last night. I believe that had you not texted him the first night to say that I was safe then my father would have been informed by the morning. At least we had *some* time.'

'You didn't get a week,' Mikael said, 'but have you had a nice few days?'

'They have been wonderful,' she said. 'You have been wonderful to me.'

Mikael made her favourite dinner—*without* setting the kitchen on fire—and she sat on the bench and watched him.

'Sick of prawns yet?' he asked.

'Never.'

They took their dinner up on deck and washed it down with champagne, and Layla shivered a bit when he asked her what would happen when she went back to Ishla.

'I know you said there would be trouble for you, but can I ask what sort?'

'I expect that my father will ban my computer,' Layla

said, 'and I will have to apologise to Trinity and Zahid, and perhaps I will not be allowed to teach...' She ran a hand through her hair and thought of the smiling faces of her students and how much they would miss her. 'I was selfish, I suppose. They will miss out because of me...'

'It might not be for long,' Mikael offered, but she shook her head.

'My father has already told me that my future husband might find it offensive if I work...I expect that decision will be made for him.' She told Mikael the truth then. 'My father will bring my wedding forward, I expect. I have been trying to avoid it, but he will say I have given him no choice.'

'Layla...'

'Please don't ask that question again.'

He let out a tense breath in exasperation, but she had not finished speaking yet.

'I am so loved and so happy at home,' she said. 'I wanted adventure—just one big adventure—and I have had that, I just forgot the first rule of chess.'

'Tell me.'

'To look to more than the next move,' she said. 'I planned and researched escaping, being here, and all the things I wanted to do, but I forgot to consider the leaving part. I never thought it would hurt—it never even entered my head that I might prefer to live life here.' As Mikael went to speak she shook her head. 'I would never do that to my father, to my country, to my people.'

'Even if you won't be happy?'

'Of course I will be happy. I will just miss things here,' she said, and tried to hold back on just how much she would miss Mikael. It would not be fair to either of them.

She had not lied to him that first day. Revealing her thoughts always got her into trouble, and possibly never more so than now. It was imperative that she did not break down and tell him just how she was feeling.

'I wanted tonight to be wonderful,' she said, 'but all I feel like doing is crying.'

'Come here,' Mikael said and led her to the day bed where they lay for a lovely while.

'Do you have any regrets?' Mikael asked and she shook her head.

'You?'

'None,' Mikael said and then thought for a moment. 'I wish that I'd got you that joint.'

'I don't need it now,' Layla said because lying here next to Mikael with the stars shining so brightly and the feel of being in his arms she had her high. It was a gorgeous navy sky, so dark except for the stars and just the tiniest sliver of moon.

'That's the first thing I thought of when I saw you,' Mikael said, gazing up at the moon and remembering walking into his office and seeing her standing there in her silver dress. 'Make a wish on the new moon,' he said.

Perhaps he should not have said that, because he had just managed to get her to smile.

'I just made it,' Layla said, and turned her head and looked at him.

'You can't tell me what your wish is,' he warned.

'Okay.'

She looked up at him and thought how lucky she was to be here even if just for a little while. 'I've done everything,' Layla said. 'I have danced...'

'You can *really* dance!' He nodded approvingly.

'I have had a romantic dinner with a very romantic man. We have held hands, touched knees, kissed...' she looked over at him. 'We have exceeded my list with orgasms.'

'Good.'

'I have had flowers, a whole day in bed...' She counted things off. 'A day out sightseeing.'

'What was your best bit?'

'Apart from the orgasms? Then your verdict party,' she answered immediately. 'Have *you* enjoyed it, Mikael?'

'Very much?'

'What was *your* best part?'

He paused as he tried to think, but he could not choose a best part, from her biting her teeth at him on the day they met, taking out that ruby—there was not one part that he could list above another.

'It's all been good,' he settled for saying. 'Though I do feel bad about our row.'

'Mikael!' she scolded. 'I *loved* our row. If it wasn't for our row you wouldn't have had to calm me down and agree to bring me to your home...'

Mikael actually laughed. 'Were you manipulating me *then*?' He was impressed rather than annoyed. 'Do you ever stop?'

'Never.' She grinned. 'Every word I say is with the intent to get what I want...' She looked over to Mikael, still smiling and looking a whole lot happier than he had on the day they'd first met. 'Can we have sex like the actors do?'

That was the wish she had made.

And he would make it come true.

'Yes,' he said, and decided that for however long they had left he would simply let himself love her.

'You could film it with your phone and then we could watch it together afterwards,' Layla said as he led her down to the cabin.

'No!'

'It would be fun.'

'Not a chance,' Mikael said, and he meant it even though he was laughing.

He would miss her so.

'You are so good to me,' she said as she sat on the edge of the bath and watched him shave just so that he wouldn't mark her.

'Why wouldn't I be good to you, Layla?'

'All the people who think you are a savage bastard...' she said. 'They don't know you.'

'I don't want them to,' Mikael said.

He'd liked living under his lonely rock—a career that consumed nearly all of him and pretty meaningless sex had been enough till now. But tonight, for one last night, he stepped out into the sun.

'You remember what I said back at the car?' she said as he dried his face. 'That even if I beg...?'

'Layla, you don't have to worry about that,' he said. 'Right—where do you want me?'

'Sorry?'

'Am I coming home from work, or are we already in bed? What was happening in the episode of that TV programme you saw?'

She started laughing—on a night she'd thought she never would. It was a side to Mikael she had never seen.

They were drunk on lust and enjoying it.

'We're on a boat and sailing for ever,' Layla said

as he took her face in his hands. 'Tomorrow never comes.'

They had shared many, many kisses, but she had never tasted him so tender as his hand traced her spine and then unhooked her bra. She felt her breasts naked against his skin; it made her ache from the inside.

It was Layla who went for his belt but then changed her mind. Her hand held him through the fabric, growing him, holding him, stroking him, till Mikael pushed her hand away and led her to the bed.

Layla lay there, watching him undress, and she slid under the sheet as a naked Mikael joined her.

He kissed not her mouth but the breasts he had never tasted, and Layla relished the gentle licks and soft sucks, looking down at his lips as he blew her nipple to a painful peak and then kissed down her stomach and then back upwards.

'Take them off,' she said as his fingers stroked her through her bikini bottom; she wanted to feel him there.

But Mikael would not.

And so she did.

She undid the sides as he kissed her, and they wrestled just a little with each other, and with self-control—and then Layla's hand went where it must not, and she held him with no barrier this time.

Mikael rose to his knees and Layla looked at him.

'Just a little way?'

'Not a chance,' he said, and his hand was over hers this time as she stroked him, feeling the soft, soft skin that encased his manhood, moving him closer to where she wanted him. And it was cruel, for they deserved more.

Mikael moved down the bed and kissed along her

thighs, over and over, till she pleaded with him to taste her *there* again.

This time he pulled her legs so that they lay over his shoulders and down his back, and she felt every breath from him; the flicks of his tongue were intense and they made her sob with both need and frustration, for she wanted him inside.

He struggled to stay gentle, not to bury his face in her mound and suckle and nip and probe her till she was ready—for that was where his mind was, and so too was Layla's.

'I don't care, Mikael…' she said as her fingers tried to pull his head from her, as she tried to move her legs so he would slide up the bed and take her. 'I don't care what happens when I get back…'

But his arms held her legs down, and his tongue was more rapid and probing, and he took her from the edge of potential disaster to temporary oblivion. Yet even as she came to his mouth, even as her body rode the high, somehow it was not enough.

She still wanted more.

'I want to taste you,' she said, and she smiled as she felt him moan with want between her legs.

'You said…'

'I can do this,' she said—for she would make her own rules. She would never do it with another…she would marry Mikael the only way she could: with her mouth. 'Please, Mikael, I will only ever do this with you.'

He lay on his back and Layla lay astride him, lowering her head to the base of him and slowly kissing the long way up.

'My hair…'

She lifted it and tied it into a knot.

'That is better,' Layla said. 'Now I can concentrate.'

She kissed him with her eyes open—not just his lovely shaft but down to his balls, which she took one by one into her mouth and sucked gently, because every bit of this she wanted to remember for ever.

He tasted clean, and she was about to give thanks for all the showers he took, but the moan from him and the slight pressure on her head told Layla he might not appreciate a break for conversation.

She was as turned on as she had been when his mouth had been on her, and she felt one hand cupping her bottom as his other hand guided her just a little further down.

She ran her tongue around the top and then swallowed him a little way down, and then more, over and over, working him with her hand, somehow imagining that the hips that bucked in her mouth bucked between her legs.

Yes, she married him—for she would never be as intimate with another, would never moan and purr in pure pleasure.

She forgot her stride for a second, coming herself as he moved in her mouth, and just as it subsided Layla got the shock of her life as he swelled and started thrusting and she felt the first splash of Mikael.

He had meant to warn her. Instead he'd been taken back at the speed and strength of his orgasm.

He heard a small gasp from Layla—and even in the throes of his pleasure she made him smile. Kneeling up, holding her mouth closed with her cheeks bulging, she was the only woman in the world who could be about to spit and somehow not offend.

But instead she took a deep breath and swallowed.

'Oh, Mikael!' She was truly stunned for a moment, but then she smiled. 'That was fantastic.'

'It was.'

'A little more practice and I think…' Her voice faded. They had almost run out of time.

'Come here,' he said, and brought her back to his arms for their last night on earth together.

Neither wanted the morning.

CHAPTER FOURTEEN

MIKAEL DID NOT sleep.

All night he heard the buzzing of a helicopter and wondered if it was for them—or more likely an air search that had nothing to do with Layla.

As she started to stir he kissed her head and smelt her hair. It smelt of the ocean and their time had run out.

She woke but did not open her eyes, because she didn't want it to be today.

'Layla?' He turned. 'I know you're awake.' He watched her smile with her eyes closed and he smiled at her too. 'Do you want breakfast?'

'No, I feel too sick to eat.'

Her eyes were still closed and he saw just the tiniest glimmer of moisture at the edge of them. He did not want to make this harder for her, even if it was almost killing him.

'Thank you for giving me a lovely last night,' she said.

'It was my pleasure.'

She opened her eyes and knew she wanted to open her eyes to him every morning; it felt as if this was the way the world should be for ever, with Mikael on the pillow beside her.

His eyes roamed her face and he took her hand. He

had never wanted love and yet here it was now—and he was about to lose it.

'Marry me?'

She heard the words and they made her chest hurt. They made her eyes sting and they made her heart soar—and yet it plummeted in the next instant at the absolute impossibility of any future for them, so she answered him in the way that must serve them best.

She laughed.

'Layla…' He would not be swayed. 'I will sort it with your family. I will speak with your brother…'

'Mikael, you would be bored without your cases.'

'I mean marry me and live *here*,' he said, and she sat up and hugged her knees to her chest.

'Mikael, I live in a palace. As beautiful as your home is, do you really think I would want to give up my life?'

He said nothing.

'Will you give up *your* life and live in Ishla?'

He took a breath. 'If you let me speak with your family we can work out exactly what we want.'

'You really think my father would entertain the idea?' Again Layla laughed. 'Of course not. And so it is time for me to return to my family. I told you that if you gave me one more night then I would return happy. Now I keep that promise to you.'

Mikael sat as she headed to the bathroom. There was no request for assistance this time; in fact she closed the door.

Layla stared at her reflection for a very long time, telling herself over and over that she could do this. Reminding herself that she was going back to a family whom she loved very much.

Except on the other side of the door was a man she

loved in a different way; he was there in her heart, and she felt right now as if that heart was breaking.

She pulled on her silver dress and slippers and felt as if she was dressing for her own execution.

Mikael!

She wanted to scream his name, to plead for him to sort this, to go to bed now and wake up in a year in his arms to find out that it was all somehow over.

Instead she pushed open the bathroom door.

'Can you take me back to my family now?' she said. 'I want my father to know that I am okay.'

Even the ocean was against them, for they slid through the water with rapid ease. Mikael wondered if there might be police waiting at his car—if their good-bye would take place right here—but as he approached, there his car was, as he had left it.

Layla looked at the silver car that had caught her eye before she had even met him, and as they approached Mikael examined the huge scrape down its side and tried to tell himself his more ordered life could return soon.

'I loved driving,' she said as he opened the door and she slipped into the passenger seat. 'I have done all the things on my list and more.'

She put on her own seatbelt, albeit a bit clumsily, but if he neared her she would bury herself in his arms and plead for him to keep her for ever.

Wendy called on Mikael's private number to say that the police had been in touch and had asked that he call them.

'Thank you.'

He did not relay the news to Layla, and neither did she ask what the call was about; instead they drove in near silence, but as the city approached she turned the radio on.

'Don't.'

Mikael went to turn it off but she stopped him.

'Let me hear.'

She was the headlines.

He heard her snort as the newsreader said that Princess Layla of Ishla suffered from seizures and might need urgent medical attention, but her mirth turned to a strangled sob as an interview with her father was played.

Even before the translation Mikael could hear grief and bewilderment in the old King's voice.

The translation even procured a sniff from Mikael— for, as cynical as he was, and as much as he wanted to be angry with the man, he could hear the love.

'I love my daughter; she is my most precious possession. Please, Layla, come back to your family. Please, whoever is hiding her, make sure she is safe. There is nothing for me if there is no Layla.'

Then there was a statement that said if there was no news by morning the King would travel to Australia to help in the search for his daughter.

It would be morning in Ishla in a few short hours, and at the sound of her father's promise Layla issued her instructions.

'Drop me near the hotel that Trinity and Zahid are staying at.'

'I'm not just dropping you off,' Mikael balked. 'I will come and speak with your brother.'

'No!' she shouted. 'No, you will not!'

'You really think I'm just going to let you out of the car and drive away…?'

'If you care about me that is exactly what you will do.'

It wasn't supposed to end like this, Layla thought, resting her head on the window. It was supposed to end happily; she was supposed to leave smiling.

She wanted to cry, wanted Mikael to turn the car around and drive her to his home, but she must never let him see that.

'Here!' she said as they passed the café where she and Mikael had once shared breakfast. She knew the way to their hotel from there. 'Drop me here.'

'I can't just—'

'It was fun,' she interrupted, her heart breaking. 'Can we please just keep it at that?'

'Layla—'

'Please,' she broke in, 'stop the car and let me out.'

It was the hardest thing she had ever done.

Followed by the hardest thing Mikael had ever done.

Watching her get out and simply leave.

He walked into chambers and didn't even have to tell Wendy not to speak. One shake of his head was all she got and he stepped into the cool dark of his office, trying to fathom that a few days ago he hadn't even known her.

The best thing that had ever happened in his life had gone and he had had no choice but to let her go.

He felt as if there had been a death.

Yet he'd never mourned like this before.

He was breathing hard, just trying to get used to the idea of fifty or so years on the same planet as Layla without ever seeing her, when his intercom buzzed.

He ignored it.

'Mikael?' Wendy knocked at his door.

'I don't want to hear it!' he shouted, and then turned as the door opened.

'Yes, you do,' Wendy said. 'The café where you have breakfast just called. Layla's there, apparently. They saw her on the news but instead of calling the police they have called you.'

'Tell them to take her out to the back!'

'They've tucked her away in a booth and put reserved signs on all the tables near her. Layla doesn't know that they've called you.'

Mikael ran.

He almost flew into the café, to see the smile of Joel.

'Layla's fine,' Joel said as he walked Mikael over. 'Well, she's crying. She came and asked if we had any coffees on sub. I don't think she really gets the concept, but she's so gorgeous who could say no to her?'

Not Joel—and certainly not Mikael.

Tears were streaming down her cheeks as she nursed her coffee and Mikael knew he was glimpsing the real Layla—the one who hid deep beneath the shining surface, the Layla he had been so privileged to get to know even just a little.

'Why are you crying in your coffee?' he said, and saw her jump a little.

And then she looked up and did not even try to wipe her tears.

'I'm very confused, Mikael,' she admitted. 'It was supposed to be fun. I did everything I ever wanted and I don't understand why I feel so sad.'

Mikael moved into the seat opposite and took her hands without thought.

He looked at the little circular scar on her wrist and knew that even if it hurt them both he would try one more time—because not only did he not want her to go back, his guts folded over at the thought of her with another man, going through the trauma of having babies she simply wasn't ready for and might never be ready for.

He did not want her scared—and if she had to be then he did not want her scared in the world without *him*.

'Layla, I meant what I said this morning—will you marry me?' he asked again. 'I will sort it all out. I will speak with your brother, your father…'

'No.' She looked at him. 'It can never happen.'

'Layla—'

'Please, Mikael, you are making this worse for me. I just wanted to sit with my coffee and my thoughts before I face my brother. I am more scared than I thought I would be, and I am so cross with them for telling my father.'

Her tears ran silent now and he did not want her to leave. It was the last thing on earth he wanted, and yet he needed to do as she asked and somehow make this better for her, not worse.

Mikael knew he needed to make this about *her* now, rather than them.

'Is there anything I can do that will help?'

'There is.' She gulped. 'Will you speak with Zahid? Can you tell him that nothing happened between us…? Can you tell him that I stayed with your married friends and that you were not with me when you texted in the evenings and nights, that your friends let you know how I was…?'

'Will that make it easier on you?'

'Much,' Layla said. 'If my father thinks I was alone with a man…' She shook her head. 'He cannot know. But please only agree if you are sure you can act as though you have no feelings for me—as though I am the trouble you first thought I was.'

He moved into the seat beside her and she felt his

arms around her for the last time, then his mouth on hers. It was a very tender kiss, for Mikael had not shaved, but it was so loaded with passion it would burn her lips every time she remembered it.

'I don't know how to let you go,' he admitted.

'If you care for me you will. I love my family. They will be cross, yes, but you are not sending me to savages, Mikael—you are returning me to my family and to people who love me.'

He thought of her kitten-soft feet and how pampered and looked-after she had been, and of her father, who was devastated that she was missing and in agony that he might have lost her.

Mikael was in agony too.

'Please, Mikael—please don't make this worse for me than it already is.'

He couldn't say no to her, and so he said yes to the most impossible task of his life.

'We'll do it at my chambers.'

CHAPTER FIFTEEN

THEY WENT OVER and over their stories before Mikael would call Zahid.

'I'll have Wendy make up a bill for units of time.'

'Reduce them!' Layla gave a thin smile.

'Yep—and I'll add the hotel costs…'

'The hotel?'

'I'm sure they would have remembered you and called the police—your family will know by now that you stayed there, I'll tell Zahid that you stayed between there and Demyan and Alina's.'

He missed nothing.

Mikael called the hotel and asked them to send an amended bill—with the alcohol removed.

'Thank you.'

He even rang Demyan and Alina, just to firm up her alibi.

'*Every* night,' Mikael reiterated to Demyan in English, so that Layla heard it too, 'and you or Alina would call me and say that she was okay, and then I would text Zahid. The other night the baby was upset and crying and you simply forgot till much later to call me.'

'Okay,' Demyan said. 'Mikael, is there any way Layla can stay…?'

Mikael switched to Russian and Layla closed her

eyes at his angry voice as he swore at his lifelong friend—because if there *was* any way Mikael would be utilising it now.

When he had ended the call Mikael switched back to being impassive, but Layla had glimpsed his anger and his pain and she knew he was hurting just as much as she was.

'Okay, Demyan and Alina know what to say if asked.'

'What if they mess up?'

'Forget that,' he said. 'They'll do the right thing by you.'

'You need to call my brother now.' Layla's voice was suddenly urgent. 'My father will be flying from Ishla if there is no news by morning. I want him to know as soon as possible that I am safe. He is ill…' She was starting to panic—not for herself but her father. 'Mikael, my father is sick and no one must know that. I should not have done this when he is so ill…'

'Calm down,' he said. 'I'll call Zahid now.'

'I have been trouble, remember?' she said as he punched in the numbers.

Zahid answered on the first ring. Mikael was certain he must have spent the last few days with his phone permanently to hand.

'Your sister has asked that you collect her,' Mikael told Zahid, and gave his address. 'She's fine,' he said. 'Yes, I put her in a hotel, but you were right—she's completely incapable and so I had a couple I know looking out for her.' His voice changed to irritated. 'They happen to have just had their first baby, so having your sister dumped on them was a huge inconvenience—'

Mikael pulled the phone from his ear. Zahid had hung up on him.

'How did he sound?'

'Relieved—which will soon turn to angry,' Mikael warned. 'But that's normal, and it will be the same for your father. It was the same for me when you didn't come back to the hotel that night.' He took her in his arms. 'Then, when they've calmed down, they'll remember how relieved they are because they love you. As do—'

'No.' She stopped him before he could say it. 'Those words belong between a husband and wife.'

He poured two glasses of sparkling water, added lime and ice and placed one either side of the desk as they took their seats.

'Have you any mints?' she asked, and he took a packet from his pocket and rolled them across the desk.

She didn't take one; instead she put them in her tunic—she would keep them for ever.

She wrote him a note and folded it. 'Read it when I am gone.'

'Is it in English?'

'No,' Layla said as he pocketed it, and tried with all she had to make their parting easy on him. 'It will be good to get back to my students.' She gave him a smile, for it was surely kinder to do that than to cry. 'And you can get back to your cases and your blonde girlfriends.....'

He said nothing—just looked at her for the very last time.

Sooner than they could ever be ready the intercom buzzed.

'They're here,' Wendy said.

Mikael knew he was tough, but he wasn't a patch on Layla. She put on her brightest smile and sat, her eyes rolling, as a furious Zahid marched in.

Then she stood and screamed at him in Arabic.

'English, please!' shouted a blonde woman—presumably Trinity. 'I want to know what the hell has been going on too!'

'I want to know why you called Father!' Layla shouted. 'All this could have been kept between us…'

'We didn't call your father,' Trinity said. 'Zahid said to leave it, to keep it between us. It was Jamila who couldn't…'

'How *dare* she step in?' Layla flared. 'How dare a lowly servant—?'

'That so-called *lowly* servant held you the day you were born.' Zahid was livid. 'That *lowly* servant loved you when your parents…' He halted.

Mikael noted it.

'Go and take your fury to Jamila, Layla. Go and shout at an old woman who has been weeping for days over you,' Zahid said. 'You are a spoiled brat and you always have been. Well, you got your way again—no matter the cost to everyone else. So, what have you been doing?'

'Having fun!' Layla shrugged. 'The same sort of fun you and Trinity have always had.'

'What sort of *fun*?' Zahid demanded.

'Expensive fun,' Mikael said.

'And you've paid for it for she had no money with her?' Zahid's eyes narrowed as he looked at Mikael. 'Why would you do that?'

'I had a retainer.' Mikael opened the safe and displayed the ruby. 'I'd prefer a wire transfer.'

The room was starting to calm down.

'Can I see your expenses?'

Mikael buzzed Wendy and asked her to bring in the current bill for Layla.

'Today hasn't been added yet,' Mikael said, and handed the paper to Zahid, who scrutinised it for a few moments. So too did Trinity, who frowned.

'How can you spend more than five hundred dollars on apples?' Trinity asked, but that was the least of Zahid's concerns.

'These friends of yours…?' He turned to Mikael. 'I wish to speak with them.'

'I doubt that they wish to speak with *you*,' Mikael responded coolly. 'Layla says that you two are expecting a baby of your own. Remind me to dump a problem like Layla in *your* lap a couple of days after your baby is born.'

'Zahid…' Trinity was the voice of reason. 'She's safe—that's all you need to know.'

Mikael watched as Zahid's jaw gritted and knew that Layla's brother was struggling to hold back tears of relief.

Layla was right: they loved her.

'We will go,' Zahid said, and glanced briefly over to Mikael. 'Your account will be settled as soon as I return to Ishla. Or now, if you—'

'When you return to Ishla is fine.'

'Come,' Zahid said to Layla. 'We do not discuss our business in front of strangers.'

Mikael handed over the ruby and glanced at Layla, who looked defiant, angry, happy—a strange combination only she could manage.

She shot him a brief smile.

'Thank you for your assistance, Mikael.'

'You're welcome.'

That was it.

The coolest goodbye ever.

She turned and simply dismissed him, and Mikael

stood there as they all walked out and did not flinch. He kept his face impassive.

For her sake.

Only when she was gone did he pull out her note and stare at the pretty curves and dots. He had no idea what she'd written.

Whatever it meant, Mikael felt it too.

For the first time in his life he did not have a solution.

For the first time in his life Mikael cried.

CHAPTER SIXTEEN

LAYLA RETURNED INTACT.

A little swollen, the doctor commented as she examined her.

'I know!' Layla said. 'There was no one there to bathe me! The hotel refused to send someone, and the baths are high there and not sunken. I slipped getting out. I am still very sore.'

She spoke with the same authority she always did and looked the doctor in the eye as she lied.

'Does my father have to know about that?'

The doctor hesitated, for perhaps King Fahid *should* know. Yet she was a kind woman, and she had been the one who had delivered Layla the awful day that her mother had died, and she had also fabricated the story about a seizure just to help Layla.

'Of course not.'

The King breathed out a long sigh of relief when it was reported that there was not a bruise nor a cut on his daughter's skin and that it appeared no harm had come to her. He sent for her and Layla stood, resigned, staring above and over his shoulder as her father delivered a very stern lecture and demanded more details as to what had happened in her time in Australia.

'You lied to me,' Fahid said. 'Even now you lie. What

was the whole point of running away if all you were going to do was sit with people who have just had a baby? You don't even like babies.'

Layla breathed out through her nostrils.

'I want the truth, Layla,' her father demanded. 'Did you dance?'

'Yes, I danced,' she said.

'And drink alcohol?'

'Once.' She'd admit to once. 'I had an Irish coffee. I have wanted to try one since Zahid told me you could have whisky in coffee and the cream stays at the top.'

'What else?'

Layla said nothing.

'What else?' the King demanded. 'What else did you get up to?'

'I tried to get a joint.'

'A joint?'

'Weed,' Layla said. 'The same stuff that was found in Zahid's locker at school! I had always wanted to try it.'

'And did you?'

'No one would let me.'

'What about men?' the King demanded—for, like her mother, Layla had always dreamed of romance. 'Did you do anything of which you are ashamed?'

'No, Father.'

Her answer was the truth.

'Layla?'

'No, Father, I did nothing of which I am ashamed.'

'I'm *very* disappointed in you, Layla.'

'I know that you are.'

'Are you disappointed in yourself?'

'No.' She shook her head. 'I am proud of myself and

glad that I did it. I've had my rebellion. I am sorry that it had to hurt you.'

'You are supposed to say *yes*, you *are* disappointed in yourself.'

'But I'm not.'

'You won't be teaching,' he said, and saw her lip tremble. 'Who knows what you might suggest...?'

'I would never encourage poor behaviour in my students,' she said, 'but I *am* an adult—'

'Enough!'

The King went through her punishments.

'No more teaching...' He saw her chin jut. 'No phone.'

'I never had one in the first place.'

'No letters.'

Layla was relieved. Otherwise poor Mikael might need to get a wheelbarrow for the thousands of letters in Arabic that might be delivered to him—letters he could never understand. Her heart squeezed as she thought of the small note she had left him and wondered if he would ever work it out.

Perhaps it was better to have their contact severed so brutally.

'No internet—ever!' Fahid continued.

'What about chess?'

'You can play chess with me,' Fahid said. 'And next week you will select a husband.'

Layla said nothing.

'You don't argue?'

'I knew the consequences when I ran away,' she said. 'I knew what would happen when I got back.'

'And was it worth it?'

It was the only time the King had glimpsed a flash of tears.

'Yes.'

* * *

She was back, and plans had been made for Princess Layla to choose her husband tomorrow.

She was well, she was safe, she had returned.

The palace felt like a funeral parlour though.

The King looked out to the gardens below his study and saw Layla walking when usually she would have run.

She looked cold, even though the evening sun was still blazing before dipping below the horizon.

'How has she been?'

He turned when Jamila entered; he had asked to speak with her.

'She is very polite, she is doing everything that has been asked of her and she has given me no cheek—but she is very angry with me. I know that, even if she doesn't say so.' Jamila started to cry. 'I am sorry for interfering…you might never have known.'

'You were scared for her,' Fahid said. 'You were right to call me.'

He looked to the woman who had been like a mother to his child—Layla's only parent when he had not been able to be one.

'You were brave to go against Zahid and call me.'

He sat down, for he could not stand to look out of the window and see Layla so unhappy.

Fahid closed his eyes. He wanted this sorted. 'I have not got long…'

'Don't say that, Your Highness.'

'It is true, though. I just want to know she will be taken care of.'

He looked over, because again Jamila was crying.

'Jamila…?'

'I don't want you to die, Fahid.'

She was no longer speaking with the King but with the man who had come to her at night a year after his wife had died.

The man who had made love to her as Layla slept in her crib beside the bed.

The man who still came to her at times, even now.

Times that must never be discussed, for she was a servant—that was all.

Yet the King and Layla felt like Jamila's family, and she wanted more time with him—especially now.

'Perhaps the treatments will give me more time,' he said, and took his lover in his arms.

And if they did give him more time, Fahid thought, then perhaps he should use it wisely.

Fahid watched as Layla pushed her *hashwet-al-ruz* around her plate. It was her favourite—spicy rice with minced lamb and mint—and Jamila had told the kitchen to add extra roasted pistachios, which Layla loved.

Not tonight, though.

'You are not hungry,' the King observed.

'Not really.' Layla attempted a smile. 'Do we have prawns here?'

'Prawns?' The King frowned. 'You mean shrimp?'

Layla shrugged. She didn't know.

'We do, but I don't like it,' the King said, and waited for the smart answer that the old Layla would have given—something along the lines of, *So you don't like it and that means that I don't get to try it?* But instead she just carried on pushing her food around her plate.

'We could play chess tonight,' the King offered, but she shook her head.

'May I be excused?'

'Layla...' the King started, but then he halted. 'You may.'

'Am I allowed to go for another walk?'

'Of course,' he said. 'Enjoy.'

Abadan laa tansynii.

Mikael had managed to work out what the first part of her note meant and it had been painstaking. He could ask someone to translate it, but he wanted to do it himself and finally he had managed a little of it.

Don't ever forget me.

He never, ever could.

So much so that as Mikael read the brief for a new client he felt nauseous.

'He needs to find someone else,' Mikael said to Wendy.

He simply couldn't do it any more; he'd assuaged his guilt over Igor and now he was going to use his power for good.

What had Layla done to him?

He just had to know that she was okay.

He took out his phone and stared at it for a long time. He was worried that his calling might make things worse for Layla, but the payment of his fees had gone in today so there was almost a valid reason to call. He would keep his voice brusque, Mikael decided. He would thank Zahid for the payment and check that she was okay.

He just had to do *something*.

Layla walked through the palace gardens and had never felt more confused—because she had done more than she could ever have dreamed of in her few days away and so surely she should be happy. As she walked she remembered dancing and laughing with Mikael, and she remembered his kindness too. How he had come back for her that night and stopped her going out. How he had bathed her and watched over her.

She had laughed when he had asked her to marry him and yet it was the nicest thing that had ever happened to her. What she wanted more than anything in the world was to be his wife.

Yet it was impossible. For even if somehow—impossibly—her father agreed, imagine Mikael here, in Ishla...

She could not.

Oh, at first it would be bliss. But without his cases, without the life he had built from nothing, that bliss would surely fade. Layla could not do that to him; she could not bear to think of him living here, with his opinions invalidated by the King and later by Zahid.

No palace would be big enough for such strong men.

A sob came and she could no longer hold it in.

Her father might be watching her from the window, Layla knew, and she fled down a hidden path towards the second palace, where Trinity and Zahid lived. But she did not run to them. Instead she sat on a stone bench and wept and sobbed as she never had in her life—not even when she had gone to choose her suitor. This evening Layla cried not just for herself but for Mikael, for he had no family and yet it felt as if he was a part of hers, and she would never see him again.

'Layla!'

Trinity had been walking, and at first had thought an animal must be trapped, such was the distress she'd heard. Trinity put her arms around Layla's heaving shoulders and tried to find out what was wrong, but Layla shook her head at everything Trinity asked.

'Is your father still cross?'

Layla shook her head.

'Are you scared of choosing a husband?'

'No.' Layla gulped.

There was no room in her heart left to be scared.

'I fell in love.' Her tears calmed just a touch with the terrible admission. 'I always thought I wanted to fall in love but it is horrible…it is agony. Please, *please*, don't tell Zahid.'

'He might understand.'

'Even if he could understand it would make no difference, Zahid is not yet King.'

'Who?' Trinity asked. 'Who did you fall in love with?'

'Mikael.'

Trinity blew out a breath. Perhaps Layla was suffering from a serious case of a crush, because if Mikael loved her in return surely he would not have let her leave?

'I begged him not to let Zahid know there had been anything between us.'

'He's a brilliant actor, then,' Trinity said, remembering Mikael's bored expression.

'He did it for me,' Layla said. 'No one ever knows what he's thinking, yet he tells *me* how he feels.'

'He feels the same about you?' Trinity checked, and then double-checked again. 'You're sure that Mikael loves you?'

'He asked to marry me.'

'Mikael asked you *that*?'

'Yes.' Layla said. 'And I laughed because it is so impossible. I love my family. I did not know how to say yes to what I want without hurting all the people I care for. He tried to tell me that he loved me and I would not let him, because those words only belong in marriage. But I want to hear those words now, and I want to tell him I love him too. I wish I had at least said that. If I could speak with him just one more time…'

'Do you have his phone number?'

'No, he gave it to me but I tore it up.' Layla turned and managed a smile. 'I don't want his number—there would be too much temptation.' The tears had stopped but the sadness was still there and very possibly would never leave. 'I should get back to the palace.'

'Stay and talk,' Trinity said, but Layla shook her head.

'I had better not take too long…'

All the fight had gone out of her, Trinity thought sadly as Layla headed back.

Trinity walked into the second palace and looked at her husband. His back was to her as he gazed out to the ocean and his shoulders were set rigid. Trinity wondered if it would make things better or worse for Layla if she told Zahid.

She did not have to tell him, though—it would seem that he already knew.

'I think something went on with Layla and her barrister.' Still Zahid did not turn. 'He has called to see how she is.'

'Perhaps it was just a follow-up call,' Trinity said, not sure how to tread here. She loved her husband so much, but some of the ways in Ishla she would never understand.

'I don't know if it was poor reception, but…' Zahid could not explain, and neither did he want to acknowl-

edge the sudden husk in Mikael's voice near the end of
his call. 'He asked to speak with her.'

'What did you say?'

'That it would not be wise. That she was happy to
be back with her family.' Zahid turned then. 'She's not
happy, though, is she?'

'No.'

'Has she spoken to you about what went on while
she was away?'

'A little,' Trinity said. 'Zahid, please don't ask me to
break her confidence.'

'I shan't.' He looked at the wife he cherished, despite
once fearing love. 'Layla is very different to me,' he explained. 'She has always craved love. From the day she
was born she screamed for it. She wanted to be held, to
be cherished. Jamila did her best for her. I was seven
when Layla was born, and I tried to be a comfort to her,
but she wanted her mother. She wanted my father too,
but she got neither...'

'Is there anything you can do to help her?' Trinity
asked.

'I have tried.' Zahid sighed. 'You remember I had
already agreed to choose a bride when we met again
in London?'

Trinity nodded.

'The reason I had agreed to choose a bride was in
order to postpone a wedding for Layla. I knew my father did not have much time. I wanted to change the
rules for my sister.'

Zahid was conflicted too—angry with the man who
had looked him in the eye as he'd lied to him.

'Have you seen the scum that Romanov defends?'
Zahid sneered. 'I have looked him up and his reputation with women is—'

'I had a *terrible* reputation,' Trinity broke in. 'We both know that what people said about me was wrong.' She took a breath as she saw her husband waver. 'Layla herself says that they can never be together—she simply wants to speak with him one more time.'

Zahid did what he knew he should not: he handed Trinity his phone.

Trinity almost flew from the second palace. She chatted politely with the King for a few moments and then asked how Layla was.

'She is very…' The King halted. 'Layla has accepted all her punishments instead of fighting me.'

'Can I speak with her?'

'Of course—she is not a prisoner.'

Trinity smiled at Jamila, who opened the door of Layla's room as Trinity approached.

'I don't want to talk about it any more,' Layla said. She was lying on her stomach, reading the card Mikael had sent with the flowers. 'If I do I will cry, and I don't want to be sad when I think of him. I have this.' She handed Layla the card. 'This makes me smile.'

'Do you want me to read it to you?' Trinity offered.

'No, Mikael did, and I remember every word. *"Layla, thank you for an amazing end to a difficult day and an even more amazing night. Mikael."* And he gave me three kisses.'

Trinity smiled, but then frowned at the 'amazing night' part. 'I thought the doctor said…?'

'Trinity…' Layla would let her in on a very big secret! 'You don't have to have sex to have an orgasm—there are other things you can do.'

'I'll bear it in mind.' Trinity laughed—she just *loved* Layla.

She handed her Zahid's phone.

'You wanted to speak with him one more time,' Trinity said as Layla stared at it. 'Mikael just called Zahid to see how you were and asked if he could speak with you.' She put the phone down on the bed. 'I will go out on the balcony.'

Trinity couldn't hear the words, just the love and tears in Layla's voice as she tried to be brave and not break down, as she tried to sound upbeat for Mikael.

It was enough to make Trinity cry as she did her best not to listen to one side of their final conversation...

When his phone rang and he saw that it was Zahid Mikael answered it on the first ring—and then nearly folded when he heard Layla's voice.

'Mikael.'

'Layla.' *Thank God.* 'Are you okay?'

'Of course I am.'

'How was your father?'

'Disappointed, cross. I am to choose a husband tomorrow...and I cannot use my computer ever again. But I will work on that soon. Trinity has smuggled me Zahid's phone. This will be the last time we speak.'

'Don't say that.'

'It will be,' Layla said, and knew, for his sake, that she had to somehow keep this a little light—for even Mikael could not fix this. 'Our minds might meet now and then, but we won't speak or see each other again.'

Mikael frowned. Was she talking about dreams?

But Layla had changed the subject. 'How is work?'

'I don't want to talk about work. What do you mean, our minds will meet?'

'You will work it out,' Layla said. 'Now, I want to know about your work—how is it?'

'Nauseating,' Mikael admitted. 'I'm crossing to the other side.'

'Meaning?'

'Prosecuting the bastards.'

'Go you…' Layla smiled.

'How are your students?'

'I am banned from teaching at the moment. After the wedding perhaps I will get to teach again, but I don't think so.'

'Layla?' he asked, and she closed her eyes at the depth of his voice. 'Did I look after you?'

'Beautifully.'

'Is there anything you regret?' he said, for he worried that they might have gone too far.

'Just one thing,' Layla said. 'That I laughed when you proposed. Mikael, I laughed only at the impossibility, not the sentiment.'

'Can I *please* speak to your father?'

'You will not get a fair hearing.'

'I thought he was a fair man?'

'Not about this,' Layla said. 'There is something else I regret—that I did not let you say *I love you* and that I did not tell you that I love you, and that I shall for the rest of my life.'

Mikael felt his heart squeeze in pain, and then the knife in it twisted as she continued.

'I wish you had been my first. Then I could perhaps have been punished and made a spinster…'

'Layla…'

'I have to go. Jamila is knocking at the door. *Abadan laa tansynii,*' Layla said.

'I'll never forget you either,' Mikael replied.

'And I will love you for ever,' she said.

'I'll love you for ever too.'

Mikael's answer was honest. His response immediate.

He walked out and past Wendy and gave a shake of his head that said *not now*.

He went straight to his car and smiled at the scratched paintwork before gunning it to the airport.

Layla loved him.

Which meant he was going to Ishla to plead his case.

CHAPTER SEVENTEEN

'RETURN OR ONE-WAY?'

'Return,' Mikael said, and then changed his mind, for he could not imagine returning without Layla by his side, and in dark superstition he said, 'One-way.'

'It's actually cheaper to buy—'

'False economy,' Mikael interrupted. 'I'm going to be fed to the dogs when I get there.' As he had with Alina, Mikael smiled again at another woman who was not Layla—for that was what Layla had done. She had been in his life for less than a week but, despite the pain of living apart from her, in ways he was happier than he had ever been for she made the world a nicer place.

'Enjoy!' The stewardess smiled back and handed the good-looking man his first-class one-way ticket to Ishla.

Mikael would not be enjoying the flight.

He would be working the hardest that he ever had in his life.

He asked for sparkling water with lime—their first drink.

And he asked for a peeled and finely sliced apple and raspberries.

He knew that he worked better hungry.

As he prepared for the biggest case of his life he had no distractions. He would focus purely on Layla, on every meal, every conversation they had ever had—and he did.

He went over and over it all in his mind, honing in on words, recalling with intricate detail every conversation that had been shared, and he worked out, too, who he might have in his defence.

Trinity was a given, Mikael immediately decided, for she had smuggled the phone.

Zahid?

He loved his wife and had caused controversy himself, given that Trinity had been pregnant when they'd got married, and with Trinity buzzing in his ear... Mikael asked for more water and recalled proud Prince Zahid close to tears when he had been reunited with Layla and knew that he loved his sister.

Yes, he had Zahid.

But it was Layla's father, the King, whose consent he required.

What did Mikael know?

He remembered Layla's eyes filling with tears, for her father was sick.

Noted.

It wasn't enough, though, Mikael knew. There was something he was missing—there just had to be more.

Jamila?

He thought of the old lady, who must surely love Layla, but she was set in her ways and would perhaps want tradition to be followed.

There *was* something missing, but Mikael did not know what. He was going into the biggest fight of his life and yet he felt unprepared.

Mikael pulled out his wallet and stared at the piece of paper she had given him and the dots and swirls that had proved so hard to decipher.

Intensely private, he did not like to ask for help, and he had done his best to work her words out for himself, quite content to spend the rest of his life learning Arabic if that was what it took. But now Mikael needed every detail.

When the stewardess came round to ask if he would like his bed prepared for sleep, Mikael shook his head and said that he would be working through the flight.

'Would you mind translating this note for me?'

'Of course.' She read it and smiled. '"Don't ever forget me",' she said. 'It is a love saying,' the stewardess explained. 'Then it reads, *"Wahashtini Malikah"*, which means *I miss you, Queen.*'

'Princess, perhaps?' Mikael checked.

'No.' The stewardess shook her head. 'That would be *Wahashtini Ameera.*'

It didn't make sense, but Mikael tried to work it out with the stewardess's help. 'Could it mean: I miss you, *from* your Queen?' Mikael frowned, for Layla had never said that in marrying Hussain she would one day be queen.

'No.' Again the stewardess shook her head. 'I don't really understand what is being said—just that it reads, "I miss you Queen".'

It was then that he understood her words.

His heart was thumping in his chest as he took the small note back and stared at it with a smile.

Clever, *clever* Layla, he thought. So *that* was what she'd meant about their minds meeting at times...

It was her online chess name, Mikael was positive about that, but more than that— more than a future meeting of minds—he was starting to see that it was the Queen who was missing in his argument.

The Queen who, despite her absence, was still a huge presence in Layla's life.

A queen who had apparently been very similar to the daughter she had never met—a woman Layla herself had said would approve of her plans.

Mikael rested back in his seat and closed his eyes for a moment as his thoughts started to align.

If she *had* been like Layla it must have killed the King to lose her. Mikael was certain of that, for in the days since Layla had been gone, despite the joy she had brought, his heart had closed, his curtains had been drawn, and the world seemed a very dark place.

Mikael recalled Zahid's words in chambers when he had told Layla off about Jamila.

'That so-called *lowly* servant held you the day you were born. That *lowly* servant loved you when your parents...'

Zahid had halted.

Now Mikael was starting to understand Zahid's hesitation.

In his grief, had the King turned his back on his daughter?

Did Layla not even know that he had?

As the plane began its descent still Mikael continued working, examining every angle, refusing to let up as he prepared for the most important case of his life.

The plane was on its final approach, but Mikael saw not the desert or the ocean, nor the clusters of buildings and streets, but the huge palace that looked out to its people.

In there was Layla, preparing to choose the man with whom she would spend the rest of her life.

It had to be him.

He had to be right.

The plane landed and the passengers disembarked, and Mikael was searched at Customs and asked the reason for his visit to Ishla.

'I have heard it is a very beautiful land.'

'You have no luggage.'

'I want to wear robes,' Mikael said. 'I would like to blend in.'

A female customs officer was going through his wallet and pulled out Layla's note. She looked to Mikael. 'Do you know anyone in Ishla?'

'I have a friend who I play chess with,' he said, and told himself not to break out in a sweat. He told himself not to falter or blink or react as the officers chatted in Arabic and laughed for a moment.

'You are here for romance?'

'Hopefully,' he said, wondering if it was the right answer, if he would even get into the country, if this was the end of the line.

'Enjoy your stay in Ishla,' the female officer said, and handed the wallet back to him.

He arranged a hire car and then stepped out into the fierce sun. But before heading to the palace he rang Zahid. As expected it went straight to voicemail.

'I am in Ishla.' Mikael left a message. 'I suggest that next time you pick up.'

He gave it five minutes and then called Zahid again. This time his call was answered.

'It is better that you stay away,' Zahid said, by way of introduction.

'I am not staying away,' Mikael said. 'I am here to speak with your father.'

'I cannot suggest strongly enough that you get on a plane and leave now.'

Zahid was speaking the truth. If his father found out

that Layla had been in any sort of relationship while overseas then all hell could break loose—not just for Mikael, but for Layla.

'You need to leave Ishla.'

'That is not going to happen without my first speaking with your father,' Mikael said.

Zahid looked over to Trinity and then looked away.

'My sister chooses her husband this day.'

'Then I need to speak with your father before she does—and you shall arrange it.'

Zahid's jaw gritted. There were few who would speak to him like that, and his temper was starting to rise at Mikael's arrogance.

'It is not just my father you need to speak with.' Zahid's voice was black with anger. 'Layla is my sister and you will speak with *me* and explain yourself. How dare you lie to me and tell me she was nothing but an inconvenience? I want to know exactly what went on. I will send a car to collect you.'

'No need.' Mikael's smile was also black, for he did not trust Zahid not to have him driven out to the desert and left there. 'I'm in a car and on my way.'

He would shout to Layla from the palace gates if he had to.

Zahid ended the call and still he did not look at Trinity. Instead he called for Abdul.

'We have a visitor arriving shortly,' Zahid said. 'His name is Mikael Romanov and he is to be brought straight to the King's office, but he is not to be taken through the main entrance. You will tell my father to meet me there now.'

'Your father is entertaining Princess Layla's suitors and their families…'

'This is not a discussion,' Zahid said.

Now he spoke to Trinity. 'He wants to speak with my father. I will be there.'

'Can I be there too?'

'No.' Zahid shook his head.

'Why?'

'Because he does not need to convince *you*,' Zahid said. 'You have already made up your mind.'

'Zahid, please...'

'Trinity, you do not understand how delicate this is.'

'Your father has accepted me.'

'Layla is his *daughter*!' Zahid said. 'You came and moved to Ishla—do you think Mikael will do the same? Do you think my father will let Layla leave the country?'

Trinity blinked as it dawned on her just how impossible this situation was.

'Never.' Zahid shook his head. 'My father will never agree to a commoner marrying his daughter, let alone taking her to live overseas. Go and help Layla get ready. You are not to let her know that Mikael is here.'

'Zahid, surely she should be able to see him? Even if nothing can come of it!'

'Trinity, I know my father and sister best, and I am asking you...'

'Or *telling* me?' Trinity challenged.

'Both,' Zahid said. 'You have to trust that I will try to do the right thing by my sister.'

Trinity did trust that Zahid would do his best.

She just didn't know if it would be enough.

Jamila handed Layla a cloth to wash her private parts as she readied herself to choose her future husband.

'You get to wear make-up today for the first time,' Jamila said.

'The second time,' Layla corrected.

'Ah, yes, you were wearing make-up that time you had a seizure.'

Layla turned at the slightly wry note in Jamila's voice and for the first time since she had returned to her family they shared a small smile. And then Layla's eyes filled with tears, because Mikael was right: she loved Jamila too.

Horrible, *horrible* love, Layla thought, hugging her handmaiden.

'Please come with me when I marry,' Layla begged.

'You know that I can't,' Jamila said. 'On your wedding day it will be my time to retire. Hussain will give you new maids and a new handmaiden. A young one who will help you with your babies.'

'I don't want babies,' Layla said, and then defiance crept back as Jamila helped her out of the bath. 'Anyway, who says that I am going to *choose* Hussain?'

'You will do the right thing by your father and King, I am sure,' Jamila said as she started to pull out all the rags that had been put in Layla's hair the night before.

'Have you ever been in love, Jamila?' Layla asked.

'I have never been married.'

'Nor have I,' Layla said, but she had been in love— she *was* in love and for ever would be—and she did not want to be with another man.

'You are in a funny mood today, Layla,' Jamila observed.

'I don't feel funny,' she said as Trinity came in.

It was a dangerous mood she was in, and Jamila had every reason to be worried—for she knew that Layla was volatile at the best of times.

'Your hair's so curly,' Trinity said when she saw Layla. 'It looks wonderful.'

Layla said nothing, though her eyes glittered with suppressed rage as she forced a smile for Trinity.

'How is Zahid?' Layla asked.

Trinity swallowed. 'He is fine.'

'Does he send his best wishes for me today?' Layla asked with spite in her voice, for she was so jealous of Trinity and Zahid, and so cross that the rules were different for them. 'Does he hope that my marriage will be as blessed and as happy as his? Because if he does he's a hypocrite—as are you.'

'Zahid loves you.'

'So many people who love me!' Layla shrugged. 'Aren't I lucky?'

Trinity was close to tears. Just knowing that Mikael was on his way and that Layla did not know had her heart racing.

Jamila painted Layla's eyelids and eyelashes till they glittered as much as the Opium ruby that she would hand to the man she chose.

'I wonder what gift Hussain will have for me,' Layla said. 'I doubt he will bring flowers.'

'You are to behave today,' Jamila said.

Layla swallowed down tears and then nodded, for she had promised that if she could just have her freedom for a short while then she would marry with dignity and grace.

Oh, it was *hard*, though.

'I shall do your lips and cheeks after you are in your robe,' Jamila said.

Layla stood and lifted her arms, and tried not to shake as the white and gold robe was slipped over her head.

She opened her eyes and saw Trinity was looking out of the window. And then she turned and stared at

Layla, and there were tears in Trinity's eyes, and Layla could no longer be angry.

It was not Trinity's fault; it was just ancient rules that had to be obeyed.

Now was the time to be brave.

'I will be okay.' Layla smiled, for she loved Trinity, even if she was cross and so very scared. 'I always knew that this day would come.'

CHAPTER EIGHTEEN

MIKAEL GAVE HIS name at the palace gates and drove slowly forward when they opened.

He was nervous.

He had not lied to Layla that day in the café. Until she had come into his life he had never cared about anybody enough to be nervous.

Mikael drove through the gates and climbed out of the car. He looked up to the gleaming palace and saw a blonde-haired woman step back from a window.

So, Trinity knew that he was here.

A small door carved within the huge main ones opened and a robed man who did not introduce himself gestured for Mikael to follow him. He led him around the side of the palace and to another door.

From there he was taken through a labyrinth of corridors to doors that had guards beside them. When they were opened, Mikael stepped in to face his judge and jury.

'It is customary to bow when you greet the King,' Fahid said. He sat at his desk and Zahid stood behind him, a little to the side.

Mikael bowed.

He could see the fury in the King's eyes and indeed Fahid *was* furious—for Zahid had just told him that

Layla had possibly been friends with the man they had just paid. A man they had thought had taken care to ensure that Layla was safe and looked after.

Layla had told him herself that she had danced, and of other things that she had done.

'You are dismissed,' Fahid said to Abdul, and when it was just the three of them he addressed Mikael. 'I assume you are not here to discuss your fees?'

'That is correct,' Mikael said.

Ill, old, Fahid was still very much a king, and he looked with distaste at this man who came from a country with the most expensive apples in the world.

'Why are you here?' the King demanded. 'What is it you want?'

'Permission to ask Layla to be my wife.'

Mikael heard an angry breath from the King before he responded.

'A commoner does not ask royalty to marry him. It is for Layla to choose…'

The King halted then. He was an honest man, but as he met Mikael's eyes he looked away, for the truth was that Layla did *not* truly choose.

'I went through your bill very carefully and I also spoke with Layla. She says that she drank alcohol and danced. Were you with her when she did these things?'

Fahid did not give Mikael time to answer.

'The fact you are here must mean that something more went on in those days that she was away.' The King was almost shaking in fury. 'Or is she such an amazing dancer that you want to marry her? *Was* there a romance?' Fahid demanded.

Mikael looked briefly to Zahid. He was terrified now for Layla, for the damage his being here might cause her, but Zahid gave Mikael the slightest nod.

'Yes,' Mikael said. 'There was a romance.'

'Have you any idea how foolish of you it is to admit that?' The King stood. 'What went on between the two of you?' he demanded.

Mikael's face was as impassive as it was in court. He watched every flicker of the King's reaction as he used one of the few weapons he had against this powerful man.

'Your Highness, just as you must have the moment you saw Layla, I fell in love.' He watched as the King's hand moved to his ear. The slight telling gesture told Mikael he was right and so he continued. 'The first time I looked into her eyes I knew I would do anything to save and protect her.' He looked to Zahid, who stared straight ahead. 'I knew that Layla would do those things with or without me, and I considered her safer with me than without.'

'Oh, so you did *not* lead my daughter to do these things? You are telling me that it was all Layla's fault...?' He cursed at Mikael, but Zahid spoke to his father in Arabic.

'Father, I realise now that Layla had been planning this escape for some time. She tried to go to London with me once. She would have done those things there.'

Fahid felt sick at the thought of Layla in London, trying those things, doing those things, and he looked to Mikael again, who had returned her with not so much as a bruise. Here was a man he begrudgingly admired for having the nerve to stand before him and admit to these things.

'Did she ask you to get her a joint?' Fahid asked.

'She did.'

'And you said no to her?'

The King frowned, for very few people said no to his daughter.

'Did she remind you she was a princess?' Fahid watched the slightest smile twitch on Mikael's lips.

'She did.'

'But still you said no.' Fahid thought for a moment and then turned and spoke to his son in Arabic.

'I should have him removed.'

Very possibly he could have Mikael killed, Zahid guessed, for he doubted it had been such a sweet romance as the one Mikael depicted.

'You could pardon him for ensuring she returned safely,' Zahid said.

'King Fahid.' Mikael pulled out his final weapon. 'I understand you know nothing about me. And I cannot imagine raising a daughter alone, as you have done. It must be unbearable that your wife is not here to discuss this with—'

'There is nothing to discuss!' Fahid snapped.

But Mikael knew that the seed had been sown, for the King closed his eyes and breathed in for a moment, and it was as if Annan had stepped into the room to plead for their daughter's freedom. Mikael could see the struggle on Fahid's features as his once wild wife fought from the grave for her child.

The King spoke some more in Arabic to his son and Zahid translated his words to Mikael.

'My father says you are as arrogant as a rooster, and if you did marry her it would mean you would bow to him, obey him…' Zahid challenged.

'I would.'

Zahid crossed the room and walked till he was in Mikael's face. 'Given that one day I will be King, are you therefore saying you would also bow to *me* and obey?'

A muscle flickered in Mikael's cheek but he had planned his closing argument and was prepared.

'I will be more obedient to you than to my own right hand.'

Mikael watched the slight flare in Zahid's eyes as he answered him with an Arabic saying that might just mollify the King, but then Zahid closed his eyes in regret as Mikael qualified it slightly.

'When I am in Ishla.'

Zahid knew the King would never let Mikael take her away, as he was clearly hoping to do.

'If Layla moved to Australia I would do my best to give her a wonderful life and return here often. When here, I will wear robes and bow and do everything that is expected. It would be my pleasure to do so.'

'You will not take her overseas,' Fahid said.

'All I want is for Layla to be safe and happy—as must you.' He knew the King was ill, and yet he pushed on. 'I know how nervous she must make you, for I felt the same fear. She is independent and strong, and she insisted I leave her so she could enjoy her freedom, and yet...' He looked right at the King and both matched and voiced what was surely the King's greatest fear. 'I was scared at the thought of her in the world without me.'

'She is the end of the vine...' Fahid's voice wavered. 'My daughter, my precious. I don't want her overseas.' The King looked to his son and then back to Mikael. 'I am not just talking about tradition...'

'I understand that fear,' Mikael said. 'Your daughter is trouble. I wanted her off my hands, and yet I felt ill at the thought of her coping in a city she wasn't used to. If Layla came to live in Australia then I would take time off from work—however long it takes—to ensure she understands all that your son does, having lived overseas. Layla could still work, still see her students…'

'I don't want to lose her.'

For the first time in more than two decades Zahid watched as his father struggled not to break down.

'You could never lose Layla,' Mikael said.

It was then that Mikael was glad that Trinity was not there. She did not understand just how ingrained these traditions were. She would have argued Layla's case, interrupted him; instead Mikael had stated his own case to a king who was listening.

'You couldn't lose Layla,' he reiterated, and then admitted what he perhaps shouldn't. 'I have already asked her to marry me and she laughed in my face. She said she would not turn her back on her country and you. I am as sure as I can be that Layla would only ever leave with your blessing—and, if she did, she would return often with love and gratitude to you.'

Mikael had nothing left. He had used every argument he could, every weapon in his arsenal, had planned every move to the endgame.

It was as if the Queen that Layla so sorely missed had nudged him to checkmate.

Yes, it was for the King to decide now—but before he did, Mikael voiced the one united thought of everyone present in the room.

Even Queen Annan.

'I love Layla.'

CHAPTER NINETEEN

'READY?' TRINITY ASKED.

'I am,' Layla said, though her heart was breaking.

Of course she was ready, she told herself. She had known for ever that this day had to come.

'I have my memories and I have all my dreams…'

'You do.'

Trinity was torn. It was like taking a beautiful lamb to slaughter; how she wanted to tell Layla that Mikael was here, and yet Zahid had told her not to.

In this she had to trust that her husband knew best.

Layla walked down the palace stairs, determined to see this through without breaking down—and then she saw the closed doors and thought of the men behind it, and Hussain.

She looked down to her wrist, at the tiny little mark there, and knew that the match had burned more than twice for now it flared again.

'No!' Layla screamed, and went to run up the stairs.

Jamila grabbed her arms and a guard caught her by her dress as she dropped to the floor.

'She's having another seizure!' Jamila shouted.

'No!'

She kicked and she fought and Mikael, who was kneeling with the other suitors as the King sat on his throne, lowered his head and smiled as he heard her scream his name, weep and beg that she wanted to die a virgin spinster if she could just dream of him each night. It was the sound of torture, but it came from love.

Mikael lifted his head and looked to Hussain, who was kneeling to his right. It had to be him, for he was an arrogant and pompous git, but he was sweating now as he was shamed for a second time. Mikael felt another gaze on him then, and looked over into the tired eyes of the King as Layla's screams continued to fill the palace.

'Perhaps you can handle her?' the King said to Mikael.

Fahid was weary and, though he would never admit it, it was quite a relief that Mikael was here today—especially now, as Mikael stood and took over the rebel princess.

He would take care of her, Fahid knew, and he felt the first glimmer of peace as they walked out of the room to the spectacle that awaited. He loved his wild daughter so...

'Layla...' Mikael's fingers gripped her cheeks just in time to stop her biting a guard. 'It is time to choose your husband.'

Layla thought she was dreaming—for dressed in robes of white and gold, and just so beautiful, was the man who would for ever live in her dreams. Not a night had passed since their parting that hadn't been spent together in her mind.

'Mikael...' She stood for a sixth of a second, then leapt like a cat into his arms.

'Layla!' her father scolded as Mikael put her down. 'You are to follow tradition.'

'Father, I don't understand...' She frowned. She could barely make sense of anything; she looked to her father and simply didn't understand how Mikael was here or what was going on.

'Mikael has spoken with Zahid and me today. He wants to give you a life in Australia but you shall return here often. It is up to you if you choose this man as your husband.'

'Oh, but I do.'

'Layla...' The King's tone warned her of their traditions. 'What do you do now?'

As she had on the day they had first met, she took the precious stone from her tunic and placed it down.

'You have to offer your gift to me now,' Layla said.

Trinity saved the day and retrieved Mikael's jacket from the room where he had changed into traditional robes.

'My wallet.' Mikael handed it over and smiled at the dark bastard he had once been, for he had sworn that if this day ever came there would be a watertight prenup; instead he handed her the keys to his home, his passport—she could have the lot.

'That's a black credit card,' he said as she went through his wallet.

'What's a credit card?' she asked.

'It means I can keep you in peeled, thinly sliced apples prepared by gourmet chefs.'

'Good.' Layla smiled.

Then she took out the folded piece of paper that told him she would never forget him, and the online chess name that she had thought might be their only link, and she looked up as Mikael spoke for the first time in Arabic. It was her favourite saying—one Layla had never thought could apply to the man who would be her husband

'Hayet albi enta,' Mikael said.

'And me.' Layla smiled again. 'You are the life of my heart too.'

CHAPTER TWENTY

MIKAEL BOUGHT A return flight this time, when he went back to Sydney without her.

There was an appeal to be lodged for his bastard client, and a lot of desk to be cleared—especially given that Mikael would be changing career direction when next he returned.

He poured a glass of sparkling water and even the bubbles seemed to fizz in delight as he acknowledged that when he returned it would be with Layla.

It was time to make a call.

'Demyan.' Mikael followed protocol. 'How is the baby?'

'Her name is Annika.'

'How is Annika?'

'She is awake for twenty-three hours a day,' Demyan said. 'I forgot how much noise babies make. So, where have you been? What happened with you and Layla?

'Well, as Layla would say, we are betrothed!'

Demyan laughed as he heard that Mikael would be getting married in Ishla and that it would be a very traditional wedding.

He'd laugh even more, Mikael thought privately, if he knew he was marrying a virgin. In fact Demyan might drop the phone if he found out that it was Mikael who had insisted that Layla save herself for their wedding night.

'Layla is going to be living here after we marry, but her father is not well so we shall be returning to Ishla often. I am not taking any more cases for now. I'm going to take a few months off to teach her about traffic lights and currency and such things.'

'You have it bad,' Demyan said, for he could hear the adoration in Mikael's voice even as he tried to keep it light.

'I have it so *good*,' Mikael said. 'Demyan, I understand it is short notice, and you have Annika, and things might be difficult to arrange, but—'

'We will be there.'

They had grown up on the streets together; they were family—just not by blood.

'Will you be part of the wedding party?' Mikael asked. 'You would have to frock up.'

Demyan said something very rude in Russian, and then laughed and said that he would be delighted.

'I need another favour,' Mikael said.

'Apart from my wearing a dress?' Demyan checked.

'I need to speak with Alina.'

'Alina?'

'Women's business.'

'Very well.'

It was possibly the most awkward conversation of Mikael's life, but for Layla he pushed through it.

'But, Father...'

They were waiting for Mikael to arrive back at the palace—not that Layla was allowed to see him till their wedding day. She was more excited than she had ever thought possible about her wedding, and yet it was dawning on her that she was moving far, far away.

'Jamila will be so bored without me, and she will fret and worry. I think it would be good for her if she came to live in Australia with me.'

'Jamila deserves to retire!' the King snapped.

'The car has just arrived!' Trinity walked in, smiling, and Layla started hopping on both legs.

'Five minutes?' she pleaded with her father. 'Please, can I just have five minutes alone with Mikael?'

'You will see him on your wedding day.'

'*Please...*' Layla begged. 'To know he is in the palace and not be allowed to see him is very cruel to me. Please...'

'Five minutes.' Her father gave a weary sigh. 'You,' he said to Trinity, 'go with her. And...' But then Fahid rolled his eyes What was the point? Trinity's chaperoning skills had got them to this place. 'Five minutes.'

Four were spent kissing, which left one minute to quickly take her contraband from Mikael's toiletries bag.

'You have no idea how hard it was to get these...'

Mikael rolled his eyes because, just as Layla had on her way to Australia, Mikael had had a little flutter of anxiety at Customs, wondering how he'd explain what he had in his bag.

Yes, he had packed it himself?

'I had to ask Alina to get them for you...'

'Are she and Demyan here.'

'Yes, and baby Annika. You will see them all at the wedding.'

He felt more than a touch uncomfortable, handing the packet of pills over, but Layla had insisted she wanted a perfect wedding night and had started retching when

Mikael had tried to explain condoms. And she didn't want a baby just yet.

'You get twelve repeats.'

'Repeats?'

'Twelve months before you go to the doctor. Layla, I am fine if you decide that you do want a baby...'

'I don't want one yet.' She popped the shiny packet in her bra. 'So, a year of taking this every day and there'll be no baby—it's like magic...' She was ecstatic! 'We can party, we can swim, we can dance.' But then her face was serious. 'Thank you. This means a lot to me.'

Mikael knew she was scared about having a baby, and was just so grateful that he would be there for her if she ever wanted to address those fears.

Now, though, wasn't the time.

There was a wedding to get ready for.

Layla was far from the blushing bride.

She was glowing and smiling as she walked through the scented gardens on the arm of Fahid towards Mikael, who was dressed in gold robes and a headdress with Demyan and Zahid in silver beside him.

Trinity was in silver too, and Zahid remembered the last time she had been a bridesmaid as she walked towards him.

Demyan tried not to catch Alina's eye, because she kept laughing at the sight of him in robes and head-gear.

Mikael saw no one except Layla.

Her dress was gold, and she had on a gold veil, and as she stood beside him Mikael saw that her eyelids had been painted gold too.

The first time he had seen Layla he had been reminded of the beauty of a new moon.

Now it felt as if the sun was stepping into his life.

It was a very short ceremony and there was no kissing the bride! The formal service was followed by a long meal, with laughter and love at the top of the menu and all the promise of the desert for the night.

As darkness descended Jamila handed Layla a goblet of liquid that should ensure their wedding night was a fertile one, and for the first time Layla's smile faltered.

Mikael watched her cheeks burn as she drank it down. She swallowed the drink and then looked to him, and she had never been more grateful for a person who understood her—a person she could be herself with and a wedding night that she did not fear now.

I feel guilty, her eyes told him.

It's fine, said his small smile.

As they went to leave and say their goodbyes again Layla's smile wavered as she embraced Jamila, and both women started crying.

'Thank you.' Mikael said it in Arabic to the old lady, and wished he could say more, but still Layla did not know that there had been a time when Jamila's love had been all she had had. 'Thank you for taking such good care of her.'

'Father, please!' The emotion of the day was catching up with her now, and at the thought of leaving Jamila behind Layla was crying. 'Why won't you let Jamila come to Australia with me…?'

For the last time the King stepped in.

'Layla, Jamila is staying here. You do not have to worry—she will be kept in splendour…'

'But I want her with *me*!'

'Well, you can't have her,' Fahid said. 'For Jamila has agreed to be my bride.'

There was a very stunned silence, followed by a shocked gasp from Layla.

Mikael dared not look at Demyan, for he knew his lips would be twitching—as were Mikael's.

Trinity smothered a laugh and Zahid closed his eyes as Fahid broke with tradition and in view of everyone kissed his future bride.

'Congratulations!' Alina beamed, delighted to see the couple looking so very happy and not comprehending what an incredible shock this was.

'We were going to wait till after the wedding,' Fahid explained. 'But you all have what you want, so why not us?'

'Congratulations.' Zahid spoke next, and even if his voice was a touch strained he was always polite, and he followed tradition and kissed Jamila's hand.

'Congratulations!' Trinity was more effusive, and she kissed not just Jamila's hand but the King's cheek too, for she had told him herself once that she hoped he would again find love.

'Congratulations,' Mikael offered, and Jamila raised her hand to him and he did as he had promised he would when in Ishla and followed tradition.

It was the Princess to his right, though, who was struggling with the news.

Layla felt Mikael's hand nudge the small of her back and she looked at Jamila, who gave her a nervous smile which she did not return.

As more congratulations were offered there were tears filling Jamila's eyes as still Layla stood rigid.

'This is *not* Planet Layla,' Mikael said in a very low voice, and his hand nudged the small of her back again.

'Congratulations,' Layla forced out through very tense lips, and then kissed Jamila's hand.

Fahid gave a small nod of gratitude to Mikael.

'I don't want to talk about it,' Layla said as she and

Mikael headed to a helicopter, and she shook her head, as if to clear it from the unwelcome images dancing before her eyes. 'I don't even want to think about it.'

She let rip, though, when they were in the desert, in their tent and alone.

Mikael opened champagne as Layla stood swaying in stunned fury. 'He's marrying *Jamila*!'

'Layla…' Mikael warned.

'Has he lost his mind?' Layla said.

'Layla, he loves her.'

'My handmaiden——a *queen*!'

Mikael had heard enough.

'Layla, you will walk back into that palace happy for them,' he told her. 'Your father has done everything to ensure his children are happy—*everything*…'

He pointed his finger at her, and when she didn't smile, when she didn't make the biting noise she had on the day they had met, Mikael knew she was hurting inside.

'Now you ruin our wedding night,' she accused him.

She huffed off to the sleeping area and Mikael called to her.

'It won't work with me, Layla…'

He followed her in and was momentarily sidetracked, for he had never seen anything like it. There was nothing more luxurious than a desert sky at night, and with the tent's roof pulled back they would sleep under the stars in the vast marital bed.

'We are not married till we sleep together,' Layla said. 'You can still change your mind.'

'Nobody's talking about changing their mind, but your father deserves to be happy too.'

'What about my mother?' Layla asked. 'How long has this been going on?'

'That's none of our business.'

'Oh, but it is!' Layla roared. 'Has he forgotten his Queen?'

'Of course not,' Mikael said, and he took his bride in his arms and felt her heart racing as she struggled to process the news. He had guessed that it was this, not Jamila's lowly status, that was at the heart of her distress. 'Your father loves your mother and always will. I am quite sure of that.'

'How can you be?'

'When I tried to convince your father to allow you to marry me it was as if she was there in the room— talking to him, guiding him. Nothing will take their love away...'

The most cynical man in the world had confirmed what Layla felt in her heart—that her mother was somehow still there.

Layla thought about how happy she was and wanted everyone to feel the same—to feel as loved and as content and as excited about the future as she felt now.

'I am happy for Jamila and my father,' she said. 'I think it will be awkward, but I am going to try.'

'That's all you have to do.'

'Will you one day have forgotten *me*?' Layla asked.

'Never.'

'What if you hadn't come for me...?'

And there was her real fear—and it was scary even to voice it. But they had barely spoken since she had chosen Mikael and now, in his arms, she dared to face up to how terrible tonight might have been had it not been for Mikael.

'I was always coming for you,' he said to the shell of her ear. 'I'd have worked out your note, we'd have met online, I'd have lived in Ishla just to be near you...'

Mikael told her his truth—just not all of it, for he knew he would have appealed to Zahid on the death of the King and, whether she'd been married to another or not, he would one day have made Layla his.

'I would have spent the rest of my life either working out how to be with you or ensuring that you were happy.'

'What made you come when you did?'

'When I found out you loved me there was no question.'

'How could you not have known I loved you?' Layla frowned. 'Even if I could not say it, surely you knew...?' She pulled her head back and saw his eyes. He did not comprehend her words—but then how could he? Layla thought. For Mikael had never known love.

He would know it every day now.

It would not just be a year of dancing and kissing, Layla thought as her mouth moved to his. It would be a year of learning about a man who had never loved another—and what a privilege that would be.

Their first kiss as husband and wife was from another dimension, and knowing they did not have to halt, that they had the blessing of the desert, made it all the more sublime.

His chin was rough and it did not matter—for they were here in the desert for as long as they desired... and desire they did.

At every turn, in every intimate moment, Mikael had resisted—and now he did not have to.

Her tongue was the instigator, for it suckled his, and then she glimpsed Mikael without restraint. He was raising her robe and her hands lifted above her head, for she wanted it gone too.

She stripped, and so did he, and she stood as his

mouth kissed her breasts till she could stand no more, and then they were side by side on the bed.

He tried to soften the mouth on her breasts but Layla pushed at his head in consent, for she had loathed how they had always had to hold back.

No more.

His mouth returned to hers and Layla was breathless—even more so as his hand slid between her thighs, stroking her clitoris as he swallowed the tiny shallow breaths that made Layla dizzy. And as his fingers slowly probed not even his kisses could temper the feel of him stretching her.

There would be no babies, Layla thought, for she could barely stand one finger…now two…

'It's okay,' he said to her grimace, and he was right.

His mouth was gentle balm as intimately he explored her, and soon it turned divine. Layla felt as if there were a key in the very small of her back that Mikael wound ever tighter with each deep stroke inside. Over and over he stroked, till the key was so taut she thought it might snap, but there was no fear.

Mikael wanted to ensure she was oiled and ready.

'Please…' Layla said, because she could not be more ready.

She was pulling him on top of her, for she wanted to be crushed by him—she wanted Mikael in the most basic of ways that till this moment they had had to deny.

She made an involuntary biting noise as she felt the first stretch of him and Mikael halted, but then he remembered that was what she did when she was overexcited. He waited for a moan, a protest—for anything that might indicate he should take it more slowly as for the first time he filled her—but Layla was lost in her own pleasure.

Mikael gave her a moment to acclimatise to the burning inside her body and she didn't know if her eyes were open or closed, for there were stars on either side.

'I like,' Layla said, and felt the soft shudder of his half-laugh. And then he started to move and she *still* liked.

He moved within her so slowly that she moaned in increasing want. She tasted salt on his neck and passion on his tongue and her hands pressed him in as her hips started to beg.

'I don't want to be a princess...'

It was a language of their own. She was not glass—and, though she loved that he treated her as such, in this moment there was no need to. There was just need.

He had accepted her password, Layla knew, because she felt this most guarded man unwind within her. He gave her himself and no longer held back, each thrust a shot of passion that drove her higher, wound her tighter, until that key was released and Layla's mind spun as her body concurred with Mikael's. Even her arms were trembling as he locked her into ecstasy and made her for ever his.

'Now you cannot change your mind,' Layla said as they came back to earth.

'I was never going to,' Mikael said, for he needed no get-out clause. He did not care about the small print of the contract they had entered into. 'Did I hurt you?' he asked, concerned he had not been gentle enough.

'Hurt me?' Her eyes widened. 'That is not hurt. Those nights I thought I had lost you—that was hurt...'

'You'll never lose me, Layla,' he said, and he meant it.

'I think we have to do this more than once a week.'

Mikael stared at the sky and the very full moon and held in his laughter before speaking. 'Once a *week*?'

'Jamila said that once a week would suffice. Can we do it more than that?'

'Absolutely.'

'How much more?'

'Much, much more.'

'What if those herbs make the pill not work?'

He looked over to her. 'I doubt that very much,' Mikael said, 'but what do you think would happen if it *didn't* work?'

She thought for a very long time about how she felt right now.

No, this wasn't Planet Layla, and yet since she had arrived on Planet Earth something had been missing.

There had been an ache.

She didn't really know what it had been, and now it was as if warm cement had been poured and that void was for ever filled. There was nothing she could not face with Mikael by her side.

'We'd get through it,' Layla said.

'We would,' he agreed, and he took her hand and she felt his fingers close around hers.

'I would probably be difficult to live with,' she warned, and Mikael rolled his eyes as he thought of life with a pregnant Layla.

'Yes, you would be *very* difficult to live with,' Mikael said, and then smiled as he thought about the day she had stepped into his chambers and claimed his black heart. 'But impossible to live without.'

'You say the nicest things.' She smiled. 'You are the nicest man.'

'Just make sure you don't tell anyone,' Mikael said, 'or you'll ruin my reputation.'

'It can be our secret,' she said, and then stamped her feet in pleasure and did a little horizontal dance in bed as happiness consumed her—for Layla knew she had met true love.

And Mikael watched on and let her be—delighted by his family.

* * * * *

"I will not marry you."

"Then you will enjoy prison."

The look on Samarah's face nearly destroyed what little was left of Ferran's humanity. A foolish thing—to pity the woman who'd just tried to kill him. And she might have succeeded. He had no illusion of her being a joke just because he was a man and she a woman. He had no doubt that the only thing that had kept him from the end was her moment of hesitation. Seconds had made the difference between his life and death.

He should not pity her. He should not care that he'd known her since she was a baby. That he could clearly picture her as a bubbly princess who had been beautiful beyond measure. A treasure to her country.

That was not who she was now. As he was not the haughty teenage boy he'd been. Not the entitled prince who'd thought only of pursuing pleasure.

Life had hit them both, harsh and real, at too young an age. He had learned a hard lesson about human weakness. About his own weaknesses. Secrets revealed had sent her father into the palace in a murderous rage...one that had, in the end, dissolved a lineage and destroyed a nation.

She was a product of that, as was he. And her actions now had nothing to do with that connection from the past. He should throw her in a jail cell and show her no mercy.

And yet he didn't want to.

USA TODAY bestselling author **Maisey Yates** lives in rural Oregon, USA, with her three children and her husband, whose chiselled jaw and arresting features continue to make her swoon. She feels the epic trek she takes several times a day from her office to her coffee-maker is a true example of her pioneer spirit.

In 2009, at the age of twenty-three, Maisey sold her first book. Since then it's been a whirlwind of sexy alpha males and happily-ever-afters, and she wouldn't have it any other way. Maisey divides her writing time between dark, passionate category romances, set just about everywhere on earth, and light, sexy contemporary romances set practically in her back yard. She believes that she clearly has the best job in the world.

Recent titles by the same author:

ONE NIGHT TO RISK IT ALL
PRETENDER TO THE THRONE *(The Call of Duty)*
FORGED IN THE DESERT HEAT
A HUNGER FOR THE FORBIDDEN
  (Sicily's Corretti Dynasty)

**Did you know these are also available as eBooks?
Visit www.millsandboon.co.uk**

TO DEFY A SHEIKH

BY
MAISEY YATES

Published in Great Britain 2014
by Mills & Boon, an imprint of Harlequin (UK) Limited,
Eton House, 18-24 Paradise Road, Richmond, Surrey, TW9 1SR

© 2014 Maisey Yates

ISBN: 978-0-263-25026-8

Printed and bound in Spain
by Blackprint CPI, Barcelona

TO DEFY A SHEIKH

To Megan Crane, who said "Obviously you have to write this book" when I told her about my idea.

There are few things that are more valuable than the encouragement of friends.

CHAPTER ONE

SHEIKH FERRAN BASHAR, ruler of Khadra, would not survive the night. He didn't know it yet, but it was true.

Killing a man was never going to be easy. But that was why she'd trained, why she'd practiced the moves over and over again. So that they became muscle memory. So that when the time came there would be no hesitation. No regret.

She waited by the door of the sheikh's bedchamber, a cloth soaked in chloroform in one hand, a knife stowed securely in her robe. There could be no noise. And she would have to surprise him.

How could she have regret? When she knew what his legacy had brought onto hers. Tradition as old as their kingdoms demanded this. Demanded that his line end with him.

As hers had ended with her father. With one lone, surviving daughter who could never carry the name. With a kingdom that had lost its crown and suffered years of turmoil as a result.

But now was no time for emotion. No time for anything but action. She'd gotten herself hired on at the palace a month ago for this very purpose. And Ferran had been no wiser. Of course he hadn't. Why would he ever look at her? Why would he ever recognize her?

But she recognized him. And now, she'd observed him. Learned him.

Sheikh Ferran was a large man, tall and lean with hard

muscle and impressive strength. She'd watched him burn off energy in the courtyard, hitting a punching bag over and over again. She knew how he moved. She knew his endurance level.

She would be merciful. He would feel nothing.

He would not know it was coming. He would not beg for his life. He wouldn't wait in a cell for his life to end, as her father had. It would simply end.

Yes, unlike him, she would show mercy in that way at least.

And she knew that tonight, she would win.

Or she would be the one who didn't live to see morning. It was a risk she was willing to take. It was one she had to take.

She waited, her muscles tense, everything in her on high alert. She heard footsteps, heavy and even. It was Ferran, she was almost positive. As sure as she could be with footsteps alone.

She took a deep breath and waited for the door to open. It did, a sliver of light sliding across the high-gloss marble floor. She could see his reflection in it. Broad, tall. Alone.

Perfect.

She just needed to wait for him to close the door.

She held her breath and waited. He closed the door, and she knew she had to move immediately.

Samarah said a prayer just before she moved from the shadow. One for justice. One for forgiveness. And one for death, that it would come swiftly. For Ferran, or for her.

He turned as she was poised to overtake him, and her eyes met his. It stopped her, dead in her tracks, the glittering in those dark depths so alive. So vibrant. He was striking, beautiful even.

So very familiar.

In spite of all the years, she *knew* him. And in that moment, all she could do was stare, motionless. Breathless.

That moment was all it took.

Ferran stepped to the side, reaching out and grabbing her arm. She lifted and twisted her wrist, tugging it through the weak point of his hand where his fingers overlapped, as she crossed one leg behind the other and dipped toward the floor, lowering her profile and moving herself out of harm's way.

She turned and sidestepped, grabbing his shoulder and using his thigh as a step up to his back. She swung herself around, her forearm around his neck, the chloroform soaked rag in her hand.

He grabbed her wrist, a growl on his lips, and she fought to tug out of his grasp, but this time, he held fast. This time, he was expecting her escape.

She growled in return, tightening her hold on his neck with her other arm. He backed them both up against the wall, the impact of the hard stone surface knocking the air from her.

She swore and held fast, her thighs tight around his waist, ankles locked together at his chest. His hand wrapped around her wrist, he took her arm and hit it against the wall. She dropped the rag and swore, fighting against him.

But her surprise was lost, and while she was a skilled fighter, she was outmatched in strength. She'd forfeited her advantage.

She closed her eyes and imagined her home. Not the streets of Jahar, but the palace. One she and her mother had been evicted from after the death of her father. After the sanctioned execution of her father. Sanctioned by Ferran.

Adrenaline shot through her and she twisted to the side, using her body weight to put more pressure on his neck. He stumbled across the room, flipped her over his shoulders. She landed on her back on the floor, the braided rug doing little to cushion her fall, the breath knocked from her body.

She had to get up. This would be the death of her, and

she knew it. Ferran was ruthless, as was his father before him, and the evidence of that was the legacy of her entire life. He would think nothing of breaking her neck, and she well knew it.

He leaned over her and she put her feet up, bracing them on his chest and pushing back, before planting her feet on the floor and leveraging herself into a standing position, her center low, her hands up, ready to block or attack.

He moved and she sidestepped, sweeping her foot across his face. He stumbled and she used the opportunity to her advantage, pushing him to the ground and straddling him, her knees planted on his shoulders, one hand at his throat.

Still, she could see his eyes, glittering in the dark.

She would have to do it while she faced him now. And without the benefit of chloroform either putting him out cold or deadening his senses. She pushed back at the one last stab of doubt as she reached into her robe for her knife.

There was no time to doubt. No time to hesitate. He certainly hadn't done either when he'd passed that judgment on her father. There was no time for humanity when your enemy had none.

She whipped the knife out of her robe and held it up. Ferran grabbed both of her wrists and on a low, intense growl pushed her backward and propelled them both up against the side of the bed. He pushed her hand back, the knife blade flicking her cheek, parting the flesh there. A stream of blood trickled into her mouth.

She fisted his hair and his head fell back. She tried to bring the blade forward, but he grabbed her arm again, reversing their positions. He had her trapped against the bed, her hands flat over the mattress, bent a near-impossible direction. The tendons in her shoulders screamed, the cut on her face burning hot.

"Who sent you?" he asked, his voice a low rasp.

"I sent myself," she said, spitting out the blood that had pooled in her mouth onto the floor beside them.

"And what is it you're here to do?"

"Kill you, obviously."

He growled again and twisted her arm, forcing her to drop the knife. And still he held her fast. "You've failed," he said.

"So far."

"And forever," he said, his tone dripping with disdain. "What I want to know is why a woman is hiding in my bedchamber ready to end my life."

"I would have thought this happened to you quite often."

"Not in my memory."

"A life for a life," she said. "And as you only have the one, I will take it. Though you owe more."

"Is that so?"

"I'm not here to debate with you."

"No, you're here to kill me. But as that isn't going to happen—tonight or any other night—you may perhaps begin to make the case as to why I should not have you executed. For an attempt at assassinating a world leader. For treason. I could. At the very least I can have you thrown in jail right this moment. All it takes is a call."

"Then why haven't you made it?"

"Because I have not stayed sheikh, through changes in the world, civil unrest and assassination attempts, without learning that all things, no matter how bad, can be exploited to my advantage if I know where to look."

"I will not be used to your advantage."

"Then enjoy prison."

Samarah hesitated. Because she wouldn't forge an alliance with Ferran. It was an impossible ask. He had destroyed her life. He had toppled the government in her country. Left the remainder of her family on the run like dogs.

Left her and her mother on the streets to fend for themselves until her mother had died.

He had taken everything. And she had spent her life with one goal in mind. To ensure that he didn't get away with it. To ensure his line wouldn't continue while hers withered.

And she was failing.

Unless she stopped. Unless she listened. Unless she did what Ferran claimed to do. Turn every situation to her advantage.

"And what do I need to give in exchange for my freedom?"

"I haven't decided yet," he said. "I haven't decided if, in fact, your freedom is on the table. But the power is with me, is it not?"

"Isn't it always?" she asked. "You're the sheikh."

"This is true."

"Will you release me?"

He reached behind her, and when he drew his hand back into her line of vision, she saw he was now holding the knife. "I don't trust you, little desert viper."

"So well you shouldn't, Your Highness, as I would cut your throat if given the chance."

"Yet I have your knife. And you're the only one who bled. I will release you for the moment, only if you agree to follow my instructions."

"That depends on what they are."

"I want you to get on the bed, in the center, and stay there."

She stiffened, a new kind of fear entering her body. Death she'd been prepared for. But she had not, even for a moment, given adequate thought and concern to the idea of him putting his hands on her body.

No. Death first. She would fight him at all cost. She would not allow him to further dishonor her and her family. She would die fighting, but she would not allow him inside of her body.

Better a knife blade than him.

Ferran wouldn't...

She shook that thought off quickly. Ferran was capable of anything. And he had no loyalty. It didn't matter what he'd been like in that other life, in that other time. Not when he had proven all of that to be false.

She didn't move, and neither did he.

"Do we have an agreement?" he asked.

"You will not touch me," she said, her voice trembling now.

"I have no desire to touch you," he said. "I simply need you where I can see you. You're small, certainly, and a woman. But you are strong, and you are clearly a better fighter than I am, or I would have had you easily beaten. As it is, I had no choice but to use my size advantage against you. Now I have the size advantage and weapon. However, I still don't trust you. So get on the bed, in the center, hands in your lap. I have no desire to degrade or humiliate you further, neither am I in the mood for sex. On that score, you are safe."

"I would die first."

"And I would kill you first, so there we have an agreement of sorts. Now get up onto the bed and sit for a moment."

He moved away from her, slowly releasing his hold on her, the knife still in his hand. She obeyed his command, climbing up onto the bed and moving to the center of the massive mattress. Beds like this had come from another lifetime. She scarcely remembered them.

Since being exiled from the palace in Jahar she'd slept on raised cots, skins stretched over a wooden frame and one rough blanket. In the backs of shops. In the upstairs room of the martial arts studio she'd trained in. And when she was unlucky, on the dirt in an alley. When she'd arrived in the Khadran palace, as a servant, she'd slept in her first bed since losing her childhood room sixteen years ago.

The bed here, for servants, was much more luxurious than the sleep surfaces she'd been enjoying. Sized for one person, but soft and with two pillows. It was a luxury she'd forgotten. And it had felt wrong to enjoy it. The first week she'd slept on the floor in defiance, though that hadn't lasted.

And now she was on Ferran's bed. It made her skin crawl.

She put her hands in her lap and waited. She had no reason to trust his word, not when his blood had been found so lacking in honor. And not when he'd carried that dishonor to its conclusion himself.

The execution of her father. The order had been his. And no vow of bonds between royal families, or smiles between friends had changed his course.

As a result, she did not trust his vow not to touch her either.

"I'll ask you again," he said. "Who sent you?"

He still thought her a pawn. He still did not realize.

"I am acting of my own accord, as I said before."

"For what purpose?"

"Revenge."

"I see, and what is it I have not done to your liking?"

"You killed my king, Sheikh Ferran, and it was very much not to my liking."

"I do not make a habit of killing people," he said, his tone steel.

"Perhaps not with your hands, but you did set up the trial that ended in the execution of Jahar's sheikh. And it is rumored you had part in the overtaking of the Jahari palace that happened after. So much violence…I remember that day all too well."

He froze, the lines in his body tensing, his fist tightening around the knife. And for the first time, she truly feared. For the first time, she looked at the man and saw the ruthless desert warrior she had long heard spoken of. Thirty days in the palace and she had seen a man much more civilized than she anticipated. But not here. Not now.

"There were no survivors in the raid on the Jahari palace," he said, his voice rough.

"Too bad for you, there were. I see you know from where I come."

"The entire royal family, and all loyal servants were killed," he said, his voice rough. "That was the report that was sent back to me."

"They were wrong. And for my safety it was in my best interest that they continued to think so. But I am alive. If only to ensure that you will not be."

He laughed, but there was no humor to the sound. "You are a reaper come to collect then, are you? My angel of death here to lead me to hell?"

"Yes," she said.

"Very interesting."

"I should think I'm more than interesting."

He stilled. "You made me fear. There are not many on earth who have done so."

"That is a great achievement for me then, and yet, I still find I'm unsatisfied."

"You want blood."

She lifted her chin, defiant. "I require it. For this is my vengeance. And it is all about blood."

"I am sorry that I could not oblige you tonight."

"No more sorry than I."

"Why am I the object of your vengeance?" he asked. "Why not the new regime? Why not the people who stormed the palace and killed the royal family. The sheikha and her daughter."

"You mean the revolutionaries who were aided by your men?"

"They were not. Not I, nor anyone else in Khadra, had part in the overthrowing of the Jahari royal family. I had a country to run. I had no interest in damaging yours."

"You left us unprotected. You left us without a king."

"I did no such thing."

"You had the king of Jahar tried and executed in Khadra," she spat, venom on her tongue. "You left the rest of us to die when he was taken. Forced from our home. Servants, soldiers…everyone who did not turn to the new leader was killed. And those who escaped…only a half life was ever possible. There was no border crossing to be had, unless you just wanted to wander out into the desert and hope to God you found the sea, or the next country." As her mother had done one day. Wandered out into the desert never to return. At least, in recent years it had eased. That was how she'd been able to finally make her way to Khadra.

"I am not responsible for Sheikh Rashad's fate. He paid for sins committed. It was justice. Still, I am regretful of the way things unfolded."

"Are you?" she spat. "I find I am more than regretful, as it cost me everything."

"It has been sixteen years."

"Perhaps the passage of time matters to you, but I find that for me it does not."

"I say again, I did not give the order to have your people killed. It is a small comfort, certainly, as they are gone, but it is not something I did. You aren't the only one who doesn't believe. I am plagued by the ramifications of the past."

She curled her lip. "Plagued by it? I imagine it has been very hard for you. I'm not certain why I'm complaining about the fate of my country. Not when it has been so hard for you. In your palace with all of your power."

"It is hard when your legacy is defined by a human rights violation you did not commit," he bit out. "Make no mistake, I am often blamed for the hostile takeover of your country. But I did not send anyone into the palace to overthrow your government. Where have I benefited? Where is my hand in your country? What happened after was beyond my reach. And yet, I find I am in many ways responsible for it."

"You cannot have it both ways, Sheikh. You did it, or you did not."

"I had choices to make. To stand strong for my people, for my father, for my blood. Had I foreseen the outcome, as I should have done, my choices might have been different."

"Are you God then?"

"I am sheikh. It is very close to being the same."

"Then you are a flawed god indeed."

"And you? Do you aspire to be the goddess?" he asked, moving to the foot of the bed, standing tall, proud and straight. He was an imposing figure, and in many ways she couldn't believe that she had dared touch him. Not when he so obviously outmatched her in strength and weight. Not when he was so clearly a deadly weapon all on his own.

"Just the angel of death, as you said. I have no higher aspiration than that. It isn't power I seek, but justice."

"And you think justice comes with yet more death?"

"Who sent the king of Jahar to trial, Sheikh? Who left my country without a ruler?" *Who left me without a father?* She didn't voice the last part. It was too weak. And she refused to show weakness.

"I did," he said, his tone hard, firm. "Lest we forget the blood of the king of Khadra was on his hands. And that is not a metaphor."

"At least Khadra had an heir!"

His expression turned to granite. "And lacked an angry,

disillusioned populace. Certainly the loss of the king affected Jahar, but had the people not been suffering…"

"I am not here to debate politics with you."

"No, it is your wish to cut my throat. And I must say, even politics seems preferable to that."

"I am not so certain." She looked away for a moment, just a moment, to try and gather her thoughts. To try and catch her breath. "You left a little girl with no protection. A queen without her husband."

"And was I to let the Jahari king walk after taking the life of my father? The life of my mother."

"He did not…"

"We will not speak of my mother," he said, his tone fierce. "I forbid it."

"And so we find ourselves here," she said, her tone soft.

"So we do indeed."

"Will you have me killed?" she asked. "As I am also an inconvenience?"

"You, little viper, have attempted to murder me. At this point you are much more than an inconvenience."

"As you see it, Sheikh. The only problem I see is that I have failed."

"You do not speak as someone who values their preservation."

"Do I not?"

"No. You ask if I aim to kill you and then you express your desire to see me dead. All things considered, I suppose I should order your lovely head to be separated from your neck."

She put her hand to her throat. A reflex. A cowardly one. She didn't like it.

"However," he said dryly. "I find I have no stomach for killing teenage girls."

"I am not a teenage girl."

"Semantics. You cannot be over twenty."

"Twenty-one," she said, clenching her teeth.

"Fine then. I have no stomach for the murder of a twenty-one-year-old girl. And as such I would much rather find a way for you to be useful to me." He slid his thumb along the flat of her blade. "But where I could keep an eye on you, as I would rather this not end up in my back."

"I make no promises, Sheikh."

"Again, we must work on your self-preservation."

"Forgive me. I don't quite believe I have a chance at it."

Something in his face changed, his eyebrows drawing tightly together. "Samarah. Not a servant girl, or just an angry citizen. You are Samarah."

He'd recognized her. At last. She'd hoped he wouldn't. Not when she was supposed to be dead. Not when he hadn't seen her since she was a child of six.

She met his eyes. "Sheikha Samarah Al-Azem, of Jahar. A princess with no palace. And I am here for what is owed me."

"You think that is blood, little Samarah?"

"You will not call me little. I just kicked you in the head."

"Indeed you did, but to me, you are still little."

"Try such insolence when I have my blade back, and I will cut your throat, Sheikh."

"Noted," he said, regarding her closely. "You have changed."

"I ought to have. I'm no longer six."

"I cannot give you blood," he said. "For I am rather attached to having it in my veins, as you can well imagine."

"Self-preservation is something of an instinct."

"For most," he said, dryly.

"Different when you have nothing to lose."

"And is that the position you're in?"

"Why else would I invade the palace and attempt an assassination? Obviously I have no great attachments to this life."

His eyes flattened, his jaw tightening. "I cannot give you blood, Samarah. But you feel you were robbed of a legacy. Of a palace. And that, I can perhaps see you given."

"Can you?"

"Yes. I have indeed thought of a use for you. By this time next week, I shall present you to the world as my intended bride."

CHAPTER TWO

"No."

Ferran looked down at the woman kneeling in the center of his mattress. The woman was, if she was to be believed, if his own recognition could be believed, Samarah Al-Azem. Come back from the dead.

For surely the princess had been killed. The dark-eyed, smiling child he remembered so well, gone in the flood of violence that had started in the Khadran palace, ending in the death of Jahar's sheikh. What started as a domestic dispute cut a swath across the borders, into Jahar. The brunt of it falling on the Jahari palace.

It was the king of Jahar who had started the violence. Storming the Khadran palace, as punishment for his wife's affair with Ferran's father. An affair that had begun when Samarah was a young child and Ferran was a teenager. When the duty to country was served by both rulers, having supplied their spouses with children. Or so the story went. But it had not ended there. It had burned out of hand.

And countless casualties had been left.

Among them, the world had been led to believe, Samarah.

Was she truly the princess?

A girl he'd thought long dead. A death he had, by extension, caused. Was it possible she lived?

She was small. Dark-haired. At least from what he could

tell. A veil covered her head, her brows the only indicator of hair coloring. It was not required for women in employment of the palace to cover their heads or faces. But he was certain she was an employee here. Though not one who had been working for the palace long. There were many workers in the palace, and he didn't make it his business to memorize their faces.

Though, when one tried to kill him in his own bedchamber, he felt exceptions could be made. And when one was possibly the girl who had never left his mind, not ever, in sixteen years…

He truly had exceptions to make.

He was torn between rage and a vicious kind of amusement. That reckoning had come, and it had come in this form. Lithe, soft and vulnerable. The most innocent victim of all, come to claim his life. It was a testament, in many ways, to just how badly justice had been miscarried on that day.

Though he was not the one to answer for it. His justice had been the key to her demise. And yet, there was nothing he could do to change it. How could he spare the man who had robbed his country of a leader, installed a boy in place of the man.

The man who had killed his family for revenge.

They were two sides to the same coin. And depending upon which side you looked at, you had a different picture entirely.

Also, depending on which version of events you heard…

He shook off the thoughts, focused back on the present. On the woman. Samarah. "No?" he asked.

"You heard me. I will not ally myself with you."

"Then you will ally yourself with whomever you share a cell with. I firmly hope you find it enjoyable."

"You say that like you believe I'm frightened."

"Are you not?"

She raised her head, dark eyes meeting his. "I was prepared for whatever came."

"Obviously not, as you have rejected my offer. You do realize that I am aware you didn't act on your own. And that I will find who put you up to this, one way or the other. Whether you agree to this or not. However, if you do… things could go better for you."

"An alliance with you? That's better?"

"You do remember," he said, speaking the words slowly, softly, and hating himself with each syllable, "how I handle those who threaten the crown."

"I remember well. I remember how you flew the Khadran flag high and celebrated after the execution of my father," she said, her tone ice.

"Necessary," he bit out. "For I could not allow what happened in Jahar to happen here."

"But you see, what happened in Jahar had not happened yet. It wasn't until the sheikh was gone, the army scattered and all of us left without protection that we were taken. That we were slaughtered by revolutionaries who thought nothing of their perceived freedom coming at the price of our lives."

"Thus is war," he said. "And history. Individuals are rarely taken into account. Only result."

"A shame then that we must live our lives as individuals and not causes."

"Do we?" he asked. "It doesn't appear to me that you have. And I certainly don't. That is why I'm proposing marriage to you."

"That's like telling me two plus two equals camel. I have no idea what you're saying."

He laughed, though he still found nothing about the situation overly amusing. "The division between Khadra and Jahar has long been a source of unrest here. Violence at the borders is an issue, as I'm sure you well know. This could change that. Erase it. It's black-and-white. That's how I live my life. In a world of absolutes. There is no room for gray areas."

"To what end for me, Sheikh Ferran? I will never have my rightful position back, not in a meaningful way. The royal family of Jahar will never be restored, not in my lifetime."

"How have you lived since you left the palace?"

"Poorly," she said, dark eyes meeting his.

"This would get you back on the throne."

"I will not marry you."

"Then you will enjoy prison."

The look on her face nearly destroyed what little was left of his humanity. A foolish thing, to pity the woman who'd just tried to kill him. And she could have succeeded. She was not a novice fighter. He had no illusion of her being a joke just because he was a man and she a woman. He had no doubt that the only thing that had kept him from a slit throat was her bare moment of hesitation. Seconds had made the difference between his life and death.

He should not pity her. He should not care that he'd known her since she was a baby. That he could clearly picture her as a bubbly, spoiled little princess who had been beautiful beyond measure. A treasure to her country.

That was not who she was now. As he was not the haughty teenage boy he'd been. Not the entitled prince who thought only of women and what party he might sneak into, what trouble he might find on his father's yachts.

Life had hit them both, harsh and real, at too young an age. He had learned a hard lesson about human weakness. About his own weaknesses. Secrets revealed that had sent her father into the palace in a murderous rage...one that had, in the end, dissolved a lineage, destroyed a nation that was still rebuilding.

She was a product of that, as was he. And her actions

now had nothing to do with that connection from back then. He should throw her in a jail cell and show her no mercy.

And yet he didn't want to.

It made no sense. There was no room for loyalty to a would-be assassin. No room for pity. Putting your faith in the wrong person could have a disastrous end, and he knew it well. If he was wrong now...

No. He would not be wrong.

This was not ordinary compassion leading him. There was potential political gain to be had. Yes, Jahar had suffered the most change during that dark time sixteen years ago, but Khadra had suffered, too. They had lost their sheikh and sheikha, they had been rocked by violence. Their security shaken to its core.

The palace had been breached.

Their centuries-old alliance with their closest neighbors shattered. It had changed everything in a single instance. For him, and for millions of people who called his country home.

He had never taken that lightly. It was why he never faltered. It was why he showed her no mercy.

But this was an opportunity for something else. For healing. One thing he knew. More blood, more arrests, would not fix the hurts from the past.

It had to end. And it had to end with them.

"Can you kill me instead?" she asked.

"You ask for death?"

"Rather than a prison cell?"

"Rather than marriage," he said.

Her nostrils flared, dark eyes intense. "I will not become your property."

"I do not intend to make you my property, but answer me this, Samarah. What will this do to our countries?"

"I almost bet it will do nothing to mine."

"Do you think? Are you a fool? No one will believe one girl was acting alone."

"I am not a girl."

"You are barely more than a child as far as I'm concerned."

"Had I been raised in the palace that might be true, but as it is, I lived on the streets. I slept in doorways and on steps. I holed up in the back rooms of shops when I could. I had to take care of a mother who went slowly mad. I had to endure starvation, dehydration, the constant threat of theft or rape. I am not a child. I am years older than you will ever live to be," she spat.

He hated to imagine her in that position. In the gutter. In danger. But she had clearly survived. Though, he could see it was a survival fueled by anger.

"If you kill me," he said, "make no mistake, Khadra will make Jahar pay. If I imprison you…how long do you suppose it will take for those loyal to the royal family to threaten war on me? But if we are engaged…"

"What will the current regime in Jahar think?"

"I suppose they will simply be happy to have you in my monarchy, rather than establishing a new one there. I suspect it will keep you much safer than a prison cell might. If you are engaged to marry me, your intentions are clear. If you are in jail…who knows what your ultimate plans might have been? To overthrow me and take command of both countries?"

"Don't be silly," she said, her voice deceptively soft. "At best, I'm a lone woman. Just a weak, small ex-royal, who is nothing due to her gender and her gentle upbringing. At worst…well, I'm a ghost. Everyone believes me dead."

"I am holding a knife that says you're far more than that."

"But no one will believe otherwise."

"Perhaps not. But it is a risk."

"What do you have to gain?" she asked.

It was a good question. And the main answer was balm for his guilt, and he had no idea where that answer had come from. The past was the past. And yes, he had regretted her death—a child—when he'd thought she'd been killed. But it had not been at his hand. He would have protected her.

He would protect her now. And in the process, himself, and hopefully aid the healing of a nation too long under a shadow.

"Healing," he said. "What I want is to heal the wounds. Not tear them open again. I will not have more blood running through this palace. I will not have more death. Not even yours," he said, a vow in many ways.

Sheikha Samarah Al-Azem was a part of a past long gone. Tainted with blood and pain. And he wanted to change something about it. He wanted more than to simply cover it, and here she presented the opportunity to fix some of it.

Because it had not been her fault. It had been his. The truth of it, no matter how much he wanted to deny it, was that it was all his fault.

It was logic. It was not emotion, but a burning sense of honor and duty that compelled it. He didn't believe in emotion. Only right and wrong. Only justice.

"What's it to be, Samarah?" he asked, crossing his arms over his chest.

"Prison," she said.

Anger fired through him, stark and hot. Was she a fool? He was offering her a chance to fix some of this, a chance at freedom. And she was opting for jail.

She was not allowing him to make this right. And he found he didn't like it.

"So be it," he growled, throwing the knife to the side

and stalking to the bed, throwing her over his shoulder in one fluid moment.

She shrieked. Then twisted, hissed and spit like a cat. He locked his arms over hers, and her legs, but she still did her best to kick his chest.

"I think, perhaps, *habibti,* a night in the dungeon will cool your temper."

He stalked to the far wall of his room and moved a painting, then keyed in a code. The bookshelf swung open. "We've modernized a bit here in Khadra, as you can see," he bit out, walking through the open doorway and into a narrow passageway. "Though these tunnels are quite new."

"Get your hands off of me!"

"And give you a chance to cut my throat? I highly doubt it. You were given another option and you chose not to take it. No one will hear you scream, by the way. But even if they did…I am the sheikh. And you are an intruder."

He knew every passage that ran through the palace. Knew every secret. A boy up to no good would have to know them, of course, and a sheikh with a well-earned bit of paranoia would, naturally, ensure the passages were always kept up. That he knew the layout of the castle better than anyone, so that the upper hand would always be his in the event of an attack.

He had lived through one, and he was the only member of his family who had. He felt he had earned his feelings on the matter.

In any case, he was well versed on where every dark, nondescript tunnel in the palace led. And he knew how to get down to the dungeon. It wasn't used. Hadn't been in ages, generations. But he would be using it tonight.

Because if he left her free, she would no doubt kill him in his sleep. And that he could not have. Either she formed an alliance with him, or he put her under lock and key. It was very simple. Black-and-white, as the world, when all was in working order, should be.

"I will kill you the moment I get the chance!" she spat, kicking against his chest.

"I know," he said. "I am confident in that fact."

He shifted his hold on her, his hand skimming the rounded curve of her bottom as he tried to get a better grip on her. The contact shot through him like lightning. This was the closest he'd been to a woman in…much too long. He wouldn't count how long.

You know just how long. And if you marry her…

He shut off the thought. He was not a slave to his body. He was not a slave to desire. He was a slave to nothing. He was ice. All the way down.

He took them both down a flight of stone steps that led beneath the palace, and down into the dungeon. Unused and medieval, but still in working order.

"Let me go."

"You just threatened to kill me. I strongly doubt I'm letting you go anytime soon."

He grabbed a key ring from the hooks on the back wall, then kicked the wrought iron door to the nearest cell open. Then he reached down and picked up a leg iron and clamped it around her ankle.

She swore, a violent, loud string of profanity that echoed off the walls.

He ignored her, slung her down onto the bench and moved quickly away from her range of movement before shutting the door behind him.

"You bastard!" she said.

He wrapped his fingers around the bars, his knuckles aching from the tight grip. "No, I am pure royal blood, Sheikha, and you of all people should know it."

"Is the leg shackle necessary?"

"I didn't especially want to find myself overpowered and put in the cell myself."

She closed her mouth, a dark brow raised, her lips pursed. A haughty, mutinous expression that did indeed remind him of Samarah the child.

"You do not deny you would have." He walked to the side of the cell so that he could stand nearer to her. "Do you?"

"Of course not," she said.

"Come to the bars and I will undo the leg shackle. It is unnecessary now that you're secured."

"Do you think so?" she asked.

He stared at her, at those glittering eyes, black as midnight in the dim lighting of the dungeon. "Perhaps I do not now. You truly need to work on your self-preservation. I would have made you more comfortable."

Her lip curled, baring her white teeth, a little growl rumbling in her chest. "I will never be comfortable in your prison."

"Suit yourself. Prison is in your future, but you may choose the cell. A room in the palace, a position as sheikha, or you may rot in here. It is no concern of mine. But you will decide by sunset tomorrow."

"Sunset? What is this, some bad version of *Arabian Nights?*"

"You're the one who turned back the clock. Pursuing vengeance in order to end my bloodline. Don't get angry with me for playing along." He turned away from her, heading back out of the dungeon. "If you want to do it like this, we will. If you want to play with antiquated rules, I am all for that. But I intend for it to go my way. I intend to make you my wife, and I doubt, in the end, you will refuse."

CHAPTER THREE

FERRAN PACED THE length of his room. He hated himself in this moment, with Samarah behind the secret passage doors, down in the dungeon.

She did not deserve such treatment. At least, the little girl he'd known had not.

Of course, if they were all paying for the sins of their fathers, she deserved the dungeon and then some. But he didn't believe in that. Every man paved his own road to hell. And he'd secured his sixteen years ago.

And if he hadn't then, surely now he had.

Marriage. He had no idea what he'd been thinking. On a personal level, anyway. On a political level he'd been thinking quite clearly.

But Samarah Al-Azem, in his life, in his bed, was the last thing he'd been looking for. In part because he'd thought she was dead.

Though he needed a wife, and he knew it. He was long past due. And yet…and yet he'd never even started his search. Because he was too busy. Because he had no time to focus on such matters.

Much easier to marry Samarah. Heal the rift between the countries, ensure she was cared for. His pound of flesh. Because it wasn't as though he wanted this for himself.

But then, it was better that way. He didn't allow himself to want.

This was about atonement. About making things right.

Want didn't come into it. For Ferran, it never had. And it never would.

Samarah woke up. She had no idea what time it was. There was no natural light in the dungeon. If there had been a torch on the wall, she wouldn't have been terribly surprised.

But then, that might have been a kindness too many. Not that Ferran owed her a kindness at this point.

Not all things considered.

But she hadn't been looking to repair bridges. She'd been looking to finish it all.

You can't finish it from in here...

"No," she said out loud. "Fair enough."

But the alternative was to agree to marry him. Or to give the appearance of an alliance.

Anger, revulsion, burned in her blood.

She could not ally herself with him. But...

But every predator knew that in order to catch prey successfully, there was a certain amount of lying in wait involved.

She squeezed her hands into fists, her nails digging into her palms, the manacle heavy on her ankle. Diplomacy was, perhaps not her strongest point. But she knew about lying in wait. As she'd done in his room last night.

This would be an extended version of that. She would have to make him trust her. She would have to play along. And then...then she could have her revenge before the world if she chose.

The idea had appeal. Though, putting herself in proximity with Ferran, pretending to be his fiancée, did not.

She lay back down on the bench, one knee curled into her chest, the chained leg held out straight. She closed her eyes again, and when she opened them, it was to the sound of a door swinging open.

"Have you made up your mind?"

She knew who the voice belonged to. She didn't even have to look.

She sat up, trying to shake out the chill that had settled into her bones. She looked at Ferran's outline in the darkness. "I will marry you," she said.

The room Ferran showed her to after her acceptance was a far cry from the dungeon. But Samarah was very aware of the fact that it was only a sparkling version of a cell. A fact Ferran underlined as he left her.

"You will not escape," he said. "There are guards around the perimeter. And there will be no border crossing possible for you as my patrol will be put on alert. You will be trapped in the country should you decide to try and leave, and from there, I will find you. And you will have lost your reprieve."

He was foolish for worrying, though. She had nothing to go back to. No one waiting for her. And she had arrived at her goal point. Why would she go back to Jahar with nothing accomplished?

It was true that Jahar was not as dangerous for her as it had once been. In the past five years there had been something of an uneasy transition from a totalitarian rule established by the revolutionaries, who had truly only wanted power for themselves, into a democracy. Though it was a young democracy, and as such, there were still many lingering issues.

Still, the deposition of the other leaders had meant that she no longer had a target on her back, at least. But she had no place, either.

That meant she was perfectly happy to stay here, right in Ferran's home, while she thought of her next move.

Well, perhaps perfectly happy was an overstatement,

but it was better than being back in an old room in a shop in Jahar.

She looked around, a strange tightness in her chest. This was so very familiar, this room. She wondered if it was, perhaps, the same room she'd sometimes stayed in when she and her family had come to visit the Bashar family. In happier times. Times that hardly seemed to matter, given how it had all ended.

Lush fabrics were draped over marble walls, the glittering red and jade silks offering a peek at the obsidian and gold beneath. Richness layered over unfathomable richness. The bed was the same. Draped yards of fabric in bold colors, the frame constructed around the bed decorated with yet more.

Divans, pillows, rugs, all of it served to add softness to a room constructed from stone and precious gems.

And the view—a tall, tower room that looked beyond the walls of the palace gardens, beyond the walls of the city and out to the vast dunes. An orange sun casting burning gold onto the sands.

There was a knock on the grand, carved double doors and she turned. "Yes?"

One door opened and a small woman came in. Samarah knew her as Lydia, another woman who worked in the palace, and with whom Samarah had had some interaction over the course of the past month.

"Sheikha," Lydia said, bowing her head.

So it had begun. Samarah couldn't deny the small flash of…pleasure that arched through her when the other woman said her title. Though it had been more years gone than she'd been with it, it was a title that was in her blood.

Still, she was a bit disturbed by the idea of Lydia knowing any details of what had passed between Ferran and herself. More disturbing though was just what she'd been led to believe about their relationship.

The idea of being Ferran's wife…his lover…it was revolting.

She thought of the man he was. Strong, powerful. Broad shoulders, lean waist. Sharp dark eyes, a square jaw. He was clean shaven, unusual for a man in his part of the world, but she couldn't blame him. For he no doubt used his looks to his advantage in all things.

He was extraordinarily handsome, which was not a point in his favor as far as she was concerned. It was merely an observation about her enemy.

Beauty meant little. Beauty was often deceitful.

She knew that she was considered a great beauty, like her mother before her. And men often took that to mean she was soft, easy to manipulate, easy to take advantage of. As a result some men had found themselves with a sword trained at vulnerable parts of their body.

Yes, she knew beauty could be used to hide strength and cunning. She suspected Ferran knew that, as well.

She had spent the past month observing his physical strength, but she feared she may have underestimated the brilliance of her adversary.

"I have brought you clothes," Lydia said, "at the sheikh's instruction. And he says that you are to join him for dinner when the sun sinks below the dunes."

She narrowed her eyes. "Did he really say it like that?"

"He did, my lady."

"Do you not find it odd?"

A small smile tugged at Lydia's lips. "I am not at liberty to say."

"I see," Samarah said, pacing the width of the room. The beautifully appointed room that, like Ferran and herself, was merely using its beauty to cover what it really was.

A cage. For a tigress.

"And what," Samarah continued, "did he say about me and my change in station?"

"Not much, my lady. He simply said we were to address you as sheikha and install you in this wing of the palace. And that you are not to leave."

"Ah yes, that sounds about right." She was relieved, in many ways, that he hadn't divulged many details. "So I am to dress for him and appear at this magical twilit hour?"

"I shall draw you a bath first."

Samarah looked down at herself and put a hand to her cheek, her thumb drifting over the small cut inflicted by her own knife. She imagined she was a bit worse for wear after having spent the night in a dungeon. So a bath was likely in order.

"Thank you. I shall look forward to it."

Minutes later, Samarah was submerged to her chin in a sunken mosaic tub filled with hot water and essential oils. It stretched the length of the bath chamber, larger than many swimming pools. There were pillars interspersed throughout, and carvings of naked women and men, lounging and tangled together.

She looked away from the scenes. She'd never been comfortable with such things. Not after the way her family had dissolved. Not when she'd spent so many years guarding her body from men who sought to use her.

And certainly not when she was in the captivity of her enemy. An enemy who intended to marry her and…beget his heirs on her. In that naked, entwined fashion. It was far too much to bear.

She leaned her head back against the pillow that had been provided for her and closed her eyes. This was, indeed, preferable to the dungeon. Furthermore, it was preferable to every living situation she'd had since leaving her family's palace.

And of course he'd planned it that way. Of course he would know how to appeal to certain weaknesses.

She couldn't forget what he was.

When she was finished, she got out and wrapped herself in a plush robe, wandering back into her room.

"My lady," Lydia said. "I would have helped you."

"I don't need help, Lydia. In fact, and this is no offense meant to you, I would like some time alone before I go and see the sheikh."

Lydia blinked. "Of course, Sheikha." Samarah could tell Lydia was trying to decide whom she should obey.

Ultimately, the other woman inclined her head and walked out of the chamber.

Samarah felt slightly guilty dismissing her, but honestly, the idea of being dressed seemed ridiculous. Palatial surroundings or not. She picked up the dark blue dress that had been laid out on her bed. It was a heavy fabric, with a runner of silver beads down the front, and a scattering of them across. Stars in a night sky. Along with that were some silken under things. A light bra with little padding, and, she imagined, little support, and a pair of panties to match.

She doubted anyone dressed Ferran. He didn't seem the type.

She pondered that while she put the underwear and dress on. He had not turned out the way she might have imagined. First, he hadn't transformed into a monster. She'd imagined that he might have. Since, in her mind, he was the man who killed her father.

He also hadn't become the man she'd imagined he might, based on what she remembered of him when he'd been a teenage boy.

He'd been mouthy, sullen when forced to attend palace dinners and behave. And he'd often pulled practical jokes on palace staff.

He didn't seem like a man who would joke about much now.

Well, except for his 'when the sun sinks beneath the dune' humor. She snorted. As if she would be amused.

She considered the light veil that had been included with the dress. She'd chosen to wear one while on staff, but in general she did not. Unless she was headed into the heart of the Jahari capital. Then she often opted to wear one simply to avoid notice.

She would not wear one tonight. Instead, she wandered to the ornate jewelry box that was situated on the vanity and opened it. Inside, she found bangles, earrings and an elaborate head chain with a bright center gem designed to rest against her forehead.

She braided her long dark hair and fastened the chain in place, then put on the rest of the jewelry. Beauty to disguise herself. A metaphor that seemed to be carrying through today.

She found that there was makeup, as well, and she applied it quickly, the foundation doing something to hide the cut on her cheek. It enraged her to see it. Better it was covered. She painted dark liner around her eyes, stained her lips red.

She looked at herself and scarcely knew the woman she saw. Everything she was wearing was heavy, and of a fine quality she could never have afforded in her life on the street. She blinked, then looked away, turning her focus to the window, where she could see the sun sinking below the dunes.

It was time.

She lifted the front of her dress, her bangles clinking together, all of her other jewels moving with each step, giving her a theme song composed in precious metals as she made her way from the room and down the long corridor.

She rounded a corner and went down a sweeping staircase into a sitting area of the palace. There were men there, dressed in crisp, white tunics nearly as ornate as her dress.

"Sheikha," one said, "this way to dinner."

She inclined her head. "Thank you."

She followed him into the next room. The dining area was immaculate, a tall table with a white tablecloth and chairs placed around. It was large enough to seat fifty, but currently only seated Ferran. There were windows behind him that looked out into the gardens, lush, green. A sign of immeasurable wealth. So much water in the desert being given to plants.

"You came," he said, not bothering to stand when she entered.

"Of course. The sun has sunken. Behind the dunes."

"So it has."

"I should not like to disobey a direct order," she said.

"No," he responded, "clearly not. You are so very biddable."

"I find that I am." She walked down the edge of the table, her fingertips brushing the backs of the chairs as she made her way toward him. "Merciful even."

"Merciful?" he asked, raising his brows. "I had not thought that an accurate description. Perhaps…thwarted?"

She stopped moving, her eyes snapping up to his. "Perhaps," she bit out.

"Sit," he commanded.

She continued walking, to the head of the table, around the back of him, lifting her hand the so she was careful to avoid contact with him. She watched his shoulders stiffen, his body, his instincts on high alert.

He knew he had not tamed her. Good.

She took a seat to his left, her eyes on the plate in front of her. "I do hope there will be food soon. I'm starving. It seems I was detained for most of the day."

"Ah yes," he said, "I recall. And don't worry. It's on its way."

As if on cue, six men came in, carrying trays laden

with clay pots, and clear jars full of frosted, brightly colored juice.

All of the trays were laid out before them, the tall lids on the tagines removed with great drama and flair.

Her stomach growled and she really hoped he wasn't planning on poisoning her, because she just wanted to eat some couscous, vegetables and spiced lamb. She'd spent many nights trying to sleep in spite of the aching emptiness in her stomach.

And she didn't have the patience for it, not now.

She needed a full stomach to deal with Ferran.

"We are to serve ourselves," Ferran said, as the staff walked from the room. "I often prefer to eat this way. I find I get everything to my liking when I do it myself." His eyes met hers. "And I find I am much happier when I am in control of a situation."

She arched a brow and reached for a wooden utensil, dipping it into the couscous and serving herself a generous portion. "That could be a problem," she said, going back for some lamb. "As I feel much the same way, and I don't think either of us can have complete control at any given time."

"Do you ever have control, Samarah?"

She paused. "As much as one can have, Sheikh. Of course, the desert is always king, no matter what position in life you hold. No one can stop a drought. Or a monsoon. Or a sandstorm."

"I take it that's your way of excusing your powerlessness."

She took a sharp breath and turned her focus to her dinner. "I am not powerless. No matter the situation, no matter the chains, you can never make me powerless. I will always have choices, and my strength is here." She put her hand on her chest. "Not even you can reach in and take my heart, Sheikh Ferran Bashar. And so, you will never truly have power over me."

"You are perhaps the bravest person I've ever met," he said. "And the most foolish."

She smiled. "I take both as the sincerest of compliments."

"I should like to discuss our plan."

"I should like to eat—this is very good. I don't think the servants eat the same food as you do."

"Do they not? I had not realized. I'll ask the chef if it's too labor intensive or if it's possible everyone eat as I do."

"I imagine it isn't possible, and it would only make more work for the cook. Cooking in mass quantities is a bit different than cooking for one sheikh and his prisoner."

"I've never cooked," he said. "I wouldn't know."

"I haven't often cooked, but I have been in the food lines in Jahar. I know what mass-produced food is."

"Tell me," he said, leaning on one elbow. "How did you survive?"

"After we left the palace—" she would not speak of that night, not to him "—we sought asylum with sympathizers, though they were nearly impossible to find. We went from house to house. We didn't want people to know we'd survived."

"It was reported you were among the dead."

She nodded. "I know. A favor granted to my mother by a servant who wanted to live. She feigned loyalty to the new regime, but she secretly helped my mother and I escape, then told the new *president*—" she said the word with utter disdain "—that we had been killed with the rest."

"After that," she said, "we were often homeless. Sometimes getting work in shops. Then we could sleep on the steps, with minimal shelter provided from the overhang of the roof. Or, if the shopkeeper was truly kind, a small room in the back."

"And then?" he asked.

"My mother died when I was thirteen. At least…I as-

sume she did. She left one day and didn't return. I think…
I think she walked out into the desert and simply kept
walking. She was never the same after. She never smiled."

"I think that day had that effect on us all. But I'm sorry
to hear that."

"You apologize frequently for what happened. Do you
mean it?"

"I wouldn't say it if I didn't."

"But do you feel it?" she asked. He was so monotone.
Even now, even in this.

"I don't feel anything."

"That's not true," she said, her eyes locked with his.
"You felt fear last night. *I* made you fear."

"So you did," he said. "But we are not talking about me.
Tell me how you went on after your mother died."

"I continued on the way I always had. But I ended up
finding work at a martial arts studio, of all places. Master
Ahn was not in Jahar at the time of the unrest, and he had
no qualms about taking me in. Part of my payment was
training along with my room and board."

"I see now why you had such an easy time ambushing
me," he said.

"I have a black belt in Hapkido. Don't be too hard on
yourself."

"A Jaharan princess who is a master in martial arts."

She lifted a shoulder. "Strange times we live in."

"I should say. You know someone tried to murder me in
my bedchamber last night."

"Is that so?" she asked, taking a bite of lamb.

"I myself spent the ensuing years in the palace. Now
that we're caught up, I think we should discuss our engagement."

"Do you really see this working?" she asked.

"I never expected to love my wife, Samarah. I have long
expected to marry a woman who would advance me in a

political fashion and help my country in some way. That is part of being a ruler, and I know you share that. You are currently a sheikha without a throne or a people, and I aim to give you both. So yes, I do see this working. I don't see why it shouldn't."

"I tried to kill you," she said. "That could possibly be a reason it wouldn't work."

"Don't most wives consider that at some point? I grant you, usually several years of marriage have passed first, but even so, it's hardly that unusual."

"And you think this will…change what happened? You think what happened *can* be changed?" she asked. And she found she was honestly curious. She shouldn't be. She shouldn't really want to hear any of what he had to say.

"Everything can be changed. Enough water can change an entire landscape. It can reshape stone. Why can't we reshape what is left?"

She found that something in her, something traitorous and hopeful, something she'd never imagined would have survived all her years living in the worst parts of Jahar, enduring the worst sorts of fear and starvation and loss, wanted to believe him.

That the pieces of her life could somehow be reshaped. That she could have something more than cold. More than anger and revenge. More than a driving need to inflict pain, as it had been inflicted on her.

"And if not," he said. "I still find the outcome preferable to having my throat cut. And you will have something infinitely nicer than a storeroom to sleep in. That should be enough."

And just like that, the warm hopefulness was extinguished.

Because he was talking as though a soft bed would fix the pain she'd suffered. The loss of her family, the loss of her home.

He didn't know. And she would have to force him to understand. She would make him look at her pain, her suffering. And endure it as she had done.

"Yes," she said, smiling, a careful, practiced smile, "why not indeed?"

CHAPTER FOUR

NOT FOR THE first time since striking the deal with Samarah, Ferran had reservations. Beautiful she was, biddable she would never be.

She was descended from a warrior people, and she had transformed herself into a foot soldier. One he'd rather have on his side than plotting his death.

She'd been a little hermit the past few days. But he was under no illusion. She was just a viper in her burrow, and he would have to reach in and take her out carefully.

Barring that, he would smoke her out. Metaphorically. He wasn't above an ironhanded approach. He supposed, in many ways, he was already implementing one. But the little serpent had tried to kill him.

There was hardly an overreaction to that. Though, there was a foolish reaction. Proposing marriage might be it. And there were the reservations.

He walked up to the entry of her bedchamber and considered entering without knocking. Then he decided he liked his head attached to his shoulders and signaled his intent to enter with a heavy rap on wooden doors.

"Yes?"

"It's Ferran," he said.

He was met with silence.

"If you have forgotten," he said, "I am the sheikh of Khadra and your fiancé. Oh, also your mortal enemy."

The left door opened a crack, and he could see one brown eye glaring at him through it. "I have not forgotten."

"I haven't seen you in days, so I was concerned."

She blinked twice. "I've been ill."

"Have you?"

"Well, I haven't felt very well."

"I see," he said.

"Because we're engaged."

"Did my proposal give you a cold?"

The eye narrowed. "What do you want?"

"I did not propose to you so you could nest in one of the rooms in my palace. We have serious issues to attend to. Namely, announcing our engagement to the world. Which will involve letting the world know that the long-lost, long-mourned sheikha of Jahar lives."

"Can't you write up a press release?"

"Let me in, Samarah, or I will push past you."

"Would you like to try?"

"Let me in," he repeated.

She obeyed this time, the door swinging open. She held it, her arm extended, a dark brow raised. "Enter."

"Why is it you make me feel like I'm a guest in my own palace?"

"These are my quarters. In them, you are a guest."

"This is my country, and in it, you are a prisoner." Her shoulders stiffened, her nostrils flaring. "Such an uncomfortable truth."

"I can think of a few things more uncomfortable."

He arched a brow. "Such as?"

"If I planted my foot between your ribs," she said, practically hissing.

"You and I shall have to spar sometime. When I'm certain you don't want me killed."

"You'll be waiting a long time."

"Careful. Some men might consider this verbal foreplay." He said it to get a reaction. What disturbed him was that it did seem that way. It made his blood run hotter. Made him think of what it had felt like to hold her over his shoulder, all soft curves and deadly rage.

He gritted his teeth. He was not a slave to his body. He was a slave to nothing. He was master. He was sheikh. And with that mastery, he served his people. Not himself. That meant there was no time for this sort of reaction.

Her upper lip curled into a snarl. "You disgust me. Do you think I would sleep with the man who ordered my father killed?"

"For the good of our people? I would sleep with the woman whose father caused the death of my parents." The man who had wrenched the bars open that held Ferran's demons back from the world. The man who revealed what it was Ferran could be with the restraints broken.

He ignored those memories. He ignored the heat that pooled in his gut at the thought of what sleeping with her would mean.

She blinked. "I feel as though we have an impossible legacy to negotiate. I have, in fact, been thinking that for the past few days."

"To what end?"

"To the end that in many ways I understand what you did." Her dark eyes looked wounded, angry. "But I don't have to condone it. Or forgive it."

"Your father killed mine. Face-to-face and in cold blood. My mother…"

"I know," she said. "And…it is a difficult set of circumstances we find ourselves in. I realize that."

"Not so difficult. Marriage is fairly straightforward." It was a contractual agreement, nothing more. And as long as he thought of it in those terms, he could find a place for it in his ordered world.

Both brows shot up. "Is it? As our parents' deaths were

a result of marital infidelity I think it's a bit more complex than you're giving it credit for."

"Passion is more complex than people give it credit for. Passion is dangerous. Marriage on the other hand is a legal agreement, and not dangerous in the least. Not on its own. Add passion and you have fire to your gasoline."

"Okay, I see your point. But are you honestly telling me you act without passion?"

He lifted a shoulder. "Yes. If I acted based on passion I would have had your pretty head for what you tried to do. Lucky for you, I think things through. I never act before considering all possible outcomes." He studied her, her petite frame hinted at by a red, beaded tunic that hung to her knees, her legs covered by matching pants. Her dark hair was pulled back again, the top of her head covered by a golden chain that was laced over her crown. He wondered what her hair might look like loose. Falling in glossy black waves over her shoulders.

And then he stopped wondering. Because it was irrelevant. Because her hair, her beauty, had nothing to do with their arrangement. It had nothing to do with anything.

"Are you passionate?" he asked, instead of contemplating her hair for another moment.

She cocked her head to the side, a frown tugging down the corners of her lips. "About some things," she said. "Survival being chief among them. I don't think I could have lived through what I lived through without a certain measure of passion for breathing. If I hadn't felt burning desire to keep on doing it, I probably would have walked out to the desert, lain down on a dune and stopped. And then there was revenge. I've felt passion for that."

"And that's where we differ. I don't want revenge, because the purpose it serves is small. I want to serve a broader purpose. And that's why thinking is better than passion." Passion was dangerous. Emotion was vulnerability. He believed in neither.

"Until you need passion to keep air in your lungs," she said, so succinct and loud in the stillness of the room. "Then you might rethink your stance on it."

"Perhaps. Until then…in my memory, passion ends in screams, and blood, and the near destruction of a nation. So I find I'm not overly warm to the subject."

"But you don't anticipate us having a marriage with passion?" she asked.

He looked at her again. She was beautiful, there was no question, and now that she didn't have a knife in her hands it was possible to truly appreciate that beauty. She had no makeup on today, but she was as stunning without it as she'd been with her heavily lined eyes and ruby lips.

"Perhaps a physical attraction," he said.

He wasn't sure how he felt about that. The truth of the matter was, he'd given up women and sex that day his family had been killed. That day he'd been handed the responsibility of a nation full of people.

His father had been too busy indulging his sexual desires to guard his family. To guard his palace. And then he had seen what happened when all control gave way. When it shifted into unimaginable violence. When passion became death.

He'd turned away from it for that reason. But he'd known that when he married he wouldn't continue to be celibate. He hadn't given it a lot of thought.

But he was giving it thought now. Far too much.

Those beautiful eyes flew wide. "I hardly think so."

"Why is that?"

"I despise you."

"That has nothing to do with sex, *habibti*. Sex is about bodies. It is black-and-white, like everything else." She looked away from him, her cheeks pink. "You expect a celibate union? Because that will not happen. We need children."

Something changed on her face then. Her expression going from stark terror, to wonder, to disgust so quickly he wondered if he was mistaking them all. Or if he'd simply hallucinated it. "Children?"

"Heirs."

Now her unpainted lips were white. "Your children."

"And yours," he said. "There is no greater bond than that. No greater way to truly unite the nations."

"I…"

Samarah was at a loss for words. She'd been thrown off balance by Ferran's sudden appearance, and then…and then this talk of marriage. Of passion and sex. And then finally…children.

The word hit her square in the chest with the force of a gun blast.

Terror at first, because it was such a foreign idea.

Then…she'd almost, for one moment, wanted to weep with the beauty of it. Of the idea that her love might go on and change. That it might not end in a jail cell of Ferran's making. That she might be a mother.

On the heels of the fantasy, had come the realization that it would mean carrying her enemy's baby. Letting the man who had ordered her father's death touch her, be inside of her. Then producing children that would carry his blood.

Your blood.

You wouldn't be alone.

No. She couldn't. Couldn't fathom it.

And yet, there was one thing that kept her here. That kept her from fashioning a hair pick into a weapon and ending him.

When he'd said, cold, blunt, that her father had killed his, that he had been responsible for the death of his mother as well, she'd realized something for the first time.

She would have done the same thing he had done. Given the chaos her father had caused, were she in Ferran's position, the newly appointed leader of a country...she would have had her father executed, too.

That shouldn't matter. The only thing that should matter was satisfying honor with blood. She could have sympathy for his position without offering him forgiveness or an olive branch of any kind.

But it sat uncomfortably with her. Like a burr beneath her rib cage. And she didn't like it. But then, she liked this whole marriage thing even less than the murder thing.

She was undecided on both issues presently.

And he'd confused her. With his comfy mattresses, delicious food and offers of a life she'd never imagined she could have.

A chance to be a sheikha. To do good in the world. To remember what it was to be poor, starving and homeless, and to have a chance to make it better for those in this country who were currently suffering in poverty.

A chance to be a mother.

A chance to live in a palace with everything that had been stolen from her.

She would not feel guilty for wanting that. Not even a little. Not when she'd spent so many years as she had. She'd been spoiled once, and after all the deprivation, she felt she could use a return to spoiling.

It was all so tempting. Like a poisoned apple.

But she knew it was poisoned. Knew that while it looked sweet it would rot inside of her.

"I can't discuss this just now," she said.

"You've already agreed. It's the only reason I've not had you arrested."

Yes, she had agreed. But inside she didn't feel as if it was a done deal yet. It didn't feel real, this change in her fate. She'd done nothing but focus on her revenge for so many years. Revenge and survival. They'd kept her going. They were her passion. She had nothing else; she cared for nothing else. Food, shelter, safety, sleep, repeat. All in the aim of making it here, and from there? She'd had no plan. She'd imagined…well, she'd hardly imagined she would survive this.

He was offering her something she'd never once imagined for herself: a future. One that consisted of so much more than those basic things. One that gave her the chance to add something to the world instead of simply taking Ferran from it.

He wasn't a monster. And that she'd known since she first came to live at the palace a month ago. It had been uncomfortable to face that. That it was a man she fought against, not a mythical being who was all terror and anguish. Not the specter of death himself, come to destroy her family.

She hated this. She hated it all. She hated how it tempted her.

"I suppose I have," she said, "but I'm still processing what it means."

It was the most honest thing she'd said to him in regards to the marriage. There were implications so far-reaching that it was hard for her to see them all from her room here in the palace.

"As am I. But one thing I do know is that marriage means heirs. I'm a royal, so there is no other aspect of marriage that's more important."

"Certainly not affection," she said.

"Certainly not. I doubt my father had much if any for my mother. If he did, he would not have been with your mother."

"Or perhaps they were simply greedy." She looked down, unsure if she should say the words that were pounding through her head. Because why talk to him at all? Why discuss anything with him? "I think my mother loved them both."

It was a strange thing to say. Especially when love had been utterly lacking in her life. But this was, in part, her theory why.

"What?"

"I think she loved my father and yours. She was devastated to lose them both. That her husband, whom she loved, was killed in the same few days that her lover was killed…I don't think she ever recovered. I don't know that she ever loved anything as much as she loved the two of them." Certainly not her.

He paused for a long moment, his eyes on the back wall. "That's where you're wrong."

"Is it?"

"Yes. I don't think your mother ever loved anyone more than she loved herself."

"You aren't fit to comment on her," she said, but there was something about his words that hit her in a strange way. Something that felt more real than she would like.

"Perhaps not." The light in his eyes changed, and for a moment, she thought she almost saw something soft. "No child should have to see what you did."

She looked away. "I hardly remember it."

Except she had. She and her mother had been staying at the palace. Visiting. Of course, she figured out that meant they'd been sneaking time in for their affair. At the time it had all been so confusing. She'd been a child who hadn't known anything about what had passed between the sheikh and sheikha and why it had caused the fallout that it had.

Honestly, at twenty-one, she was barely wiser about it than she'd been then.

In her mind, male desire wasn't a positive thing. It was something she feared. Deeply. Living unprotected as she had, she'd had to respond with fierce, single-mindedness to any advances.

It didn't take long for the men in the city to learn that she wasn't worth hassling.

And in her life, there had been no place, no time, for sexual feelings.

It made it hard to understand what had driven their parents to such extremes. What had made her mother feel her husband, her only daughter weren't enough for her. What had made her cast off a lifetime of perfect behavior, a marriage to a man she'd seemed to love, and for her father to react with mindless violence. She'd long been afraid that desire like that was some sort of demon that possessed you and left you with little choice in the matter.

But she didn't fear it now. Obviously, it wasn't a concern for her. Particularly not with a man like him.

"I am glad for you," he said. "I remember it with far too much clarity."

"You didn't...you didn't see..."

He swallowed, his eyes still focused on a point behind her. "I saw enough."

All she could remember was being pushed behind a heavy curtain. She'd stayed there. And she'd heard too much.

But she hadn't seen. She'd been spared that much.

"What is your timeline for this marriage?"

"The sooner the better. You're certain no one is going to come for you?"

"You mean am I sure no one will come and save me? Yes, I'm certain. There is no one like that in my life." What a lonely thought. She'd always known it, but saying it out loud made it that much more real, sharpened the contrast between what he offered with marriage, and what she would get if she used him and went ahead with her plan.

It was simple. A chance at a future, or nothing at all.

The offer of a future was so shiny, so tempting, so breathtakingly beautiful....

"That is not what I meant."

"What did you mean?"

"Are any of the old regime, the revolutionaries, still after you in any regard?"

"Not that I'm aware of. The old leader was killed by one of his own, and that ushered in a completely new political era in Jahar. Things are better. But there is still no place for me."

"As a symbol, you would shine beautifully," he said.

The compliment settled strangely in her chest. Lodged between rage and fear. "Thank you." The words nearly choked her.

"It is true. I think people would look at you, at us, and see echoes of a peaceful time. Of a time when our nations were friends. Sure, you won't be sheikha of Jahar, but you will still matter to the people there. They suffered when the royal family was deposed. They will be happy to know that you've risen up from that dark time, as will they. As they have."

"It is an idealistic picture you paint."

"I'm not given to idealism. This is how it will be."

"You seem very sure," she said.

He lifted a shoulder. "I am the sheikh. So let be written, et cetera."

"I didn't imagine you would have a sense of humor."

"I don't have much of one."

"It's dry as the desert, but it's there."

The left side of his mouth curved upward into a smile. "I see, and what did you imagine I would be like?"

"I had imagined you were a *ghul*."

"Did you?"

She shifted uncomfortably. Because sadly, it was true.

In her mind, he'd become a great, shape-shifting creature. A blood-drinking monster.

"Yes."

He reached his hand out, and she swiped it away with a block. He lowered his head, his dark eyes intent. "Permit me," he said, his voice hard.

She froze and he lifted his hand again. She stayed there, watching him. He rested his hand on her cheek, his thumb sliding over her cheekbone, over the cut he'd inflicted on her.

"I suppose," he said. "To a child who saw me as the one who took her father from her, as the one who stole her life, I would seem like a monster."

"Are you not?" she asked, unable to breathe for some reason, heat flooding her face, her limbs shaking.

With one quick movement, she could remove his hand from her face. She could break his thumb in the process. But she didn't. She allowed this, and she wasn't sure why.

Perhaps because it felt like something from another time. When Ferran hadn't been scary at all. When she hadn't hated him. When he'd simply been the handsome, smiling older son of her parents' best friends.

But he isn't that boy. That boy was a lie. And he's now a man who must answer for his sins.

"I suppose it depends," he said. "I am a man with many responsibilities. Millions of them. And I always do what I must to serve my people. From the moment I took power." He lowered his hand, heat leaching from her face, retreating with his touch. "I will always act in the best interest of my people. It depends on which side of me you fall on. If you are my enemy…if you hurt those I am here to protect, then I am most certainly a monster."

"And that," she said, her words clipped, "is something I can respect."

It was true, and it didn't hurt to say. There was honor

in him, and she accepted that. The only problem was, it clashed with the honor in her. With her idea of what honor needed in order to be satisfied.

"Get yourself ready," he said.

"What?"

"I intend to take you out into the city."

"But…no announcements have been made."

"I am well aware of this. But a limo ride with a woman who is hardly recognizable as the child sheikha who disappeared sixteen years ago isn't going to start a riot."

"A limo ride?"

"Yes. A limo."

"I haven't been in a car…well, I rode beneath the tarps in a truck to get across the border into Khadra. Then I got a horse from some bedouins out in the desert and rode here."

"What became of the horse?"

"I sold him. Got a return on the money I spent on him."

"Enterprising."

"I am a woman who's had to create resources, even when there were none. Other than that ride in the truck though, I've not been in a motorized vehicle in years."

"You haven't?"

"I walk in Jahar. I rarely leave the area I live in."

"Then decide what you think would be best for a limo ride. And by all means, Samarah Al-Azem, try to enjoy yourself."

CHAPTER FIVE

SAMARAH MADE HERSELF well beyond beautiful for their outing into Khajem, the city that surrounded the palace. It was hard to believe that the child he had known had grown into the viper that had tried to end him. And harder still to believe that the viper could look so soft and breathtaking when she chose. Hard to believe that if he leaned in to claim her mouth he would probably find himself run through with a hairpin.

Today she was in jade, hair constrained, a silver chain woven through it, and over her head, a matching stone resting in the center of her forehead.

"This is all so different to how I remember it," she said, once they were well away from the palace.

"It is," he said. "Khadra has been blessed with wealth. All I've had to do is…"

"You've been responsible with it. You could have hoarded it. God knows my country had wealth, and it was so badly diminished by the regime that came after my parents. Spent on all manner of things, but none of them ever managing to benefit the people."

"As you can see, we've followed some of what Dubai has done with development. New buildings, a more urban feel."

"But around the palace everything seems so…preserved."

"I wanted to build on our culture, not erase what came

before. But Khadra has become a technology center. Some of the bigger advances are starting to come from here, and no one would have ever thought that possible ten years ago. The amount of Khadrans going to university has increased, and not universities overseas, to take jobs overseas, but here. Some of the change has been mine, but I can't take credit for that."

"I wish very much Jahar could have benefited from this," she said, her words vacant. As though she had to detach herself in order to speak them. "You have done…well."

"You didn't know about the development happening here, did you?"

"I saw from a distance. From in the palace, but I didn't know the scope of it. I didn't know what these buildings accomplished." She leaned against the window and looked up at a high-rise building they were passing. "How could I have known? We were cut off from the world for years, not just my mother and I, but the entire country. We were behind an iron curtain, as it were. And in the years since it's lifted…well, the rest of the country may have made a return to seeing the world, but mine has stayed very small."

"I think it's time it grew a little, don't you?"

"Why are you doing this?" she asked, turning to look at him.

It was a good question, and he knew she didn't mean why had he improved his country, but why was he showing her. Why was he trying to change her mind about him.

It had less to do with self-preservation than he'd like to believe.

Perhaps it was because he wanted to return something to her that, no matter how justified he thought it might be, he'd taken from her.

Perhaps it was simply a desire to see some of the sparkle return to her dark eyes.

Or maybe it was just that he truly didn't want a wife

who had more fantasies about killing him than she had of
him in bed.

Would he truly make her his wife? In every sense of
the word?

He looked at the elegant line of her neck, her smooth,
golden skin, dark glossy hair. And her lips. Red or plain,
they were incredible. Lush and perfectly shaped. He had
not looked at a woman in this way in so long. He hadn't
allowed himself to remember what desire was. What it
was to want.

So dangerous. So very tempting.

If he married her, it would be his duty. His heart rate
quickened, breathing becoming more difficult.

Yes, he would make her his wife. In every sense. He
was decided.

She would be perfect. Because of who she was. Because she knew. She knew about the danger of passion.
She would be the kind of wife he needed. The kind of wife
that Khadra needed.

"Have I suitably impressed you?" he asked.

She nodded slowly. "In some ways. It cannot be denied.
But I find I'm in need of...something."

"What is that?"

"I've been idle for too many days. You promised me a
sparring match. I think I will have it now."

He looked at the lovely, immaculate creature sitting
across from him, her elegant fingers clasped in her lap as
she asked him to spar with her in much the same tone she
might have used to ask him to afternoon tea.

He thought of what she would look like if they sparred.
Her hair in disarray, sweat beading on her brow. He gritted his teeth and fought to suppress the rising tide of need
that threatened to wash him away.

"If you think you're ready, Sheikha."

"Only if you think you are, Sheikh."

* * *

Samarah was surprised to discover that Ferran had provided her with clothes. Well, he'd already been providing her with clothes, so she didn't mean it that way. But the fact that he'd provided her with clothes for the gym was surprising.

A pair of simple black shorts and a matching tank top. After all the layers she was used to—for protection on the streets, for her disguise in the palace, and then...with all of her beaded gowns now she was in position as Ferran's... whatever—she felt nearly naked in the brief clothing.

She opened the door to her chambers and saw Lydia just outside. "How do I get to the gym?"

"The general facility or Sheikh Ferran's private facility?"

"I...assume the sheikh's private facility."

"Near his quarters. Down this hall, and down the staircase, all the way at the far end. It's the last set of doors."

Dear Lord, he'd put her a league away from him. Probably because he feared for his safety. The thought made her smile as she started the trek down to his quarters. That she had succeeded in unsettling him would do for now. It wasn't revenge, but it was in the right vein.

She moved to the red double doors and pushed them open slowly. And stopped cold when she saw Ferran, his back to her as he punched the large bag hanging from the ceiling.

He wasn't wearing a shirt. The only clothing on his body was a pair of black shorts that looked a lot like hers. Though, they covered more of his legs.

His back was broad. Shockingly so, tapering down to a slim waist. Everything on him was solid. Ridges of muscle shifting beneath skin as gold as desert sand.

She'd known he was strong. She'd come up against him already and seen just what a worthy opponent he was, but seeing him now...she could see why her hesitation had meant the end of her plan.

She could see it in every line of his body as his fist hit the bag and sent it swinging. He was powerful. A weapon. That was the basis upon which she admired him. What warrior, what martial artist, would not appreciate such a finely honed instrument? That was why she stared. It could be the only reason.

Samarah took a breath and assumed her stance, raising her leg high, bringing it down softly between his shoulder blades. A muted outside crescent kick.

He whirled around, reaching out and grabbing her wrist, tugging her forward, her free arm pinned against his solid chest.

"You're here," he said, cocking his head to the side, his eyes glittering.

"You had your back to the door."

"So I did. I suppose I deserved that."

"I could have hurt you," she said. "I didn't skim you on accident."

"I understand that," he said, his breath coming in hard bursts from the exertion, fanning hot across her cheek.

"Are you ready?"

"Just quickly." He released his hold on her and ran his hands over her curves, light and fast. Her heart slammed against her breastbone when his fingertips grazed the sides of her breasts. "I had to check," he said.

Her breath escaped her throat in a rush. "Check what?"

"To see if you had a weapon."

"I have honor," she said. "If I was going to kill you, it wouldn't be during a planned sparring match."

"I see. You'd do it while I slept then."

"Honor," she repeated.

"Clearly. Shall we go to the center of the mats?"

He gestured to the blue-floored open room and turned away from her again, walking to the center of the mats.

She followed and took her position across from him, her hands up, ready to strike or block. "Are you ready?" she asked.

"When you are."

"Are you giving me the handicap because I'm a woman?"

"No, I'm giving you the handicap because you're tiny and I must outweigh you by a hundred pounds."

"I'll make you regret it," she said.

She faked a punch and he blocked high. She used the opportunity to score a point with a side kick to his midsection and a follow-up palm strike to his chin. She wasn't hitting with full force, because she honored the fact that this was for points, not for blood.

He blocked her next hit, gripping her arm and holding it out, miming a blow that would have broken her bones at the elbow if he'd followed through.

One for him, two for her. Her mental score sheet had her in the lead, and she was happy with that, but unhappy that, in reality, that would have been a disabling hit. Points aside, had it been a real battle, she would have crumpled to the ground screaming.

They hit gridlock, throwing hits, blocking them, then one of them would slip a blow through.

He was using a mixed fighting style, while she was true to her discipline. Her training was more refined, but his was deadly.

She was faster.

Only a few minutes in, she had him breathing hard, sweat running down the center of his chest, between hard pectoral muscles. She watched a droplet roll over his abs, and she was rewarded with a swipe of the back of his hand across her face.

She let out a feral growl and turned, treating him to a spinning back kick that connected with the side of his cheek. It wasn't as pulled as she'd meant it to be, and his head jerked to the side, a red mark the lingering evidence of the contact.

He growled in return, gripping her forearm and flipping her over his back. She hit the soft mat and rolled backward, coming to her feet behind him and treating him to a sweep kick under his feet so that he kissed the mat just as she'd done.

He got to his feet more slowly than she had, and she was facing him when he came up, her breathing coming sharp and fast now. She hadn't fought anyone this hard in a long time. Maybe ever. Sparring in the studio had never been quite this intense. There had never been so much on the line.

She wasn't sure exactly what was happening here. Only that it seemed essential she show him who she was. That she was strong. That she wasn't someone he could simply manipulate and domesticate. That no matter that she was, for now, going with his plan, he should never take for granted that she was tame.

It was a warning to him. A reminder to herself. She might have put on some beautiful dresses this week; she might have been impressed with the changes he'd made in the city. She might enjoy the soft bed she had now.

But she could not forget. She was not a princess anymore. Life had hardened her into more. She was a warrior first. And she could never forget that.

She prepared to strike again, and he reached out, his hands lightning fast, his fists curled around her forearms, pushing her arms above her head.

She roared and pulled her hands down, twisting them as she did, but he was expecting it. She'd done this to him once before, and she wasn't able to break through his hold.

She pulled her *kiai* from deep inside her, her voice filling the gym. The sound startled him enough that she was able to pull one hand free, and she used it to land another palm strike against his cheek.

He twisted her captured arm behind her back and propelled her forward so that she hit the thankfully padded wall.

She was pinned.

She twisted, scraped her foot along his instep—somewhat ineffectively since she was barefoot. But she was able to use his surprise again to free herself and reverse the positions. His back was to the wall, his arms in her hold. But that wasn't what kept him still, and she well knew it.

It was her knee. Poised between his thighs, ready to be lifted and to connect hard with a very delicate part of his anatomy.

"I would keep still if I were you," she said.

"We're sparring," he said, his chest rising and falling hard with each breath. "You're not supposed to do full contact hits."

"But I could," she said, smiling.

He leaned forward, angling his head and she stopped breathing for a moment. He was making eye contact with her, and it made something in her feel tight and strange. She looked down, her vision following a drop of sweat again, this time as it rolled from his neck, down his chest.

She found herself fascinated by his chest. By each cut muscle. By the way the hair spread over his skin. So unique to a man's body. These shapes, the hair, the hardness of the muscle.

She looked down farther. At the well-defined abs, the line of hair that disappeared beneath the waistband of his shorts. And she nearly choked.

She'd never been this close to a man. Not for this long. She'd fought them off before, but this was different.

She looked back up at his face, breathing even harder now. Her limbs tingling a bit. From the lack of oxygen, she was certain. Since she was breathing hard. And there was certainly no other explanation.

He leaned forward and bit her neck. It wasn't painful, the sensation of his teeth scraping against her skin. It was something else entirely. Something that made her flail, stumble and fall backward onto the mat.

"I say we call it even, little viper," he said, looking down at her.

Rage filled her and she popped back to her feet. "Of course you'd say that because I won. That was…not a move I recognize."

"You didn't say no biting."

"One shouldn't have to say that!"

"Apparently one did," he said, breathing out hard, the muscles in his stomach rippling.

"I demand a rematch."

"Later," he said, "when I can breathe again. You are a fierce opponent. And considering I do have a major size advantage, I cannot overlook the fact that, were we the same size, you would have destroyed me."

"I very nearly destroyed you as it is," she hissed.

"Very nearly."

"Don't sound so dry. I could have ended you."

"But you will not," he said. "Not now."

"You don't think?"

"No," he said, shaking his head. "Because I can offer you life. Ending me means ending yourself, too."

Her throat tightened, her palms slick. "I was prepared for that."

"I understand," he said, his tone grave. "But I think now that you've been given another opportunity you might see things differently?"

She looked down, hating that the war inside her was

transparent to him. Hating that he could see her weakness. That he could see she *wanted*. That his poisoned apple was indeed shiny and tempting.

A future. One with power. One where she wasn't starving, or freezing or afraid.

One where she lived.

Yes, she was starting to want that. But what it came with…that she wasn't sure of. But the cost would be her honor. The cost would be letting her enemy into her bed.

If it's for the greater good?

That was hard. She'd never much thought of the greater good. Only her own. That was what survival mode did to a person.

But this served the greater good and her personal good.

Weakness. Are you certain this isn't just weakness?

It very likely was. But then, she was tired of being strong. At least in this way. Tired of having to be so strong she didn't care for anything but living to the next sunrise, but living long enough so her life could end in Khadra when she'd ended Khadra's ruler.

Perhaps, in the end, that was the weakness. To aspire to nothing more than revenge, because wanting anything more had always seemed impossible. Too far out of her reach.

She shoved that thought aside.

"Perhaps," she said. "You have to admit, life is a very enticing reward."

"It is," he said. "I was personally prepared to beg for it sixteen years ago."

She blinked. "Were you?"

"It turned out I didn't have to," he said. "I simply hid… and I was able to escape."

She nodded slowly. "That's what I did."

"You were a child."

"You were young."

"I did my best to atone," he said. "Though, in the end it was too late."

"You couldn't have saved them. If your father wasn't strong enough to save them, a boy of fifteen with no fighting skills certainly couldn't have."

It was nothing more than the truth, and she wasn't sure why she was speaking it. Wasn't sure exactly why she wasn't letting him marinate in his guilt. Only that, from a purely logical standpoint, he was wrong. Because, had he not hidden, as she and her mother had done, he would not have lived.

She took a sharp breath and continued. "It would have done your country no good to have you killed that day."

The left corner of his mouth lifted. "Perhaps not. But it would have saved you a trip."

CHAPTER SIX

IT WAS TIME for him to announce his impending marriage. And Ferran could only hope his viper bride cooperated with him.

She'd been in the palace for nearly a week, and their contact had been minimal since that day in the gym. Partly because he'd found the physical contact a temptation he did not need.

It had put a fire in his blood that he didn't like to remember existed. When he'd been a boy, he'd been all about himself. All about pleasure. Lust, and satisfying that lust.

But then he'd seen the devastation such things could bring. So he'd stopped acting that way. He'd stopped indulging his flesh.

Now Samarah was unearthing feelings, desires, best left buried.

Her father wasn't the only man he'd killed that day. He'd destroyed everything he'd been, everything he'd imagined he could be, in that moment too.

His rage had been regrettable but no matter how things played out, the end would have meant death for her father. But he had never been able to forgive himself for the deaths of Samarah and their mother.

Finding out she was still alive gave him a chance to soothe parts of him he'd thought would never heal.

But attraction, like the kind he'd felt in the gym, sparring with her, biting her…that had no place in this arrangement. They had no place in him.

They would have to consummate, and they would have to have children, but beyond that, Samarah would be free to live as she chose, and to be the symbol he needed.

He hardly needed her in his bed. He ignored the kick of heat that went through his body at the thought. When they'd fought, she'd been passion personified. And it had been beautiful and terrifying in equal measures. Because there was more conviction in her movements than existed in his entire body.

But then, he didn't need conviction. He just needed to do right. He needed to do better than his father. He needed to do better than he'd done at fifteen.

He'd lied to Samarah when he'd spoken of her father's fate. When he'd spoken of simple justice and black and white. So much of that reasoning had come from rage.

Ferran curled his hands into a fist, a spike of anger sending adrenaline through his veins. When he thought of his mother…cold and lifeless… Innocent in every way.

And then he thought of the spare moments before that. When Samarah's father had wrapped his fingers around her throat and Ferran had acted. For his mother. And for him.

But he had been too late. His violent rage utterly useless. In the end, none of his life was the same. Nothing of those whom he loved remained. Not even the good pieces of himself.

That day had destroyed so many things. And it was why he had to guard his emotions, why he must never allow his demons free rein. Ever again.

He rapped on Samarah's door and it opened slowly. Lydia, the maid, peered out. "Sheikh," she said, inclining her head.

"Is the lady ready?" he asked.

"Yes, Sheikh."

"I can speak for myself." Samarah's voice came from beyond the door.

"Leave us please, Lydia," he said.

The other woman nodded and scurried out of Samarah's chamber and down the hall. He walked in, and she looked at him with an expression reminiscent of someone who'd been stunned.

"What?"

"You're in a suit."

"So I am," he said, looking down at his black tie and jacket. "This shocks you?"

"I didn't expect Western attire."

She was elegant, in a long-sleeved black dress with a swath of white silk draped across the skirt and a gold belt around her waist. Matching gold decorated the cuffs of her sleeves, and there was gold chain woven through her hair. Which was still back in a braid.

He felt like making it a personal mission to see her hair loose.

Though, he shouldn't care about her hair. It had nothing at all to do with honor.

"You look perfect in Eastern attire," he said.

She pursed her lips. "I would think you might have liked us to look united."

"Perhaps you wanted it to look as though we got dressed together?"

Her cheeks turned a burnished rose. "That is not what I meant."

"Perhaps one day we will dress together." Though there would be no purpose behind that in their marriage, either. He would go to her at night when it was necessary. They wouldn't share a life. Not in those ways.

"This is not…an appropriate…I don't…"

"Do I fluster you, Samarah?" He did, he could see it. And he had no idea why he enjoyed it. Only that he did.

And he enjoyed so few things, he felt driven to chase it. If only for the moment.

"No," she said, dark eyes locking with his, her expression fierce. "It would take much more than you to fluster me, Ferran Bashar. I remember you as a naughty boy, not simply the man you are now."

"And I remember you as a girl, but I think we're both rather far removed from those days, are we not?"

"Maybe."

"I think we're a whole regime change, an execution and a revenge plot away from who we were."

"And a marriage proposal," she said.

"Yes, there is that. Though you seem to object to all mentions of marital related activities."

"I'm not ready to think about it," she said.

"I see." Heat burned through him, reckless and strange. Nothing like he'd experienced in his memory. Arousal was familiar. But there was a way he handled it now. And that was: alone.

He didn't act on reckless impulse. He didn't try to make the heat burn brighter. He extinguished it as quickly as possible. By working out until he dropped from exhaustion. By submerging himself in cold water.

He'd managed to diminish the desire for release until it was simply a physical need. Like hunger for food, thirst for water. There was no need for fanfare or flirtation. He had successfully managed without another person for years.

But there was a reality before him now. A woman he would marry. A woman who he would share his body with. And he was fascinated by her, by the thought. Now that sex was on the horizon he was finding it a difficult desire to ignore.

Especially with all the questions he had about her hair. How long it was. How it would feel sifting through his fingers.

Yes, he was curious about many things. He looked at her, at the exquisite line of her neck, the curve of her lips. His heart rate sped up. His fingers itching with the need to touch her.

"Tell me, Samarah," he said, ignoring his reservations and chasing the fire, "in all of your time spent on vengeance training and nurturing your rage, did you make time for men?"

She blinked. "No."

"Women?"

She blinked again. "No."

"Have you ever been kissed, Samarah?"

She stepped back as if she'd been shocked, her eyes wide. And he should be thankful she had. Or years of restraint would have been undone. "We're going to be late."

"The press will wait. We're what they're there for."

"I don't like to be late." She strode past him and out the door. "Are you coming?" she asked, out of view.

"Yes," he said, trying to calm the heat that was rioting through him.

They had to present a united front for the nation. He only hoped she didn't decide to attempt to give him a public execution.

Samarah looked out at the sea of reporters and felt the strong desire to scurry off the podium and escape so she could indeed do what Ferran had already accused her of doing. Nesting in the palace. Hiding away from everyone and everything.

She wasn't used to being visible like this. It felt wrong. It felt like an affront to survival.

But then, this pounding, wild fear she was experiencing was much better than the strange, heated fear she'd felt in her bedroom.

Have you ever been kissed, Samarah?

What kind of question was that? And why did it make her feel like this? Edgy and restless, a bit tingly. If this was rage, it was a new kind. One she was unfamiliar with. And she didn't like it one bit.

"It is with great happiness," Ferran said, his tone serious and grave and not reflecting happiness in the least, "that I announce my upcoming marriage. It is happy, not only because marriage is a blessed union—" Samarah nearly choked "—but because I am to marry my childhood friend—" she mentally rolled her eyes at his exaggeration "—who was long thought dead. Sheikha Samarah Al-Azen."

The room erupted into a frenzy, a volley of questions hitting like arrows. Samarah hadn't been the focus of so much attention in her memory. As a child, she'd been shielded from the press, and as an adult, she'd spent her life in hiding.

This wasn't anything she was prepared for. Fear had a limited place in her life. It acted only as a survival aid. To be heeded when she needed to heed it, and ignored when something larger than survival commanded she ignore it.

She never felt as if she was a slave to it.

Until now. Until she found herself doing something that went beyond explanation.

She put her hand on Ferran's arm, her fingers curling into his firm, warm flesh, and she drew nearer to him, concealing part of herself behind his body.

She felt him tense beneath her touch, saw a near-imperceptible shift in the muscles on his face. "I will take no questions now," he said. "I will add only this. I am regretful of the history that has passed between Khadra and Jahar. As are we all. I hope that this ushers in a new time. A new era. We are neighbors. And when children come from this union, blood. And while things will never be as they were, perhaps we can at least forge a truce, if not an alliance."

He put his hand on her back, the touch firm, burning her through her dress. He propelled her from the podium and away from the crowd, who were being managed now by his staff. "I have briefed them on what to say," he said when they were back in the corridor. "They have a nice story about how we reconnected at a small event we both attended in Morocco six months ago."

"That's quite the tale," she said, feeling shivery now, though she wasn't sure why.

"You have not been in front of people in that way before, have you?"

"I'm used to being anonymous," she said. "Actually, I'm used to needing anonymity for survival. This runs...counter to everything that I've learned."

That was a truer statement than she'd realized it was going to be. A far deeper-reaching statement.

Everything she'd been experiencing here this past week countered everything she knew about life. Everything she'd known about Ferran.

And about herself.

It was a lot to take in.

"This is my world," he said. "Everything I do needs a press conference."

"I'm not sure how I feel about that. Well, no, that's not true. I'm certain I don't like it." Because if she was really doing this sheikha thing, she wasn't sure how she would survive something like that all the time. "I feel too exposed."

"You're perfectly safe," he said.

"I'm standing there being useless in formal attire and I'm not at all ready to defend myself if something should happen."

He frowned and took a step toward her, and she took a step back, her bottom hitting the wall behind her. "It's something you'll have to get used to. This is only the be-

ginning. We'll be planning a formal ball after this, to cel-
ebrate our upcoming marriage. And then the wedding. I
am not going to hurt you," he said. "Stop preparing to col-
lapse my windpipe."

"Should the need arise, I must be prepared."

One dark brow shot up. "The need will not arise."

"Says you."

He planted a hand by her head, leaning in. "I am here
to protect you. I swear upon my life. In that room, where
the conference is being held, there are always guards. They
are ready to defend us should anything happen. And if they
should fail, I am there. And I will guard you. I failed you
once, Samarah. I let you die, and now that you've come
back from the grave I will not allow you to return to it."

She felt the vow coming from his soul, from that place
of honor he prized so dearly, and she knew he spoke the
truth. So strange to hear this vow when part of her had
still been ready to exact the revenge she'd come to deliver
from the first.

She looked up and met his gaze. It was granite. And she
felt caught there, between the marble wall and the hardness in his eyes. Between the honor he had shown since
her return, and the growing respect she felt for that honor,
and the years-long desire for a way to repay the devastation
he'd been part of wreaking on her life. She couldn't look
away, and she didn't know why. She was sent right back to
the moment in his room, when she'd been poised, ready to
take his life, and she'd seen his eyes.

There was just something about his eyes.

"I have never been able to trust my safety to another
person," she said. Even when she'd had her mother with
her, she'd often felt like the one doing the protecting. The
parenting.

"Entrust it to me," he said. "I've already entrusted mine
to you."

She turned that over for a moment. "I suppose that's true. But then, I am a prisoner of sorts."

"Instead of a leg shackle you'll have a ring."

"Sparklier anyway," she said, flexing her fingers, trying hard not to picture what it might feel like to wear a man's ring.

"You don't sound thrilled."

"Jewelry was never an aspiration of mine."

"I dare say it wasn't."

"So you can hardly expect for me to get all girlish over it, now can you?"

"Oh, Samarah, I don't expect that. No matter how much you make yourself glitter, I'm not fooled."

"Good," she said.

"You are a feral creature," he said, leaning in slightly, the motion pulling the breath from her lungs.

"And you think you'll tame me?"

He put his hand on her cheek, his thumb tracing the line of her lower lip. She could do nothing. Nothing but simply let him touch her. Nothing but see what he might do. She was fascinated, in the way one might be of something utterly terrifying. Something hideous and dark that all decent people would turn away from. Her stomach twisted tight, her lungs crushed, unable to expand.

"Have you ever seen exotic animals that were caged?" he asked. She shook her head. "The way they pace back and forth against the bars. It's disturbing. To see all that power, all that wildness, locked away. To see every instinct stolen from them. I do not seek to tame you. For those very reasons. But I do hope we might at least come to exist beside one another."

"We might," she said, the words strangled.

"I will take that as an enthusiastic agreement coming from you. I know this is not ideal but can't you simply…"

"Endure for the greater good?" she asked.

"Yes."

"Is that what you will be doing?"

"It's what I've always done," he said. "It's what I must do. This is the burden of a crown, Samarah. If you do it right, you're under the power of the people, not the other way around."

"Let me ask you this, Ferran," she said. And she didn't know why she was keeping the conversation going. Didn't know why she was standing in the hall with him, backed against a wall, allowing him to keep his hand on her cheek. But she was.

She knew she was extending the moment, extending the contact, but as confused as she was by her motivations, she didn't feel ashamed.

"Ask away," he said.

"You consider me feral."

"I do."

"Does this mean you're domesticated? As you've been brought up in captivity?"

"Of course I am," he said. "I'm the ruler of this country, and I have to be a diplomat. A leader. I have to be a man who acts rationally. With his mind, with his knowledge of right and wrong."

She narrowed her eyes and tilted her head, the motion causing his fingers to drift downward to her jawline. He traced the bone there. Slowly. It felt like the long slow draw of a match. Burning. Sparking.

"That's not what I see," she said.

"Oh no?" he asked. "What is it you see?"

"A tiger pacing the bars."

CHAPTER SEVEN

SAMARAH WAS IN the garden doing martial arts forms when Ferran found her.

"I'm pleased to see you're out enjoying the scorching heat," he said.

She wiped the sweat from her forehead. "It's the desert. There is no other sort of weather to enjoy. It's this or monsoons."

"You don't get so much of the torrential rains here. But if you go west, toward the bedouin camps…there you find your monsoons."

"Then I suppose here at the palace, heat is my only option."

"Mostly."

He watched her for a moment longer. Every graceful movement. Precise and deadly. She was a thing of beauty. A thing of poisoned beauty.

He was much more attracted to her than he'd anticipated. Because he hadn't anticipated it at all. This strange, slow burn that hit him in the gut whenever she was near. He'd never experienced anything like it. He wasn't the kind of man who burned for one woman. For any woman.

He scarcely remembered his past lovers. He'd had one year of his life devoted to the discovery of women. At fifteen, he hadn't been able to get enough. Such a spoiled, stupid boy he'd been. He'd been granted almost his full height then, and he'd had more money and power than a boy his age knew how to wield. That had meant he'd discovered sex earlier than he might have otherwise.

But women had only been a means to him finding release, and nothing more. He'd never wanted one much more than any other.

But here and now, he burned.

It was not at all what he wanted.

Then there was her bit of insight.

A tiger pacing the bars.

When she'd said that, he'd wanted to show her—while he kept himself leashed, he was not in a cage. He could slip it at will, and he'd had the strong desire to make sure she realized that.

To press her head against the wall and let her feel just what he was feeling. To tilt her head back and take her lips with his.

To show her just what manner of man he was.

But that was passion driving that desire. And he didn't bow down to passion. It was too exposing. And he would not open himself up in that way again.

This deadly, encroaching *feeling* had fueled his plan for the day, too. It was time for both of them to get out of this palace, this mausoleum that held so many of their dead.

He would get them both out into an open space for a while.

"I had thought you might like a chance to go out in it for a while."

"Out in it?"

"The heat," he said.

"Oh." She stopped her exercise. "For what purpose?"

"There is a large bedouin tribe that camps a few hours east of the palace at this time of year, and I always like to pay them a visit. See that their needs are being met, what has changed. They have an ambassador, but I like to keep personal touch, as well."

"Oh. And you would...bring me?"

"You're to be my wife. This will be a part of your duties. You will be part of this country."

"It's hard to imagine being a part of Khadra," she said. "Being somehow a part of you."

"And yet, that is to be our future," he said.

"So it appears."

"So it is."

"So let it be written, et cetera."

He smiled. "Yes. I think you just bantered with me."

She frowned in return, the golden skin on her forehead creasing. "I did not banter with you."

"You did. For a moment there, you thought of me as a human being and not a target you'd like to put an arrow through."

"Lies. I am imagining breaking your nose as we speak."

"I don't think you are, princess."

"Don't let my naturally sweet demeanor fool you."

"There is no chance of that," he said.

He didn't know why, but he wanted to tease her. He wanted to make her smile. Because she never did. It was less perturbing than wanting to feel how soft her skin was beneath his fingers, anyway. So perhaps for now he would just focus on the smile.

"How will we get there?" she asked.

"By camel."

An air-conditioned, luxury four-wheel drive SUV was hardly a camel. She realized, the moment the vehicle pulled up to the front of the palace, that Ferran had been...teasing her.

Strange.

He probably wasn't afraid of her anymore, since he

seemed content to poke at her with a stick. Which, all things considered, wasn't the worst thing. That he wasn't afraid of her, not that he felt at liberty to stick-poke her.

Though, she couldn't remember the last time someone had teased her. Maybe no one ever had. Dimly, she recalled a nanny who had been very happy. Smiling and singing a lot. But Samarah couldn't even remember the woman's name. And she was more a misty dream than an actual memory.

Master Ahn had been kind. But he hadn't had much in the way of a sense of humor. He'd been quiet, though, almost serene and it had made a nice counterweight for Samarah's anger. He'd helped her channel it. He'd helped her find some measure of peace. Had helped her put things in their proper compartments.

But he hadn't teased her.

Ferran held the door for her and she got inside, the rush of cold air a nice change from the arid heat. She wasn't used to being able to find this kind of reprieve from the midday sun. It was…luxury.

"This is not a camel," she said.

"Disappointed?" he asked, as he took his place in the driver's seat and turned the engine over.

He maneuvered the car out of the gates and toward and around back behind the palace, where the city thinned out, and there was a gap in the walls. Walls that were left over from medieval times. More of the old mixed with the new.

"I'm not particularly disappointed by the lack of camel, no."

"They aren't so bad once you learn to lean into the gait."

"They are so bad, Ferran. I remember."

"Do you?"

She leaned back against the seat and closed her eyes. "Vaguely. We did a…caravan once. We rode camels. And picnicked out in the sand beneath canopies. It seems like…

like maybe it was a dream. Or another person told me this story. It hardly seems like me. But I remember the rocking motion of the camel so…if I know that, then it had to have been real, right?"

He nodded. "It was real. Your father hosted a picnic like that for visiting dignitaries every year."

"Oh, is that it? I couldn't remember. Weird how you know more about my past than I do. I was so young and my mother never talked about it."

Weird was…too light of a word. It was…everything. Horribly sad. Happy, in a strange way, to hear about her past finally instead of just having vague memories seen through the lens of a child.

But so odd that she was dependent on the man she saw as her enemy to learn the information.

"We used to go to the palace by the seaside," she said.

"My parents' home. Mine now. Ours. Or it will be."

Her stomach tightened. "I'm not sure if I want to go there."

"Why not?"

"I was so happy there," she said, closing her eyes. "It almost hurts to think about it. Like someone scooped out my stomach." She opened her eyes again and looked out at the desert. "I don't think I want to go," she said again.

They were silent for the rest of the drive. Samarah trying to focus on the view and the air-conditioning, rather than the heat the man beside her seemed to radiate. It was stupid. His body temperature should be ninety-eight point six, just like hers. So why did he always feel so damn hot? It was irritating beyond measure.

So were the feelings that he called up out of her. Effortless. Like he was some sort of emotional magician. Creating emotions when there had been none, at least no refined, squishy ones, for years.

"Do you see?" he asked.

She looked up and out the front windshield at the tents in the distance. "Yes."

"That's the encampment. And there's smoke. Likely they're cooking for us. If not, we're in trouble because it means they aren't happy with me."

"Do they have reason to be unhappy with you?"

"People are unhappy with the leader of their country most of the time for various reasons, are they not?"

"I suppose they are. Though, I've had more reason to be unhappy with mine than most."

"Given the circumstances, yes."

"They stole my life from me," she said, looking up and meeting his gaze. "They stole my life."

"*They* did?"

And not him. She didn't miss the unspoken part of the sentence.

"Do not read too much into that. It was a complex situation, that's for sure," she said. "Many people could be assigned portions of blame. Except for me," she said, feeling the familiar anger welling up in her. "I was a child. I was six. It wasn't my fault. And I've still had to live it."

"You have," he said. "And it is a crime, because you're right. You had no fault in it. You had no part in the play and yet you were forced to deal with the consequences. So now…accept this. Accept this life. Live something different."

His words curled around her heart. Sticky, warm tentacles that wrapped her up tight and made her feel secure. And trapped. And she wasn't sure if she should fight or give in.

"Are you ready?" She knew he was talking about getting out and meeting the people, but it had another meaning for her.

She nodded slowly. "I'm ready."

She thought, for the first time, she might truly mean it.

* * *

The people did rush to greet them. And there was dinner prepared. They hurried to make a spot at the head of the table not just for Ferran, but for Samarah.

Ferran was pleased that everyone here seemed happy with his choice of bride. Because for the desert people who often traveled near the borders of the neighboring countries, the relations between Khadra and surrounding nations was even more important than to those who lived in the cities.

For them it wasn't about trade. Or import tax. Or the ability to holiday where they pleased. For these people, it was often about survival. To be able to depend on the friendliness of their neighbors for food, shelter, water if there was an emergency. Medical help. It was essential.

For his part, Ferran provided what he could, but if there was ever an emergency on the fringes, then there would be no way for the government to provide aid in time.

He looked at Samarah, who was curled up next to him, her feet tucked beneath her bottom, her hands in her lap. She looked much more at ease in this setting than she had at the press conference, but he still wondered if all of the people looking at her with obvious interest were bothering her.

He didn't like for her to be afraid. That realization hit him hard. But he wasn't sure why it did. Of course he shouldn't want her to be afraid. She was to be his wife, and it was his duty to ensure his wife was protected, regardless of how they'd gotten their start.

Perhaps you find it strange because you know you can't really protect her?

Not from the truth. Not if it ever came out.

He shut down his thoughts and focused on what was happening around them. Most of the tribe was sitting in the mobile courtyard area for dinner. Families in clusters, children talking and laughing, running around on the outskirts of the seating area.

The elders were seated with him and Samarah, on cushions, their food in front of them on a wooden mat that would be easy to roll up and transport. It was nothing like the heavy, grand dining table in the palace that his father had had brought in. So formal. Custom made in Europe.

Ferran found that in many ways, he liked this better. This spoke of Khadra. Of its people. Its history.

"Sheikha."

Ferran watched Samarah's dark head snap up when the tribal elder to his right addressed her. "Yes," she said, seemingly shocked to have been spoken to.

"How do you find the political climate in Jahar at present?"

She blinked rapidly. "I... It has improved," she said. "The sheikhdom is never going to be restored, not as it was. The new way of doing things is imperfect. But since the death of the previous leader, there is something of a more...legitimate democracy in place. All things considered, that is perhaps best for the country."

"And do you think this will unite the countries again?"

Her brow creased. "It's difficult to say. But I do think that the current government won't perceive me as a threat now that I'm marrying into the Bashar family and making my home here. So that is helpful for me. As for everyone else? I think if nothing else it will help old wounds heal."

Ferran nodded slowly. "If she can forgive me, then perhaps Jahar can forgive."

"And," she said, her words slow and steady, "if Ferran can lay aside the pain my family caused him, perhaps Khadra can forgive the pain, too."

"It was a great loss, that of your mother and father," the elder said to Ferran.

"Yes," he said. "It was."

"But you have done well. You've made them proud. You've made us all proud."

Ferran watched Samarah's face. He wondered if she thought he'd done well. Or if she still thought he was the worst sort of man.

The funny thing was, Samarah was more right about him than any of the leaders here. Yes, he'd done some good for his country. That was true. But in many ways he was no less than the murderer Samarah believed him to be.

"You do well in your choice of bride," the man continued. "It is truly a wise choice for us all."

"That," Ferran said, "I will wholeheartedly agree with you on."

And he did. Samarah was a choice he couldn't have foreseen having the chance to make. And she was certainly the best one.

"Well," she said. "Thank you."

"It's the truth," Ferran said.

The other man turned his attention back to the man to his right and Ferran continued to keep his focus on Samarah.

"I'm pleased to be a handy political pawn."

"Better than an instigator of war. You see what might have become of these people if you'd succeeded in executing me? Or if I'd imprisoned you. Marriage is preferable to either of those things."

"Marriage is preferable to death or imprisonment? Someone should embroider than onto a pillow."

"Poetic, I think."

"Very."

"Neither you or I are romantics," he said, watching her very closely, trying to gauge her response. She was so very hard to read. Such a guarded creature. And he shouldn't care about whether or not he was able to break that guard.

It had nothing to do with their arrangement. And neither did his fascination with her. Though, being able to read her might come in handy, just in case she ever got it in her mind to try and kill him again.

"Obviously not," she said, her face remaining impassive.

"Do you ever smile, *habibti*?" he asked.

"That's…an improvement over *little viper,* so I won't push the issue. And no, I don't often smile.

"I think that's too bad."

"Do you ever smile, Ferran?"

"Not often."

"Then don't concern yourself with my smile. I thought you said you weren't a romantic."

"Is smiling a romantic notion now?"

"Maybe just a luxury you and I haven't been able to afford?" she asked, cocking her head to the side.

"Perhaps that. Though, I am a sheikh,"

"As you've reminded me many times."

"It is the most defining part of me."

"Is it?"

"Yes," he said. "If I weren't a sheikh…things would be very different. But I am. And as such I can afford a great many things. Perhaps I should invest in smiling."

"Investing in frivolity? That seems like a recipe for disaster."

"Or at the least a recipe for…shenanigans."

The left side of her mouth twitched. "Shenanigans?"

"Yes."

"You said *shenanigans.*"

"I did," he said.

"Have you ever said that word before in your life?"

"No. I haven't had occasion to."

"It's a good word," she said. "And you got up to a lot of them when you were a teenager. I…I remember."

"I hope you don't remember in very great detail," he said. "I wasn't the best version of myself then."

She frowned. "So…this is the best version of you then?"

"Obviously." Her shoulders shook, her lips turning upward, a choked noise escaping. "Did you just…laugh at me? Is that what that was?"

"I think so," she said.

"You nearly smiled."

"I…did." She looked confused by that.

"I wish for you to do that again," he said. And he meant it. Not because he was being emotional, but because it wasn't fair that a woman like her, one so beautiful, one who should have been happy, had ended up with so few things to smile about.

"Perhaps I shall."

"Consider it at least." The corner of her mouth twitched again. "We will retire to bed soon."

Her eyes flew wide. "We?"

"I have brought my own tent, and it was graciously set up for us. Don't worry, it has rooms. And you will get your own."

"I had better."

"You will have to get over your aversion to sleeping with me." His pulse quickened. He was quickly discovering he had no aversions to sleeping with her. And why should he? Marriage made sex expected. It justified the desire.

As long as desire didn't rule in him, as long as he kept control over his weaknesses, there was no harm in being with his wife.

Her eyebrows lowered. "I am not having this conversation with you," she said, her voice a furious whisper, "sitting next to all these men."

"Your point is taken," he said. "But I come back to the issue of smiling."

She looked hesitant for a moment. As if she was trying to decide if she should say something else to him or bolt off into the desert. "What about it?"

"I should like the chance to try and make you smile tomorrow." Because he wanted to give her something. To give her more than he'd taken away.

"How will you do that?"

"There is an oasis not far from here. It is a place I frequent. I would like to show you."

"I…" He could tell she was considering telling him where to put his offer. But she swallowed her initial response. "All right," she said.

"We will have to ride horses, though, as you cannot drive in with a car."

"Horses?" she asked.

"Yes, horses. Can you ride?"

"I…I don't know."

"Well, you can share mine. I intend to ask for the use of one here."

"All…all right."

"No argument?"

She shook her head. "No. I think…perhaps I might make an attempt to smile."

CHAPTER EIGHT

SAMARAH HESITATED NEXT to the big black horse that was saddled and ready for their ride to the oasis. Ferran was already seated and she was meant to…get on there with him somehow. There was no way to avoid physical contact.

And frankly, physical contact with him was disturbing.

Though, the fact that it was disturbing…disturbed her. Because there was no reason for it to be quite so unsettling.

Sure there is. He ordered your father to his death. He's partly responsible for much of the misery in your life. Of course it's uncomfortable.

Yes, but it wasn't only that.

She wasn't used to touching men. And he was very much a man. So very different from the way she was built. So hard. So…so warm. She always came back to how damn warm he was. Perhaps he had a fever.

He lowered his hand and she stared at it.

"You're meant to take it," he said.

"Take it where?" she asked, crossing her arms beneath her breasts and turning her shoulders in.

"Grasp my hand, Samarah."

She reached out and curled her fingers around his, heat exploding against her palm and streaking up her arm. She didn't even have time to process it before she found herself getting hauled up onto the horse, behind Ferran.

Reflexively, she wrapped her arms around his waist and

leaned into him. Then she started to ponder which was more frightening. The idea of falling onto the sand, or continuing to cling to Ferran and his unnaturally warm back.

His back won. For now.

She should have asked to sit in front. It might have been a bit less disturbing.

But then…then she could have been between his thighs. Though, for the moment, he was between hers. There really was no winning in this situation. At least the current seating arrangement gave her an upper hand of sorts. If she wanted to jump off and run, she could. That was a comforting thought.

"It is not a long ride," he said, "an hour perhaps."

"I'm not concerned," she said, holding her head away from the hollow between his shoulder blades that looked like a very nice place to rest her cheek.

But she would not. She didn't need to use him as a headrest.

"You seem stiff," he said, spurring the horse into a trot.

"I am on a horse. How would you like me to behave?"

"Rest against me."

"I hardly think that's necessary."

"Suit yourself."

"Nothing about this suits me," she said.

"That's not good. Because I'm attempting to make you smile, and if nothing suits you, I won't be able to accomplish that."

"You're making me sound difficult."

"That's not my intent. You are much less difficult than when we first met and you attempted to stab me. That considered, I would hate to get on your bad side again."

"Who said you were off of it?"

Their conversation faded out and she settled into the horse's gait. And eventually, she settled into him. Her neck got stiff, a kink forming in the side, and she looked at the perfect pocket, just there, between his shoulder blades.

It would alleviate the pain. If she could just rest against him for a second.

She lowered her head. He was solid, but it wasn't uncomfortable at all. The fabric of his shirt was damp with sweat, and she didn't find it at all disagreeable.

That only increased her discomfort.

She could hear his heart, thundering in his chest. Could feel the shift of his muscles as he moved with the horse over the desert sand.

She turned her face slightly and caught the scent of his skin. Of the sweat. Really, none of it was disagreeable at all. Which…made it disagreeable in its way.

Samarah shifted and tightened her hold on him, her palms flat against his stomach. He was hard there, too. And she could feel his muscles, the definition of them, even with the fabric of his shirt separating her hands from his flesh.

She'd seen his muscles, so she knew just how very defined they looked. And she also knew about the body hair. Which she found much more fascinating than she should.

She stared at the horizon line after that, trying her best not to think too hard about Ferran's body, and the way it felt beneath her hands. Or the way it looked without his shirt.

It was only because she was trapped against him that she was thinking this way.

The ride stretched on forever. She got hotter, and she got more restless. And her thoughts weren't calming down. Her body wasn't, either. She would have thought you just got used to being pressed against someone eventually, but apparently you didn't.

At least not when that someone was Ferran.

"We're here," Ferran said, his tone hard, tugging back on the horse's reins, bringing his behind pressing hard between her thighs and sending a jolt through her body.

She curled her fingers into his shirt, desperate to hold on to him. And desperate to jump off and run screaming into the desert until she could figure out what the hell was wrong with her.

She looked around his shoulder, and her body slowly released the tension it was holding fast to. The oasis was beautiful. A lush green blot of ink against a dry, pristine background of bone-white sky and pale sand.

"Hang on to the saddle," he said.

She obeyed and he slid down off the horse, then held his hands out.

"Seriously?" she asked.

"What?"

She swung her leg over the side of the horse and slid down onto the sand, landing deftly on her feet. "I'm not a delicate flower, Ferran. Do not treat me like one."

"I wouldn't dream of it."

"You just tried. Now, where is it we're staying?"

"Are you wilting?"

"Be careful, or I will bite you. I believe I owe you on that score."

His expression sharpened, the look in his eyes intensifying. "I can't say I'm entirely opposed to you biting me."

"That makes no sense."

"Perhaps not to you, *habibti*. But if I conduct our marriage in the proper manner, it will make sense to you soon."

"I don't see how it could."

He just looked at her, and he appeared to be amused. And she felt heat—both anger and other sorts of heat, sorts she didn't want to contemplate—rising in her.

"Your imagination is sadly lacking."

"You bit me once already," she said. "I felt nothing."

Her stomach pitched, both because she was lying, and because she was reliving the scrape of his teeth over her skin. It was such an intimate thing. And right then, she started connecting all the dots.

"Surely people don't bite each other when they…" She snapped her mouth shut.

"Not always. And I meant no more than I said."

"I don't believe that," she said. "About there being no hidden meaning, not…not about the biting. I believe that, I just… Where are you going?" He'd taken the horse by the reins and started leading him away.

"I thought you wanted to see where we were sleeping tonight?"

"Fine. Lead the way."

"I am."

They walked farther into the oasis, shielded by a rock formation, and by a thick growth of trees that grew taller as they edged closer to the waterline.

The water was like a sheet of glass. Reflecting the trees, the sky and sun from the still surface.

"This is incredible," she said. "Are there…don't a lot of animals come here?"

"I've never seen many, not when I have a fire going at night. And it's rained recently, so this isn't the only water. Though, you should watch for snakes."

"I don't like snakes," she said, her focus going to the ground as she watched the placement of each of her steps.

"I'm not a huge fan of them, to be honest, but for the most part, you won't be bothered by them."

"Yes, well, sometimes in floods, they would slither into the rooms I was staying in. Fortunately, not usually poisonous ones. But…but sometimes the odd viper would pay me a visit. So, your nickname for me is somewhat fitting."

"You don't have to worry about snakes tonight," he said. "I'll build a fire now."

"It's hot still."

"A precaution. The tent is this way."

She followed him down the well-worn trail that led deeper into the trees, and out to the far side of the small lake. She stopped when she saw it. "It is not exactly a tent."

The "tent" had permanent walls, with windows, and what appeared to be a broad canvas stretched over the roof and anchored into the ground. There was a small deck off the front that went over the water.

"What is this?" she asked.

"My escape, I suppose. Something much simpler than the palace. And quiet. I come out here whenever I visit the tribe. And sometimes for no reason at all."

"Do you bring women here?"

She was curious. Fascinated by who Ferran was as a man. Not as the monster she'd built up in her head, and not even as the man he was around her. But the man he'd been for the past sixteen years. The man who, apparently, had a retreat. And who knew biting was a thing that could be exciting. And who undoubtedly *had* been kissed many times. And had lovers.

Yes, she was very curious all of a sudden, who this man was. Because she had to know her enemy. The enemy she was preparing to ally herself with.

"No," he said. "I don't bring women here."

"Where do you bring women?" she asked.

She was curious now. And she wanted to know the answer. She wanted to know about these women, who knew about how it felt to be pressed up against his back, and to feel his stomach. And…more.

She despised the fascination. It was like giving in to the desire to watch a fight breaking out on the streets. To take in the horror, the anger and blood. To be both drawn to and repulsed by what she was seeing.

"Why do you want to know?" he asked.

"Because I do."

"Why?"

"Because...because I am supposed to be your wife." It was the first time she'd said it. The first time she'd felt like that position might matter. Like it might really be real. Like she was making real steps toward their treaty, rather than just standing in a holding pattern, contemplating the merit of escaping, or exacting revenge of some kind. "It seems like I should know these things about you."

"I don't," he said, his tone hard.

"What?"

"I don't...conduct affairs."

"Never?" she asked.

"No."

"I...I don't..."

He swept past her and into the dwelling.

She looked inside. "This is very much not a tent. Just as your car was not a camel."

Yes, the ceiling was swaths of draped fabric; beneath it stretched canvas that she imagined was completely water-proof, but that did not make it a tent.

There was formal furniture. It was spare, but very expensive looking. Wood and plush fabrics. Nothing as ornate as the palace. This seemed to speak more of Ferran, and not the rulers that had come before him. This was the man, and not the legacy.

At least, it was a piece of him.

She was digging for other pieces.

"I confess, calling it a tent was slightly misleading."

"And the car?"

"Yes, that, too."

"You're telling me you don't conduct relationships with women?" she asked. "I assumed..."

"Why would you assume, Samarah?"

Her cheeks heated. "I would have thought a man such as yourself would have lovers. Several of them. I remember how you were. Though, I suppose being naked with someone makes you very vulnerable to them. Sleeping with someone—they could kill you while you dreamed. I suppose…I suppose that means you have to be selective about lovers."

She wanted to know the answer because if she really was to be married to this man then it seemed like this was important information for her. It seemed she should know how he viewed sex. Why he had no lovers. If he was being truthful. Because if they were going to be married, they would share the marriage bed and all the intimacies that entailed.

Intimacies she was woefully uneducated about.

She'd heard sex spoken of in vile, crude terms. Had heard men make threats that were disgusting. Had heard prostitutes make allusions to things she hadn't fully understood.

She hoped there was more to marital activities than all of that. Really, she knew there had to be, because it was the thing that had driven their families to destruction.

That was the part that scared her. The part of her that feared she would become a slave to it…the part that feared there was a part of herself that was undiscovered that would change completely when she finally found it.

"Being naked with someone does not really make you all that vulnerable to them. And I never slept with any of my lovers."

"You didn't? I was under the impression that…" She trailed off, not liking how innocent she was revealing herself to be.

In so many ways she had no innocence. She'd been in the palace during all that horrible destruction. And then, back at home she'd survived the siege. There had been so much violence on both of those days. She'd survived homelessness, hunger, cold, heat, fear. Grief. So much more grief than one person could be expected to bear.

But she didn't understand the kind of connection that

drove two people to pursue a romantic relationship. She didn't understand sexual desire. Not in a specific way that existed between two lovers.

It was her only piece of innocence really. Her physical innocence. Her emotions were jaded, her mind inundated with the cold ugliness of the world. It was only her body that remained untouched and she had fought fiercely for that. For her body was the one thing she had left that hadn't been violated by the world.

Still, she didn't especially want him to know all of that.

Have you ever been kissed, Samarah?

She had a feeling he might know already. But she didn't need to go revealing herself.

"You do not have to sleep with someone just because you have sex with them. Though, perhaps in your case, since you lacked a steady bed it was easier to stay."

She didn't know what to say to that. She wasn't sure if he was digging for information or not. And she wasn't sure if she wanted to give him any.

"We aren't talking abut me," she said.

"No. We are not. But that should answer your questions."

"It doesn't really."

"Then perhaps you should speak more plainly so I can answer them. I am not playing guessing games with you, Samarah."

"When you say you do not conduct affairs…you are not…I mean, you have been with…"

"I am not a virgin," he said, the word dripping with incredulity. "I slept with enough women that they blurred together during my teenage years, but there was an inciting incident that put me off passion. I had a job to do, and I have not had the time to lose myself in pleasure since I overtook the throne." His expression was hard, a dark, frightening rage filling his eyes. "Do you now feel suitably informed, Samarah?"

No. Now she wanted to ask about the pleasure. The pleasure he was afraid to lose himself in. Wanted to ask what that meant to a man like him. Sixteen years of celibacy. What it would mean when he broke it. And if he really intended to break it with her. For them to... Now she wanted to ask a whole lot of questions, but she was stuck because if she did then she really would give herself away. And then she would be standing in a remote location talking about sex with the man who was caught in a fog in her brain. Somewhere between enemy and ally. Somewhere between monster and fiancé.

It was all too weird.

"I feel more informed. Yes. Are you going to start a fire?"

"Yes," he said. "I'll bring you your things. Why don't you get settled."

"Where is my room?" She wondered for a moment if he would suggest they share. And that terrified her. And made her feel something else that she couldn't quite place.

"Whichever one you choose, I will take the other. Does that suit?"

"As much as anything in this arrangement does."

"You flatter me," he said, his voice clipped.

Now he sounded annoyed with her, and she couldn't for the life of her figure out what she'd done. And she shouldn't care. So she wouldn't.

"All right, I will arrange my things. Enjoy building your fire."

"I'll see you again for dinner," he said. "If it rains, I will cook indoors."

"Do you expect it to rain?"

"I always prepare for a potential catastrophe. Rain, flooding."

"All right," she said, waving her hand, already going off to explore other rooms of the house. She badly needed a reprieve from his presence. He was making her say—and think—crazy things.

She needed to get her head on straight. She needed to remember what it was she was doing here.

That thought deflated her. She sank to the couch. What she was doing here was marrying Ferran Bashar, the man she'd sworn to kill. Because it was the right thing to do. For their countries. It was a greater good she couldn't simply ignore.

This was a true sacrificial act, not just something that would assuage the burning anguish inside of her. She'd talked herself into thinking his murder, and her subsequent death, a death she'd been nearly certain of, would be sacrificial. But perhaps not. Perhaps it had only been an act born of blinding rage and desperation.

The same sort of rage that had driven her father.

The thought hit her hard, a realization she slid sickly through her veins like cold tar. She was not her father. She was not a mindless rage machine who would destroy all simply to get revenge upon his wife and her new lover.

And on the heels of that realization, the other was cemented.

She was going to marry Ferran. She was going to be his wife.

God help her. It was real.

A tear slid down her cheek and dropped onto her hand. And for the first time since her mother wandered into the desert and never returned, Samarah Al-Azem let herself cry.

When she stumbled outside an hour later, she didn't feel any less stunned, but she did feel a renewed sense of purpose. Determination. She felt…she felt as if she was truly on a new path. As if she'd reconciled this change.

At least in part.

She looked up at the sun, which was resting low over the horizon now. A chill spread over the desert sand, along with a hazy blue blanket that seemed to thicken the air. Gnats swarmed over the reeds, and she batted them away from her face as she walked through the tall plants down to the water.

She grabbed a large stick and let it go before her, doing a sweep for snakes as she went along.

Thankfully, none had seen the need to get in her path.

She came to the damp, cold mud and stopped, looking out at the water. The surface rippled, then broke, and Ferran appeared. He stood, his back to her, water droplets rolling through the valleys in his flesh, created by the hard-cut muscles that she'd been enjoying on the ride over.

He took a step up toward the bank that was to the left, and the waterline lowered on his body, so that it revealed two deep grooves in his lower back before showing his...oh.

He took another step and the water slid off his skin. And she could see now that he was naked. And he was...

She'd never really looked at a man's butt before. Not like this. Not one that was bare, and muscular and...well, bare.

More importantly, she'd never been given to the urge to simply stare at a man like this, clothed or not. As a man and not a threat. As a man and not a mere weapon. But flesh and blood. He was fascinating. Especially with their earlier conversation playing through her mind, combined with the close proximity of the horse ride.

And her recent acceptance, full acceptance, of the fact that she was to be his wife.

Yes, it was all that that had her there, staring and unable to stop. Her mouth was agape. Truly. Her face felt like it was on fire and her heart...her heart was beating faster than she'd thought was physically possible.

The only time it had ever come close to this was in moments of sheer, unadulterated terror. Those she'd had.

Those she was familiar with. This? This was something else. Something new. Something that had nothing to do with the past.

He turned to the side and she couldn't breathe. It all just gathered in her chest like a ball and stopped. She was completely frozen, held captive by him. She wanted to see him. All of him. She wanted so badly for the mystery to be solved. To know now what he looked like. All over. Because not knowing…it made her more afraid of the future. She just needed to know.

She tried to swallow, but it got caught with the knot of air.

Then he turned to face her, dark eyes boring into hers. But she only met his gaze for a moment. Then, completely without thought, she was looking down.

She bit her lip, taking the moment to study him in detail. It was her first glimpse of a naked man and she found she could only stare. And that she could not remain wholly detached.

"See something you're interested in."

She wasn't sure *interested* was the word. She forced her gaze back to his. "I'm sorry."

He lifted one shoulder and the muscles in his chest shifted. Fascinating. "No need to apologize. I didn't hang a sign out."

"Do you…do you have a sign?" she asked, feeling slow, her brain processing things at half the speed. The lack of oxygen was probably to blame.

"No, I don't have a sign."

"It would be the best way to warn people."

"I could have sent you a text."

She blinked slowly. "I don't have a phone."

"That will change."

"Will it?"

"Of course," he said, still standing there. Casually naked.

She didn't feel casual at all. There was so much skin on display it made her want to slip out of her own and run away.

"There's no *of course* about any of this. Not to me and I—I can't just stand here and talk to you while you're naked."

"That will change, too."

"I do not think," she said, turning around and heading back up the path, sweeping her stick through the grass and quickly following behind.

She had no desire to run away from a naked man, only to step on a snake. Out of the frying pan and all that.

And it wasn't as if Ferran's nakedness put her in any danger.

The heat in her cheeks, the pounding of her heart, said otherwise. It felt a lot like fear. She knew fear well. Much more intimately than most.

Though, there were subtle differences to this feeling.

Such as the not entirely unpleasant feeling between her thighs.

She wasn't that innocent. She knew what that was. Why was this happening to her now? With him?

You are marrying him....

Yes, but she'd intended to deny sex as part of the equation for as long as possible and then submit to it when she had no other option. Her plan, thus far, hazy as it was, had been to just lie there and think of Jahar, so to speak. As far ahead as she'd thought in the past hour, when she'd finally decided that yes, she would be his wife. Really. Not just as a reprieve to a sentence or until she could kill him.

Even so, she wasn't ready to contend with the idea that she might...desire him.

No. This was just garden variety, biologically inspired arousal that had nothing to do with desire. It was the first time she'd been exposed to a man, an attractive man, and not been worried about him being something of a threat in the back of her mind.

So that was all it was.

She frowned as she shut the door to the dwelling. When had she stopped perceiving Ferran as a threat? She was certain he wouldn't harm her. Certain he would never force himself on her. And she wasn't sure what he'd done to earn that measure of trust, when only two weeks ago she'd cowered in the middle of his bed, her own weapon in his hands, fearing he would kill her or use her body.

She didn't now. Not in the least.

Strange how things had changed. How they were changing.

Now, that made her feel afraid. Because without all the anger at Ferran, she wasn't sure what she had left. It had insulated her, consumed her, for so long, she felt almost bereft without it.

"I apologize that my body offended you."

She turned and saw Ferran in the doorway, tugging his shirt over his head. His pants were already on, riding low on his lean hips. Not that any of it helped now, since she could so clearly visualize how he looked without the clothes on. Problematic.

"It was not...offensive," she said. "I just am not accustomed to having conversations with nude men. Out in the open."

"You only have conversations with them in the enclosed?"

"Well, where else would I have them?" she asked.

"Outside, it turns out."

"No. That's why I came in."

"Stubborn creature. Since you're in an enclosed space now, I could always take my clothes off again as I know you find this preferable."

She held up her hands, her heart scurrying into her throat. "No!"

"Then perhaps you might like to come outside and have dinner."

"Clothed?"

"Only if you want. I have no such rules about women and nudity."

She narrowed her eyes. "But you aren't naked with women at all, if what you say is true."

"Come back outside, Samarah."

"I will require we both remain clothed." She walked out the door and followed the rising smoke, back down to the pond where he'd been swimming only a few moments earlier. The ground was damp here, but there were blankets and pillows spread out already. There was a pan over the fire, resting on a grate.

"You've cooked?"

"I come here alone often, as I said. I could cook inside, but I quite like to eat out here." He took the pan from the grate and moved it to a small, low table that was next to his seat.

"Obviously."

There was rice and meat in the pan, and he handed her a bowl filled to the top. It was much simpler than the way they ate at the palace. She liked it. It reminded her of who she was apart from all the comforts. Of the way she'd grown up.

But this was a piece of that memory with the absence of that wary feeling. The fear. The anger. This was different. This felt like they were totally set apart from the world. From reality.

It was nice, because she'd had far too much reality in her life.

Something about this felt much more like a fantasy. Strange, because never in all her life away from the palace had she imagined spending time with Ferran being part of a fantasy. In her life at the palace, perhaps. She'd been fascinated by him then. The handsome prince who was always in trouble. Always up to mischief.

He lifted his head, and the disappearing sunlight cast a glow on his face. She remembered then. An image pulled from deep in her mind. Standing in the palace in Khadra, watching him stride into the room. The way he'd smiled. He'd reached out his hand on her head and ruffled her hair.

And she'd been certain he was the most beautiful person she'd ever seen.

She didn't know why she was only remembering this now.

Or maybe she did. Maybe because her anger, her determination for revenge, wouldn't let her have a memory of him that was so...precious.

It was precious because it was a part of where she'd started, and she had so few memories of that time in her life. The time where things had been right. Before it had all gone to hell.

"I remember you," she said, allowing real memories to mingle with her words. Allowing herself, for the first time, to really remember the people they had been. Before their parents had destroyed everything.

"You should. I've been sitting here with you the whole time."

"From before," she said. "I remember you." It made her feel so strange. To connect him, suddenly, much more strongly with that boy than with the monster she'd made in her mind.

"And what do you remember?"

"I thought...I thought you were beautiful." They were true words, forgotten thoughts that rose up in her mind and poured from her lips, filled her chest with a strange warmth.

"Did you?" he asked. "That is...not the description one might hope for."

"I was a little girl. I thought you were fascinating." She looked down into her bowl. "And you were very nice to me." Little wonder she hadn't let herself remember that. Because it did not fit with the stories she'd told herself about Ferran the monster. But here and now, those legends were being overridden with something more powerful. With memory.

"It was impossible not to be. You would not be ignored, and being unkind would have been like kicking a puppy."

In this moment, she decided she would pretend there was nothing away from this fire. She would allow them to have nothing but these good, shared memories. A truce.

"Well, I appreciate it, anyway. I had a...nice memory just now. I'm short on those. I don't remember very much about my life before my father died. And I think a lot of that isn't so much because I was too young—I was six. I feel I should remember some things—but because I forced myself to stop trying to remember. Because it hurt so bad. Because it...made me hate where I was even more. Those memories didn't serve a purpose, so I didn't let myself have them." She looked up. "I'd like to have them again. I'd like to have...something normal."

"I'm afraid I'm not the man for that," he said.

Of course he wasn't. How could he be? Given the way things were all tangled up, he couldn't be. And still, she pressed. "Why?"

"I'm not sure I know what normal is. Though, I'm not sure either version of our lives, on this side of the tragedy or the other, were normal."

"Maybe not. But one was happy. In one, I did smile."

"And you're looking for your smile."

"I am. Currently seeking any emotion other than anger

or fear, actually. That's basically been my life for the past sixteen years."

His expression changed, hardened. "I cannot imagine all that you've been through."

"It's okay. I mean, it's not okay. But it's what is. And there is nothing that can be done about it now."

"I wish there was more I could do."

She laughed suddenly. So suddenly not even she expected it. "It's so strange. I never thought I would sit across from a campfire with you while you offered to try and fix things for me. Not so long ago, I would have cried death before dishonor but…I feel like I was wrong about you."

"Samarah…"

"I don't see how either of us could have won in the situations we were put in, Ferran. You were a new ruler and you had to act as a king. And that day my father did not act as a king. He was simply a jealous man. Ruled by emotion." She took a breath and tried to loosen the tightness in her chest. "He was tried fairly, and found guilty of a crime he absolutely committed. What happened to my mother and I was less just, but it wasn't by your hand."

It nearly pained her to say it. But there was no honor in misdirected rage. She knew that better than most. And yet she had spent sixteen years clinging to it.

It didn't make her friends with Ferran, but…but it made her feel as though a truce that extended beyond the moment might be possible.

"Samarah," he said again, "there are things… I am not a hero."

"Neither am I. I'm a victim. And I think you are, too. But isn't it time to stop?"

"You're not a victim now," he said, the words coming slowly. "You will never be again. You're a sheikha. And you have power in this country. You have power now."

"I think I've proven that I've always had power. Though,

it's nice to have that power backed up by...the law. And the army."

"Don't get too power mad."

"I can make no guarantees." She looked out across the water, dark blue now with the sun gone behind the horizon line. "Do you know, these past weeks with you...before them, I can't remember the last time I sat and just had a conversation with someone. I can't remember when I had the time for something so casual. Master Ahn was very good to me. The closest thing I ever had to a friend, but we didn't have many conversations. He instilled in me the will to survive, the sense to think with my head and to act with honor in all things. To know what was right, so deeply that it would be an instinct to act upon what's right when the time comes...." She paused. "Maybe...maybe that's why I hesitated in your room that night. Because something in me knew it was wrong. Because something in me knew I couldn't possibly be serving justice if I hurt you."

"A bold statement, Samarah."

"I realized something today. I was allowing rage to dictate my action. And in that, I was no better than my father. For all that I wished to avenge his death, I have never condoned his actions. My anger was for me. For my mother and our country. But revenge was never going to make that right. Rage would never do anything but lead to more devastation. I'm ready to let go. Even if that makes me weak." She looked down at her food, then back up at him. "Does it make me weak?"

"You have never been weak," he said. "Never."

"You say that with such confidence. But I've always been scared."

"Is that a weakness?"

"Not when it keeps you alive, I suppose."

He set his food down, then stood. "I'm going to bed,"

he said. "Tomorrow we'll stay for breakfast and then head back to the bedouin camp."

For some reason, the thought of leaving made her feel sad. "Okay."

"See you tomorrow, Samarah."

Another chance to simply sit. To be with another person. To live. She found she was looking forward to it.

CHAPTER NINE

SAMARAH WOKE UP to the sound of rain on the canvas roof-top. She slipped out of bed and looked outside. It was gray out, the sun trying to pierce through the heavy blanket of clouds that had rolled in overnight.

She ran her fingers through her hair and leaned forward, the silken strands sliding over her shoulders.

She looked out the window, at the rain pelting down, hitting the parched earth, large droplets creating ripples on the surface of the lake. And she had the sudden urge to go out in it.

She'd hated the rainy season when she'd lived in Jahar. Hated having to hide in rooms that were muddy and flooded. Hated looking for shelter during the day wher-ever she could find it, or more often, just spending most of the afternoon feeling like a drowned rat.

But it was different now. She wasn't forced to stand out in the rain. She had a choice. She could stay in here where it was dry, or she could dance in the water drops. It was up to her. Because shc had a home now. She had shelter.

Everything had changed. There was more than survival. There was…enjoyment. Happiness. Something about yes-terday's realization, yesterday's acceptance, had allowed her to capture these things. Or at the very least the possi-bility of them.

She stood and walked to the window, pressing her palm

against the glass. Then she turned and walked out into the living area. It was still hazy, and the house was dark. She hadn't checked the time but it had to be early.

She padded to the front door and pressed down on the handle before going out onto the deck. She was wearing only a nightgown, a soft, silken one with very little in the way of adornment. It had been provided for her at the palace and she'd packed it for the trip. It wasn't designed to be flashy, just to be comfortable.

Normally, she wouldn't go walking outside in it. And she wouldn't go walking out with her hair down, simply because there was too much of it, and letting it free was much more trouble than it was worth.

But right now she didn't care.

She stepped down onto the wet sand; it stuck to her feet while the raindrops poured down over her body, making her nightgown stick to her skin. She looked up and let the rain drop onto her face, sliding down her cheeks and her neck.

How different it was to stand in the rain when it was your choice. When you knew you could go back inside and get dry.

She spun in a circle, her arms held out wide. She felt like the child she had been. As if she was free. As if rain was just rain, and she didn't have to worry about the cold, or the discomfort, the mold or the damp. All of the cares she normally carried were washed away.

She walked along the path they'd taken last night, to the ashes of the fire from the night before, and to the edge of the water. She looked out across the surface, continually being shattered by heavy drops of rain and tilted her face upward again.

"You'll catch your death."

She turned and saw Ferran, and immediately the child-like joy, the simplicity of it, faded. And she realized she was standing there with nothing but a thin nightshirt clinging to her body, and her hair wet and stringy down her back.

"You're out here, too," she said.

And in nothing but a pair of jeans. He was wearing jeans. And no shirt. But he hadn't worn jeans to bed so that must have meant he'd been...well, he'd likely slipped the jeans on before coming outside.

"Yes, but you're...you're beautiful," he said.

"I'm wet."

"Yes." He took a step toward her and she looked behind herself, her heel at the edge of the water. There was no backing away from him. And she didn't feel very inclined toward punching him in the face, either. Which was new. He extended his hand and took a strand of her hair between his thumb and forefinger, twisting it lightly. "I wondered what your hair looked like down."

"It is also wet. Therefore not the most flattering representation."

"I disagree," he said, leaning in closer. "Do you know how much of your body I can see through that nightshirt?"

She looked down at the fabric, which had shaped itself to her figure. She could clearly see her nipples, hardened from the cold. The nightgown provided no coverage there.

"I have an idea," she said, looking back up.

"And do you know what it does to me?"

She started to speak, then closed her mouth. Then she blinked and shook her head. "No."

"I have not touched a woman in sixteen years. I... Right now I feel like the ground here. Like I've been too long without water, and it's finally here in front of me."

"Oh...Ferran...I don't...I..." She didn't know what to do. She wasn't sure what he wanted. She wasn't sure she could give it.

He hadn't touched a woman in sixteen years, and now he was here, his hands on her hair. Touching her. So much pressure on her, when she had no idea what might happen next.

"I'm going to ask you again, Samarah." His dark eyes were level with hers. "Have you ever been kissed?"

She felt as if the breath had been pulled from her lungs. "Not exactly," she said.

"And by that you mean?"

Samarah hesitated, her heart fluttering in her chest. She knew this admission would change things. That in a few moments, the answer to the question *have you ever been kissed*, would not be the same. Even with no experience, she knew it. In her bones. In her blood. And she wanted it. "Not by anyone other than my family. Never by a man. Never in the way you mean."

He put his hands on her cheeks and brushed the water drops away. Was she really going to let him kiss her?

He's going to be your husband.

He was your enemy.

He'll be your lover.

Her brain was fighting with itself. And she had no idea which voice to listen to. But she felt her lips parting, her eyes slipping closed as she tilted her face upward.

To know what was right, so deeply, that it would be an instinct to act upon what's right when the time comes...

"I have waited for this," he said, his voice a growl, "for longer than you can imagine."

And then his lips met with hers. They were hot beneath the sheen of rain that covered them. Slick from the water. And firm. But more so than she'd imagined they might be. He held her face steady, then tilted his head, opening his mouth and touching the center of her upper lip with the tip of his tongue.

A simple, delicate touch that sent a flash of heat, like lightning, through her body.

He pulled back slightly, his hands still on her face, holding her. "Kiss me back, Samarah."

"I don't know…how. I don't know…" Desperation grew wings and fluttered in her chest, fear and need gripping her tight.

"What do you want to do?"

"I…" She looked at his chest, at his stomach, and she put her hands on him, one palm resting against the hard ridge of his abs, the other just above his heart. She wanted to touch him. To feel those muscles with no clothing between them. She'd known that for a while now, even though she hadn't quite understood it.

Or, more to the point, she hadn't wanted to understand it.

Now she did. Now she wanted to understand it all. All this depth and nuance of being human, of being alive. This rich tapestry that existed beyond mere survival.

There was so much more than just drawing breath. There was the feel of Ferran's skin beneath hers. The rough hair, the heat of his body, the hard definition of his muscles. And there was the need it created in her. Reckless and heady. A high like nothing else she'd ever experienced. The adrenaline rush that accompanied fear coupled with a much more pleasant emotion.

So this was lust. Real, raw lust, so much more potent than she'd ever imagined it could be. Even though she'd known it must be something so very strong, there was a difference from knowing that and having lived it. She was living it now.

She leaned in and kissed him, freezing when her mouth touched his, a raindrop rolling between their lips and sliding onto her tongue. She laughed, then pulled back. "Sorry, I don't think you're supposed to laugh when you kiss."

He moved his hands from her face and wrapped them around her waist, pulling her against his body. "Why not?" he asked. "I like that you're finally smiling."

He closed the distance between them, his kiss harder this time. His lips moved over hers, his tongue sliding against the seam of her mouth before she opened and gave him entry. Then he took her deep, long. The sensual friction sending a deep, sharp pang of longing through her. An arrow of pleasure that shot straight to her core and left a hollow pain in its wake.

She fought to free her hands from where they were trapped between their bodies and wrapped her arms around his neck, holding him to her. She tried to match his movements, to make her lips fit against his. He adjusted some of what he was doing, and she adjusted, too. And then they found a way to make their lips fit together just right.

He moved his hands down over her back, her butt, and down to her thighs. Then he gripped her tight, tugging her up into his arms, the blunt tips of his fingers digging into her flesh, the points of pressure adding pain into the mix with the pleasure.

She clung to him, wrapped her legs around his waist so that she didn't fall back down to the ground, and the motion brought the heart of her into contact with his hard stomach. A short, shocked moan climbed her throat and escaped.

He growled and angled his head, biting the side of her neck, harder even than he'd done back in the gym.

She whimpered, and he slid his tongue over the spot, soothing the sting, ramping up her arousal. She kissed him back, feeling confident now. Maybe because he seemed as if he was on the edge of control, too. She certainly was. Because this wasn't necessary, or useful. And yet it felt essential. And she wanted it. More than she could ever remember wanting anything.

He cupped her bottom and pulled her hard against him. At the same time he bit her lip, then soothed it away. Pleasure rocketed through her. She curled her fingers tightly into his shoulders, understanding perfectly now why some people actually enjoyed biting.

There was so much more to this than she'd ever thought possible. To wanting a man. To sexual desire. It wasn't just nice feelings, or pleasure, or whatever it was she'd imagined it might be.

It was need, so deep and intense it made you burn. It was pain. Pain because there was too much pleasure, pain because you wanted more.

Kissing Ferran was both the best and the worst kind of torture.

It was everything. It filled up the moment. It filled her up. And yet, it wasn't enough. It hinted at things she didn't know about, made her desire things she didn't understand. Made her body crave something she wasn't certain existed. Tipped her beliefs on right and wrong onto their heads and twisted her into a stranger she didn't know, and wasn't certain she liked.

But she didn't care.

She rocked her hips against him and a low, feral growl rumbled in his chest. He moved quickly, decisively, lowering them both down to the ground. To the sand. And she didn't care that she was going to get dirty. That she would get wetter. It didn't matter as long as he kept kissing her.

He adjusted their positions, forking his hands through her hair, tilting her head back, tugging slightly. He slid one hand down her back, cupping her rear and lifting her up against him. And she wasn't pressed against his stomach anymore, but the hard line of his shaft. She'd seen him naked yesterday, but it hadn't prepared her for this. He hadn't been aroused yesterday in the lake.

Instinct, and need, had her flexing her hips against him, each movement making the ache inside her build, grow, until she thought she was going to die.

She was sure no one could withstand this kind of sensual assault. The rough sand beneath her; Ferran, hot and hard above her; the rain, cold against her skin.

He moved his hand to cup her breast, drawing his thumb slowly across her nipple, before pinching her lightly. She was still covered by the damp fabric of her gown. He lowered his head and sucked her deep into his mouth.

He pushed against her, the hard ridge of his arousal hitting her just where she needed it.

And the dam burst inside of her. A hoarse cry escaped her lips, much like the sound she made when she fought. Raw, passionate, bold.

Pleasure poured through every part of her. She arched against him, holding tight to his shoulders as the waves crashed over her, her eyes squeezed shut, her fingernails digging into his shoulders.

She just lay there for a moment, feeling spent, the fog slowly clearing. And then she started to feel other things. Shame. Embarrassment.

He moved against her again, kissing her neck, his hands firm on her breasts.

She shoved at his chest.

"What?" he asked. "Samarah, did I hurt you?"

"No…I…no…"

She couldn't tell him. She couldn't tell him that she'd had what she suspected was an orgasm from kissing him. That was…it was terrifying and way past the point of embarrassing straight into humiliating. Because how could that be? How? With him…with anyone, but especially with him.

This was not lying back and thinking of Jahar. This was not a truce. It was somewhere far over that line, and it was one she couldn't believe she had crossed.

He moved away from her and she scrabbled to her feet, her nightgown sticking to her legs, tugging upward, the sand caked over her skin, in her hair. "I just…I have to go back inside now."

"You do?" he asked, still on the ground, breathing hard. He looked nearly as shocked as he had the night she'd tried to kill him.

"Yes. I do. I...thank you. For the kiss. I have to go. I'm cold."

She turned away from him, her arms wrapped around her waist, and she ran back toward the house, then into the bathroom. She locked the door behind her and turned the water on, stepping inside fully clothed and watching the sand wash down the drain.

Then she started to shiver.

She'd never felt anything like this before. And it was much too big for her to deal with. Too big for her to process.

There was a whole new depth to life, and she'd just discovered it. And now she was terrified by what might come next. By what it meant about who she was.

Because once upon a time, Ferran might have been able to have lovers without feeling connection. But in that moment she knew for certain that *she* couldn't.

She thought of her mother, the author of her own destruction, and everyone else's, so desperately in love with two men that she couldn't give either of them up.

As much as she didn't want to be her father, she didn't want to be her mother. And God help her, she would not be a fool over Ferran Bashar.. And until she figured out how to get a handle on her emotions, she couldn't allow Ferran to touch her again. It was as simple as that.

Ferran called himself every kind of bastard as he kicked over the cooking grate that was still set up over the dead coals from last night's fire.

He was an animal. Of the worst kind. He'd known she was a virgin, hell, he knew she'd never been kissed. She'd been badly handled all of her life. Thrown out onto the streets when she was a child so that she could escape a grisly death.

He was responsible for every bad thing that had happened in her life. And now he'd added another thing to the incredibly long list.

He'd allowed himself to be ruled by passion. Had let the floodgates open after keeping them firmly closed for so many years.

No.

He was not that man. Not anymore. He would not allow it. Not again.

He had been rough with her. He'd been ready to take her, take her virginity, in the sand, in the rain. Without talking to her. Without making sure she was ready.

You're using your need for control to hold her captive.

He shrugged the thought off, turning his self-disgust to the more specific events at hand.

He'd led with his own desire, and had given no thought to anything else. He'd thought he was better than that now. He had to be. The alternative was unthinkable.

He stalked into the water, in spite of the fact that he was already wet, and submerged himself. It was much colder today, with the sun behind the clouds and the rain pouring down.

It didn't do anything to assuage his arousal. He was still so hard it hurt, need coursing through him like a current. He ground his teeth together and walked back out of the water, his jeans heavy and tugging downward, chafing against his erection.

That had been a stupid, damn idea. And it hadn't even worked.

He walked back toward the house and shrugged his jeans off at the door. Hopefully Samarah wasn't around because he didn't really want to ambush her with his body like this.

He could hear the shower running and he said a prayer of thanks for small mercies.

He went into his bedroom and started digging for dry clothes. They needed to get back to the palace. Back to civilization and back to sanity.

There, he would be reminded to keep his distance. He would be reminded of all the indignity she'd already suffered without him adding to it.

His weakness had caused her suffering.

He paused at that thought. She deserved to know. Because if there was one thing Samarah truly cared about it was honor. It was doing right.

Though, there was a limit to what he could say without adding to her pain. Without uncovering himself completely.

One thing was certain. Before he tied her to him for the rest of her life, before he jailed her in a whole different way than she'd originally threatened, she had to know at least in part, what sort of man it was she was tying herself to.

CHAPTER TEN

THEY ARRIVED AT the palace late that evening. The ride back had been torturous. Samarah had spent so much of her life without human interaction, she'd never fully understood just how awkward it could be to sit in an enclosed space with another person when you had nothing to say.

And when you had something obvious and tense hanging between you.

That morning seemed like a lifetime ago, and yet it had only been about fifteen hours since Ferran had held her in his arms. Since he'd pulled her against him and kissed her. Since he'd brought her to the peak of pleasure on the ground outside in the rain.

She could hardly believe that had been her. And that it had been him.

In the cold of the night, she could not understand what had possessed her to go outside in a rainstorm. What had possessed her to fall into his arms and kiss him as if he was the only source of water in the desert.

She moved through her chambers and stopped cold when she saw Ferran in the doorway. "What are you doing here?" she asked.

"I came to speak to you about tomorrow. We're to have lunch with the palace event planner. To speak to her about the upcoming engagement party and the wedding."

"Oh," she said. "I had forgotten about the party."

"As had I. Since I'm not particularly interested in parties, it was easy to let it slip my mind."

"I can't say I'm a real party animal, either," she said, her tone dry.

"I imagine not. I have brought you something."

"Oh?" She really had to try and find something more intelligent to say than that.

"I feel we got off track today."

"Oh." Well, dammit. That was not more intelligent.

"I should not have touched you like that. Not knowing how innocent you are. And I regret that I frightened you."

It was on the tip of her tongue to say he hadn't frightened her at all. She'd frightened herself. But honestly, his assumption was so much less revealing that she felt like letting him have it.

Coward.

Yes. But so what? He was about to apologize and since he owed her many, in reality, she would take one for this. Even though he didn't owe her one for that incident in particular. She bore the full weight of the consequences for the foolishness of her body.

"I lost sight of what it is we are doing. This marriage is to benefit our nations. And to heal the past. What I did accomplished neither of those things."

"Well…no I suppose not."

"This is to remind you, to remind me, of what this is about." He reached into his pocket and pulled out a small black box. "I spoke to the palace jeweler, and he managed to come up with something very quickly. It is not my mother's ring. All things considered I felt no monuments needed to be built to that marriage." He opened the lid of the box and revealed an ornate, sparkling piece of art. Gold with diamonds set into an intricately carved band. "But this is from the crown jewels, as it were. And it has been in my family for many generations. It's lasted longer than a marriage. Than the rule of any one sheikh or sheikha. And I hope what we build forges a bond between our countries that is the same. I hope that what we build transcends a simple marriage, and becomes something lasting that benefits both of our people."

"Oh that's…that's perfect," she said, banishing images of them kissing, of the heat she'd felt in his arms, and bringing to the front pictures of their country. Of their people. Of all that could be built between the nations if they followed through with this union.

"I am prepared to ask you to wear it."

"Of course," she said.

She waited for him to do something. To get on one knee or put the ring on her finger. She wasn't sure if she wanted him to do that.

He did neither. He simply stood there with the box held out in front of him until she reached inside and took the ring, putting it on her own finger.

"You may not want to do that just yet, princess," he said.

"Why not?"

"I am prepared to ask you to wear it. But only after this. I want to talk to you about what happened at the oasis."

"Oh," she said, looking down, heat bleeding into her face. "You know what? I'd rather not."

He took her chin between his thumb and forefinger and tilted her face up so that she met his gaze. "Did I hurt you?"

"What? No." She shook her head and took a step back. "No, you didn't hurt me."

"Did I frighten you?"

"I…I…no." It wasn't him that scared her. It was herself. The way he'd made her feel. The fact that he'd commanded a response from her, with such ease that she hadn't even realized she was capable of feeling.

"Then why did you run?"

"I didn't…run. I was cold and I went back in the house."

"You were right to be afraid," he said.

"I wasn't afraid."

"Then you should have been."

"I'm sorry—I should be afraid of you? I beat you in hand-to-hand combat, lest we forget."

"I believe I beat you," he said. "Both times."

She scowled. "You cheated. You bit me."

"It was not cheating. But that's beside the point. I have something to tell you about that day. And you won't like it. But I have to tell you before you concede to marrying me. Because it will change things. I owe you this explanation. Though I'm certain I will regret giving it."

"Then why give it?" she asked. She suddenly felt afraid. Because she was starting to feel at ease with this man. With this situation. With the fact that she was to be his wife.

More than finding ease…she was starting to want things. From him. From life. And she was afraid that whatever he said next might take it all away.

"Because you have to know. Because if you aren't afraid, then you need to understand that you should be. You need to understand why I can never be allowed to lose control. Why I have spent sixteen years doing nothing more than ruling my country. Why I despise passion so very much."

"The same reason we both have to distrust it," she said. "Because it led our parents to a horrible end. The only innocent party involved was your mother, and yet, she suffered just as badly for having been there as any of them."

"It is true," he said. "She was the only innocent party. She was true to her marriage vows. She didn't attack anyone. She was simply there when your father and his band of men decided to make my father pay for what he'd done."

"It was wrong, Ferran. All of it. And I'm willing to put it behind us." And she meant it. This time, she meant it for real. "Because…it has to be. It can't keep being my present and my future. I can't allow it. Not anymore. I want something different. For the first time I just want to move on from it and please…please don't take that from me."

"It is not my intent to take anything from you. But to inform you of the manner of man you're to marry."

"Does it matter what manner of man?" she asked. "If I have to marry you either way, does it matter?"

"You spoke to me of honor when we first met, Samarah. You were willing to die for it, so yes, I think it matters. I feel I have to tell you. For my honor at least. What little there is."

"And I have no choice?"

"This is giving you a choice. So that you know who you let into your body at night once you're my wife. I owe you that. Or I at least owe it to my sense of honor."

Her face heated. "That was unnecessary."

"It hardly was. I nearly took you this morning at the oasis. I nearly took your virginity on the ground. Do you understand that? Do you understand that I am capable of letting things go much too far when…when I am not in control."

"You didn't."

"You stand there and blush when I talk about being inside of you. It would have been a crime for me to do that there. In that manner."

It wouldn't have been. And part of her wanted to tell him that. That she was blushing because she was inexperienced. Because she was embarrassed by her response to him. Confused by the fact that she felt desire when she'd expected to endure his touch. Not because she found the idea of being with him in that way appalling.

"I don't…I don't think I would have stopped you. And if you say I couldn't have, I'm going to do my best to remind you that I, in fact, could have. Don't ever forget what I can do, Ferran. Who I am. I am not delicate. I am not a wilting flower that you've brought out to the desert. I survived that day. I survived every day after. You don't need to protect me, and I refuse to fear you."

"I killed your father," he said, his dark eyes boring into hers.

"I know," she said.

"No, Samarah, you don't. I did not have your father arrested. I did not send him to trial. I was hiding. In a closet. I heard everything happening out in the corridor and I hid. That is when your father burst into the family quarters. And he attacked my father with a knife. I stayed hidden. I did nothing. I was afraid. I watched through the partly open door as he ended my father's life. My mother was in the corner. A woman, unarmed, uninvolved in any of it. And then he went for her and...I didn't hide anymore. She begged, Samarah. For her life. She begged him to spare her. For me. For my sake and the sake of our people. For the sake of his soul. But he didn't. I opened the closet door and I took a vase off of one of the sideboards and I hit him in the back of the head with it. I was too late to save my mother. She was already gone. And I...disarmed him."

"Like you did me," she said, feeling dizzy. Feeling sick.

"Yes. Exactly like I did you. But unlike you...he ran. And I went after him."

She tried not to picture it, but it was far too easy. Because she'd been there that day. Because she'd heard the screams. Because she knew just how violent and horrible a day it had been. It was so easy to add visual to the sounds that already echoed in her head.

"Ferran..."

"I was faster than he was. Because of age or adrenaline, I'm not sure. But I want you to know that I didn't even give him the chance to beg for his life. Because he never knew I had caught him. I ended him the moment I overtook him. I stabbed him in the back."

Samarah took a step back from him, her eyes filling

with tears before she could even process what he was saying. She shook her head. "No…Ferran don't…don't…" She didn't know what she wanted to say. Don't say it. Don't let it be true. *Don't tell me.*

"It is the truth, Samarah. You should know what kind of man you're going to marry. You should know that I am capable of acting with no honor. There was no trial. He was not given a chance. I acted out of emotion. Out of rage. And it is one thing I refuse to regret. You need to know that before you agree to bind yourself to me. I killed your father and I will not regret it."

She growled and ran forward, shoving his chest with both hands. "Why must you do this now?" she asked, her voice breaking. "Why did you make me care and then try and rip it away?"

"I'm being honest," he said, gripping her arms and holding her so that she couldn't hit him again. "You have to know. Am I the man you want in your bed? Then you must know the man I am."

She fought against him, not to break free, but just because it felt good to fight against something. Because it was easier than standing there passively while all these emotions coursed through her. Grief, rage, anguish, panic. All of it was boiling in her, threatening to overflow. And she didn't know how to handle it. She didn't know how to feel all of this.

This wasn't simply breathe in, breathe out. This wasn't a calculated plan for revenge and satisfaction of honor. This wasn't even the low hum of sixteen years of anger. This was all new, and shocking and fresh.

And horrible.

Because she hurt. For what she'd lost. For her father. For the man he truly was. A man who killed an innocent woman because he was scorned. A man who was not the one she'd loved so much as a child.

And she hurt for Ferran. As horrible as it was to imagine him being involved as he had been, she hurt for him. The boy whose mother had died before his eyes. The boy who had avenged her.

As she would have done.

Oh, as she would have done to him if he'd allowed it. And then what? Would she be the one standing there with nothing but a scorched soul? With haunted eyes and the feeling that she had no honor left because in her rage she'd allowed herself to justify taking the life of someone else?

"You see now," he said, "who I am. And why I cannot permit myself to be led by my emotions? I am no better than they are, Samarah. I am no better. I am not stronger."

And neither was she. Not really. Because she'd been prepared to act as he had, but not in the heat of rage. Not in the midst of the fight. With years to gain perspective, she'd been ready to behave as her father had done.

As she looked at Ferran, at the blank, emotionless void behind his eyes, she felt she could see the scars that he'd been left with that day. It had been so easy for her to imagine him as the one who'd come out of it whole. He'd had his country. He'd had his palace. Hadn't that meant in some way, that he had won? That she had lost and therefore was owed something?

But when she looked at him now, she didn't just understand, she felt, deep down in her soul, that he'd lost, too. That there had been nothing gained for him that day. Yes, he'd ascended the throne, a boy forced to become a man. Yes, he had a palace, and he had power. But he had lost all of himself.

That was why he looked so different than the boy she'd known. It wasn't simply age.

She struggled against him, and he held her tight, his eyes burning into hers. "How dare you make me understand you?" she asked, the words coming out a choked sob.

"How dare you make me feel sorry for you?" Tears rolled down her cheeks, anger and pain warring for equal place in her chest. And with it, desire. Darker now, more desperate than what she'd felt at the oasis.

And she knew it now. There was no question. It was what she'd felt that first moment, in his bedchamber when their eyes had met. What she'd felt watching him shirtless in the gym, fighting him, getting bitten by him.

It was what she'd felt every time she'd looked at him since returning to the palace. It had just been so expertly mixed with a cocktail of anger and shame that it had been impossible to identify.

But now that she'd tasted him, she knew. Now that she'd gone to heaven and back in his arms, she knew.

Now that she understood how you could long for a man's teeth to dig into your flesh, she knew.

"How dare you?" she asked again, the words broken. "How dare you make me want you? I should hate you. I should kill you."

She leaned in and claimed his lips with hers, even as he tried to hold her back. He released one arm and reached around to cup the back of her head, digging his fingers deep into her hair, squeezing tight and tugging back, wrenching her mouth from his.

"Why are you doing this, Samarah?" he growled.

"Because I don't know what else to do," she said. "What else am I supposed to do?"

"You're supposed to run from me, little girl," he said, his expression fierce. He was not disconnected now—that was certain. He wasn't hollow. Her kiss had changed that. It had called up something else in him.

Passion.

Passion that he thought she should fear, and yet she didn't. She found she didn't fear him at all.

"I don't run," she said, her eyes steady on his. "I stand

and meet every challenge I face. I thought you knew that about me."

"You should run from this challenge," he said. "You should protect yourself from me."

She pushed against him, and he pushed in return, propelling her backward until she butted up against the wall. "You don't scare me, Ferran Bashar," she said.

"As far as your family is concerned," he said, "I am death himself. If you had any sense at all, you would run from this room. From this palace. And you would not wear my ring."

Her heart was raging, each beat tearing off a piece and leaving searing pain in its place. And she couldn't turn from him. It would be easy to get out of his hold if she really wanted to. A well-placed blow would have him at her feet. But she didn't want to break free of him. Even now.

"You need me to run, coward?" she asked. "Because you fear me so? Because I am such a temptation?"

That was the moment she crossed the line.

His lips crashed down on hers, his hold on her wrists and hair tightening. It wasn't a nice kiss. It was a kiss that was meant to frighten her. A show of his dangerous passion, and yet, she found it didn't frighten her at all.

She kissed him back. Fueled by all of the emotions that were rioting through her, fueled by the desire that had been building in her from the first moment she'd seen him again. From the moment she'd walked into the palace, with vengeance on her mind.

She had wanted him then, but she'd been too innocent to know it. And desire had been too deeply tangled in other things. But she knew now. The veil had been ripped from her eyes. And all the protection that surrounded her heart seemed to have crumbled.

Because she couldn't hate him now. Not even with the newest revelation. All she could see was what they'd both lost. All she could do was feel the pain of losing her father over again. The man who'd been a god in her mind transforming into a monster who would kill an unarmed woman. And all she could do was let it all come out in a storm of emotion that seemed to manifest itself in this.

At least a kiss was action. At least a kiss wouldn't end with one of them dead.

Though now, with all of the need, all of the deep, painful desire that had possessed her like a living thing, like a beast set on devouring her insides if she didn't feed it with what it wanted, she wondered if either of them would survive.

He pulled his mouth from hers, his hands bracing her wrists against the wall behind her head, dark eyes glaring, assessing her. "Why do you not run from me?"

"Because I am owed a debt," she said, her breath coming in short, sharp bursts. "You stole my life from me. You stole this," she said, speaking of the need she felt now. "I had never even kissed a man because I could afford to feel nothing for men but distrust and fear. I had to guard my own safety above all else because I had no one to protect me. I could never want, not things beyond food and drink. So you owe me this, Sheikh. I will collect it. I will have you, because I want you," she said. "It is your debt. And you will pay it with your body."

"So you want my passion, Samarah? After all I have told you?"

"Is it not my right to have it? If it has been used so badly against me? Should I not be able to take it now, when I want it, and use it as it would satisfy me?" Anger, desire, anguish curled around her heart like grasping vines. Tangled together into a knot that choked out everything except a dark, intense need.

"You want satisfaction?" he asked, his voice a low growl, his hips rolling against hers, his erection thick and hard against her stomach.

"I demand it," she said.

He leaned in, his breath hot on her neck, his lips brushing against her ear. "Do you know what you ask for, little viper?"

"You," she said. "Inside my body. As discussed. You seem to think I don't know what I want, but I will not have you disrespect me so."

"No, Samarah, I am of the opinion that you likely always know what you want, at the moment you want it." That was not entirely true, because she hadn't realized how badly she wanted him until today, when she knew it had gone on much longer than that. "But what I am also sure of, is that sometimes you don't always want what is good for you."

"Who does?" she asked.

"No one, I suppose."

"We all want things that will harm us in the end. Cake, for example. Revenge for another."

"Sex," he said.

"Yes," she said. "Sex."

"That's what you want? You want sixteen years of my unspent desire unleashed on you?"

"That's what I demand," she said.

He tugged her away from the wall and scooped her into his arms in one fluid movement, carrying her across the room. She put her hand on his chest, his heart pounding so hard she could feel it pressing into her palm.

"Then you shall have what you demand," he said, depositing her onto the mattress before tugging his shirt over his head and revealing his body to her. So perfect. So beautiful. Not a refined, graceful beauty. His was raw, masculine and terrifying. So incredible she ached when she looked at him. "But know this, my darling, your command stops here. For now you are mine." He let his finger trail over her cheek, his dark eyes boring into hers. "If you want this, I will give it you. But the terms will be mine."

"This is my repayment," she said. "I agreed to nothing else."

"And that is where you miscalculated, my little warrior. For in this, I am nothing short of a conquerer."

"And I no less a warrior."

"I would expect nothing else. But in the end, I will stake my claim. Run from me now, if you do not want that."

She could hardly breathe. Could hardly think. But she didn't want to think. She wanted to focus on what he made her body feel. Because this, this release that she was chasing with him, overpowered the feelings in her chest.

This desire won out above all else, and she so desperately needed for it to continue to do so. And she did not want to run.

His hands went to the waistband of his pants and he pushed them down his legs. She did gasp, virginal shock coursing through her, when she saw him naked and erect.

This was different than when she'd seen him in the lake, but she hadn't been prepared for just how different. Just how much larger he would be.

Neither had she been prepared for her body's response. She might not know exactly what she wanted, but her body did. Her internal muscles pulsed, the ache between her legs intensifying.

"Let me see you," he said. "I am at a disadvantage, for you have seen me twice, and I have only ever been teased by promises of your body."

She just sat there, staring at him, feeling too dazed to follow instruction.

He approached the bed, his hands going to the front of her dress, where it was fastened together with hooks and eyes. "Consider this *my* payment," he said. "For all that was stolen from me. For I have not touched a woman since that day. And it is fitting that you are the one who has returned desire to me."

"A fair exchange then," she said. "And in the end, perhaps neither will owe the other anything?"

"Perhaps," he said, his tone raw.

He pushed the little metal clasps apart at the front of her dress and started to part the silken fabric, slowly and deliberately. Her breasts were bare beneath the heavy material. She wasn't generously endowed there, so unless she was engaging in physical combat, there was little need for her to wear undergarments.

She wished for one now. For one additional buffer between her skin, the cool air of the room, and Ferran's hot gaze.

He pushed the dress from her shoulders, leaving her in the light pants she'd been wearing beneath them, and nothing more. He looked at her breasts, his admiration open. "You are truly beautiful. Let your hair down for me."

She pulled her braid from behind her and took the band from around the bottom, sifting her fingers through the black silk and letting it loose to fall around her shoulders, all the way down to her waist. She let the loose strands cover her breasts.

"That's a tease," he said. "Giving me only one thing that I want at a time. I want it all. I have waited long enough. Stand."

She obeyed the command, because she was more than willing to follow orders now. She was not the expert here. She had nothing but a deep, primal instinct pushing her forward, and if she stopped to think too hard, nerves were waiting in the background to take hold. They had no place here. They were not allowed to overshadow her desire.

He remained sitting at her feet on the mattress, and he reached up and tugged her pants down, along with her underwear, leaving her completely bare before him, with him on his knees, right at eye level with the most secret part of her.

"Ferran…"

He leaned forward and pressed a kiss to her thigh, then to her hip bone, his lips perilously close to…to…her. To places on her she didn't know men might want to kiss.

"You want my passion used for your pleasure, Samarah? You demand it? Then you must submit to it."

"I…I will," she said.

"Do not fight me."

"I won't."

He tightened his hold on her. "Do not fight what we both want. I feel that you're about to flee from me."

"I'm not," she said, her throat tightening, her heart fluttering.

"Liar," he said, his lips skimming the sensitive skin on her inner thigh. "Spread your legs for me," he said.

She obeyed. Because he would know the best way to do this. That she did trust. And he was right, if she wanted his passion, demanded it, then she had to accept it. Not try to control it.

He leaned in again, his tongue sliding through her inner folds, across the sensitive bud there before delving in deep.

"Ferran." She grabbed hold of his shoulders to keep herself from falling, her legs shaking, the mattress wobbling beneath her feet. He anchored her with his hands, holding tightly to her hips as he pressed in deeper, increasing the pressure and speed of his strokes over her wet flesh.

Her stomach tightened, pleasure a deep, unceasing pressure building deep inside of her until she thought she might not be able to catch her breath. Everything in her tightened so much she feared she was turning to glass, so fragile and brittle she would shatter if he pushed against her too hard.

He kept going, adding his hands, pushing a finger deep inside of her, the sensation completely new and entirely different to anything that had come before.

He established a steady rhythm, pushing in and out of

her, the friction so beautiful, so perfect, she very nearly did break. She held back, rooted herself to earth by biting her tongue, by gritting her teeth so hard she feared they'd crack.

Because she was afraid to let herself go over the edge again. Afraid of what her release would bring this time.

"Give it to me, Samarah," he said. "Give me your pleasure."

"I can't…I can't."

"You can," he said, adding a second finger as he continue to lick and suck her. He stretched her, a slight pain hitting as he did, and she used that to help pull her back again.

"I'm afraid," she said.

"Don't be. I will catch you."

He leaned in again, the hot swipe of his tongue hitting just the right timing with his fingers, and then, she couldn't fight it anymore. She let go. Her hands moved away from his shoulders as her orgasm crashed over her. Only Ferran kept her on her feet. Only Ferran kept her there. And she trusted him to do it.

She didn't try to keep herself standing, because she knew he would. Because he'd promised her.

He laid her down on the mattress afterward, rising up to kiss her lips, deep and long. She could taste her own desire there, mingled with his. His shaft was hard and hot against her hip, evidence of the fact that he'd given, again, while taking nothing for himself.

Evidence also, of the fact that he'd enjoyed what he'd done for her. A sweep of heat, of pride, pure feminine power, rolled through her. He had enjoyed doing that to her. Had relished the taste of her. He wanted her, even as he told her to run.

She didn't know why it made her feel the way it did. Didn't know why it made her feel so powerful. Only that it did. Only that it spurred her on. And this time, she didn't want to run after her climax. She wanted to stay. She wanted more. Because she couldn't be embarrassed by what he'd made her feel.

Not when he was feeling it, too.

She shifted their position and parted her thighs, the blunt head of his erection coming up against the slick entrance to her body.

"I tried to prepare you," he said, his voice strangled. 'But it will still hurt."

"I am not afraid of pain, Ferran," she said, sliding her hands down his back, feeling his muscles shift and tense beneath her fingertips. "I am not afraid of you."

"I do not wish to hurt you."

"But in order for us to join, you have to. So don't worry. Please, Ferran, I want you. I want this."

He started to push inside of her, slowly, gently. He stretched her, filled her. It did hurt, but not as much as she'd expected. It was only foreign, and new. But wonderful. Like every other pain he'd caused her physically, it was good.

He started to pull back and she locked her ankles over his, their eyes meeting. "Ferran, don't stop."

"I won't," he said, thrusting back inside of her, deep and hard, filling her completely.

She held on to him, getting adjusted to having him inside of her. She tilted her head and looked at him. His eyes were closed, the veins in his neck standing out, his jaw clenched tight. He looked as if he was in terrible pain. She kissed his cheek and a rough sound rumbled in his chest.

"Don't hold back now," she said.

"I am trying not to hurt you," he said, kissing her hard and deep.

When he separated from her lips, she was breathless. "You aren't."

He seemed to take that as permission. He started to move inside of her, slowly at first. Achingly so. Building all of that lovely, orgasmic tension in her again. Starting from the beginning, and this time, he brought her even higher. Further. Faster.

His rhythm grew fractured, his breath shortening. She shifted her legs, wrapped them higher around his waist and moved with him. He braced one hand on the mattress, by her head, and wrapped the other around her, pulling her against him, his movements hard and fast.

His eyes met hers, and she slowly watched his control break. She could see it, in the dark depths. Could see as he started to lose his grip. Sweat beaded on his forehead, his teeth ground together.

Watching him, seeing him like this, so handsome, so on edge, pushed her closer, too. Then he thrust inside her, hard, his body hitting against the part of her that cried out for release. As it washed over her in waves, she leaned in and bit him on the neck.

A harsh, feral sound escaped his lips, and he stiffened above her, his shaft pulsing deep inside of her. And she relished it. Reveled in his utter loss of control.

He moved away from her as if he'd been shocked, his chest heaving, his muscles shaking. He got off the bed and started collecting his clothes.

"Ferran…"

"That should not have happened."

"But it did," she said, the words sounding thick and stupid. She sat up and pushed her hair out of her face. "It did." A strange surge of panic took hold as Samarah tried to process what had happened. As she tried to deal with the fact that he was regretting what had passed between them.

She had given him, the man who had been her enemy all her life, her body, and now he was telling her what a mistake it had been. Shame lashed at her as she remembered the first night she'd met him.

I would sooner die.

And I would sooner kill you.

Oh, how she had fallen.

You did not fall. You jumped.

"You don't know what you want," he said. "You're an in-nocent." He tugged his pants on and turned away from her.

Even as she battled with the shame inside of her, his words ignited her anger. "Hardly. I was a virgin, but that does not equate to innocence."

"Well, I am a murderer." He pulled his shirt over his head, concealing his body from her view. "Compared to me, everyone is an innocent. Good night, Samarah. In the morning, if you are still here, and if I am still here, we will speak."

"Are you afraid I'll kill you?"

He lifted a shoulder. "I trust you to act in an honorable manner."

He walked out of her bedroom and closed the door be-hind him. Leaving her naked. And very, very confused.

She had slept with her father's murderer. She had wanted him.

She had laid herself bare to her enemy and joined her-self to him. The man she had sworn to kill. The man she had agreed to marry. The man who heated her blood and showed her desire she'd never known possible.

Why could things never be simple? This future he had offered had seemed such a miraculous thing in many ways, but the strings attached were different, unexpected. The war, the one she had sought to wage in a physical manner, had moved inside of her body.

What she wanted, right now, was to forget everything. To process what it meant to be intimate with another per-son for the first time. But her lover was gone. And even if he were here, it wouldn't be that simple.

He would still be Ferran. She would still be Samarah. She had never felt more alone than she did in that mo-

ment. She had spent years in near isolation, with no friends
and no family, and here, with the imprint of his fingertips
still burning on her skin, she felt completely abandoned.

She rolled over onto her stomach and curled up into a
ball.

She felt utterly changed. By Ferran. By his confession.
By his touch. And she would have to figure out what to
do about both.

One thing she knew for certain, she would not allow
his touch to transform her into a quivering mass. She had
survived all manner of things; she would not allow herself
to implode now.

She repeated the words she'd said to Ferran, just before
he had touched her. Before he'd altered her entirely.

"I am still a warrior."

CHAPTER ELEVEN

FERRAN SUPPOSED HE shouldn't be too surprised by Samarah storming into the dining room early the next morning in her workout gear, her long dark hair restrained in a braid.

He also supposed he shouldn't be too surprised by the feral, tearing lust that gripped him the moment he saw her. Sixteen years of celibacy, burned away by this fearsome, beautiful creature.

"You're not exactly dressed for our meeting with the event planner," he said, gritting his teeth, trying to get a handle on himself.

"And you're not exactly dead, so perhaps you should just be grateful."

"It's true," he said, lifting his mug to his lips, "I suppose after last night, I should be happy that you allowed that."

"Again, I find myself merciful."

"I have no doubt. And are you here to tell me you're leaving, Sheikha? Though, I must warn you, I will not allow it."

"A change in tune from last night."

"After what happened, there is no way you can go."

She held up her hand and showed him the ring on her finger. "As it is, I've decided to stay."

"How is this possible?"

"I have nowhere else to go. I get thrown in your dungeon, I get sent back to the streets of Jahar, and neither option is entirely palatable to me. So I'm staying here. I find sheikha-hood much preferred to street urchinhood. Imagine that."

"I would ensure you were cared for."

"And I would live on your terms. This way I have my own source of power and visibility in the public eye. I have my rightful position. It is the only way."

"Why are you not angry with me?"

"Perhaps I am," she said, her expression cool, impassive. "Perhaps this is simply me lying in wait."

There was something about the way she said it that sent a slug of heat through him, hitting him hard in the gut. Because it made him think of last night. Of her soft hair sifting through his fingers, of her softer skin beneath his palms.

It made him think of what it had been like to be inside her. A storm of rage and fire, of all the passion she'd asked for.

And in that passion, he had dishonored her. At least, he had not done what his mother would have expected from him with the daughter of their neighboring country. A virgin princess. He would have been expected to honor her. To never touch her until marriage vows had been spoken, until she was protected.

Now, he could not send her away. It was impossible. A bigger sin than the one he'd already committed.

More weakness. How he despised it. How he despised himself. A jailer now, by necessity, because he had ensured now that they must marry.

"If so, then I suppose it's no less than I deserve," he said. "Although, marriage is a life sentence, and some might argue a life sentence is more of a punishment."

"Glad to be your punishment," she said. "I always knew I would be your reckoning. Why did you leave me alone last night?"

"What?"

"You heard me. Why did you leave me alone last night?"

"Because, it was a shameless loss of control on my part."

"You made me feel ashamed," she said.

"That was not my intention."

"Regardless," she said, her voice trembling. "You did. We have a history thick with death and hatred. But in that moment, I was just a woman. And seeing your disgust—"

"At myself. One moment I confessed to stabbing your father in the back, the next you begged me to have sex with you. It was, without a doubt, the strangest encounter I've ever had with a woman."

She frowned, her cheeks turning a dark rose. "I'm not sure how I feel about my only experience with a man being called strange."

"Do you think it's common to go from death threats to making love?"

"Does it matter what's common?"

"I handled you too roughly."

"You handled me in exactly the right way," she said. "During sex. Not after. After…I find you in much fault on the way you behaved after."

"How would you know I treated you in the right way?"

"Because. I know what feels good to me. I know what creates…release."

"Orgasms," he said, not feeling in the mood to be considerate of her inexperience. If she thought she could handle it, then she'd have to be able to handle the discussion of it in frank terms.

"Yes," she said, the color in her cheeks deepening. "Obviously I know what gives me orgasms, and clearly, it is something you know how to accomplish. So you handled me correctly. I think we can both agree on that."

"Do you know what virgins deserve?"

"Do you even remember being one? How would you know?"

"This isn't about me," he said.

"Like hell it's not," she grumbled.

"Virgins deserve candles, and lovemaking and marriage vows."

"Do they? Did your first time come complete with those things? If so, I feel I should tell you, I've no interest in sharing you with another wife. And I find candlelight overrated."

"I'm a man. It's different."

"Oh? Really? Because I'm a woman and therefore must be coddled? Because for some reason my body is your responsibility and not mine?" Her face wasn't smooth now, not unreadable. She was angry. Finally. "If that's the case, where were you when I shivered in the cold? Where were you when I was alone and starving? Where the hell were you when men approached me and offered me shelter for sex? Or just demanded that I lie down and submit to them? Or perhaps, I should have taken them up on it? Since I clearly don't know what I need, perhaps they did?"

"That is not what I'm saying, Samarah," he said. "Hell. I didn't know.... I didn't..."

"Because in so many ways, you are the innocent here, Ferran. I have lived in the dark. You only played in it for the afternoon."

"The thing about something like that is that it never leaves you," he said. "On that you can trust me. You know, even if you've cleaned blood it shows beneath fluorescent lights. That's how I feel. That no matter how many years pass, no matter how clean I think I am, how far removed... it doesn't ever really go away. The evidence is there. And all I can do is make sure I never become the man I was in that moment ever again."

"This is one of the many things about my association with you that troubles me, Ferran," she said, grabbing her braid and twisting it over her shoulder.

"Only one? Do you have a list?"

She lifted her brows. "It's quite long. I made it last night. About what I want. About what all this means for me. And about what I find problematic about you."

"Is it a physical list?"

She nodded. "But this is just one of the things. Before you, everything was black-and-white to me. I hated you for what you did. I didn't have to know your side. I didn't have to see multiple angles. I just had to know you were responsible for the death of my father. But now I know you. Now I've heard your side. I should hate you more, knowing you ended my father's life, and yet I find it only makes me feel worse for you. Because coupled with it, comes the revelation that my father killed your mother. That you saw it. That…in your position, I would have acted the same, and that in many ways, had you not made him pay for what he'd done, I would have judged you a coward."

"I should have had him go to trial, Samarah. That would have been the right thing to do in the black-and-white world. In the one I aspire to live in."

"I think of that day like being in the middle of a war zone. It's how I remember it. I was just a child, and I saw very little. I was so lucky to be protected. My mother ensured that I was protected though…have you ever considered my father would have come for us next? For her? Would he have come for me too, Ferran, ultimate vengeance on my mother, if you hadn't acted as you did?

"Samarah…you're assigning heroism to me, and that is one thing you should never do. It's conjecture. Who knows what would have happened?"

"Yes, who knows? I only know what did. But now I know it from more angles. I miss my blinding conviction. The less I knew, the easier it all was. I could just…focus on one thing in particular."

"Your rage for me."

"Yes. And I could move forward, using that as my target. And now? Now everything has expanded and there are so many more possibilities. For what my life could be. For what I could do with myself and my purpose. But it's scarier, too."

"Scarier than gaining access to my palace? Being thrown in a dungeon? Facing possible trial?"

"Yes. Because when I was in that state I didn't want anything. I had accepted that I would probably die carrying out my mission, and that meant an end to... Life has been so hard. I've had no great love for it. But you came in and you offered me more, and the moment you did...things started to change. Now...now I don't want to turn away. I don't want to go back to how it was. And yet...and yet in some ways I do. It makes no sense to me, either."

He laughed. It was an absurd thing to do under the circumstances. Neither he nor Samarah had anything to laugh about. And yet, he couldn't help it. It was as if she was discovering emotions for the first time. Discovering how contrary it could be to be human.

"Is this your first experience with such confusion?" he asked.

"Yes," she said. "Emotions are wobbly. Conviction isn't."

"I'm very sorry to have caused you...feelings."

"Thank you," she said. "I'm...sorry in many ways to be experiencing them. Though not in others. Really, is it always like this?"

"Not for me," he said. "I'm not overly given to emotion."

"I suppose you aren't. Though, passion seems to be a strong suit of yours."

"No, it's a weakness."

She let out a long breath. "You're getting off topic. I have my list." She reached into the pocket of her athletic shorts and pulled out a folded piece of paper. "Now that I'm not merely surviving, there are some things I would like. I would like to be comfortable," she said, unfolding the paper and looking at it. "I would like to be part of something. Something constructive. Something that isn't all about breaking a legacy, but building a new one."

"Lofty," he said, standing, his stomach tightening as he looked at her, his beautiful, brave fiancée, who didn't seem to be afraid of anything, least of all him. She should be. She should have run. He'd given her the chance and she had not.

Why had she not run? Any normal woman would have turned away from him. From the blood on his hands.

She should be afraid.

He moved nearer to her, fire burning through his blood. A flame to alcohol, impossibly hot and bright. She should be afraid. He wanted to make her afraid. Almost as badly as he wanted her to turn to him and lean in, press her lush body against his chest.

"Is that your entire list?" he asked.

"No," she said, her voice steady. "I want to feel like I have a life. Like I have…"

"Sex," he said, leaning in, running his thumb over the ridge of her high cheekbone. "Is sex on your list?"

He let his hand drift down the elegant line of her neck, resting his palm at the base of her throat. He knew that she wouldn't fear his wrath. She would fight him to the death if need be. Here was where he had the undisputed upper hand. Here was where his experience trumped hers.

He felt her pulse quicken beneath his thumb. "I don't know."

"If you stay, there is no option, do you understand?" He slid his thumb along her tender skin. "You are my prisoner in many ways."

And it was true. A hard truth that settled poorly.

"It is better than the streets," she said, arching a brow.

"A high compliment," he said.

"It is," she said. "For in the beginning, I would have said death was better than this."

"Oh, my little viper." He moved his hand upward and cupped her jaw. "You are so honest."

"I am not," she said.

"Your eyes. They tell me too much." Liquid, beautiful and dark as night, they shone with emotion. Deep. Unfathomable. But the presence of that emotion twisted at his gut. Convicted him.

"Do not trust me, Samarah," he said, his voice rough. "I don't trust me."

"I don't trust anyone."

"See that you don't. You may be a warrior. You may be a strong fighter. You may not hesitate to cut my throat… now. But in the bedroom, I have the experience."

"Sixteen years celibate," she said.

He wrapped one arm around her waist and drew her to him, holding her chin tight, pressing her breasts tight to his chest. "And yet," he said. "I had the power over your body. Do you deny it?"

Dark eyes shimmered, her cheeks turning pink. She caught her breath, pressing her breasts more firmly against him. "No," she said, her voice choked.

Oh, Samarah. She revealed too much to him.

He wanted to press her back against the wall, wanted to take her. To show her that he was not a man to toy with. To prove he wasn't a man to trust.

He released her, moved away from her. The distance easing his breath. "Now, unless you're planning on wearing workout clothes to meet with the event coordinator, you may want to go change."

"Yes, I may. Thank you. How thoughtful." She turned away from him, head down, and walked out of the room.

The twisting sensation in his gut intensified. He was her jailer. Not her fiancé. Being with her…it was akin to force.

He gritted his teeth as pain lashed through his chest. No. He would not force her. He had not. What had happened last night could not be changed, but the future could. At the very least, he would begin showing her the respect a sheikha was due.

CHAPTER TWELVE

SAMARAH HUNG OUT in the corridor, listening to the sounds of people inside the grand ballroom of the palace. She was still a little bit nervous in large gatherings like this. More so now that she was a focal point for attention. And she felt as if there was nowhere to hide.

As palace staff, no one had noticed her. As the sheikh's fiancée? Yes, she was certainly going to be noticed. Especially in the green-and-gold gown that had been sent for her. It had yards of fabric, the skirt all layered, billowing folds. The sleeves went to her elbows, sheer and beaded, with matching details on the bodice, disappearing beneath the wide, gold belt that made her waist look impossibly small. It also kept her posture unreasonably straight, since it was metal.

A matching chain had been sent for her hair, an emerald in the centerpiece that rested on her forehead. She *did* like the clothes, but less now when she felt so conspicuous. And without Ferran.

She relied on his presence much more than she'd realized until this moment. Of course, after she'd gone and read him her list she felt more than a little embarrassed to see him again.

Though, really, she'd been naked with him, so nothing should embarrass her with him now. It did, though, because he'd run afterward. Because, when they'd spoken earlier, his intensity had unsettled her.

He was right. In this, this need, he was the master. And he could easily use it against her.

How sobering to realize that if the sheikh of Khadra were to defeat her, it wouldn't end in screams of terror, but in pleasure.

Just then, she saw him. Striding down the hall. He was wearing white linen pants and a tunic, his concession to traditional dress. She'd noticed that he never seemed to bother with robes.

She didn't feel so conspicuous now. Because surely everyone's eyes would be on Ferran. He was taller than most men, so he always stood out for that reason. But he was also arrestingly handsome. She'd kissed his lips, touched his face, his body. And she was still struck to the point of speechlessness by his beauty.

Or maybe it was even more intense now. Because she'd been with him. Because she knew what wicked pleasure his perfect lips could provide. Because she knew what a heaven it was to be in his strong arms, to be held against his muscular chest.

"You're late," she said, clasping her hands in front of her.

He paused, his dark eyes assessing. "You're beautiful."

She blinked hard. He'd said that to her before. But for some reason it hit her now, how rarely she'd heard that in her life. Not when it was said in a nonthreatening tone. Men on the streets had called out to her, but they had frightened her. Her father and mother had called her beautiful, but when she was a child.

Ferran said it to her just because. Because he believed it. Because it was what he saw when he looked at her. And for some reason, just then, it meant the world to her.

"Thank you," she said. "I think you're beautiful, too."

"I'm not often called beautiful," he said, one corner of his mouth lifting.

"Well, neither am I."

"That will change."

"Have you accepted than I'm not leaving you?" she asked.

"I'm not sure," he said, holding his arm out to her.

She took a step forward and curled her fingers around his forearm. "You have my word," she said. "My word is good. I want you to know that, at first, I didn't intend to marry you."

"Is that so?"

"I intended to bide my time. And carry out my plan."

He tightened his hold on her, his other hand crossing his body and settling over hers. "I had a feeling that might be the case."

"But it's not the case now. I will marry you," she said. "I will be your wife. And I will not leave you. So don't try to scare me away. You'll only be disappointed."

"Is that so?"

"Yes. Because I do not scare. And just because I don't intend to kill you doesn't mean I won't punch you in the face."

"I'll endeavor to avoid that," he said. "Are you ready to go in?"

"What are we supposed to do?"

He lifted a shoulder. "Wave. Eat some canapés. Dance."

"I have never danced with anyone."

"I'll lead," he said. "You have nothing to worry about. You are strong, Samarah, I do know that. But there's no shame in letting someone else take control sometimes. It can even be helpful."

"All right. In the bedroom and on the dance floor, you may lead," she said, testing him. He had tried to prove his power over her earlier, and while he had done so, while he had left her quivering, aching and needing in a way she hadn't thought possible, she rebelled against it. She wanted to push back.

Because if there was one thing in life Samarah didn't understand, it was defeat. She had spent her life in a win or die battle, and as she was here, breathing, living, it was clear she had always won.

And that meant, in this moment, she was determined to keep fighting.

"We'll discuss the bedroom later," he said. "After our wedding."

"What?" It was such a stark contrast to what he'd said earlier. To the implied promise in his words.

"We have to go in now."

"Wait just a second. You said..."

"Did you think you were going to seize control back?" he said, dark eyes glittering. "You, and my body, no matter how it might ache for you, do not control me."

His words, the intensity in his eyes, stopped her voice, stole her breath.

"You do not want me out of control," he said, his face hard. "I remind you. Now, come with me."

He led her into the ballroom, and as they drew farther in, nearer to the crowd of people, panic clawed at her. How was she supposed to smile now? How was she supposed to deal with all those eyes on her after what Ferran had just said?

They were formally announced, and Ferran lifted their joined hands, then bowed. She followed suit and dipped into a curtsy, shocked she remembered how, everything in her on an autopilot setting she hadn't known she'd possessed. Her muscle memory seemed to be intact. Princess training obviously lurked in the back of her mind.

"Who are all these people?" she asked, still reeling from the change. From his uncivilized words in the hall to this venue that was all things tame and beautiful.

"Dignitaries, diplomats. From here and abroad. Anyone who feels they may have a political stake in our union."

"Including the Jaharan rulers, I imagine?"

"Yes," he said. "This is the first time they've been at a political event in Khadra since…"

"Yes. Obviously."

"Already, we have done some good."

"I guess that remains to be seen," she said. "Just because they're here doesn't mean… Well, I guess I'm pessimistic when it comes to politics."

"I can see how you would be."

"But I can see that people are happy to be here. I feel like…I feel like this is good."

They spent the next hour wandering through the party, making light conversation with everyone they came across. This wasn't the time for any heavy-hitting, political negotiation, but everyone seemed very aware that it was the time to get on Ferran's radar.

And people seemed to want to talk to her, as well. As if she carried influence. As if she mattered. It was so very different to the life she'd had before she'd come here. So very different to the life she'd ever imagined she might have.

"Now," Ferran said, "I think it's time for you to dance with me."

"I think I could skip the dancing," she said, looking out across the expanse of marble floor, to where gorgeous, graceful couples twirled in circles, in eddies of silk and color. She doubted very much she would be that graceful. Martial arts was one thing. She kept time to the beat of the fight. Of her body.

She wasn't sure if she could follow music.

"I will lead you," he said. "As I think I've established."

"So you have," she said, but in this instance she was grateful.

Sex and dancing were Ferran's domain, it seemed.

He led her through the crowd, and to the center of the floor. The other dancers cleared extra space for them, as if in deference to Ferran's royal personage.

He grasped her hand, his arm curling around her back as he tugged her against his chest. She lost her breath then, captivated wholly by the look in his eyes. So dark and intense. Simmering passion. The kind he'd unleashed last night. The sort she craved again.

And he was telling her now that they would wait. That he could control himself.

She didn't like it. It made her feel powerless. It…hurt her. And she would not have it.

She'd waited all of her life. She'd spent countless nights cold and alone, and she'd be damned if she'd spend any more that way, not now that she'd been with him.

"I think we need to discuss what you said in the hall," she said.

"Which thing?"

"About abstaining until the wedding," she said.

He looked around them. "Are we having this conversation now?"

"I take your point. However, you just said some very explicit things in the hall and then we were cut off. And I'm not done. I just thought I should tell you that I'm not doing that."

"Excuse me?"

"It might interest you to know that I have obtained some very brief underthings."

"Samarah…"

"They're intended to arouse you, and I have it on good authority they will."

He looked torn between anger, amusement and, yes, arousal. "Whose authority?"

"Lydia's. She provided them for me when I asked."

"And they are meant to…"

"Arouse you," she said, her face heating. "I had thought, seeing as I was to be your wife, I should set out to…behave like a wife. And then you told me…you told me no."

"Tell me about them," he said, his voice lowering, taking on that hard, feral tone he'd had in the hall, as he leaned nearer to her.

"The uh…the bra is…made of gems. Strung together. It shows…a lot of skin."

"Does it?"

"Yes," she said, swallowing hard, her face burning.

"And the rest?"

"I don't feel like you deserve to know," she said, lifting her head so she was looking in his eyes, so their noses nearly touched. "If you want abstinence, you don't want to know about my underwear."

"That isn't the case. And I never said I *wanted* to abstain. Only that it's the right thing."

"For who?"

"For you."

She growled. "Stop doing that. Stop trying to protect me. I don't want you to protect me I want you to…to…"

Love me.

Where had that come from? She did not need that thought. No, she didn't. And now she would forget she'd ever had it. And she would never have it again.

"I just need you to be with me," she said, which was much more acceptable. "I'm tired of being alone. Now that I don't have to sleep by myself anymore I would just… rather not."

He pulled her closer, his lips pressed against her ear. "Yes, *habibti*, but do you want me? Do you want my body? Do you want me to touch you, taste you. Be inside you. If all you want is companionship, I would just as soon buy you a puppy."

"I want your body," she said, leaning in and pressing a

kiss to his neck. "I want you. I don't want a puppy. I'm a woman, not a child. I know the difference between simple loneliness and desire."

"And you desire me?" he asked, his eyes growing darker.

"Yes."

"Tell me what you desire."

"Here?" she asked, looking around them.

"Yes. Here. Tell me what you want from me. What you want me to do to you. You said you wanted my passion. You said you weren't afraid. Now tell me. Remember, I have much more practice than you at abstaining when temptation is present. So if you intend to break my resolve, you'd better damn well shatter it. If you want to take my control, you prepare for what you will unleash."

"I…" She felt her cheeks get hotter, and she wanted to shrink away. To tell him nothing. To tell him something quick, and unexplicit. Something dishonest that had nothing to do with what she'd actually been thinking about doing with him.

But then she remembered her own words.

I do not run.

She tilted her head up and leaned in so that her lips were near his ear, her heart hammering hard.

"I want to take this dress off for you," she said. "While you sit and watch. I want to watch your face as your need for me takes you over." She swallowed hard. "Then…then I want to…I want to get onto the bed, on your lap, and kiss your lips."

"You want to do all of that?" he asked.

"I'm not finished."

"I may need to be," he said. "This doesn't sound very much like you're planning to let me lead."

"You were the one who said I should let you lead in the bedroom. I never agreed to it."

"We were not taking a vote," he said, his tone hard.

"I deserve to get what I want from this marriage, too."

"You aren't talking about marriage. You're talking about now."

She lifted a shoulder. "Don't I deserve to be certain of the manner of man I'm binding myself to? You said that yourself."

"And you think seducing me will reveal me to you more than my confessions already have?"

"It's the one thing you've held back for the past sixteen years. That makes me feel like it's important."

Ferran wanted to turn away from her, and yet, he found it impossible. She was too beautiful. Too powerful. It wasn't simply beauty. It never had been. She was a glittering flash of temptation that could easily be his undoing.

But she was also to be his wife. And that meant he had to get a handle on himself with her, didn't it? That meant that he had to be able to sleep with her, to make love with her, without losing himself.

Here before him was the challenge. If he turned her away now, then he proved that she held the power to take him back to where he'd been before.

She didn't. No matter how strongly she called to him. No matter how much he wanted her, he could control it. He could have her tonight, and feel nothing beyond release.

It didn't matter what she wore, what she did. He would prove to himself he had the control.

"All right, Samarah. You want me? You want my body? Tonight?"

"Yes."

"Now?" he asked.

"Now…we're…Ferran, not now."

He pulled her closer, staring down into her wide, dark eyes. "If you want me, *habibti*, you will have me on my terms."

He released her from the close hold they were in, then

laced his fingers through hers, drawing her through the crowd of people, out into the gardens. The night was cool, the grounds insulated from view by palm trees and flowering plants.

And no doubt his security detail had seen him exit with Samarah. If for no other reason, no one would be following them out here.

He tugged her to him and kissed her, hard and deep. If this was what she wanted, it was what she would have. But he wouldn't be at her mercy. He wouldn't be taking orders from her. If she wanted him, she could have him.

And he would make her understand what that meant.

He cupped her chin, his thumb drifting along the line of her jaw as he continued to kiss her. To taste her. He could drown in it. He very nearly had before. Both when they'd kissed in the rain, and last night.

There were things about kissing a woman he hadn't remembered. How soft feminine lips were, the sounds they made. How it felt to be so close to someone living. To feel their heartbeat against your own.

Or maybe he hadn't forgotten. Maybe he'd just never noticed before.

But he did now. It was like slowly having feeling return to frozen limbs. To places that had been numb for years. So much so, he'd forgotten they were even there.

In his quest to be the best sheikh, to choke out all of his weaknesses, he'd forgotten he was a man. And the touch of Samarah's lips in his brought it all back with blinding clarity.

And with the clarity came a host of other things he'd spent years trying to deny. Fear. Anger.

He backed her against one of the walls that enclosed the garden from the rest of the world, taking her mouth with all the ferocity he possessed.

"You want this?" he asked again, kissing her cheek, her

neck, moving his hand to her breast. His whole body was shaking. He could hardly breathe. He could barely stand. Touching her like this…

It had nothing to do with how long it had been since he'd touched a woman. If he was honest, he had to confess that.

It was more. She was more.

He slid his palm over her curves, to the indent of her waist, over the rounded flare of her hip. He gathered up the material of her dress, curling his fingers around the heavy, beaded fabric.

"Ferran…"

"Scared, *habibti*?"

"No," she said. "But we're in the garden and…"

"And you said you wanted me. You do not get to dictate all the terms. If you want me, you will have me now."

He moved his hand between her thighs, felt the thin silk that separated the heart of her from his touch. He pushed it aside and growled when his fingertips made contact with slick flesh. "You do want me," he said, moving his thumb over the source of her pleasure.

She arched against him, her breathing coming in short, sharp bursts. More evidence of her need for him. He suddenly felt that he might require her more than air.

"Samarah," he said, sliding his fingers through her folds.

She pushed her knees together, forcing his hand more tightly against her body, her head falling back against the wall, her lips parted, an expression of ecstasy.

If he took her now, it would be over quickly. It would be so easy to undo his pants and thrust deep inside her, take them both to release.

But then he couldn't see her body. He couldn't touch her as he wanted, taste her as he wanted.

"I want to take you to bed," he said.

"I thought you wanted me here?"

"I do," he said. "Here and now, but I also want to be able

to see you." He moved his hand from between her thighs.
"I want to touch you. I want to take my time."

He tugged her dress back into place.

"You can't expect me to walk back through there. We
look...well, we must look like we've been doing exactly
what we've been doing."

"I am certain we do. But I have no issue with it."

"I cannot figure you out."

"I've made the decision," he said, looking at her eyes,
which were glittering in the dim lighting. And he could
feel the desperation within himself. Could sense his own
biting need to justify his actions.

But he'd decided he would do this. So surely that made
it okay. Surely that meant he had reasoned it out. She was
to be his wife. He repeated that fact in his mind. She was
to be his wife, and that meant that he could be with her.
That meant he had to be. It was duty and honor, and it had
nothing to do with the heat in his blood.

And making sure he took his time and enjoyed it was
for her. For his wife.

"Come with me," he said, holding out his hand.

She took it, delicate fingers curling around his. He
flashed back to the moment in his bedroom, when those
hands had struck at him. When she'd looked at him with
fear and loathing. It was gone now. All of it. Replaced by
a desire he wasn't certain he deserved from her.

But he needed it. Because they were getting married.

That was the only reason. For his people.

Not for himself.

But either way, he needed it.

He led her back through the garden, and into the brightly
lit, glittering ballroom. She was flushed, her eyes bright.
She looked very much like a woman who was on the brink
of release, and suddenly, he was afraid that everyone in the
room would know.

Not for himself, but for her. He didn't want to humiliate Samarah. He didn't want to expose her or hurt her. And yet, he feared that was what he'd done. All he would ever do.

Not tonight. Tonight she would be his, and he would worry about the rest later.

He gritted his teeth and battled with himself. With his reasoning, his justifications.

Spare me. Spare us.

No. There was no place for that memory. Not in this. This wasn't the same. He could keep control, and have this.

He could keep her.

He led her out into the hall, then down the corridor, toward his chambers. Halfway through, he swept her up in his arms. "I have no patience," he said, striding onward.

"I doubt this is faster," she said, her arms looped around his neck.

"But you are near me," he said.

Why had he said that? Why was he feeling this. Why was he feeling anything? Why did it matter?

He kicked the door to his bedchamber open and Samarah jumped in his arms. "I found that arousing," she said, her eyes locked with his.

"Did you?" he asked.

"I like your intensity," she said. "I like that you want me. No one has wanted me in so long."

He set her down and she leaned into him, curling her fingers into the lapels of his shirt. "No one has wanted me in longer than I can remember. Until you. You want me. And that matters, Ferran…"

He bent and kissed her, slamming the bedroom door as he did, the sound echoing in the cavernous space. "My wanting you is not necessarily something to rejoice in," he said, dragging the edge of his thumb along her cheek. "I am broken, Samarah, in every way that counts."

And there was more honesty than he'd ever given even to himself.

"I don't care," she said. "I don't care."

"Samarah…"

She took a step away from him and reached behind her back before unclasping her belt and letting it fall to the ground. The top layer of her gown fell open and she shrugged it off, letting it slither to the floor, revealing the simple shift beneath.

The heavy silk conformed to her slender figure. It revealed very little skin, and yet he found the sight erotic. So sexy he could hardly breathe.

She started on the little buttons on the front of her garment. She let it fall away, revealing another layer beneath. A skirt with a heavy, beaded waistband that sat low on her hips, strips of gauzy, nearly translucent fabric covering her legs. Every movement parted the fabric, showed hints of tanned, shapely thighs.

The top was exactly as advertised, and yet, nothing she'd said had prepared him for the deep, visceral reaction he had to it. Glittering strings of beads strung across her golden skin, conformed to the curve of her breasts, hints of skin showing through.

It wasn't the gems that held him captive, not the sparkling. No, he was trying to look past that, beyond that, to her. Because she was more beautiful than any gem.

"Sit on the bed," she said.

"I told you this would be on my terms."

"And I did not agree. I have a fantasy that I wish to fulfill."

"You have a fantasy?" he asked, his heart rate ticking up.

"Yes. You know, Master Ahn rented out the studio several nights a week to a dance teacher. I never took lessons, but I did watch. Sit on the bed."

He obeyed, his eyes on her, a ferocious tug in his gut.

"Take your shirt off," she said.

He tugged at his tie, then worked the buttons on his shirt before shrugging it, and his jacket off onto the bed.

She shifted her hips to the side, slowly, then back the other way, the motion fluid, controlled. "I used to practice in my room sometimes," she said. "But there was no practical use for dancing in my life. Still, I know what my body can do. I know how to move it. How to control my muscles. Dancing came naturally in many ways."

She shifted her shoulders, then reached behind her head and released her hair, letting it fall in loose, glossy waves. She kept her hips moving in time with a rhythm that was all in her head. But he could feel it. He could feel it moving through her body and on into his.

She rolled her shoulders, down her arms, to her wrists, her fingertips curling upward, her head falling back. He shifted in his seat, desire rushing through his veins, beginning to push at the restraint that he prized so much.

That he depended on.

She met his eyes, then tipped her head back, her shoulders following, bending back until he was sure she would break herself if she went farther. She held the pose steady, no strain in her muscles, then she lifted herself back up slowly.

Such a fierce, wild creature she was.

A tiger pacing the bars...

"You did pay attention during the lessons."

"Yes," she said. "But I've never had anyone to dance for. I've never had any real reason to dance. But I did it anyway. Alone. Now...now I can do it for you. I don't understand this...how you've become the most essential person to me. But you have. I almost robbed myself of you."

"You almost robbed *myself* of me," he said, gritting his teeth, trying to keep from telling her to stop talking. Trying to keep himself from accepting what she was offering. From begging her for more.

"I did," she said, walking toward the bed, each movement a temptation. Another hit against the barricade. She put her hand on his cheek, her fingertips dragging across his skin, sending a sensual spark down into his gut that ignited, desire burning hot and hard, threatening to rage out of control.

She reached behind herself and released the hold on her top, the jewels sliding down to her waist before she managed to free herself of it entirely. She put one knee on the bed beside his thigh, her breasts so close one movement would allow him to suck a caramel nipple deep into his mouth.

But if he moved, he wouldn't be able to find out what she had planned next.

The temptation was torture. Sweet, perfect torture. He'd held himself back for years, but it had never felt like this. It had never been physical pain. To have so much beauty in front of him and to refuse to allow himself to touch it, to test himself in this way…it was intoxicating. A rush he couldn't define or deny.

She leaned in, putting her hand on his belt, her beasts so near his lips his mouth watered. She worked at his belt, her fingers deft, confident, like all of her movements.

She freed him from his slacks, her palm hot on his erection. He couldn't hold back the tortured sound that climbed his throat and escaped his lips.

"Do you like me touching you?" she asked. "No other woman has done this in a long time…" She squeezed him gently and he swore. "Did I hurt you?"

"No," he said. "And yes. You're right…it's been a long time. It makes it… No, I don't think it's the time. It's you. Because nothing ever felt like this before."

She smiled, her dark eyes glistening. She looked at him

as if he was a god. As if he was her hero, not her enemy. And he felt like the worst sort of bastard for stealing that moment. One he didn't deserve. One he could never hope to earn.

And for what? Because he had given her shelter when she had none? Because he had offered her prison or marriage? He should stop her. But he didn't. Instead he watched her face and soaked in the adoration. The need. He didn't deserve it. Dammit, he didn't deserve a moment of it and he was going to take it anyway.

Such was his weakness.

"I want to…could…" She slid down, her movements graceful, her knees on the floor, her body between his thighs. "I want to taste you."

"Samarah…" He should not allow this.

"Please." She looked up at him, and he knew he couldn't deny her. What man could deny a woman begging to allow her to take him in her mouth? Certainly not him. He had established that he was weak.

Maybe for the moment he would let his guard down fully. Maybe he would let her see it all. He forked his fingers through her silky hair, curling them inward, making a fist. Holding her steady.

She lowered her head and he allowed it, holding her back only slightly so he could catch his breath. So he could anticipate the moment she would touch him.

But when she did, it was nearly the end of it. Because there was no bracing himself for this. For the sheer, blinding pleasure of her hot, wet tongue on his skin. For the unpracticed movements she made, so sincere. Only for him.

She dipped her head and took him in deep. His hold tightened on her hair, his other hand holding tight to the bedspread. Trying to anchor himself to earth. To something.

"Samarah…" He said her name like a warning. A curse. A prayer. He needed her to stop. He needed her to keep going. He needed this because it made the past feel like less. Made it feel like maybe this need wasn't so wrong. Like maybe he wasn't so wrong.

Pleasure rushed up inside of him. Hot. Dangerous. Out of control.

He tugged her head upward and tried to catch his breath, tried to get a handle on the need that was coursing through his veins like fire.

"Not like that," he said, his words harsh in the stillness of the room. "I want to be inside you. Just like you said. You said you wanted that. Wanted me."

"I do."

"Show me, *habibti*. Show me."

She rose up slowly, her hands on the beaded band of her skirt. She pushed it down her hips slowly, then stepped out of the fabric, leaving her bare to him.

"You are water in the desert," he said, pulling her close, his face pressed against her stomach. He kissed her tender skin, tracing her belly button with the tip of his tongue. "You are perfection."

She put her arms around his neck, one knee pressed onto the mattress beside his thigh. Then she shifted and brought the other one up, too. "I want you, Ferran Bashar. You are not my enemy."

Words he didn't deserve. Words he would never deserve. And yet, he did not have the strength to turn her away.

She lowered herself onto his length, slowly, so slowly he thought his head might explode. And other parts of him. But if that happened, he wouldn't get to see this through to the end. And he desperately needed to. If only to watch her face while it happened. When she reached her peak. If he could see that again…maybe he would put up the walls after. And carry that with him.

He watched, transfixed as she took him in fully, her lips rounded, her eyes closed. The pleasure there was humbling.

More than he deserved. But he was of a mind to take it all, whether he deserved it or not.

He curved his arm around her waist, his palm resting on her hip. And he put his other hand on her chest bracing her as he thrust up inside her. She gasped, her eyes opening, locking with his.

"Yes," he said. "Look at me, Samarah. Look at me."

He shifted his hold, tightened the arm around her waist, cupped the back of her head with his other hand, his thumb drifting to her mouth. She turned her head and bit him. Lightly, just enough to send a short burst of pain through him, the sensation setting off a chain of sparks.

She moved over him, with him, and he held her tight, held her against him, tried to brace them both for what was coming.

He thrust up hard as he pulled her down against him and she cried out, his thumb braced against her lips as she shuddered out her release, her internal muscles tightening around him.

He moved his thumb and claimed her mouth in a searing kiss as he thrust inside her one last time and gave in to the need that was battering him, breaking him down. And he gave in to his own need. His own desire washing over him like a blinding wall of cleansing fire. Strong enough to burn away the past. Strong enough to burn away blood.

And when they were done, he pulled her onto the bed with him and held her close, their hearts beating together.

"Don't make me go," she said, burying her face in his chest.

"I doubt I could make you do anything you didn't want to do."

"I don't know about that," she said, moving against him, her breasts against his bare chest sending a fresh shock of desire through him. He couldn't blame the celibacy. This was all Samarah.

"Maybe someday we can go back to the palace by the ocean, Ferran," she said. He stiffened, dark memory pouring through him. Like black ink on white, it stained. It couldn't be stopped. "Maybe together we can make new memories there. Memories that aren't so sad. I remember loving it. I remember…almost loving you."

Her words choked him. Made his vision blur. He didn't deserve this. A man like him. She knew he'd killed her father but she didn't know how he'd felt. The rage. The decisive, brilliant rage that had made sinking his knife into the other man's back feel like a glorious triumph…

"I don't know that we should go back, Samarah."

"We won't let the past win, Ferran. You were the one who taught me that. You were the one who made me want more."

"I should not be the one who inspires you, little viper." He was her captor, nothing more. A man who went through life ruling with an iron fist and—he envisioned the past washed in a haze of red—when he had to, blood.

And that was the man who held her.

He had enslaved her, and she was thanking him. He had robbed her of her choice, and she gave him her body. He should go. He should leave her.

He started to roll away, but she held tight to him. He felt the hot press of her lips on his back. "Don't do that," she said. "Please don't."

He put his hand over hers, pinned it to his chest. Then he turned sharply, pulling her naked body against his as he kissed her, hard and deep. He didn't deserve this. He shouldn't take it. He had no right.

But he was going to take it anyway. He lowered her back down to the bed and settled between her thighs, kissing her neck, her shoulder, the curve of her breast. "I won't do it then," he said. "Why? When we can do this instead."

"Ferran, we should talk."

"I don't want to talk," he said, his voice rough. "I don't want to talk."

"Why not?"

"Because…" He kissed her again. "Because words are dangerous, and until I'm not feeling quite so dangerous… I don't think I should speak."

"Then we won't speak," she said.

And they didn't for the rest of the night.

CHAPTER THIRTEEN

THEIR WEDDING DAY was fast approaching and Samarah felt as if she was sleeping with a brick wall.

Ferran Bashar was nothing if not opaque. He didn't want to talk. He didn't want her to talk. He wanted to make love. Frequently. Constantly, some might say, and she was okay with that. But she wanted something else. Something more.

She wanted him to feel what she did, and she had no earthly way of knowing if he did. Because she felt as if she was butting up against a brick wall whenever she tried to find out.

She thought of the woman she'd been only a month ago, and she could scarcely remember her. Angry. Hopeless.

Now her whole life stretched before her, a life with Ferran. But she was afraid it would always be like this. He talked to her more before they'd started sleeping together. At least then they'd tried. Now it felt like he only wanted to see her at night.

It could not stand. Because when she'd chosen him, she'd done so with the intent of having a life. A real life. Everything she wanted. So she would damn well have it. She was tired of feeling nothing but hunger, cold and exhaustion. Tired of only seeing to the basics.

She wanted more. Whatever *more* might be. And she wanted it with him. If she could walk away now and do anything, *be* anything. Be with anyone, she wouldn't.

She would stay here. Because her home was with him. She felt as if her heart might even be with him. And that meant it was worth pushing for what she wanted, didn't it?

Yes, it did. She would not question herself. She adjusted the tape on her fists and strode into the gym, where she knew Ferran would be. He was probably hoping for a quiet workout. But she wasn't going to allow it.

Because she wasn't simply going to accept what he gave. She was going to break through the brick wall.

"Hello, *hayati*," she said. *My life*. Because that was what he was. He'd changed her life, given her new purpose. New hope. And she would do her best to give him the same.

Ferran turned, his broad chest glistening with sweat. Samarah licked her lips. She loved him like this. It made her think of pleasure. Of being in bed with him, because he often looked like this there. Out of breath, physically exhausted.

They were an athletic couple, and they were not only athletic in the gym. The thought made her face hot, even now.

"What are you doing here, Samarah?" he asked.

"I'm sorry, were you looking for an exclusive workout time?" she asked, approaching the punching bag and treating it to a crescent kick, sending it swinging.

Ferran caught it, holding it steady, a dark brow arched. "And if I were."

"Too bad. I'm not leaving." She crossed her arms beneath her breasts and cocked her head to the side. "I want to spar."

"Do you?" he asked.

"Yes. I feel like we're both getting complacent. But when I win, I expect something in return."

"Do you?"

"Yes. I'm going to ask a question, and you will answer truthfully."

He tilted his head back, his nostrils flaring. "You think so?"

"Are you afraid I'll win, Ferran? You know my moves. I have no size advantage. But I will make a rule about biting."

"What are we playing to?"

"First to five?" she asked.

"And what do I get if I win?" he asked. "You have not offered me incentive."

"What do you want?"

"If I win, you ask me no more questions."

His expression was hard, uncompromising.

"That is imbalanced," she said. "I'm only asking for one question, and you're asking for none, ever?"

"It is not my fault if you set your sights too low."

"I do not…"

"I do not have to answer any," he said. "So I suggest you fight if you have a hope of getting even one answer. I do not live on anyone else's terms."

"All right," she said, moving into position. "We have a deal."

He took his stance, his dark eyes meeting hers. "Ready?"

Yes. She was ready to fight for her life. For this new life she wanted, with this man.

"Ready," she said. And then without waiting, she advanced on him, landing a kick that was a more of a tap, to the side of his neck. "One!" she shouted.

He narrowed his eyes and sidestepped her next move, then grabbed her arm and pulled her toward him, tapping her cheek with his fist. "One," he said.

"Bastard," she hissed, rolling out of his hold and stepping away, backhanding him gently before turning and landing an uppercut to his chin. "Two, three."

He reached for her arm again and she hopped back, side-stepping and moving to his side, flicking a snap kick into his side. "Four," she said.

He turned and countered, but she blocked. He grabbed her around the waist and tugged her against him, her feet off the ground. She wiggled, pushing herself up higher into his arms and over his shoulder. Then she shouted and felt his arms loosen, the jolt from the noise offering her just enough give to use her weight to flip herself over his shoulder, land on her feet and plant her foot between his shoulder blades "Five," she said.

He turned, his chest heaving with the effort of breathing. She knew she looked the same, sweat running down her neck, her back. But she was fighting for her relationship with him. She was fighting for a break in his facade.

She bowed, a sign of respect for him, even in his defeat. He squared up to her and did the same.

"You owe me," she said. "One question. We're getting married in two days and I require this."

He said nothing, he just faced her, his dark eyes blank. "You have earned your question. Ask."

He looked more like a man facing the justice she'd promised just a month ago.

"What are you afraid of?"

"You think I am afraid, Samarah?"

"I know you are."

"Not of anything outside myself."

"What does that mean?"

"That is two questions," he said. "But I will indulge you. Here is your prize. I have to keep control. At all costs. Because that day taught me not just what manner of man your father was. But what manner of man I was. Do you know why I keep the tiger pacing the bars?" he asked, moving to her, resting his hand on her throat. "Because if I ever let him free, he will destroy everything in his path."

"Ferran you won't…"

"You can't say that, Samarah."

"Yes," she said, feeling desperate to combat the bleakness in his eyes.

"No, because it happened before. And you can never guarantee if won't again. Unless I keep control."

He lowered his hand and turned, leaving her there, bleeding inside, bleeding for him. For wounds that hadn't healed. For wounds in both of them she wasn't sure would ever heal.

Maybe that was the problem. Maybe when she'd looked ahead and saw a life she'd never thought possible she'd only been dreaming. Maybe a life like that could never really belong to her and Ferran.

Maybe they were simply too broken to be fixed.

The day of the wedding was bright and clear, like most other days in this part of the country. Ferran didn't believe in abstracts and signs, so he considered it neither a particularly good or bad omen.

He had kept himself from Samarah's bed as a necessity ever since they'd spoken in the gym. Ever since she'd forced him to confess the one thing he wanted most to erase from his past.

The wedding was to be small out of concession for Samarah's issues with crowds. And frankly, it suited him, as well. There would be dignitaries and approved members of the press.

It suited him because he still felt far too exposed, as if his defenses had been torn down. He'd confessed his deepest sin to her, his biggest weakness. And now he felt desperate to build everything back up so no one else could see.

So that he was strong again.

So that nothing could touch him.

He strode out of his room and walked down the corridor, toward the room where the marriage would take place. It was far too hot to marry outside. They could have done so if they were by the oasis, or the ocean, but he hadn't seen the point in taking the trip out to the oasis.

He walked inside the room and looked at the guests, seated and ready. He strode down the aisle, completely deaf to the music, the faces of everyone present blurring. He had no family, so there was no one of real importance.

He took his position, his hands clasped in front of his body and waited. Only a few moments later, Samarah appeared in the doorway. She had an ornate gold band over her head, a veil of white and embroidered gold covering her head. Her gown was white, a mix of Western and Eastern traditions.

She looked like a bride. She looked like a woman who deserved to have a man waiting for her who wasn't so terribly broken.

But she did not have that. She had him. And he wondered if he'd truly spared her anything when he'd offered her marriage to him instead of prison.

She approached the raised platform and took his hand, dark eyes never wavering. He was shaking to pieces inside, and she looked as smooth and steady as ever.

The ceremony passed in a blur. He had no memory of what he said. Of what she said. Only that they were married in the end. Only that Samarah was his wife, till death ended it, and he could feel nothing but guilt.

He could give her nothing. He wouldn't. Opening himself up like that could only end in destruction.

They walked through the crowd of guests together, and he didn't know if people clapped for them or not.

"I need to talk to you," Samarah said, as soon as they were in the hall.

And he knew there was no denying her when she'd set her mind to something. Not really. She was far too determined.

"We have a wedding feast to get to."

"It can wait."

"People are hungry," he said.

"It can start without us. I have a question for you."

"I didn't agree to more questions."

Samarah tugged him down the corridor and into a private sitting room, closing the doors behind them. "I don't care if you've agreed. Here is my question. Do you know why I married you?"

"To avoid prison. To secretly plot my death? To gain your position back as sheikha."

"The first moment I agreed, yes, it was to avoid prison. And after that? To plot your doom. Then when I let that go, to become a sheikha and have a future that wasn't so bleak. But that was all why I was planning on marrying you weeks ago. Do you know why I married you today?" she asked.

"I'm damn certain I don't," he said.

"I didn't, either. I thought…well, I used all of those reasons. Until this morning. I was getting ready and I realized how much I missed you. Not just the pleasure, and you do give me that, but you. You're…grumpy, and you're hard to talk to. But you also tried to make me smile. No one else ever has. I dance for you. For you and no one else, because you make me feel like I want to dance. You've given my life layers, a richness it never had before. And I figured out, as I was going to make vows to you, what that richness is."

"What is it?" he asked, his throat tight, his body tense.

"I love you," she said. "I do. I am…in love with you."

"Samarah, no."

"Yes. I am. And you can't tell me no because it doesn't make it less true."

"You don't know what you're saying," he said.

"I do. I married you today because you're the man I want to be with. Because if you opened the palace doors and told me I could go anywhere, I would stay with you."

"And I married you not knowing you were going to say such a ridiculous thing. Did you not hear what I told you? I could end you, Samarah. What if I did? What if I lose control…"

"My father is responsible for it. I'm not listening to this nonsense."

"You're wrong, Samarah."

"Why are you so desperate to believe this?"

"Because it is truth," he said. "And I will never…I will never take the chance on failing like that again."

"Well, what does that have to do with me loving you?"

"I don't want your love. I can't have it—do you understand?"

"Too late."

"This was a mistake," he said.

"And it is also too late for you to have those concerns. We are married. And you know there is every possibility I could have a child. We've never taken precautions in all of our time together."

"I'm not divorcing you. Don't be so dramatic."

"You're rejecting my love and I haven't threatened to kill you. Considering our past history I'm not being over-dramatic. I'm not even being…dramatic."

He gritted his teeth, pain burning in his chest, a low, painful smolder. "I don't want your love. I don't love you, Samarah, and I won't."

"What?"

"I'm not loving anyone. Never again."

"But everything that we've… You wanted to see me smile."

"That's not love, *habibti*. That's a guilty conscience. I don't have love, but I do have guilt in spades."

"What about our children?"

Pain lanced at him, the smoldering ember catching fire and bursting into flame in his chest. "I don't have it in me.

What could I offer them? A father whose hands have stolen a life? A father who loses all humanity with his rage."

"Coward," she said. "You're right. You are weak, but not for the reasons you mean. You're just hiding. You're still just hiding."

"I stopped hiding. I took revenge, remember?"

She shook her head. "No. Part of you stayed back there. Hidden. You've been out here fighting ever since, but you left your soul behind."

"For good reason. It's too late for me. I'm sorry you want more than I can give." He stepped forward, cupping her cheek. He swept his thumb over her silken skin, pain shooting through him. He had a feeling this would be the last time he touched her for a very long time. "This is never going to be a real marriage."

Samarah stumbled back. "Say it again," she said.

"I don't love you."

A sob worked through her body, her hands shaking. "No. Of course not. No one ever has… Why should you be the first?"

"Samarah…you do not love me. You're a prisoner. You've had no one in your life, so you think you love me, but you've been fooled. I did put you in jail today. A life sentence. And because of the nature of things, going back now would be foolish."

"Do not tell me what I feel!"

"You need to be told. If you think you can love a man like me? If you think this is what love is, offering you a life of captivity behind bars or captivity in my bed, then you need to be told!"

"That isn't what you've done. You're just afraid. You're afraid of—"

"I do not fear you. I would have to care first."

She reeled back, her hands shaking. "I'm going to go," she said.

"We have a feast to get to."

"I don't care. I'm going to…I need to go."

She needed some space. She needed to catch her breath. She'd been right the other day. She and Ferran could never have normal. They could never have happy.

The blinding flash of joy she'd felt today when she'd realized she loved him was gone now. In that moment she'd believed that loving him would be enough. That if she loved him, regardless of what he thought about himself, it could work.

But she'd been naive. She'd never loved anyone before, and she'd felt so powerful in the moment that she'd been convinced it could conquer everything. But it hadn't. It wouldn't.

Looking back into Ferran's blank, flat black eyes she knew it.

He had chosen to hold on to the past. He had chosen to stay behind his walls. And as long as that was what he wanted, there would be no reaching him.

"I can't go to the wedding feast alone," he said, his voice raw.

"And I can't sit next to a man who's just rejected my love. I won't. Don't worry—I'm not going to kill you," she said, turning away from him and heading to the door. "I'll just leave you to wallow in your misery. And I do believe that eventually you'll feel misery, even if it's not now. We could have had something. We could have had a life. As it is, I'm going to try and have one. I'm not sure what you're going to do."

She turned away from him, not wanting him to see her break. Loving always involved loss, and right now was no exception.

She'd just spoken vows to stay with Ferran forever, and in almost the same moment, she'd lost any hope she had of forging a real bond with him.

She was a married woman now, in a palace. With servants and beautiful gowns and a man who would share her bed. And she felt more alone than she ever had in her life.

Ferran hadn't realized she'd meant she was leaving. Samarah wasn't anywhere in the palace. She wasn't in his chamber, she wasn't in hers.

Panic raged through him. Had she gone? She was his wife. She had nowhere else to go. He tore at the collar on his tunic, hardly able to breathe.

He'd gone to the feast and made excuses for her being sick, and when everyone had gone, he'd discovered this.

If she had gone, he should be pleased. He should not hold her to him. To a man who might destroy her. Not knowing she was here because of coercion, whatever she said now.

And yet the thought of losing her…

"Lydia!" He entered the servants' quarters, shouting.

Lydia appeared from the dining area, her eyes wide. "Yes, Your Highness?"

"Where is my wife?"

"You do not know?"

"I don't know or I would not have asked, obviously. Do not insult me," he growled. He was being cruel, and he knew it. But he was desperate. Panicked. For a woman he did not love.

Because of course he didn't love her. He couldn't love her.

He didn't deserve her.

It was his life. No matter what he thought, no matter how controlled he was, he hurt the people in it. He saw that now. With blinding clarity.

With all his prized control, he had held a woman captive. He had forced her into marriage.

"Where is my wife?" he repeated.

"She went to your oasis. I helped her pack. She said she

needed some time away." Lydia's eyes were serious and slightly judging.

He gritted his teeth. Damn that woman. "Thank you," he bit out, turning and walking away.

He paused in the doorway, his hand on his chest. He thought he might be dying. Or maybe that was just what it felt like when your heart tried to beat against a brick wall.

He wasn't sure what scared him more. That the wall would hold…or that it might finally break for good.

After two days away, Samarah's head didn't feel any clearer. She was just wandering through the tent, such as it was, thinking about Ferran. All he'd been through. The way her father had twisted his caring. The way he'd been made to feel responsible for an insane man's secrets.

She paused at the doorway of the bedroom, her fingers tracing the woodgrain on the door as she stared out the window at the water beyond.

Had she ever offered to make Ferran smile?

She didn't think she had. He'd given her so much, and in the end, he'd been too afraid to give it all, but she could understand why. She turned into the doorway and rested her face in her hand, stifling the sob that rose in her throat.

She hadn't cried in so long before Ferran. But he made her want more. The wanting was complicated. It wasn't all blind determination and a will to live. It was a deep, emotional need that she was sure at this point was overrated.

She wanted him so much.

She wanted him to love her.

She wanted to make him smile.

Samarah lifted her head. She shouldn't be here, hiding from him. Seeking refuge from reality. From him.

And she'd accused him of being a coward.

She'd held on to her anger toward him for years. With no contribution from him. With no action from him. No confirmation that he even deserved it, and yet she'd been willing to commit the ultimate sin for that anger.

Shouldn't she love him just as much? Shouldn't she love him no matter what he gave back? No matter if he loved her? Wasn't that real love?

Pain lanced her chest. Yes, she wanted him to love her back. But if she truly loved him—and she did—it didn't matter what he said. She was no prisoner. He was behaving as though she was weak, and she was not weak.

She had to tell him that.

She had to go back.

She pushed away from the door and turned around, immediately falling into a fighting stance when she saw the man in white standing there.

She relaxed when she was able to focus on his face. "Ferran?"

He took a step closer to her, the look on his face unsettled. "I came for you," he said, his voice unsteady.

"I'm sorry. I was about to come home."

"No. Do not apologize. I had to release the past's hold on me before I could come to you. I think…I think that this was the best place for me to do this."

"To do what?" she asked.

"I am afraid," he said. "I told myself it was because I had held you captive. Because I am a monster and if I do not keep control I could easily make the same mistakes I had made before."

"I don't believe it."

"I know," he said. "And…I do not deserve your confidence."

"You do."

"You can leave," he said. "I will release you from this marriage. From me. I will give you whatever you need to start a new life. All of your decisions are your own. You have options. Live life. Live it apart from me."

She stepped nearer to him, her heart pounding hard. "Don't you understand? You're the life I've chosen. You're the one I've chosen."

"I can't believe that," he said, his dark eyes haunted. "At my core, I am a murderer."

"No," she said, putting her hand on his face. "You're a survivor. I recognize it. Because it is what I am, too. We have survived the unimaginable. And you know what? It would have broken other people. We aren't broken."

"I am," he said.

"Only because you're too afraid to put yourself back together."

"I am," he said. "Because there is every chance it would reveal a monster."

"There are no monsters here," she said, looking around the room. "Not anymore. And we don't have to let them rule our life anymore. I am not my father. I am not my mother. I am Sheikha Samarah Bashar. My allegiance is to you."

"I don't feel I can accept your allegiance," he said.

"Do not insult me by rejecting it. Not when you already insulted me by rejecting my love."

"I don't seek to insult you. It is…this is the only way I know to love you," he said. "And I find that I do. But I want to be sure that you want to be with me. That you have chosen it. Not because you are a captive. I want… If you choose to stay, I want to be able to trust I can give you passion. That I can give you everything. And you will want it. Not just feel trapped into it."

"Oh, Ferran." She wrapped her arms around his neck and pulled him close, kissing him, deep and long. "I love you, too."

"I do not deserve it," he said, his voice rough.

"I tried to kill you. I don't exactly deserve your love, either."

"Samarah…I don't trust myself."

She stepped back, then reached down and took his hand in hers, lifting it to her throat. "I do," she said. "I have witnessed your character. The way you treated your would-be assassin. I have heard the story of how you avenged your mother. How much you must have loved her to be so enraged. You are a man of great and beautiful passion."

"I have never seen passion as beautiful."

"Neither did I. Before you." She pressed his hand more firmly against her neck. "Would you ever harm me?"

"Never," he said, his voice rough, his touch gentle. "Our children…"

"I know you wouldn't. And you will never harm our children. I know your hands have had blood on them. Blood from the avenging of those you love. Ferran, you would never harm your family. But you would kill for them if it ever came down to it. You would die for them. And there is no shame in that."

"I…I never saw it that way."

"I see it. Because I see you. You are a warrior. As am I. Together we can face whatever terrible things come."

"I've always been afraid that *I* was a terrible thing."

"There was a time when I thought you were, and I very nearly became terrible, too. But you saved me."

"We saved each other."

"There will always be ugliness in the world, Ferran, but loving you is the most beautiful thing that's ever happened in my life. We have something beautiful for the first time." A tear rolled down her cheek and splashed onto his hand. "Don't fear your passion. I want it. I crave it."

"You make me treasure it," he said. "Something I never imagined possible. You told me once that you found a passion for breathing when breathing was all you had. That your desire for revenge was a passion that kept you going. That's what it felt like when you left. I breathed for you. For the one thing that mattered. And then I knew. That this was love. That it was worth anything to claim. That you were worth anything. That I would have to give you the choice to leave even though I wanted you to stay. That I would have to expose myself even though I feared what was inside me. Every wall inside me is broken down, for you. I would rather stand here with you, exposed and vulnerable, than spend the rest of my life protected without you."

"Oh, Ferran…I'm so glad I chose you instead of prison."

He laughed and her heart lifted. "I'm glad, too. It's nice to be preferable to a dungeon."

"You smiled," she said.

"So did you," he said.

"You give me so many reasons to smile."

"And I promise to continue to, every day."

EPILOGUE

THERE WAS SOMETHING incredible about the fact that he and Samarah had created a life together. After so much loss, so much pain, they had brought something new into the world.

Ferran looked down at his son, cradled in his mother's arms, and he felt his heart expand. He reached down, running his fingers along Samarah's flushed cheek. "I will never take for granted that I have you here," he said. "Because I remember a moment when I thought I was touching you for the last time."

She looked up at him and smiled. "You have a lot of years of touching ahead of you," she said.

"And thank God for it. I would like to hold my son," he said, his throat tightening as he looked at the baby in her arms.

"Of course."

He bent down and took the swaddled bundle from her. He was so tiny, so fragile. And she was trusting him with him. Just as she trusted herself to him, and had done for the past year. "He is perfect," Ferran said.

"I know," she said, smiling.

"Who would have thought your revenge would end this way?" he asked. "The creation of a life, instead of the end of one."

"Two lives," she said, smiling. "I feel like my life became so much more that day. It became life instead of survival."

"Three then," he said, running his finger over his son's cheek. "Because I was frozen in time until you came back to me. And now…now my life has truly begun."

* * * * *

1114_ST_3

MILLS & BOON®

Want to get more from Mills & Boon?

Here's what's available to you if you join the exclusive **Mills & Boon eBook Club** today:

✦ *Convenience – choose your books each month*
✦ *Exclusive – receive your books a month before anywhere else*
✦ *Flexibility – change your subscription at any time*
✦ *Variety – gain access to eBook-only series*
✦ *Value – subscriptions from just £1.99 a month*

So visit **www.millsandboon.co.uk/esubs** today to be a part of this exclusive eBook Club!